W9-DGT-593

The Care and Taming of a Rogue

Bennett Wolfe blinked at her, then laughed. The unexpected sound shivered pleasantly all the way down her backbone and the backs of her legs to the tips of her toes. To cover her sudden discomfiture, Phillipa reached for a peach. He beat her to it, then handed it into her palm. Their fingers brushed.

"Your skin is soft," he murmured.

She had a sudden vision of his bare, callused hands roving over her naked body. "I bathe in lemon water," she stated, her voice coming out more stridently than she would have wished.

"Do you, now? Tasty."

By Suzanne Enoch

SUZANNE ENOCH

The Care And Taming of a Rogue

AVON

An Imprint of HarperCollinsPublishers

AVON BOOKS
An Imprint of HarperCollins*Publishers*
10 East 53rd Street
New York, New York 10022-5299

For Hugh Jackman,
whom I find very inspiring.
Very. Inspiring.

The
Care And
Taming
of a
Rogue

Prologue

Captain David Langley stepped down from his hired hack and gestured for the driver to help unload his things. Though it was twilight and the air smelled like rain, he took a moment to gaze at the white and gray house before him; after all, he hadn't seen it in three years.

The downstairs rooms all glowed with lamplight—his parents were in residence. More importantly, the generous lighting meant they were in tonight, thank God. "No. I'll take that one," he snapped, grabbing the large leather satchel from the driver and slinging it over his own shoulder. Then he marched up the three shallow steps and rapped the brass horse's head knocker against the front door.

It opened almost immediately. The tall, sallow-faced servant began a polite inquiry and then snapped his jaw shut, his skin paling to aged parchment. "Captain Langley!" he exclaimed. "Saints be praised!"

"Varner." David stepped past the bowing butler and into the foyer. Faithful servant or not, Varner was not whom he wanted to see. "Where might I find Lord and Lady Thrushell?"

"In the dining room, sir. Shall I see to—"

"Yes, please get my things inside before the rain begins, and pay the driver."

"Of course, Captain. With pleasure."

Passing halfway down the foyer to the closed double doors on the left side, he paused for a moment, shifting the heavy bag on his shoulder a little. Three years of hell he'd lived through, and now, by God, he had something to show for himself. Taking a breath, he pulled open the doors and strolled inside.

"Hello, Father. Mother."

"David!" His mother, her pretty hair now salt-and-pepper-colored but her figure still whip-thin, shot to her feet and rushed to embrace him. "Oh, my darling boy! Your note said you wouldn't be crossing from Calais for another two days!"

"The weather looked to worsen, and I didn't want to wait," he replied.

The sight beyond his mother wasn't the one he expected; in fact, it rather dampened his enthusiasm at the homecoming. Damned Bennett Wolfe again. From thousands of miles away, even from beyond death, the man still managed to throw rocks into his path.

He tempered his smile. "And Lord and Lady Fennington. How pleasant to see you again. I only wish the circumstances could have been more favorable."

By now everyone at the table was on his or her feet, coming forward to welcome him home. His father shook his hand, looking proud and pleased to see his son and heir again. "Home from Africa," he muttered, shaking his head. "It's a miracle." The earl sent a glance over to Randolph Howard, the Marquis of Fennington. "Especially given the difficulties you encountered."

Fennington nodded, offering his hand, as well. "Thank you for sending us word of my nephew's demise. It was very gentlemanly of you, considering that he didn't even bother to tell us where his latest adventure might be taking him." He sighed. "Truth be told, for the past four or five years I haven't been certain whether Bennett was alive or dead. Now, at least, I know."

David's mother was pulling him toward the table, informing him that he must be famished and needed to eat some good English cooking. "Have you informed anyone else of your return?" she asked, trying to push the satchel from his shoulder. "I know some ladies who will be very happy to see you. Especially back from the Congo. The only shame is that you won't be featured in one of Captain Wolfe's famous books now. Oh, that would have been marvelous, but I don't suppose he could have written a last one before he died."

Well, that was damned poor timing for this conversation. If he didn't say anything now, though, Fennington would be suspicious later. David drew another breath, trying to decipher how to navigate this particular thorny path when he'd expected to find it wide open. "As a matter of fact," he said slowly, "Bennett gave something into my care just before he died. Something that may improve all of our fortunes." Carefully he set down the satchel and untied the fastening, then flipped it open. "His journals and some of his sketches," he said.

"By God," Fennington breathed, leaning down as though he meant to touch the worn bindings of the topmost book.

Swiftly David closed the satchel again. "He gave them to *me*. And no one but I will know how to piece them together and shape them into something coherent."

"Considering that his book about adventuring in Egypt got him a knighthood and a grant of land from Prinny, those things are very nearly worth their weight in gold," his father observed, looking from him to the marquis. They were old, dear friends, but Fennington outranked him, marquis to earl. Silently David cursed his mother again for broaching a topic he couldn't set aside in the face of Wolfe's uncle.

"How piecemeal are they?" Fennington pursued, still looking as though he wanted to snatch the entire bag and make a run for it.

"Very, I'm afraid. Unfortunately the delirium completely addled his mind before he succumbed to his wound." David nudged the satchel with one booted toe. "And in any case, by the strictest interpretation of our expedition, upon his demise, Bennett's things would belong to the Africa Association. If he hadn't first given what little he'd managed to save to me, of course."

Both lords frowned at the mere mention of the Africa Association. "Damned Sommerset," Fennington grumbled. "He'd deny us any profits at all if he got his hands on anything. Science, exploration— it's easy to be philanthropic when you have more money than King Midas."

"Yes, but if the journals belonged to David," his father mused, "with of course a credit to Bennett Wolfe for his help and inspiration, and perhaps the contribution of a passage here and a sketch there, and—"

"And with a portion of the profits of course going to Bennett's only surviving family members," David took up, finally smiling again, "think of . . . of—"

"Of the contribution we would be making to science." Fennington grinned as well. "And to a very large and receptive audience." He stuck out his hand again. "Fifty percent?"

Damnation. An hour ago David had been contemplating one hundred percent, with no one the wiser. But on the other hand, with Wolfe's family adding weight to the idea that this was somehow a tribute to the famous explorer, the book sales, the speaking engagements, the fame, the invitations from Prinny . . . He reached out and shook the marquis's hand. "Fifty percent. If you'll write the foreword."

"Absolutely. After all, I can only have my nephew officially declared dead thanks to your presence, there in the Congo and back here in London. Without you, his property would return to the Crown."

"Excellent," his father said, shaking hands with both men in turn. "Varner! Some champagne! My son has returned from Africa after a three-year expedition!"

David sat at the table as two footmen hurriedly

set him a place. Thank God that Bennett Wolfe had finally overreached his own ambitions and been felled by a handful of natives carrying spears. He smiled again at the excited chatter around him. Yes, thank God that damned Bennett Wolfe was dead.

Chapter One

Unbreachable walls of rock confront us; it is no wonder that this western coastline of Africa has been so ill explored. By my reckoning we shall reach the mouth of the Congo River tomorrow. Nothing shall please me more than setting foot on the soil of this wild, mysterious land. I think I know and appreciate her more already than I do all of England.

THE JOURNALS OF CAPTAIN BENNETT WOLFE

Five months later

Bennett Wolfe stepped down from the hired hack and tossed the driver a shilling. "My thanks," he said, catching the bag the man heaved down at him and then pulling a second satchel from the shoddy interior of the vehicle. Not a great deal of luggage to show for three years away, but his trunks and specimen crates were on the way to Tesling, the small estate Prinny had given him six years ago just outside Tunbridge Wells in Kent.

"You owe me another three shillings," the man rasped, pocketing the one in his possession.

"Four shillings for five miles?" Bennett retorted. "Drive that bloody thing into the Thames and I'll pay you four shillings for the boat ride. And even that would be steep." He hefted his things out of the road and dropped them again on the bottom step of the house looming over them. He hoped the dwelling hadn't been sold as a boarding school since he'd last stopped by.

"You have two passengers there," the driver said stiffly.

"Mm hm." Bennett lowered his shoulder, and a black simian face fringed with white and gray fur appeared in the coach's uncurtained window. "Come here, Kero."

At his summons the young vervet monkey leapt onto his forearm and scampered up to perch on his shoulder. From there she chittered at the driver.

Bennett handed her a shilling, and aimed his arm at the top of the coach. "Up, Kero. *Nende juu.*" He looked at the driver as the cat-sized monkey jumped effortlessly onto the roof and sat. "If you're willing to take that from her, then it's yours."

The driver opened his mouth, frowning, until the vervet monkey yawned at him. After taking a look at her rather impressive canines he subsided, taking up the reins again. "Get that blasted thing away from me."

Chuckling, Bennett clucked his tongue, and Kero returned to his shoulder, handing him back the coin. Of course she didn't want it, because it wasn't edible. He flipped it up at the driver. "Two passengers, two shillings."

The fellow caught it, ramming it into a pocket as

he sent the vehicle back into Mayfair's early evening traffic. "I'll starve to death, I will," he muttered as he departed, "with every bloke who gets himself a monkey thinking he's some kind of daft old Bennett Wolfe and refusing to pay his full share."

That was a bit unsettling, since he *was* some kind of Bennett Wolfe, though not particularly daft or old. That having a monkey was now a requirement for being him was unexpected, since he'd adopted the orphaned vervet only a year ago and he'd been away from London for at least three times that long. He had more pressing things to see to at the moment, though, so he set that bit of oddness aside for later contemplation.

As he topped the steps and reached the house's small portico, the front door opened. A blue-liveried servant stopped well back in the doorway, eyeing him. "May I help you?" he asked, frowning either at him or at the monkey—or both.

A new fellow—not unexpected, since old Peters had been aged enough to have shaken hands with Noah. And that had been four years ago. "I'm looking for Jack Clancy," Bennett returned. "He wouldn't still happen to reside here, would he?"

"Lord *John* Clancy is entertaining at the moment," the servant said, lifting his head so he could apparently look down his nose to a greater degree. "Is he expecting you?"

Considering that Bennett hadn't set eyes on Jack since his last sojourn to London, that didn't seem likely. While it would be . . . polite to give the Marquis of Emery's fifth son a bit of warning that he stood on the doorstep, he hated ruining a surprise.

"Just tell him it's Miss Deborah Mason's brother from Oxford and I've just now tracked him down. And I'm not happy."

The door clicked closed, which was better than slamming in his face. Bennett pulled a peanut from his pocket and handed it up to Kero, who chittered at him happily as she pulverized the shell to pull out the meat.

As he was beginning to lose the small bit of patience he'd been able to summon, the door flung open again. "Deborah Mason does not have a brother, my good—" The tall, fair-skinned man, a stunning shock of short red hair atop his head, closed his mouth with an audible snap. "Good God," he whispered, going stark white.

"Hello, Jack."

A heartbeat later Lord Jack Clancy took a long stride forward and grabbed Bennett in a hard, tight embrace. Clearly alarmed, Kero squawked and jumped onto the metal stair railing. Abruptly alarmed himself but for different reasons entirely, Bennett returned the embrace, then pushed his friend back a step. "What's amiss?" he asked. "Your parents? Are they—"

"No, no." Jack clapped him hard on the shoulder and held on. "Everyone's well. By God, Bennett, if this all turns out to be some kind of jest, I'll shoot you myself."

Bennett frowned. "What kind of jest?"

"You were declared dead five months ago."

Dead? *Christ, Langley.* The realization hit him like a blow to the chest. "I didn't know," he said in a retort that came out more as a growl.

"We held a memorial in your honor. Thousands attended. I kept thinking it would be just like you to appear in the middle of it, having miraculously escaped from some disaster or other, but you didn't. And then finally . . ." His friend trailed off, swallowing. "No matter. It's damned good to see you, my friend. Come in."

"The butler said you're entertaining," Bennett countered, pulling back. He didn't like being pawed over, and certainly not when he'd had no idea what was afoot. "I'm only here because you know everyone in London, and I'm trying to find word about David Langley." If the bastard had reported him dead, it wasn't only word that he would be after now, either. Slow anger slid through him.

"Lang— Come in, Bennett. Please. No striding away into the dark just when you've crawled out of your own grave."

He nodded, though his mind was spinning out webs of now-likely circumstances. Of all the things he'd expected upon returning to London, finding out that he was dead hadn't been one of them. The Africa Association would have taken ownership of his journals, his estate had more than likely gone to his bloody uncle Fennington—and, damnation, his specimens were all headed there.

"I don't want to interrupt your festivities," he grunted, following Jack into the depths of the house. "Apparently I have to catch several people up about my not being deceased." A moment later Kero was back on his shoulder, and Bennett reached up to scratch her behind the ears. However unlikable he generally found civilization, she'd never even experienced it before. "Is Langley in Town? I'd like to flatten his face with my fist."

"We'll get to that in a moment."

Bennett took hold of Jack's shoulder and yanked him to a stop. Lord John Clancy was a tall man, but Bennett was larger—he had been since they'd met at Oxford. "I've spent the last day and a half in four different coaches, and the two months before that on a ship. And the weeks before that, flat on my back. Not pleasant. At all. Whatever patience I used to have is long gone, Jack. What is going on?"

"I haven't seen you in four years, my friend," Jack said in a quieter voice, pulling away and continuing forward again. "However off balance you feel at the moment, at least you knew you were returning to London. Until five minutes ago, I thought you were dead. So give me a damned minute, will you? Chat with my guests, say hello, and be a bit civilized, while I stop shaking in my boots."

Clearly Jack *was* shaken, and after five months, a few hours wasn't going to make a damned lot of difference. He didn't have many friends, and he valued Jack as the closest among them. "Fine."

"Thank you. Now, have you and Kero eaten?" Jack asked, turning to face them for the fifth time since they'd entered the house. "No, I don't suppose you have. You'll eat anything, I know, but what does she prefer?"

Just short of the closed doors to the drawing room, Bennett stopped again. "How the devil do you know Kero's name?"

Jack frowned. "How do you think I know? And be forewarned, we're reading the book tonight. I know it's been out for weeks, but I . . . Well, I figured I shouldn't be the last one to know what exactly happened to you. Even though it apparently didn't. Happen, I mean."

Shaking his head and beginning to wonder if the brief meal he'd eaten hours ago in Bristol had been poisoned and he was actually at this moment chained to the floor of some room in Bedlam, Bennett swallowed his frustration and growing annoyance and walked behind Jack into the drawing room. He could be patient and mostly pleasant for a few minutes. He stopped in his tracks. Or not.

"—isn't a misuse of the word 'savagery,' Flip," a hatchet-faced woman with a dress up practically to her chin was saying. "Three people were murdered. That is savage."

Nearly two dozen people, mostly female, sat about the drawing room, all of them with open books in their hands. Several of them were mumbling to one another, while closer to the door a younger man and woman made eyes at each other over the books' spines. So now he'd moved from Bedlam to some sort of lending library of the insane.

"I have to disagree, Wilhelmina," a sweet voice said from the left half of the room, somewhere he couldn't quite see. He liked the sound of the voice, though it might have been because he hadn't heard a cultured female accent in over three years. That said, the Wilhelmina chit hadn't stirred him in the slightest—though that might have been due to the excessive chin ruffles.

Chestnut hair beneath a blue hat came into view for a moment, then vanished as the wide fellow on the sofa shifted. Bennett took a step sideways, trying to get her into view again.

"Savagery implies the use of more force than is strictly necessary," she continued. "In this instance, Captain Wolfe had to kill those three men or his party would have been discovered and attacked. And he had to do it silently. Hence the knife and the spear. That is not savagery. It is practicality."

He agreed with that. Savagery was more a matter of perspective and circumstance than most people seemed to think. Again, though, that was something that could await contemplation until later—except that no one should have known that he'd faced down three men with a knife and a spear. That had happened nearly a year ago, and he'd been back in London for less than an hour. "What are you playing at?" he asked Jack in a low voice. "And who is—"

A pretty blond-haired girl with large brown eyes stood. "Who is your very handsome friend, John?" she cooed, smiling.

Ah now, that chit was worth a bit of distraction. Before he could respond, though, Jack took him by the arm and led him into the center of the room. Bennett didn't like that; it was hardly a defensible position. With a scowl, he pulled free of the grip.

Jack cleared his throat. "Friends, fellow reading club members, this is *my* friend, Captain Sir Bennett Wolfe. The news of his death was evidently premature."

In as coordinated a move as he'd ever seen from anyone other than the military, the members of Jack's book club launched to their feet. Roaring, chattering, even one shriek—good God, they looked like a pack of baboons—they surged toward him. Christ. He'd seen baboons in concert take down a leopard. Kero screeched and leapt onto the nearest shelf. For a moment he contemplated joining her there.

He'd been mobbed before by admiring readers, and he'd taken advantage of more than one female who found his books and the adventures therein heroic and arousing. But this was not fun. He'd returned too recently, and he'd been away for too long. He backed up—and knocked squarely into someone, sending her to the floor.

Bennett turned around. The chestnut-haired chit. Immediately he reached a hand down, gripping her fingers, and hauled her back to her feet. The pretty brown eyes that gazed at him made her the other lady's relation—a sister, most likely—but the similarity ended there. Where the other one had been tall and willowy and blond and stunning, she was more petite, and more . . . curved. Not fat, but she had a bit of meat on her bones. As though she enjoyed the taste of food.

For some reason he found that compelling. Of course he had quite an appetite himself. And not just for food. "You smell like lemons," he said, wanting to hear her speak again.

Lady Phillipa Eddison pulled her fingers free from the large, well-built man looking down at her and attempted to settle her nerves. "Thank you," she replied, hoping he'd just handed her a compliment.

An instant later she frowned, then had to wipe that expression away. *Thank you*. Was that what one said upon first meeting a famous explorer, a man whose work she admired and a man who, until recently—until two minutes ago, actually—had been deceased?

"You're Bennett Wolfe," she continued. *Oh, good heavens. Shut up, Flip.*

"I am," he agreed.

She looked at him again, harder. No one, Captain Wolfe included, had ever spent many words describing him, but she imagined that this man looked very much like a famous explorer should. Tall he was, but it wasn't only that. He wasn't fat at all, but he still appeared . . . mountainous. Broad-shouldered, clearly well-muscled even beneath what looked like a very well-used brown jacket and some sort of buckskin trousers and leather-looking boots.

With skin darkened by sunlight brighter than that found in England and eyes of deep, perfect, emerald, he seemed to radiate power. Confidence. And it abruptly didn't surprise her that this man could have taken on three native warriors and defeated them with a knife and a spear.

A shiver of warmth ran up her spine. Bennett Wolfe. It couldn't be he, and yet she knew it was. The man who had explored a good part of eastern Africa, Egypt, and now the Congo. Dusky hair of uncertain length that looked as though it had been combed through by, well, by a monkey, a long gait, and that air of utter self-possession. He couldn't be anyone else but himself.

"The last time Bennett Wolfe was in London I was only seventeen," she heard herself say. For a fleeting moment she wished her sister, Olivia, would walk up behind her and smack her in the head before she could say something even more idiotic.

"The last time Bennett Wolfe was in London I was only twenty-six," he commented, ignoring the questions—some of them not very polite—being put to him by the club's other members.

"I mean to say, I wasn't out yet, and that's why we haven't met. Until now, of course." She'd regretted that ever since, and especially in the five months since she'd learned of his death. A man of the Renaissance—well-educated, well-spoken, able to write very eloquently and to speak several languages. A man of science and of the arts. She swallowed. Her hero, in a manner of speaking. After all, she'd read both of his books numerous times, and even this last one, authored by David Langley but at least discussing Bennett Wolfe, had graced her bed stand for the month since it had been published. And that was despite her skepticism over some of the passages.

Phillipa shook herself. The man himself was standing there, looking at her. And now she was babbling at him like an utter Bedlamite. This was not the intellectual, scientific conversation she'd imagined having with Bennett Wolfe if they'd ever chanced to meet. "I'm reading your book. I mean, the new book. We all are. Reading it."

A furrow appeared between his eyebrows. "What new b—"

John abruptly appeared between them, making her jump. "Bennett, I see you've met Flip. Lady Phillipa Eddison, Captain Sir Bennett Wolfe."

The captain inclined his head. He still didn't seem to note that anyone else remained in the room at all. "Phillipa."

The sound made her shiver again. She was fully

aware that she had one of the least romantic-sounding names in history, with the possible exception of poor Wilhelmina, and she'd rather liked not being thought of as flighty and frilly before anyone actually met her. But she also liked the way he'd said her name, even if he hadn't addressed her properly—as though a kiss went along with it.

"Flip's something of a scholar where you're concerned, you know," John went on. "She even understood that complicated twaddle you went into in your Serengeti book about longer daylight in the equatorial regions equaling more plant growth."

"Did she now?" Captain Wolfe said smoothly, his gaze still on her. He held out one hand. "May I have a look at the book you're all reading?"

"Bennett, join me in the library for a moment, why don't you?" John broke in again.

"No." Green eyes didn't shift away from her for so much as a second.

"I have something I need to—"

"No."

Phillipa hesitated, stopped more by the tight look that John had assumed than by the fact that the book was precious to her and she didn't want to give it up, even to the man it most concerned. Well, with the exception of Captain Langley, of course. Squaring her shoulders, she set the book in his hand. Their fingers brushed, and another slight shiver went up her spine, as it had when he'd first picked her up off the floor. This was, of course, her first time meeting a dead man. A very large, vital, warm-skinned dead man.

He held her gaze for another beat, then finally he lowered his head to look at the book. His sun-darkened complexion lightened by several shades, and his fingers clenched around the book so hard that she could see the whites of his knuckles.

"*Across the Continent: Adventures in the Congo,*" he read in a hard, dark voice. "By David Langley? That damned fool couldn't put two words tog—"

"Into the library, Bennett. Now."

She'd never heard Lord John speak so forcefully. Even with that, it took Captain Wolfe a moment before he turned on his heel and led the way out of the room, John on his heels, the monkey back on his shoulder, and her book still clenched in his hand.

In the doorway John stopped to look back at the crowd still standing around them. "My apologies, everyone. We'll have to end our meeting a bit early tonight."

Whatever was afoot, and as much time as she'd spent imagining herself adventuring alongside Bennett Wolfe and David Langley, for a moment she was glad to be someone else entirely. Clearly something was wrong. More wrong, even, than Captain Wolfe being thought deceased.

"Flip, can you believe it?" her sister asked as she finally emerged from the chattering crowd. "Bennett Wolfe! And to think, I almost didn't let you talk me into joining you here tonight."

Phillipa eyed her statuesque, willowy, blond, preternaturally lovely older sister. "As I recall, Olivia, you wanted to come because Lady Emery has a new pianoforte. You kicked me in the ankle when John announced we wouldn't be meeting in the music room."

Olivia flipped a hand at her. "Oh, that hardly signifies. We were here. We witnessed Captain Wolfe's return." Livi clasped her fingers together and danced up onto her toes. "And the rest of these people don't know anyone significant, so we'll be the first to tell, oh, just everyone!"

"John and his parents are significant," Phillipa reminded her. "More importantly, John is Captain Wolfe's dear friend."

"Yes, yes, that's true!" Olivia did another little prancing step that she managed to make look elegant and impetuous all at the same time. "You know, I'm going to invite John to my picnic on Thursday. And I'll make certain he knows that the captain is to join us. After all, Captain Wolfe hasn't been in London for a very long time, and he's certain to want to make new acquaintances."

"A picnic. After braving the dangers of Africa? He'd expire from boredom, Livi."

"If you don't like it, then you needn't join us, Flip."

Of course she would attend the picnic. For one thing, she rather wanted to have an intellectual discussion with Captain Wolfe that didn't involve her sounding like someone who'd been kicked in the head by a horse. The most exciting bit of information for her, beyond the news of his return, would be the knowledge of whether he planned to write a book of his own about his and Langley's Congo experiences. Which brought her to another point. Captain Wolfe still had her book. And she wanted it back.

Chapter Two

I had thought the eastern savannahs of Africa rife with thorns, but there they were at least visible—every edible plant, covered. Here in the jungle, however, thorns are more insidious. They hide along tender-looking vines and are imbedded in soft-looking tree barks and their protruding roots, prickling and poking with reckless abandon. Damned annoying things.

THE JOURNALS OF CAPTAIN BENNETT WOLFE

N ow calm yourself, Bennett," Jack said, closing the library door behind them and then striding to the bottle of scotch sitting on the worktable. "I waited three weeks after the thing was published before I even purchased a volume. Nearly everyone else has read it by now. As I said, I didn't want to be the last man in London to know what had happened to you."

Bennett noted Jack's quick-paced confession only marginally. Mainly he glared at the book in his hands and willed it to vanish amid the smell of sulfur-scented smoke. Damned Langley. Now he needed to open it and look, even though the crawling of his skin already told him what lay inside.

"So I apologize for purchasing something that doesn't characterize you as you deserve," Jack continued, "but you honestly can't blame me for my interest."

A glass of amber-colored liquid appeared before his face. Good scotch—the only kind the Marquis of Emery ever allowed under his roof. Bennett took the glass and downed it in one burning swallow.

"See, there you are. Not so bad after all, eh?"

"Shut up for a bloody minute, will you, Jack? You chatter more than the monkey, and make less sense."

"Oh. Very well, then."

Bennett paced to the window and back again, then once more. Finally, grinding his jaw hard enough to flatten his teeth, he opened the leather-bound cover. For a heartbeat, hope touched him. A foreword from his uncle, Lord Fennington. Perhaps somewhere Langley *had* acquired a bit of literary acumen and a soul, and he'd managed to keep his eye on task long enough to write down the tale of his experiences in the Congo.

But then he turned to the first chapter. And there it was. Hope ground into burning dust and blew away. He cursed, not even certain which language he was speaking. Whatever it was, Jack took a step away from him.

"What is it?" his friend finally asked.

"You didn't happen to notice a certain similarity in style between my books and this bloody thing?"

he growled. He flipped through more pages, seeing sketches, translations, maps—all his. Except that someone else's name was printed all over them.

"A similarity? I suppose so. It's a book about adventure and exploration, and you're in it. What—"

"I wrote it. This"—and he slammed the book closed—"is mine." Snapping his arm forward, he hurled the book through the library window. Glass shattered, raining into the air and glinting red in the light from the fireplace. Kero screeched again, practically climbing onto the top of his head.

"Damnation!" Jack ran to the window, leaning outside. "What the devil was that for?"

"I'm angry."

"I see that. Thank God you didn't kill anyone," the marquis's son commented, facing into the room again. "And now you have to purchase Flip another edition. She was quite fond of that book."

"Generally I find you fairly amusing," Bennett snapped back, "but I worked for three years to put that 'edition' together. My journals, my observations, my conclusions."

"But how—"

"How do you think? Langley stole the lot of it." Kero patted him on the cheek, no doubt attempting to reassure him. He rolled his shoulders, giving her tail a gentle tug. None of this was her fault, at least.

Pouring himself another glass of scotch, Jack sat heavily in one of the hearth chairs. A second later the library door slammed open. "My lord," the butler said, an alarmed expression on his face. "I heard something break. Do you require assistance?"

"There's a book down in the garden," Jack returned. "Please have someone retrieve it for me. And we'll need to have the window replaced."

The butler nodded. "I'll see to it at once, my lord."

As soon as the door closed again, Jack took another drink. "I hope you understand," he said, "this is a great deal for me to take in this evening. An hour ago I thought you were dead, and now you're both alive *and* the victim of some sort of thievery involving the most popular book in England."

"You think I'm lying?" Bennett narrowed his eyes. He'd never been a patient man, and tonight he felt stretched beyond all tolerance. "I may have had a spear through my middle, but all of my wits survived."

"But are you certain? According to the book, you were delirious, and you both knew you wouldn't survive. It was quite touching. You insisted that Captain Langley take the few surviving notes and sketches you had, so that your journey would have some meaning. Langley sat by your bedside in a filthy jungle hut until you stopped breathing, and then he made the heartrending decision to return to England alone."

"That is a cartload of horseshit."

Jack sat silently for a long moment. "If you say your journals were stolen, then I believe you. But read the book, Bennett. Because I don't think it's anything you would have written."

"Explain."

"You . . . don't come out too well in it. In fact, if I didn't already know you or was familiar with those books you did write about western Africa and Egypt, I'm not all that certain I would be impressed to be meeting you for the first time." Jack slid forward to the edge of his chair. "That's why I was apologizing for reading the damned thing. It certainly makes clear why Langley survived while you didn't."

"Bloody wonderful." Pacing seemed to be the only thing keeping him from destroying everything in the room, so he kept his hands clenched and resumed stalking to the window and back. "Your book club guests weren't pointing at me and laughing."

"They wouldn't, would they? Not to your face. And according to Langley you were . . . reasonably capable, when led to it."

"And he led, I presume?"

"Yes."

Bennett cursed again. This was unacceptable. Three years of nearly losing his life on an almost daily basis, his plans to write the book that Langley had already written, his reputation—damnation, he should have remained in Africa. At least there he *expected* ambushes around every tree. "Where's Langley staying?" he growled.

"With his parents, at Langley House."

"Good night, then." Bennett turned for the door.

"But he's not there at the moment."

He stopped again. "Damn it, Jack, I am not playing about. You may have been surprised to see me alive, but I had no idea I was dead. It was Langley's doing. He stole from me, and now he's apparently defrauded me, as well." A grim smile curved his mouth. He did enjoy battle, at least. "I find that annoying. So where the hell is he?"

"In Dover, last I heard. He's doing some sort of tour, readings and autographs." His friend stood again. "So stay here tonight, and we'll take a fresh look at things in the morning."

"I don't see how sunlight will improve anything." Another thought occurred to him, and he cursed once more. "I need to see Sommerset. I doubt Langley's done any favors in my relationship with the Africa Association."

"The duke will be at the theater tonight. Some charitable event he's hosting. That's where my parents are, as well. See him in the morning."

Bennett took a deep breath, then nodded. "I'll need that book back myself. It seems I have some reading to do tonight."

"Just don't throw it through anything else." Jack crossed in front of him and opened the library door. "Come along. I'll find you somewhere to rest your head. Unless you'd prefer to sleep out in the garden."

"Don't tempt me."

"And you said nothing good would come of me joining a reading club," Phillipa noted, lathering her toast with butter.

"I'm the one John Clancy has been courting for five years, so you should thank me that he included you in his silly club." Olivia tapped her boiled egg and then began peeling off the shell.

"You should thank John for his tolerance and patience."

"What are you two quibbling about now?" Henry Eddison, Marquis of Leeds, strolled into the Eddison House breakfast room.

Olivia leaned up for a kiss on the cheek. "You will

never ever guess, Papa!" she chirped. "It's so exciting I can barely stand it!"

Their father came around the table to deliver another kiss to Phillipa before he made his way to the sideboard laden with breakfast foods. "Well, if it's *you* who's excited, Livi, I would say that trunk loads of Parisian hats have just washed ashore at Dover."

"Oh, that would be exciting." Olivia grinned. "But Flip is excited, as well."

"Now that's more complicated."

"If it was Flip alone," Livi continued, "it would be something dull and political or literary. But it's both of us!"

With a wink at Phillipa, Lord Leeds took his seat and nodded for a cup of American coffee from Lane the footman. "Both of you, hm? I haven't a clue."

"Very well." Olivia clasped her hands together. "Be glad you're sitting down, Papa. Because . . . Captain Sir Bennett Wolfe is . . . alive."

"*What?*" He choked on his coffee. Lane hurried over to offer him a second napkin, but he waved the servant away. "Where did you hear that?"

"We *saw* him. Last night. Flip dragged me to her bluestocking club, and he—"

"We don't call Flip a bluestocking, Livi."

"Apologies, Papa. You know I only say it around family."

"I'm sitting right here," Phillipa reminded them, scowling. It wasn't so much being called a bluestocking—she'd been saying that about herself since she was twelve. It was more the being overlooked. By her own family, this time. And she was the one who'd forced them to begin reading Captain Wolfe's books in the first place. "The point, Papa, is that he came calling on John Clancy. John introduced him to all of us. Apparently he recovered from the stab wound he suffered."

"He did look quite fit." Olivia sighed. "Quite fit, indeed." She took a sip of tea. "It's a shame we know now that he wasn't quite as heroic as he made out in his other works."

"Livi, that's not very nice."

"Oh, I'm certain he's still quite capable compared to most people. And I'm going to invite him and John to my picnic tomorrow. Isn't that wonderful?"

"I'm still trying to reconcile his being alive with what we all read in Captain Langley's book," their father returned. "That is remarkable."

"I know," Livi went on. "I'm thrilled, even though we all embroidered handkerchiefs with his initials in symbolic mourning."

"I'm certain he'll appreciate your efforts, regardless," Phillipa put in dryly.

"Oh, my goodness." Olivia abruptly fluttered to her feet. "I've just had a thought. I know something that Sonja doesn't. I must go see her at once, before she hears the news from someone else!"

Sonja Depris did seem to have a preternatural ear for news and gossip. "Don't forget to tell her that you've seen Kero, as well," Phillipa called after her sister as Olivia pranced out of the room.

"I wouldn't be surprised if that girl dances in her sleep," their father commented once Olivia was out of earshot.

"She does the waltz," Phillipa replied with a smile.

"Of course." He leaned forward a little. "So tell me, what do you make of this Bennett Wolfe business? It almost seems a shame for him to reappear after everyone's had a chance to read Captain Langley's book. He was a hero; Langley showed us his . . . mortal side."

With a frown, Phillipa stabbed at her poached eggs. "I don't know. He certainly didn't seem overly cautious or indecisive in *his* books. I didn't see any of that in him last night, either."

"He did return five months after being declared dead."

She shrugged. "He's still seen and accomplished more than anyone else I've ever met." And he still had possession of her copy of *Across the Continent*, a fact that, far from annoying her as she would have expected, had given her a rather pleasant shiver when she recalled it this morning.

"I shall not take that personally." Her father finished his breakfast, then stood to kiss her on the forehead once more. "I've a meeting. If you would, tell your mother I'll be home to take luncheon with her."

"Certainly. And I think I'll tell her about Bennett Wolfe, as well, since Livi is telling everyone else in Mayfair."

"That sounds fair enough to me."

As her father disappeared out the front door, Phillipa climbed the stairs and made her way through the maze of short hallways to the room at the far northwest corner of the house. Knocking softly on the half-open door, she entered without waiting for a response.

"Good morning," she said, smiling as she noted that the frail figure in the large bed was not only awake, but sitting upright.

"Good morning, Flip," Venora Eddison, Lady Leeds, returned, motioning her daughter closer. "Help Simpson tow me over to my sitting chair, will you? If I have to lie in bed for one more day I will expire from boredom."

"Of course." Phillipa moved to her mother's left shoulder while the lady's maid, Simpson, supported her right side. "Papa says he'll be home to take luncheon with you. And your color is much improved this morning, if I say so myself," she commented as she and the maid steadied her mother and slowly walked her to the large, overstuffed chair by the window.

"I feel much improved this morning," the marchioness agreed. "I don't think I coughed over a half-dozen times last night, and the fever hasn't returned." Clearly out of breath, she sank into the chair.

"You still need to rest, Mama, or you'll get sick all over again."

"Lady Phillipa, will you sit with my lady while I fetch her some peppermint tea and a broth?" Simpson asked, stooping to tuck a blanket around the marchioness's legs.

"Gladly." Phillipa sat in the chair opposite her mother as the maid disappeared down the stairs. "I don't suppose Livi has been in here to see you yet this morning."

"No. I did hear her running down the hallway shrieking for her bonnet. Something is stirring,

I assume? I do hope it's not another scandal for Prinny."

"If there is one, I haven't heard of it yet." Generally she wasn't much for gossip, but this was different. Firstly, she'd actually seen the man, touched him, and spoken to him, so he wasn't a figment of her imagination. And secondly, this wasn't about who was escorting whom to a dance, or who'd managed the first engagement of the Season. For once it was actually something that interested her.

"Well, don't leave me in suspense, my dear."

Phillipa drew a breath, that excitement and anticipation she'd felt on hearing the news herself last night running through her all over again. "Captain Sir Bennett Wolfe has returned to England. Alive."

Her mother's light-colored eyebrows lifted. "But Captain Langley's book describes his death. And the foreword by Wolfe's own uncle says he agreed to the publication because the captain would have wanted the discoveries they made known to the world."

"Apparently—well, obviously now—the captain and the marquis were both wrong. I saw Bennett Wolfe myself."

"And you're certain it was he?"

"He's John Clancy's friend. John introduced him to our reading club."

"Well. And they say the age of miracles is past." Her mother reached out and squeezed Phillipa's hand. "And you were able to meet a hero of yours. That is pleasant, indeed."

Pleasant. Logic-minded as she liked to consider herself, "pleasant" did not describe the tingle in her chest when Captain Wolfe had looked at her. Yes, she knew he might not be everything she'd dreamed before she'd read Langley's book, and yes, she had a question or two that she wanted him to answer, but he was still Bennett Wolfe.

"Tell me," her mother said after a moment, startling her out of her reverie, "what does the famous Bennett Wolfe look like?"

"He . . . looks like an adventurer," Phillipa replied.

"Handsome?"

Abruptly uncomfortable, Phillipa stood and went to the window. "Livi seems to think so. He has pretty eyes."

"Well. Then I hope I shall have the opportunity to meet him, as well."

"I don't know if you will or not, Mama," Olivia said, strolling into the bedchamber. "Sonja said that Lady Stevenson said that Lord Stevenson said that the last time Captain Wolfe was in London, he only stayed for a week, and then he went to his new estate. And that was with Prinny knighting him."

"In his *Golden Sun of the Serengeti* he wrote that London seems very crowded," Phillipa noted. She couldn't imagine being away for so long and then not staying home long enough to unpack a single trunk. She wasn't precisely a diamond of the *ton*— that was Olivia—but she did enjoy a great deal of what London had to offer. Theater, museums, reading clubs . . . She stifled a scowl. At times she positively *did* feel like a bluestocking, drat it all.

"Crowded or not, *I* hope he stays for a time. You should have seen him, Mama. He's an absolute Adonis." Livi turned to face her younger sister.

"Whose version of him do you believe, Flip? His, or Captain Langley's?"

His. "You care about his character, Livi?" she asked aloud, lifting an eyebrow. "Before you've learned about his yearly income?"

"Ha. He earned over five thousand last year, for your information. Both from the stipend Prinny granted him and from his book sales. And I don't want anyone making fun if I dance with him."

The smile Olivia flashed could have lit up an entire ballroom. And for the first time Phillipa could remember, she wished her sister wasn't quite so pretty, quite so vivacious, and quite so skilled at the art of idle conversation. It wasn't that she was jealous; heavens, she wouldn't know what to do with herself if everyone clamored for her company. Rather, if Captain Wolfe meant to stay in London for only a short time, she wanted more of an exchange than a passing request to borrow a book.

This man of the Renaissance, after all, had learned things in person that she had learned only from books. Some of them, from *his* books. And so she didn't want him spending all his time dancing with the belles of the ball. She wanted him to talk. To her. And she had an excuse to approach him. He did still have her book, after all.

A thrill ran through her. And only to herself would she acknowledge that perhaps it wasn't completely about the opportunity to talk to a great explorer. Perhaps a little of it was because Olivia wanted to talk to him, too, had even tried to talk to him last night, and instead he had conversed, albeit briefly, with her.

"Excuse me," she said, as soon as Simpson returned with her mother's tea.

She needed to go read through *Golden Sun of the Serengeti* and *Walking with Pharaohs* again. After all, the next time she saw him she was not going to waste the opportunity with girlish babble. She meant to have something to say.

Chapter Three

I always approach a village's chief first. It's both custom and practical; everyone to whom we speak requires a bribe, with each successive one being of higher rank than the last and thus requiring a greater treasure. Meeting the chief first means parting with a magnifying glass. If we met him last, I would be forced to hand over Langley. Or a Baker rifle, which I consider even more dear.

THE JOURNALS OF CAPTAIN BENNETT WOLFE

Bennett borrowed a horse from Jack and rode to Ainsley House, the Duke of Sommerset's London residence.

After prowling Clancy House since before dawn, by midmorning he had run through a dozen different scenarios for his first meeting in over three years with the president of the Association for Promoting the Discovery of the Interior Parts of Africa. In addition he'd frightened Jack's mother, Lady Emery, half to death when he and Kero appeared on the stairs behind her, and he'd convinced Jack that keeping him there kicking his heels wasn't a wise idea under any circumstances.

Yes, he remembered that mornings began late during the Season. But years of rising with the sun, walking for miles, and eating what he or his porters could catch had all left him with a distinct dislike of both idleness and small places. And small talk, for that matter, though he'd never had much of a fondness for that.

At least Kero seemed to enjoy the ride across Mayfair, as she clung to his jacket lapels and uttered threat hoots at every dog and cat they passed. He left the big bay, Jupiter, with a stable boy and topped the steps of the granite portico.

One side of the massive double oak doors swung open. "Good morning," the butler in fine black livery stated.

"Good morning. Bennett Wolfe to see His Grace."

The servant didn't bat an eye at either the name or the monkey; perhaps word of his non-death had begun to circulate. "Your calling card, sir?" the fellow asked, holding out his hand.

"Don't have one." As he said that, he could almost see the butler's opinion of him drop several rungs.

"No one may see the duke without a calling card," the servant said in the same even voice. "I shall inform His Grace that you stopped by."

Bennett was not about to be turned away because he lacked a bit of inked vellum. "Inform the duke that I'm here," he said evenly. "I have something urgent to discuss with him."

He kept his gaze on the servant. Evidently the fellow had enough wits to realize either his level of determination or the poor odds of keeping Bennett out if he should attempt an entry, because after a moment he nodded. "I shall inform him. Wait here."

Bennett's annoyance rose another notch. While he understood caution, he did not like being kept from a goal. And this morning, that goal was seeing the Duke of Sommerset. "You have two minutes," he said aloud. "After that, I'll be looking for him, myself."

The massive door closed again. He was armed; he didn't know of any explorer worth a hedgehog pelt who wasn't prepared at any time for an ambush of some sort. At the moment he preferred to save the weaponry for a better cause—like hunting down Langley—but one never knew. Reaching down, he loosened the knife stuck into his boot.

Kero tugged on his ear as he straightened, then leaned around to peer into his right eye. "Hungry again?" he asked, shaking out his muscles a little. No sense frightening to death one of his few allies, fur-covered or not.

She chittered, the sound altering to a contented hum as he handed her up a slice of apple. His handkerchiefs weren't good for anything but holding fruit and monkey tidbits any longer, but at least she seemed to appreciate it.

The door eased open again. "This way, if you please."

Still no *Sir* Bennett, or *Captain* Wolfe. No one in the house was convinced of his identity, then, but someone had his suspicions that he might be who he claimed, or the door would never have reopened. Grudging doubt was better than being tossed into the street on his arse, he supposed.

As the butler left him in a large sitting room, Bennett had to acknowledge that the man's face might well have been made of granite; the servant was the first person since he'd left the Congo who hadn't sent even a single glance at Kero perched on his shoulder. That was impressive, considering that he'd nearly been forced to remove himself and the monkey from the mail stage traveling from Dover after Kero took a fancy to the blue-feathered hat of a fellow passenger. Everyone noticed Kero.

Left alone in the sitting room, though, he had a sudden understanding of the reason behind the butler's lack of interest. The walls and shelves and floor were covered with items that would have looked more at home in Cairo or Nairobi or Constantinople than they did in a duke's town house in London. Carved ivory, reed baskets, fertility statues, a Masai shield and spear—so many items from so many different countries, the effect was almost dizzying.

He approached the shield and spear. The one that had caught him during that last, mad dash to the river hadn't been Masai, but it had been dipped in poison, something from a frog according to his guide Mbundi. The scarred-over wound still hurt like the devil some mornings. He supposed it always would. Carefully Bennett lifted the weapon from its rack and hefted it.

"I spent much of my youth traveling," Sommerset's low voice came from the doorway. "My father was an envoy for the king."

"This has nice balance," Bennett returned, facing the duke as the tall man strolled into the room. "How many goats did it cost you?"

Sommerset flashed a brief smile, the expression

making him look younger than the thirty-two years of age Bennett knew him to be. "Seven. And the shield was another eight."

"Well worth it." Finally Bennett set the spear back in its place. "I have one from the Ngole tribe just north of Lake Mai-Ndombe that might interest you."

"I believe it was one of those very spears that killed you," the duke returned, steel gray eyes assessing him. "According to Captain Langley, that is."

"He was mistaken."

"Evidently so—though if we hadn't met when the Africa Association agreed to sponsor your expedition, I might be more inclined to believe Langley's book and your fate therein. You've seen it, haven't you?"

"Last night." Bennett clenched his jaw. The tome was monstrous; even he had difficulty separating the truth from the tripe, and he'd written the majority of it. "A remarkable work of exaggeration and fancy."

"Mm hm. Considering that the Association's agreement was for *you* to lead the expedition and to share credit for any discoveries, papers, journals, and books with us, we expected you to be the one to keep journals and make maps and sketches."

"I remember that conversation. I did so."

"Not according to Langley. He owns all of *his* material, and believe you me, he's made a pretty penny from it. The Association, on the other hand, has been left hanging, without credit, scientific information, or income. I'm assuming that as you are not dead, you have those materials you promised us?"

While a welcome back to England and the offer

of a brandy might have been pleasant, Bennett understood the duke's anger. The Association had paid a great deal of money for ship passage, supplies, porters, and whatever incidentals he and Langley expected to come across during their time in the Congo. Langley had been his second, and of his choosing, even. He supposed he was lucky to have survived making such a half-witted decision at all.

Bennett scowled. "My crates of artifacts and specimens were sent ahead to Tesling for my later sorting and cataloguing, with the items of your choice going to the British Museum, as we agreed."

The duke sank into a chair. "And those journals and maps and sketches you're so famous for making?"

"Langley took them from me and disappeared downriver. I arrived in London yesterday to look for the miserable rat." Well, not *look for*, precisely, but saying that he intended to kill the man and take back his rightful possessions might raise some alarms.

"He's not here. His illustrious publishers are sponsoring a tour across the country for him."

"So I heard. I'd at least hoped that he'd decided to give my things over to the Association, but clearly he had other intentio—"

"I'm to believe that you're the true author of *Across the Continent*, then?" Sommerset put a finger and thumb to his chin. "I find that difficult to believe."

"Langley reversed our roles and did a bit of inventing."

"That's a great deal of invention for a miserable rat."

Bennett drew in a hard breath. "Standing here debating you about it is a bloody waste of my time, obviously. I don't actually give a damn whether you believe me or not. I'm merely reporting my return to you, as per our agreement. I'll take another path where Captain Langley is concerned." With a nod, he turned his back on the duke.

"You *should* worry whether I believe you or not."

Stopping, Bennett turned around again. "And why is that?"

"Adventuring is what you do, is it not, Captain? After reading that book, I can't imagine anyone wanting to sponsor a further expedition with you at its head." He sat forward. "In fact, how am I to know whether the fiction is Langley's, or whether you have been writing fictions all along? Have you actually been to East Africa?"

Bennett's insides clenched unpleasantly. That had been nagging at the back of his mind all night as he sat reading. "Once I gut Langley, we'll see which of us is the more capable."

"In which case he would be dead, you would be hanged, and you would still look foolish." The duke produced a handful of peanuts from the pocket of his immaculately tailored gray jacket and offered them to Kero. With an excited chirp she launched off Bennett's shoulder to snatch them and then re-treat to the top of the nearest bookcase to savor her new treasures. "Bloody and gossip-provoking, but not very practical."

"He stole from me. What the devil do you expect me to do? Sit back and smile while he takes my position and my status?"

"No." Sommerset stood again. "I expect you to keep in mind that you're in London. Not the Congo. We don't spill the blood of our peers without a trial—or at least a majority opinion."

"That's helpful. I hope you don't mind that I'll be following my own instincts and not your lecture on propriety and proper manners."

"I believe you, you know."

That stopped Bennett again. "You might have said that before I nearly gave myself an apoplexy."

The duke flashed that brief smile again. "And you might have said, 'Thank you' just then, but you didn't. Not much of one for either propriety or proper manners, are you, Captain?"

"No. In most of the places I've been, honesty and directness have served me better."

"You're not in any of those places at the moment. And if you want the opportunity to prove to whom *Across the Continent* truly belongs, you can't go about threatening everyone who looks sideways at you."

That was the rub. He hated the idea of staying about in London for no bloody good reason, but if he went home to Tesling to sort through his specimens, Langley would have free rein to destroy what little remained of his reputation. And as Sommerset had noted, at the moment no one was likely to sponsor an expedition led by him. They might never do so again.

"Any suggestions?" he finally grumbled.

"Come with me." Without a backward glance to see whether he was followed, Sommerset left the sitting room.

With an audible curse, Bennett collected Kero and strode after the duke. If it came to the worst, he could sell Tesling and take himself off to the Americas or back to Africa on his own. It wouldn't be exploring for the sake of the adventure, though, and he wouldn't be able to share anything he discovered, because no one seemed to have cause any longer to believe him. It would be running away, and he couldn't think of a way to word it that made it anything else.

The duke turned down a corridor running lengthwise across the front of the large house. Myriad servants bowed respectfully to their master, but ignored both Bennett and Kero. He wasn't certain if that spoke well for Sommerset, or poorly for himself.

Finally, at what looked to be the far east corner of the house, Sommerset stopped. "Here we are." He pushed open a door and stood aside, gesturing for Bennett to precede him.

Beyond the door a small alcove opened into a large sitting room with dark paneled walls and glowing lamps set upon tables alongside two dozen or so chairs. The entire back wall was lined with books, maps, and stacks of papers. A pianoforte stood in one corner, odd-looking beside a trio of Zulu drums. More foreign trinkets and animal skulls and furs lay scattered throughout the room, while the east wall featured a trio of tall windows overlooking what appeared to be the Ainsley House garden.

Three men sat at a distance from one another in the room, the oldest reading a newspaper, the second asleep in a chair facing the fireplace, while the third sat beneath the left-hand window and seemed absorbed in a book. None of them stirred at the duke's entrance, much less Bennett's.

"What is this?" he asked, noting a second door at the front of the room that looked as though it led directly outside. A fourth man, sitting in the shadows and so still that at first Bennett had thought him a dressmaker's mannequin, moved from his position by the door and headed in their direction.

"This is a beginning," the duke said. "I spent a year thinking about it, and the past four months having walls knocked down and the pieces gathered together."

"It's very . . . nice," Bennett ventured, "but the beginning of what? And what does it have to do with my wanting Langley's head on a platter?"

"Reading the newspaper there is Lucas Crestley, Lord Piper," Sommerset went on, as though he hadn't heard the questions. "Eight months ago he returned from a . . . secret expedition through the French-held territories of America to scout whether Britain might wish to reinstitute a presence there. Red Indians killed the rest of his party in a rather disturbing manner."

"That's—"

"The sleeping fellow," the duke continued, "just arrived in London three days ago. Colonel Bartholomew James. He—"

"The India Thuggee skirmishes," Bennett interrupted, looking again at the dark-haired man seated with a walking cane to hand. "He went missing for a time. I read something about it in this morning's newspaper." He knew them to be nearly the same age, but Colonel James looked older. By his gaunt face it didn't seem as though the colonel had done much sleeping lately.

Sommerset nodded. "And by the window we have Thomas Easton, sent to Persia in an attempt to persuade the locals to expand their silk exports. He posed as a Muslim for a year."

Easton looked up at the sound of his name, the light catching a thin scar running from his left ear down the side of his neck. "And I'm presently reading *Across the Continent*. You must be Captain Wolfe, the overly cautious fellow with the monkey. This says you're dead."

Bennett clenched his fists, stalking forward. "And I say you're the stupid bastard who speaks when he shouldn't."

Sommerset moved between them, heading Bennett off. "Not in here," he growled.

"What is 'here,' precisely?" Bennett demanded.

"I prefer to think of it as a gentlemen's club for those souls who've been forced, for one reason or another, to cast aside civilization's . . . frivolities. Souls who desperately need to find a way to exist in Society again."

"An asylum for outcasts," Bennett said dubiously.

"More of a sanctuary. I've taken to calling it the Adventurers' Club. There are currently fourteen members, which I believe makes it the most exclusive club in London. *I* decide its membership. And I'm inviting you to join us."

"Is Langley a member?"

"No."

"What about those souls who don't particularly want to rejoin Society?"

The duke eyed him. "You have a reputation to repair, Captain. You can't do that in Cairo."

Bennett took a breath, spending the moment looking about the room. The duke was correct, damn it all. He didn't care much for the obsequiousness of Mayfair, but the peers therein were the ones who could afford to sponsor his expeditions.

"If you wish to join us," Sommerset went on, "you'll find the establishment open at all times, food and spirits always available, a spare bed if you require one, and companions who see the world with clearer eyes than the rest of Society. As you do."

The man who'd been lurking in the shadows finally moved again, holding out his hand. "Hervey," he said. A key rested in his palm. With a slight frown, Bennett took it.

"Hervey will see that you receive anything you need while you are under this roof," the duke explained.

"And most mornings you'll find Gibbs here if I am not, sir," Hervey added.

"What if you decide Langley's version is the correct one, after all?" Bennett asked, pocketing the key.

"Then you'll be asked to leave."

"Asked," Bennett repeated dubiously.

"There are only two rules for membership," Sommerset continued. "Firstly, only you are granted access. No guests of either gender. The monkey, however, is permitted. Secondly, no one else hears of the Adventurers' Club. If Society at large begins clamoring for entry, we will cease to be a haven for those risking life and limb for the benefit of science and their country. Is that agreeable to you, Captain?"

Taking another long look around the large, comfortable-seeming room, Bennett nodded. For a day or two it would be acceptable to stay at Clancy House, but with Kero and his own current . . . hostility, Lord and Lady Emery wouldn't want him about for any longer than that. And the idea of having a place he could escape to in the middle of Mayfair was both unexpected and welcome. "Yes," he said aloud, on the chance that an audible agreement was required for membership. "It is agreeable to me."

"Good. This way, then." Again leading the way, the Duke of Sommerset left the club's main room through the second door. Bennett found himself outside Ainsley House, beneath a vine-covered overhang. "Use the key here. It doesn't open the main front door, or the one dividing the club from my home. I do require my own privacy."

"Understood. I have to say, though, that I'm surprised at the invitation, considering Langley's book and the Africa Association's disappointment with the results of the expedition."

"You were dead," Sommerset returned. "So you're only partly to blame. And this has nothing to do with the Association." He grimaced. "I do have a word or two of advice if you'll take it, having been stranded in Society for longer than you."

Stranded. That was an odd word, coming as it did from one of the wealthiest men in the country. "I'm listening."

"You've been very celebrated in the past, mostly because of your books. No one knows *you*. And they will judge by their most recent experience—which is the one with Langley's book. Don't react as they expect. And I suggest for that reason that you at least give the appearance of being friendly with the Marquis of Fennington."

"My uncle wrote the foreword for that damned book." Bennett clenched his jaw. That was only the beginning of the anger he felt toward Fennington, but he had no intention of delving into that quagmire in front of the Duke of Sommerset.

"Yes, he did. So if you want to discover what Langley has in mind, or even where the journals might be currently, you—"

"The friend of my enemy is my uncle," Bennett grumbled.

"Precisely. Consider it. Because I recommended you for the Congo expedition, and I don't appreciate being made to look foolish any more than you do." With a short nod, Sommerset vanished back into the Adventurers' Club and the house beyond.

Annoyed by and as unused to receiving advice as he was, he'd be an idiot to ignore what Sommerset had recommended. And he knew what it meant. In order to be other than what Society expected of him, he would have to be charming and social. And alive, of course. That at least would gain everyone's attention. Then he only had to turn them to his side and recover his journals from Langley. If he couldn't do both of those, he was likely to be as "stranded" in England as Sommerset seemed to be. And liking it even less.

Chapter Four

In the Wandui tribe, extended earlobes signify beauty.
They begin in youth by wearing small stones in each
lobe, and by adulthood some of them can pass an ostrich egg through the opening. They offered to begin
the process with me, but as I had a fortnight previously been pierced through the leg with an arrow, I informed them that I already had a plentitude of holes
in my person. Ah, the price of beauty.

THE JOURNALS OF CAPTAIN BENNETT WOLFE

Phillipa Eddison waited in the breakfast room
until her tea was as cold as a stone. "Barnes,
would you check again with Mary to see if Olivia
has risen yet?" she asked, turning in her chair to
face the butler.

Despite the twitch in his jaw that reminded Phillipa she'd already made the same request three
times, the butler nodded. "Right away, my lady."

As he opened the door to leave the room, though,
Olivia glided in. "Good morning, Flip," she said
with a smile, walking over to the sideboard to select

her breakfast while Barnes resumed his previous position.

"Is it still morning?" Phillipa asked in return, ready to smack her head against the tabletop. "I hadn't noticed."

"It's barely ten o'clock," her sister commented, sitting at the table opposite Phillipa. "One would almost think you're anxious about my picnic."

"Nonsense. I was anxious that you would sleep through your picnic, which would be rude and isn't at all the same thing you're implying."

With a grin, Livi began buttering her toast. "He hasn't replied, you know. John has, but he specifically said that he couldn't speak for Captain Wolfe. Are you going to attend anyway?"

Phillipa hid a wince. Hours in the company of Olivia's silly, gossipy friends, on the very small chance that Bennett Wolfe might make an appearance, that she would have a bare moment to speak to him, and that she could converse without making herself look like an idiot again.

"You're infatuated, aren't you?" Livi pursued. "You may pretend to be scholarly, but you blushed the other night when you met him."

"I admire his accomplishments," Phillipa returned.

Her sister looked at her for a moment. "Do you think I made a mistake in asking him to join us?" she finally said. "I mean, I read Captain Langley's book. 'A hesitant, unsophisticated follower.' That's how Langley described him."

"Well, I have read Captain Wolfe's books, and I'm forced to disagree with that assessment." Phillipa frowned. "And yesterday you were thrilled to be the first to have him attend a gathering."

"Yes, well, he's famous. And he's an absolute Adonis. I suppose if he doesn't prove to be as popular as he once was, I can always say that I had to invite him because he's residing with John Clancy." She nodded to herself. "That will suffice, I think."

Phillipa shook her head. Yes, she'd read Wolfe's two books and Langley's one. And if Captain Wolfe was unsophisticated, he was by far the most lucky, eloquent, and witty simpleton she'd ever heard of.

"Of course even if he *is* foolish," Olivia continued half to herself, "he *does* have an income of five thousand a year. And he's an adventurer. I know of several rather silly people who are quite popular. And they aren't even as handsome as Captain Wolfe."

"How can anyone be as fickle as you are and still have friends?" Phillipa asked.

Olivia grinned at her again. "I'm not fickle. I keep a large number of friends and beaux about me so that I may disappoint no one and still choose with whom I spend my time."

For a moment Phillipa considered changing her mind about attending the picnic. If Olivia had set her mind on winning Bennett Wolfe, anyone else trying to impress him, or even trying to carry on an intelligent conversation with him, would be pointless. Everyone fell in love with Olivia. And until that moment, she hadn't minded that fact at all.

After all, Olivia was three-and-twenty, and more than likely would marry within the next year or so. That would leave a great many disappointed gentlemen who knew the younger sister because of their pursuit of the older one. Some of them were pleasant, if a bit lag-brained. She knew her parents hoped that one of those disappointed gentlemen would offer for her.

She did try on occasion, but for heaven's sake, flirting was much more difficult than it was made out to be. So while at twenty-one years of age she should probably have been married already, she was quite resigned to waiting for one of Olivia's castoffs. Someone who'd seen her—unique, as Livi called it—manner, and decided her dowry made up for it, or something.

And so she kept it at the back of her mind, where it didn't interfere with the things that truly interested her. Which didn't explain why she didn't like the idea of Olivia sweeping Bennett Wolfe into her endless collection of beaux. Perhaps because he seemed a step or two above all that, and because she didn't want to be wrong about him.

By the time Olivia had gathered the necessary servants and the baskets of food and the three carriage loads of items required for hosting a picnic in the middle of Mayfair during the high Season, Phillipa was near to wishing once again that she'd just decided to stay at home. Once they arrived at the designated corner of Hyde Park close by the Serpentine and overlooking a pretty patch of roses set beneath towering elms and oak trees, she sat on one corner of the largest of the picnic blankets and opened the book she'd brought along.

She nearly always brought a book. That was why some of Livi's friends called her a bluestocking. At least they never did so to her face, and rarely to Olivia's, but she knew. And most times she didn't care, because it kept her from having to converse with them. Fashion and gossip were like foreign languages she hadn't quite mastered. She could stumble along for a bit, and then would become hopelessly lost.

"I'm glad you wore your orange and white muslin," Livi said, kneeling down beside her for a moment and planting a sound kiss on her cheek. "It makes your eyes look pretty. If you would look up from that book, everyone would see that."

Before she could reply, Olivia was up and roaming again, greeting her guests and chatting about some poor girl who'd worn the same dress twice already this Season. At least Phillipa was fairly certain it hadn't been she; Olivia wouldn't have allowed it.

A pair of long legs in blue trousers and Hessian boots sat beside her. Phillipa stiffened, not feeling up to telling Livi's latest admirer what her sister's likes and dislikes might be. Then she looked over and relaxed as she recognized the bristly red hair and light green eyes belong to the Marquis of Emery's fifth son. "Hello, John," she said, with what felt like her first genuine smile of the afternoon.

"Flip." Lord John Clancy reached across her for a biscuit. "Just how many friends did Livi invite today?"

"I have no idea, though I'm pleased she included you."

"We both know why she invited me," he returned easily. "And she nearly uninvited me when I couldn't guarantee Bennett's presence. I'm lucky to have survived at all."

She sent him another glance. Well, now *she* couldn't ask whether Captain Wolfe had decided to attend or not either, drat it all. "Speaking of you and Livi," she said instead, "I haven't seen you in her company as much this Season as I did last year. Have you given up the chase? Or has some other pretty young thing caught your eye?"

With a look of his own at Olivia, he shrugged. "Why do some women prefer lilies, while others favor roses? Livi's my lily and my rose. No rhyme or reason to it, but that's how it is. I was attempting the maxim that 'absence makes the heart grow fonder,' but I realized that could only work if she noticed that I wasn't about."

With a chuckle, Phillipa handed John a cucumber sandwich. "I missed seeing you at soirees, if that means anything. This year's crop of beaux doesn't have a brain among them. Thank goodness for the reading club or *my* brains would rot away entirely."

Six members of the brainless herd currently flirted with Olivia and her friends. From what she'd been able to overhear, whatever his current uncertain standing, all of them were rather pleased that the famous adventurer hadn't made an appearance today. While she didn't share their sentiment, she could appreciate it. After all, none of them stood up very well against him, even if he was unheroic—which he wasn't.

Perhaps she could discuss him without doing so directly. "Your friend owes me a book," she said aloud, though she'd wanted to save that bit of conversation should the captain himself appear.

"I reminded him of that this morning, though he was somewhat preoccupied with being bored. I'll replace it for you if he doesn't return it."

"Thank you, John, but that's not necessary. I'll purchase another for myself."

"I was attempting to be gentlemanly, Flip."

"Oh. I was only thinking that I could save you from having to deliver it." She paused, scowling abruptly as she realized what the slightly pained look on his face meant. "You want to deliver it, as an excuse to see Olivia. Apologies."

"No need." He grinned, leaning sideways to lift the corner of the book she held in one hand. "*Golden Sun of the Serengeti*? How many times have you read that now?"

She smiled back, pleased that she at least had one friend with whom she didn't have to dissemble about her lack of feminine charms and wiles. "I've lost count. I do still enjoy it, though."

"Mm hm. Literary skills aside, I have to say I'm ambivalent over Bennett's absence. Your sister's been raving about his godlike appearance for the past twenty minutes, which is why you find me over here in the levelheaded area of the luncheon in the first place." The marquis's son scowled. "He's not as handsome as all that, is he?"

"You've seen him."

"Yes, but I've known him since before he began to tower over mortal men. You're sensible. What do you think?"

"I have to say, he has the requisite number of eyes, and a well-centered nose and mouth." If every other female hadn't already been mooning over him— sight unseen for the most part—she might have felt freer to express her own appreciation of his appearance. But she also wanted to make it clear that she admired Bennett Wolfe for his accomplishments, not for his handsome face and physique.

"Ears?"

She shook herself. "I'm afraid I recall two of them."

"Damn. Add that in with the monkey, and I'm beginning to be ecstatic not to add him into the mix today."

"Should I leave, then?"

Phillipa jumped at the sound of the deep voice behind her. She whipped her head around to see . . . him. Captain Sir Bennett Wolfe wore a simple gray jacket, tan waistcoat that she thought she'd seen before on John, and buckskin breeches over that pair of worn-looking boots of uncertain color. Even in such relatively civilized clothing he still looked every inch the adventurer, and not just because Kero sat on his shoulder. It was those glinting green eyes, she decided. They'd seen a great deal more than hers had. A great deal more than had anyone else's here today.

"Of course you shouldn't leave," she said when she realized she was staring. "Olivia will be delighted that you've come."

He tilted his head as he looked down at her, a lock of his unruly dusky hair falling across one eye. "But you're not Olivia."

"No, I'm not."

"Then you're not delighted to see me."

Phillipa was fairly certain this time that she hadn't said anything sharp-edged. He was therefore teasing her. *Her.* She couldn't help the twitch of her lips. "I didn't say—"

At that moment Olivia squealed. "Oh, Sir Bennett! You've come after all!"

In a second the captain was surrounded in such a stampede that Phillipa half thought she might be trampled there on the ground.

"Well, this is disturbing," John noted, and stood. He offered her a hand, and she rose as well.

After five minutes of people jabbering at him, Captain Wolfe looked as though he was regretting his decision to attend the al fresco luncheon. Phillipa took Olivia's arm and leaned up to whisper in her taller sister's ear. "Have everyone sit down and let him breathe before you give him an apoplexy, for heaven's sake."

Olivia furrowed her brow, as though she couldn't fathom how anyone wouldn't enjoy being mobbed by admirers. Then she gave a dazzling smile and suggested that everyone seat themselves and eat. *Thank goodness.* Livi did have common sense. She just occasionally needed to be reminded of that fact.

Once the corner of the blanket cleared again, Phillipa resumed her seat. John sat beside her again and motioned for two glasses of Madeira from one of the footmen Olivia had brought along with them. Phillipa took a grateful swallow—and then nearly choked as Captain Wolfe lowered himself down on her other side.

As a keen-eyed adventurer, he should have seen that a half-dozen stunning young ladies waited expectantly just a few feet away, all of them armed with clever ripostes and witty, watered-down banter. And none of those women looked happy with her. She gave herself credit for at least noticing that—not that she had any intention of pointing it out to the captain.

"Jack called you Flip last night," he said, ignoring both the rest of the group and his monkey as Kero left his shoulder to head up the twisted trunk of the nearest oak tree. "A nickname?"

"Yes." She nodded. "When I was born, Livi couldn't pronounce Phillipa, so I grew up as Flip. It's what my friends and family all call me."

"I like it. But I prefer Phillipa."

She preferred it when he said her name like that, as well. It didn't sound at all practical the way he pronounced it, even though everyone knew she was eminently practical. "Then you should call me Phillipa," she said aloud.

"It's *Lady* Phillipa," John amended from her right side.

Green eyes narrowed, glancing beyond her to take in the marquis's son. "I hadn't realized that you and Jack are . . . a match."

Phillipa's cheeks heated. "Oh, no. We're not. John wants to marry Livi. He's my favorite choice for a brother-in-law, so we've formed an alliance."

Captain Wolfe looked down to select a sandwich, and Phillipa would have been willing to swear that the corners of his mouth lifted. Before she could decipher what that meant, Olivia's gossipy friend Sonja Depris gracefully seated herself opposite him.

"Sir Bennett, you must tell us how you and Captain Langley survived the wreck of your boat and the crocodiles," she urged.

The line of his mouth flattened out again. "There's nothing I could say that you haven't already read."

"Oh, but—"

"Miss Depris, did I ever tell you about my own adventures with a capsized boat?" Henry Camden interrupted. "It's very harrowing, I assure you."

As Mr. Camden went on to describe a rather dull-sounding holiday to the Lake District, Phillipa kept her attention on the captain. She could hardly do otherwise. And he continued to gaze at her, in a way that made her feel . . . not uncomfortable, but jittery.

"You didn't know you'd been declared dead, did you?" she finally asked, mostly to have something to say.

"No, I didn't. Nearly gave Jack here an apoplexy when he saw me standing on his damned doorstep."

"I still may have one," John said dryly. "I haven't decided yet."

"What about your family? Lord Fennington wrote very warmly about you in the foreword to Captain Langley's book. They must have been . . . ecstatic to learn of your return."

The captain's gaze lowered to her mouth. "You're reading my book," he commented, ignoring her question. He tapped the worn cover with one finger.

"Yes. It's fascinating." She drew a breath. This was likely to be her best opportunity for an interesting conversation with him. "I have to ask, though, what you mean by 'primitive.' You use it several times to describe tribes who've never seen an Englishman before."

His eyes lifted to hers again, brilliant green, and touched, she thought, with a small measure of surprise. "Is this like your definition of 'savagery,' where the meaning depends on the circumstances?"

"Oh. You heard that, then." Her cheeks heated again, though she fought the idea that she had anything about which to be embarrassed. She'd made a good point the other night.

"I did. Very astute, I thought." He edged the slightest bit closer to her. "So do you actually want to discuss the dividing line between primitive and civilized behavior, or is there something else you wish to know?"

Slowly he reached out again, straightening her sleeve. Where his fingers brushed her arm, warmth cascaded through her skin. She drew a quick breath in reaction. "Are you attempting to demonstrate the difference?" she asked.

Captain Wolfe lowered his hand again, only to twist his fingers into the hem of her skirt. "This is very soft," he said quietly, looking down. "Nothing in Africa is soft. It's all thorns and sharp teeth and spear points."

Oh, goodness. Phillipa cleared her throat. "I . . . I believe Captain Langley said precisely the same thing in his book."

His gaze lifted again, more sharply. "Did he? Precisely the same thing?" Somewhere during the conversation his tone had changed from distantly amused to . . . dangerous. She couldn't put her finger on it, precisely, but she realized that her muscles had tensed, readying her to flee from a predator who had only just arrived at the edge of her vision.

"I believe so. I don't have the book, so I can't cite the passage for you."

"Ah, yes. I've been reading the book you loaned me. It says several things exactly how I would say them. Odd, that."

No mention, of course, of if and when he would be returning it to her. "Perhaps you should write a book about the Congo yourself, then."

"Perhaps I already did."

Phillipa scowled. "Are we arguing about something? Because I prefer to have the topic stated before I choose a side."

Bennett Wolfe blinked at her, then laughed. The unexpected sound shivered pleasantly all the way down her backbone and the backs of her legs to the tips of her toes. To cover her sudden discomfiture, Phillipa reached for a peach. He beat her to it, then handed it into her palm. Their fingers brushed.

"Your skin is soft, too," he murmured.

She had a sudden vision of his bare, callused hands roving over her naked body. "I bathe in lemon water," she stated, her voice coming out more stridently than she would have wished.

"Do you, now? Tasty."

Good heavens. "I don't think you should be speaking to me this w—"

Something hit her in the back, then traveled up to her shoulder, tugging on her hair. As she inhaled to shriek, a small, furry arm reached out past her cheek and grabbed for the peach.

"Kero! *Utasimama!*"

Phillipa swallowed her surprised yelp. At the same moment Captain Wolfe put a hand on her shoulder and reached across her to grab the monkey around the middle. He made a low, irritated-sounding cluck with his teeth and sat Kero down on his thigh.

"Apologies," he said roughly. "She generally doesn't leap on people she doesn't know."

She abruptly wondered if *he* did, though. "There's no harm done," she returned aloud. "She only startled me." Working mightily to keep her hand steady, she offered the monkey the peach. "Here you are, Kero."

The monkey tilted her pretty gray and white head, then held out both front paws for the peach. As soon as she had it, she scampered back into the nearest tree. Phillipa watched her for a moment, then turned her attention back to Captain Wolfe to find him still gazing at her, an arrested expression on his face.

"Captain Langley's book said you found Kero in a market," she ventured, abruptly uncomfortable with his singular attention. Everyone was beginning to notice. Even Livi looked put out. "What would have happened to her if you hadn't purchased her?"

"She was only a couple of weeks old," he said after a moment. "Too young to be without her mother. She was meant for someone's dinner. Fresh meat." The captain shrugged. "Nothing out of the ordinary. I've eaten monkey myself."

"You meant to eat her?" Phillipa squeaked.

"I was purchasing supplies," he admitted. "The fellow kept shaking her stick-and-vine cage in my direction, telling me how monkey heart is a virility aid. I wasn't interested, but she kept looking at me like I was her last hope in the world."

A virility aid. And he said it so matter-of-factly. "You were her last hope," she returned.

He shifted. "I suppose so. I was also in the middle of an expedition. But I purchased her, and a female goat suckling a kid. I cut a hole in the finger of one of my gloves to feed her goat's milk, and to my very great surprise she survived." He smiled, the expression surprising her with its genuine humor. "Leaving me in the position of being her mother."

"I have to say, you're the most masculine chit I've ever met," Henry Camden chortled, while the rest of the group laughed and applauded.

Phillipa started. She'd forgotten that Olivia and her friends were there, much less that they might be listening to the captain's conversation. "I doubt many others would have been as compassionate, Captain," she stated. "It speaks well for your character."

The other ladies were nodding. Wonderful. She'd made him even more appealing, if that was possible. Now for all the conversation she would have with him, she might as well leave and go attend someone else's picnic.

"It speaks better for the fact that I wasn't hungry."

The laughter faltered, and several of Olivia's friends fluttered their hands over their faces as though they might faint.

Captain Wolfe looked utterly unconcerned by their fragile states, and in fact leaned back on one elbow. "Should I not have said that?" he asked, running his fingers again along the hem of her skirt.

Soft, he'd said. "The book only mentions that you rescued Kero from traders, not that you considered eating her. They're shocked, I think."

"And you're not shocked."

"No. Very little shocks me."

"Hm. I wonder about that," he murmured, tugging now on the bottom of her dress as it lay fanned out around her.

For a second she contemplated catching John's attention, but as he was conversing with Olivia, she decided against it. She didn't find Bennett Wolfe's attention terribly shocking, anyway; it was more . . . unnerving. After all, she knew a great deal about his rough, harrowing life abroad, and she knew that on occasion when he'd spoken of women in a foreign land, there were things that he left out. Intimate things.

Perhaps that was his difficulty. After all, he'd been away from England for a very long time, and he'd mentioned virility already. "Captain," she began, searching for a way to be delicate and diplomatic and not shocked, "I know you haven't spent much time in London."

"No, I haven't." *Tug.*

"Then if you require . . ." She stopped, clearing her throat again and then leaning closer so she could lower her voice. "If you require . . . intimate companionship, there are a plentitude of lightskirts outside the Drury Lane Theater every evening."

He lifted an eyebrow. "There are?"

"Yes. I have seen them."

The captain sat up straight again. "You *are* practical, aren't you, Phillipa?"

For a moment she thought she could hear laughter in his voice.

"I like to think so." He'd used her familiar name without permission, but considering the topic of their conversation, she wasn't about to complain about it.

"For your . . . practical information, then, there are a plentitude of lightskirts everywhere. They call them by different names in different parts of the world, but if I—how did you say it—required 'companionship,' I believe I could track one or more of them down."

"Flip, you're not fawning all over our guest, are you?" Olivia chirped, swooping in to sit beside Captain Wolfe. "You mustn't mind her, Sir Bennett. She can quote from both of your books, and does so constantly."

Phillipa's cheeks burned. "I do not do it constantly. And don't expect me to apologize for having a fair memory," she retorted. She and Livi sniped at each other frequently, but generally not in public. Why her older sister felt the need to poke fun at her now, she had no idea.

"Oh, of course not," her sister returned. "It's only that we all want to hear about Captain Wolfe's adventures. You mustn't monopolize him."

Emerald eyes studied hers for a moment. "I didn't mind," he said with a slight smile and a last soft tug on her skirt. Then he stood and moved to the far side of the blanket, all the girls chattering and following behind him like sheep after a shepherd.

Phillipa remained where she was. The portrait in her mind of Bennett Wolfe hadn't been precisely accurate. For one thing, the scholarly, rugged portrait didn't tug on her dress and make her feel very warm and breathy. And its eyes weren't nearly as compelling as those that were just now glancing again in her direction. Perhaps there was more to adventuring than she'd realized.

Chapter Five

I had Mbundi with me when I approached the hunters; he was more likely to speak their language than I. I also doubted these tribesmen had ever seen a white man before. I only realized later that I should have been more concerned over how hungry they might have been and whether they ever ate strangers. Another reason to be sure of an invitation before arriving at a party.

THE JOURNALS OF CAPTAIN BENNETT WOLFE

W ell, this is charming," Jack muttered, clapping Bennett on the shoulder. "What are you doing here, anyway?"

"I'm being social." Bennett grinned, showing his teeth in what felt more like a snarl. "It was suggested that I do that rather than hunt down Langley."

"It's a good suggestion. But *I* could have stayed at home and caught up on my mending for all the attention Livi's paying me."

"It's not my fault I'm more interesting than you are," he murmured back. "If you want to talk to her, then go talk to her."

"It's not that easy, wild man. She has to want to talk to me." Jack shook his head. "I'm heading back to Clancy House. And you need to find somewhere else to stay soon. My mother's convinced that Kero's going to tear out her throat while she sleeps."

"Do not leave me here with this pack of laughing hyenas," Bennett shot back, keeping his voice below the nearly constant giggles and chatter of the mostly female herd around him.

He wanted to talk with only one of the chits, and she was sitting behind him, reading. He knew that, because he knew everything that she'd done, everything that she'd said, everything that she'd eaten, since the moment he'd arrived at the picnic. Including her advice on where he might go to find some whores to satisfy himself. Plural. Apparently she sensed his appetite.

"Very well," Jack murmured back, doing a very poor job of hiding a grin. "But you will owe me a favor."

"Yes, yes. Just stay close by. Leopards, I can face. These people terrify me."

"I doubt that very much."

Jack was correct; it wasn't terror as much as it was insurmountable boredom. He stayed on his feet mainly because it kept him from being mobbed, and because from there he could see over the bonnets and bare ringlets to where the very unusual Lady Phillipa Eddison sat.

And he listened, as well. Not just to that Henry half-wit regaling the females with the tale of how he and eleven other riders and twenty hounds had chased down a fox and killed it, as though that was the greatest test of manhood ever conjured. He also heard the whispers, the behind-hand mutterings about how he didn't quite appear to be the character Langley so humorously described him to be, and about how even if he was a bit dilapidated, at least he had a handsome face and a fair income.

This was what Sommerset had meant, he supposed, when the duke had said he'd joined the small group of men who saw Society with different eyes than those who'd never left it. Because the idea that chasing a fox for amusement was comparable in any way with hunting down a leopard that had killed two of his porters, for example, was absurd. As for the rest, they were welcome to their opinions as long as none of them was in a position to sponsor an expedition.

He sent another glance at Lady Phillipa. Her head still bent over his book on eastern Africa, she didn't look as though she'd even listened to the foxhunt tale. It likely hadn't even occurred to her that she should be applauding or admiring Henry half-wit's courage or some such nonsense. She picked up a strawberry and slipped it between her full lips, and he felt a responding twitch in his cock.

Christ. Over the past three years he'd seen more bare breasts and bare arses than a man could count, but while he had no reservations about learning foreign practices in intimacy, neither did he have the compunction to rut with everything that moved. The tribes along the Congo had for the most part been hostile—their only and limited experience with fair-skinned men had been with Arabian slave and spice traders. And he hadn't wished to have anything cut off that he might have a use for later.

Above and beyond years and experience, though,

Phillipa Eddison was something out of the ordinary. Literally. The moment he'd heard her voice he'd wanted to see her face. Upon seeing her face, he'd wanted to talk with her. And now he wanted more. If he could decipher her character a bit better, find the best way to hunt, he had every intention of doing so. Because in his experience, practical, logical chits on the outside were anything but that on the inside.

"—for a discussion of your own discoveries in the Congo?" Lady Olivia was saying, and he shook himself. *Social.* He was supposed to be social, make a fair impression, until he could wrap his hands around Langley's throat.

"Oh, that would be magnificent! I do love Captain Langley's other stories."

"Say you will, Sir Bennett!"

"I'll talk to Papa," Phillipa's older sister went on as he attempted to decipher the conversation, "and he'll have to agree. We'll arrange for a dinner, and then you could entertain us with your own tales of grand adventure."

Phillipa lifted her head again at the discussion, and he caught the flare of excitement in her earth-colored eyes before someone else cut between them. "I'd be happy to," he heard himself say.

"Oh, I want to hear you tell the story about when you and Captain Langley encountered that quaint tribe on the river. The one who gave you the canoes," the prominent-chested Sonja Depris suggested.

Bennett frowned. He'd read Langley's watered-down tripe about that incident. The Nbule had "given" them the canoes only after they'd attempted to slaughter the entire expedition and steal their supplies. He remembered it as a night of blood and fire and screaming. It had not been quaint, and his journal had not described it that way. Perhaps Langley thought that if he stole only every other sentence of a man's work, he could claim the results as his own.

As the rest of the group began offering suggestions of the stories they wanted to hear, movement halfway around the edge of the glade caught his attention. A group of children and a harried-looking woman, more than likely their governess, danced about and pointed excitedly at a nearby tree. A quick look told him that Kero had gone exploring. *Thank God*. An excuse to escape.

He inclined his head in the general direction of the largest number of picnic-goers. "Excuse me." Taking several strides toward the monkey, he slowed as he caught the desperate look on Phillipa's face. She seemed to hate being there as much as he did. "Lady Phillipa," he said, turning around, "Kero seems to like you. Come with me, will you?" He returned to her side and held down his hand to her.

When she set aside her book and reached up to grip his fingers, warmth slid up his muscles in a pleasant, unexpected jolt. He most decidedly liked touching this woman. He wanted to touch her more intimately.

"Should we help?" the Sonja chit chirped.

"You should not," he returned, only half paying attention to the rest of them as he helped Phillipa to her feet. The top of her head just reached his chin as they stood in the grass. He hadn't realized that the other night. Today it seemed oddly significant.

"But why does Flip get to—"

"I doubt Captain Wolfe wants everyone chasing after Kero," Phillipa said, interrupting the Sonja chit before he could state that Phillipa was allowed to accompany him because she was the only female he found tolerable in the entire crowd. "She more than likely doesn't even understand English. We'll be back in a moment."

When he caught sight of Jack scowling at him, Bennett realized he still held her fingers. Belatedly he let her go. "She understands English and Swahili—when she wants to," he said, moving off with Phillipa falling in beside him. "Which is generally when food is about."

"If she understands English then I can see why she wanted to escape the picnic and all that chattering," she returned with an amused chuckle.

"I like the way you laugh," he stated. "Even if I was in the middle of the chattering."

Her fair cheeks darkened. "Oh. I didn't mean *your* chattering. That is to say, you weren't—I mean, I found your conversation very interesting. The—"

He grinned. "They sounded like a troupe of damned baboons."

Phillipa snorted. Immediately she covered her mouth with one hand. "I knew from your books that you would be very witty."

"What did you think of me after you read Langley's book?" It took some effort not to sneer as he said those two words.

Her smile faded. "Everyone has their own opinion of everyone else."

"That's diplomatic of you. What happened to the

chit who informed me where the high flyers could be found?"

For a moment he thought he'd embarrassed her into muteness—which would be a damned shame. Then she sighed, a sound that he instantly memorized, and one that he wanted to hear again. Repeatedly. "I do know what's proper and what isn't," she finally said. "Olivia says I assume most people are more intelligent than they are, and that when I speak to them that way they find me odd and incomprehensible."

"I find you to be neither."

"Then you must be one of the truly intelligent ones." She smiled again, more shyly.

"Which is why I realize that you didn't answer my question. Did Langley's book alter your very high opinion of me?"

"In all honesty, and only because you asked me, I found Captain Langley's book a bit one-sided."

He slowed, moving closer to her before he'd even realized that he'd done so. "How so?"

"I read in the newspaper that you were the leader of the expedition," she returned, gesturing with her hands as she spoke, "and yet Captain Langley seemed to do everything. He chose the path, organized the porters, decided where to camp, was the better shot, the better fighter, and the better tactician."

Bennett clenched his jaw. "And?" he prompted.

"Captain Langley wrote the book." She shrugged. "I imagine if you wrote one concerning the same adventure, it would be a bit more balanced."

"What if it simply tipped in the other direction?" he asked, feeling somewhat mollified.

"Ah, but I've read your other books, remember? You, Captain Wolfe, give credit where credit is due. In my estimation, anyway."

As they reach the twisted old oak tree, Bennett held up his arm, and Kero hopped down from the tree limb where she'd perched and sat on his shoulder. Over the past three years, and for all twenty-six before that, he'd made his way in the world by assessing swiftly and accurately the character of those he encountered.

In this instance his sentiments were likely influenced by the fact that he found Phillipa Eddison damned fascinating and he wanted her, but she also had good instincts. He wanted to trust her, and he wanted to tell her that most of Langley's book was actually his words, twisted to make David the hero and to make his heroism more important than any of the myriad discoveries they'd made along the way.

At the moment he had no proof, and he knew what a braggart he would sound like because of it. And if she told anyone else what he'd said, he would sound like a disgruntled and incompetent explorer angry at a better man for pointing out his shortcomings.

"You avoided one of my questions as well, you know," she said, shaking him out of his thoughts.

"Did I?"

"Lord Fennington. Why didn't you want to talk about how he greeted you when he learned you weren't dead?"

He gazed at her levelly. "I haven't been to see him yet."

"What? Why not? He's your family."

"I haven't set eyes on him since I was twelve years old."

She put a hand on his arm, her touch light, but he felt as though he'd been permanently marked. "But he wrote so warmly about you in the foreword of *Across the Continent*," she protested. "He seemed to know you quite well."

"Perhaps he's read my books." Abruptly he realized that his hand was halfway up to touch her cheek, and he swiftly lowered it again.

"You should go see him, Captain," she urged.

He *did* need to visit Fennington, though not to play the prodigal son returning to the family's bosom. He needed to know how complicit the marquis was in the theft and publication of his journals. "Call me Bennett, and I'll consider it."

"Bennett, go see him," she repeated, his name soft on her lips.

Slowly he nodded. "I will. And then I have a book to return to you," he said.

"May I help you?" the tall, hollow-cheeked butler asked as Bennett, Kero on his shoulder, reached the front door of Howard House, the London residence of the Marquis of Fennington and his family.

"I need to see Fennington," he said, his jaw already tight. He couldn't count the number of times he'd sworn to himself that he would never stand on this doorstep. Not for any reason. And then a brown-eyed chit with a nicely curved frame had said his Christian name, and he hadn't even returned to Clancy House to borrow a new jacket.

The butler didn't move. "Is Lord Fennington expecting you?" he asked. "Because I wasn't informed."

He was getting damned tired of being blocked from entering every house in Mayfair. And this one, especially. "No, he isn't expecting me. He thinks I'm dead."

With an abruptly hostile look, the servant took a step forward. "Not another one," he grumbled, signaling behind him. A pair of footmen joined him in blocking the doorway. "The income from Captain Langley's book that was granted to Lord Fennington will remain with Lord Fennington, and it will take more than acquiring a monkey to fool anyone in residence into thinking otherwise. Away with you."

That answered a large question. Langley had paid the marquis for his silence about the journals. Bennett rolled his shoulders, attempting to ease the tension there. "If you and your two baboons think to intimidate me, then you'd best try harder than that. I've been in the jungles of Africa for the past three years, and you're about as frightening as a kitten."

His muscles grew taut, his senses expanding as he readied for possible battle. After nearly dying in the Congo and then returning home to find his work along with his reputation and hope for selection to future expeditions all now in question, he more than welcomed the chance for a fight. He wanted one.

"The earl is not home to charlatans," the butler responded, though he took a half step backward. "For your information, you are the fourth Bennett Wolfe to appear asking for a handout since the Season began. I will grant that you have the shabbiest-looking boots of all of them, but I do not find that impressive in the least."

Bennett glanced down at his well-worn boots. He'd become a fair cobbler in an attempt to keep himself shod during the expedition, but he could admit that these Hessians had seen better days. He looked up again. "I do not want a handout from anyone," he said evenly. "I want a word with Lord Fennington. Go fetch him. Now."

The man blinked, then swallowed. "Very well, sir. If that is the way you wish to proceed, then so be it." With a muttered word to the footmen who then moved to stand shoulder to shoulder in the doorway and block Bennett from entering, the butler retreated into the depths of the house.

There should have been rumors about by now that he'd returned to London, but if Fennington didn't want him to be alive, or if, as the butler had said, they'd already encountered men claiming to be him, the household might well have disregarded the news. He didn't much care what the marquis thought of his return. What he wanted was some bloody answers.

Shifting to balance his weight more evenly over his feet, Bennett regarded the servants. If necessary he could more than likely take them both apart and be inside the house within a minute. He wanted to. At the same time, though, he was grateful that he'd sought out Jack Clancy first, and that he'd had a few days to let his surprise and anger simmer before he broached Fennington. If he hadn't, someone would have ended up bloody, and he would have been willing to wager good money that it wouldn't have been him.

He heard yelling from inside the house. A moment later a young face peered out from beneath one of the footmen's arms. Bennett estimated him to be ten or eleven years of age, with the dark hair and eyes typical of his own mother's side of the family. "You must be Geoffrey," he said to the lad, keeping the reins tight on his growing frustration. "We've never met, but I'm your cousin, Bennett."

The boy's pale face folded into a frown. "No, you ain't."

"Geoffrey, move away from the door," a new voice, deeper and more authoritative, ordered. "Go sit with your mother."

As the boy vanished, the butler half stumbled back into the doorway, clearly pushed from behind. "His Lordship says he has no time for posers and that you'll get nothing from him," the servant recited.

Now he was finished with playing. And patience. He'd had less difficulty getting in to see the damned Duke of Sommerset, for Lucifer's sake. Bennett lowered his shoulders, while Kero, apparently sensing his mood, leapt off him to scamper up a nearby tree. "I am going to count to three," he said, keeping his voice low and even. "If I am not face to face with Lord Fennington by that time, several people will get hurt." He fixed his gaze on the butler. "Beginning with you."

"By you? Against all of us?"

Resisting the urge to spit onto the granite portico beyond his shabby boots, Bennett bent down, slowly drawing from his boot a long, curved knife blade affixed to a handle made of leather and polished rhino horn. "I think I can manage," he murmured. "I killed a crocodile with this knife, you know. I doubt you'll be as much of a challenge. One."

"Hold there!" the deeper voice came again from

inside the house. One of the footmen stumbled side-ways, and a tall, sharp-chinned man with narrow shoulders and a stout middle took his place. "There's no need for violence, my good man. Do you require a meal? Go around to the kitchen entrance and my cook will see t—"

"Two," Bennett interrupted dispassionately, real-izing that the man standing before him must be his uncle and waiting for the marquis to acknowledge that fact.

Lord Fennington opened his mouth to say some-thing, then abruptly snapped it closed again. With obvious deliberation he took in Kero, the knife, the boots, and Bennett himself. As the dark-eyed assess-ment returned to Bennett's face, the marquis paled. "You do look very like my sister, Sarah," he finally uttered, his voice shaking just a little.

"My mother's name was Grace," Bennett corrected, keeping the knife loosely gripped in his hand, "as you know. She died when I was nine, so I cannot vouch for any similarity in our appearance. Is that sufficient?"

"Good God," Fennington whispered. "Bennett Wolfe. You're alive."

"Do you wish to take a moment, or might I come in so we can chat?" He might have been more sym-pathetic if the man had given a damn about him when it might actually have meant something, but there was no mistaking that the marquis's surprise was genuine. And that could be significant.

"I—no. Come in, come in," Fennington said with a scowl. "Hayling, move aside. Do you have luggage? Where are your things? See that a guest room is pre-pared, Hayling."

Bennett began to protest that, because he had no desire at all to sleep under the man's roof. But then again, he wasn't likely to find a better position from which to learn where his journals were and what else, if anything, Langley might plan to do with them. Amid the flurry of activity Kero chittered and returned to his shoulder. As the marquis motioned him to enter the house, Bennett was thankful yet again for the young vervet monkey. Yearling though she was, she seemed to have realized how effective a show of her canines could be in the supposedly civilized world, and she could sense when he didn't like someone. And when he *did* like someone.

At any rate, she yawned widely at Fennington. Bennett wondered belatedly if that empathy was also why she'd taken the peach so gently from Phillipa's fingers. Thank Lucifer he'd rescued the monkey as an infant; he would rather be confused for her mother than her mate. Especially when he had his eye on someone. He didn't want Kero pulling Phillipa's hair every time he looked in her direction.

The boy, Geoffrey, reappeared from the direction of the stairs, his skeptical look replaced by one of wide-eyed awe. The marquis stepped between them, though, before Bennett could attempt another greeting. The going was likely safe, now, but since the knife had gotten him into the house, he was disinclined to put it away. He knew quite well that no one stood in the way of the largest crocodile in the river. At the moment, he was that crocodile.

"I apologize for not recognizing you, Bennett," his uncle went on, speaking quickly, "but you have to understand my suspicions. I—we—all assumed you to be dead."

Bennett gave a short nod. "Understood. Is there somewhere we might speak in private?"

"Yes. My office. This way."

At the moment Fennington seemed friendly enough, but he was likely attempting to determine how much trouble he was in for, and what, precisely, Bennett was after. Bennett was in no hurry to put him at ease.

The knife pointing at the floor but still in his hand, he followed the Marquis of Fennington a short distance down the Howard House hallway. The walls were decorated with paintings and bright wallpaper, the cornices outlined in gold filigree. A wealthy-looking household, but then he'd known that his mother's family, and his uncle in particular, had money. And he also knew they didn't care to part with it—even for a young nephew who'd lost his mother and whose father wasn't even in the country. Had never returned to England, in fact.

"You have your father's build," Fennington said into the silence.

"Wouldn't know that, either," Bennett returned.

"He was a bear of a man," the marquis continued, glancing back at him. "You're not as broad, but at least as tall."

"I might care for your theories about my appearance if you'd favored me with them twenty years ago, Uncle. Today I only want you to answer a few of my questions."

"Yes, of course." The marquis sat behind a fine mahogany desk and folded his fingers into a steeple beneath his chin. The fox back in his hole. Clearly he felt more secure here. Bennett meant to alter his perception. "Have a seat, my boy," Fennington said.

"I'll stand, and I thought I'd made it clear that I'm not your boy."

Fennington cleared his throat. "Very well. When did you arrive back in England?"

"Three days ago. My specimens will have arrived at Tesling by now. Do I still own the estate, or have you inherited it already?"

"I . . . I signed the papers for it a month ago. I will of course return it to you immediately."

Bennett wanted to snarl that he'd damned well better, but he held himself back. They could have *that* conversation after Tesling legally belonged to him once again. "Thank you," he said instead.

"Do say you'll remain here with us, for as long as you choose. It's long past time we became acquainted."

He'd spent the majority of his adult life in hostile territory. After three years in the Congo, a fortnight at Howard House in order to reclaim his reputation and his property shouldn't be too difficult. "Thank you again."

"My pleasure." Fennington continued to eye Bennett, his expression cautious rather than either surprised or relieved—or even disappointed—at his nephew's unexpected survival. Admittedly Bennett still held the knife, but at least his own conscience was clear.

"There's one more matter," he said, watching the marquis closely. "My journals."

"They arrived safely home with Captain Langley," his uncle returned, not even blinking.

Hm. "Then I can go fetch them from him."

Now came the slight flush of Fennington's cheeks, the twitch of his steepled fingers. "He's in Dover, I believe." The marquis abruptly sat forward. "Look, Bennett. We thought you were dead. And that left David as the only one who could turn that mess you left him into something that would make sense. I wrote you a lovely foreword, and the sales have been phenomenal."

Bennett drew a breath. " 'Left him'?" he repeated.

"Yes. A selection of your journals and sketches. Everything that you were able to salvage after the canoe overturned. It was all a jumble, hardly legible."

His heart froze in his chest. "My journals weren't in the canoe that overturned," he said slowly. "How ruined were they?"

Fennington cleared his throat. "I . . . didn't get a very thorough look at them. David said, quite correctly, that the less they were handled, the more information he would be able to recover for reference."

Reference. That was a laugh; or it would have been, if it wasn't his reputation being trod upon. "Firstly, in the event of my death my journals should have gone to the Duke of Sommerset and the Africa Association. Secondly, I never gave them to Langley. He took them while I lay bleeding and half conscious in a mud hut, and then he left. Thirdly, I have read Captain Langley's *Across the Continent,* and aside from the role reversal and the embellishments of his own competency, *I* wrote it."

"But—"

"It's taken nearly word-for-word from my journals. My complete journals, and my complete sketches, and my complete maps, all of which he stole."

"I don't believe you. You're embarrassed by your inability to lead the expedition, so you feel the need to strike out at the man who is merely trying to do with this literary effort what you've already accomplished with your previous ones." He sniffed. "Apparently accomplished, I should say."

Bennett jabbed a finger into the desk directly in front of his uncle, sending the older man backward. "When Langley returns from Dover, see if you can get a look at the journals. Then you may insult me. And you'd best hope he hasn't destroyed them. I prefer to have two choices in how I proceed, but if they're gone, I'll only have one."

He straightened again. "And you'll have until then to decide whether you want to side with David Langley or with me." Shaking himself, he backed toward the door and returned the knife to his boot. "I assume you don't want to me staying here any longer. Good day, then."

"Wait, Bennett."

Bennett turned around again, his hand paused halfway to the door handle. "What?"

"Whatever your opinion of matters, a rift between us will not look well." The marquis stood again. "Hayling!"

The butler opened the door. "Yes, my lord?"

"Show my nephew to the blue room."

"But that's the—"

"Now, Hayling. It's our best room," he continued, turning back to Bennett. "Give me the address where you've been staying, and I'll send for your things."

"For the sake of appearance," Bennett said, inclining his head. He'd hoped that would be the marquis's reasoning. And he also hoped that, regardless of where his uncle fit into all this, his warning about the journals would be passed on to Langley. He needed them to prove that he wasn't the fool they made him out to be, and David would need to keep them in good condition to keep himself breathing.

Chapter Six

We approached the village cautiously, from down-wind. Despite the small chance of our porter Mhiku still being alive, I insisted that we attempt a rescue. The sight we beheld was even worse than I'd feared; human skulls atop spears circled the entire village, hundreds of skulls in all. A fresh one, flesh and hair still hanging from it, stood at the head of the trail. And the patronesses at Almack's thought *they* were unfriendly.

THE JOURNALS OF CAPTAIN BENNETT WOLFE

I still wish *I'd* thought of letting him catch me reading one of his books," Olivia said, leaning over Phillipa's shoulder for a hair clip.

"I want that back," Phillipa said. "And I wasn't trying to impress him or anything. I was attempting to keep myself entertained."

"There were six gentlemen there, and that's not even counting Sir Bennett. You chatted with John."

"John is my friend. The other men were there to see you."

Olivia scowled, then gazed into the dressing mirror

and smoothed out one of her eyebrows. "Even if that were so, Flip, you could still chat with them. How are they to know how wonderful you are if you never speak to them?"

"I do speak to them. I say, 'She's over there,' and 'No, I believe she already has a partner for this dance.'"

Her sister planted a kiss on the top of her head. "You should try harder. They aren't all bad, but you'll never see that with your nose buried in a book."

Phillipa liked the way Livi said that, as though the decision to remain unattached was completely hers, and not because most men found her odd and more than likely a bit intimidating. Of course they both knew the truth, but it meant something that her sister never said it to her face.

"Well, if I should happen accidentally to knock some man to the ground while I'm reading, I'll be certain to invite him to come calling," she returned, though for a moment dark, shaggy hair and brilliant green eyes came to her mind. *Oh, for heaven's sake.* It was simply because she admired him. Not because he'd helped her to her feet and seemed to have sought her out at the picnic.

After making reasonably certain that she wore two ear bobs and that they matched each other, she stood up and followed Olivia out of her bedchamber and downstairs to the morning room to await their parents. She picked up her book again, but couldn't quite settle herself enough to read. What if Captain Wolfe decided to attend the soiree tonight? What if he asked her to dance?

"Come here, Flip," her sister said, making her jump. Livi waved a piece of paper at her. "While we have a moment, help me decide who I should invite for the dinner and evening with Sir Bennett. That's what I'm going to call it on the invitations, you know. 'An Evening with Sir Bennett.' Doesn't it sound grand?"

Blowing out her breath, Phillipa set aside her book and took the list from her sister. "You can't invite just men," she said after a moment.

"I included Sonja."

"Livi, you need even numbers. And in all honesty, I think your female friends will be more interested in dining with Captain Wolfe than will . . . Henry Camden, for example. Unless you were worried over inviting competition, someone else possibly to catch the captain's eye."

"I am not." Clucking her tongue, Olivia took back the list. "Very well." Frowning, she crossed out half the list and began adding names.

"And you can't remove John. He's the captain's dearest friend, *and* he's actually read the man's books. Someone has to be able to ask questions other than how tall he is and what his favorite venison dish might be."

"I've changed my mind," her sister said. "*I'll* decide who I should invite."

"I was hoping you would say that." Flashing her a grin, Phillipa rose as her mother walked into the room. "You look very nice, Mama. Are you certain you feel well enough to attend a soiree?"

"I won't be doing anything more than sitting and watching my two lovely daughters dance," the marchioness returned. "And I shall be happy to see something aside from the interior walls of my own house."

"Yes, well, we will be watching you like hawks,

Mama," Phillipa returned. "At the first glimpse of a pale cheek, we are whisking you home."

"At the very first glimpse," their father said, entering the room to tuck a strand of hair behind his wife's ear.

Phillipa watched the motion. Simple as it was, it bespoke affection. She'd liked it when Bennett touched her hand, even her skirt. Whether that was affection or some sort of jungle-induced lust she didn't know, but the idea of either one excited her. Men didn't desire her. They asked her to hold their hats while they flirted with her sister. Bennett, though, had barely glanced at Olivia.

She frowned. Why was that? And why had he spent so little time chatting with any of Livi's pretty, charming friends? It didn't make sense. And she liked for things to make sense.

"Do you think Sir Bennett will attend?" Livi asked as they all climbed into the Eddison family coach.

"I'm a bit confused," Lord Leeds said, tucking a blanket around his wife's knees. "Is he still a hero, or are we somewhat distrustful and disappointed to read that he may have exaggerated some of his previous adventures?"

"We're being tolerant," Livi answered before Phillipa could, "because he was so well respected before. And because he's very handsome and he has five thousand a year from the Crown."

"He does for now," their father countered. "If he becomes an embarrassment to Prinny and the House of Lords, he'll find himself studying ducks in Devon instead of crocodiles in the Congo."

"Very nice alliteration, Henry," his wife said, smiling.

"Thank you, my dear."

"He's not foolish," Phillipa put in. "I think it's perfectly obvious that Captain Langley exaggerated incidents because he believed Captain Wolfe to be dead. It's as Marc Antony said, 'The evil that men do lives after them, the good is oft interred with their bones.' "

"Do you truly think he requires Shakespeare's assistance?" the marquis said, grinning. "That seems rather . . . serious."

She shook herself. "You know what I'm saying, Papa. Captain Langley took advantage. You should meet Bennett, Papa. He's very witty."

" 'Bennett'?"

"He asked me to call him that. I helped him find his monkey."

"Mm hm. Well, there is to be no more monkey finding, whatever the devil that means." The marquis scowled.

"You should both be wary of him," their mother put in. "He's been in savage places, and he more than likely intends to return to them. I don't believe there are any soirees to be found in the Congo."

"If he doesn't attend tonight," Livi went on, clearly oblivious to any warnings, "you'll be able to meet him on Friday when he comes for dinner."

"He at least knows how to use utensils, doesn't he?"

"Papa," Phillipa chastised, "Captain Wolfe doesn't need rumors about that starting. He has enough on his plate, don't you think?"

"Indeed, I do. No rumors about eating with sticks shall pass my lips."

She stifled a smile. The image was rather amusing. By the time she and her father found a comfortable chair for her mother inside the ballroom at the Fordham soiree, Olivia had already been swallowed up by her usual crowd of friends and admirers. Knowing that no gentlemen would come looking for her until every place on Livi's dance card was taken, she sat down as well.

"You know Livi would be happy to include you in anything you wished," her mother said, as her father went off to greet friends and look for a glass of Madeira for his wife.

"I know she would," Phillipa returned, "but most of her friends make my head ache. They're so silly."

"There's nothing wrong with a bit of silliness now and then."

"I suppose not, and I like a good jest as well as anyone, but I don't think I could titter or flutter and flirt if my life depended on it."

The marchioness shook her head. "You can, I imagine; you simply don't wish to. Yes, I know you have other pursuits you enjoy, but you won't find a husband between the pages of a book."

"I—"

"Good evening, Lady Phillipa."

Phillipa stood up so hastily that her chair would have tipped backward if it hadn't been up against the wall. "Captain Wolfe. Bennett. Hello."

He still wore his scuffed boots. The rest of him, though, was decidedly more fashionable. She thought he might have borrowed clothes from John, but the captain was the taller and more broad-shouldered of the two by several inches. Perhaps he'd been able to find a quick-fingered tailor. Because the dark blue jacket, gray waistcoat, and tan breeches were exceedingly well-fitting. Exceedingly. Only his too-long hair and the uncivilized gleam in his green eyes branded him as other than a complete gentleman. Well, that and the vervet monkey on his shoulder. "Will you dance with me tonight?" he asked.

Excitement shivered through her. "Certainly." At a bump against her ankle Phillipa started, glancing back to see her mother looking at the new arrival, one eyebrow lifted. "Oh. Captain, this is my mother, Lady Leeds. Mama, Captain Sir Bennett Wolfe and Kero."

The green gaze left her face and turned to her mother. "My lady," he said, taking her hand.

"Captain. Welcome home to England."

"Thank you." He returned his attention to Phillipa. "I wish a waltz," he stated.

The waltz. The dance where partners weren't separated, and where she had to seek the lengthiest amount of inane conversation to share. "I—"

"Give me your dance card." He held out one hand.

"You know the waltz?" she asked, belatedly fishing her dance card and a pencil out of her reticule.

The corners of his mouth lifted, amusement lighting his eyes. "The waltz didn't begin in London, you know. I may even have invented it. By accident, of course, while attempting to escape the grasp of a very friendly princess in Vienna."

She chuckled. "When were you in Vienna?"

"On an assignment during the war," he returned, taking her card and penciling in his name. He took another place, as well, and began to write his name a third time.

"Stop that," she muttered, taking the pencil from him. "Everyone will want to dance with you. I cannot monopolize your attention. And besides,

two dances is . . . is nearly scandalous. Three is un-
heard of."

He leaned closer as he handed her back the dance
card. "You already monopolize my attention," he
said almost soundlessly, then smiled. "And I hate
wasting time."

That made her smile back at him. She couldn't
help it. "Wasting time with what?"

"With c—"

"Will Kero be joining you on the dance floor?" her
mother interrupted.

Bennett cleared his throat, straightening again. "I
believe she'll be willing to spend a short time eating
a houseplant." He flicked a finger against the monkey's tail. "Or hanging from a chandelier, if that
fails."

Still grinning, Phillipa reached out a finger to the
monkey. Kero hummed at her and grasped it in a
miniature handshake. "I would suggest the plant.
Lady Fordham is very particular about her crystal
chandeliers."

"Duly noted." As the other guests began to notice
his presence and crowd in, he nodded again. "I'll
see you in a bit."

Phillipa seated herself again as he walked away,
dozens of guests trailing him and all talking at once.
Mostly it seemed to be surprise that he was alive, or
confirmation that they'd already heard of his mi-
raculous return. Farther back, where he couldn't
hear, she made out the speculation about whether
he'd read Captain Langley's wonderful book and
whether he knew he was more popular now because of his income rather than his adventures.

She frowned. He had to know what was being said,

but she had no idea how he might counter it. Standing up and reciting equations or discussing flora species in the Congo would seem too self-serving, as though he was trying too hard. It might even give credence to the book's characterization of him.

"I can see now why Livi is so taken with him," her mother said after a moment. "That is one very handsome man." She took Phillipa's hand and tucked it between hers. "So you only admire his mind, do you?"

"I admired his mind long before I met him," Phillipa countered, her cheeks warming. "But I'm not blind. He is quite . . . striking."

"Yes, he is. Please don't let him come between you and Livi. You are sisters and friends, and that must be considered. Bennett Wolfe is a . . . well, a feckless adventurer."

Her mother left the second part of that sentence unsaid, but Phillipa heard it anyway. *And you are not an adventurer. You are a book reader.* "I would hardly call him feckless," she said aloud, shifting. "He's already won his fame and fortune; his journey to Africa was done with an eye to discovery, not income."

"There you are, my dear," her father said, returning to hand the marchioness a glass of red wine. "Was that imposing fellow Bennett Wolfe, by any chance?"

"Yes. He begged a waltz of Flip. Two dances, actually."

"He asked, not begged," Phillipa corrected, though he hadn't actually given her a choice about it.

"True enough," her mother conceded. "He doesn't precisely seem the begging sort, does he?"

"Oh, bother," the marquis broke in. "Are you in-fatuated as well, Venora?"

Lady Leeds chuckled, gripping her husband's arm. "He is beautiful, in an untamed, roguish sort of way."

"That settles that. I shall have to plan an expedi-tion somewhere so my own family will notice me."

While her parents continued bantering, Phillipa looked across the dance floor. Women practically threw their dance cards at Bennett, and he wrote his name on several of them. Once. Not twice on the same card. Nor was there any attempt at a scandal-ous trio.

She had no idea why such a fascinating man claimed to be fascinated with her, but she was abruptly noticing the way that other people ex-pressed their affection for each other; a touch of the arm, a hand at the small of the back, a brush of fin-gers against a cheek. And she wondered what Ben-nett Wolfe would do if she walked up and kissed him right on the mouth. Because she'd been think-ing about doing that since the night they'd met. And she thought maybe he'd been considering the same thing, himself.

Bennett had once seen part of the great migration of the wildebeests, thousands, millions of animals all herding together, following the same miles-wide trail through the savannah, over rivers, and out beyond where white men had ever traveled. Tonight he felt as though he was in the midst of the herd, being driven toward the edge of a cliff with no way to stop without being trampled.

What the devil had he been thinking, to come to a

place where the well-dressed horde gathered? Half the guests seemed to be speculating over whether he'd entirely invented the two books he'd written, while the rest wondered if he now meant to give up his life of adventuring and settle down to his estate in Kent with a wife.

He sent a glance across the ballroom. Phillipa Eddison stood out like summer, her yellow gown with its generous curves practically glowing among the more restrained colors of her peers. Heat slid through him, dark and primitive and undeniable. She knew all the rules of proper behavior, but thus far he'd observed that she had some difficulty following them. And he wondered how far astray he could lead her before she attempted to find the path again.

One of the chits bobbed a curtsy, blocking his way. "This is our dance, Sir Bennett," she said, smiling brightly.

Already? He knew enough about propriety to realize that he couldn't dance only with Phillipa, but neither did he have to like it. With a sigh he set Kero into the leaves of a large potted palm. "Behave," he said, placing a handful of peanuts into the hollow at the base of the fronds. "Let's go, then," he continued, glancing at the girl, and turned for the dance floor.

She fell in behind him, then hurried over to stand in the line with the other chits while he took his place with the gentlemen. For a moment he attempted to remember what the devil her name had been, but in truth the crowd had been so dense that he'd barely been able to glimpse the ladies who belonged to the dance cards he'd signed.

As the music began he bowed and turned, then held

out his hand for her. "I read Captain Langley's book," she chirped as he circled her. "I would have been frightened at being stalked by a leopard, as well."

"Mm." He walked down the line, turned, and came back to her side.

"I've been wondering why you didn't ride horses there? It would have been much faster than walking all that distance."

"They wouldn't fit in the canoes," he commented, his jaw beginning to clench again.

"Oh." She laughed uncertainly. "But you wouldn't have needed the canoes if you'd had horses."

Good God. "I'll consider that for next time."

She smiled cheerily. "I'm so pleased I could help."

He'd be more pleased when the dance ended. By the time it did, he'd heard all about English weather, as though he hadn't grown up with it, and a listing of the young men whom she would consider should they ask for her hand in marriage. He was dismayed to hear that he'd made it onto that list.

As soon as the dance ended he collected Kero and resumed walking. He'd managed to avoid the quadrille, next, and then came his waltz with Phillipa. If he didn't slow down until then, hopefully no other female would be able to maneuver him into the torture.

As he began another circuit of the room, he caught sight of the Duke of Sommerset cutting a swath in his general direction. For a man who'd spent so much time traveling to rather harrowing places under less than ideal circumstances, Nicholas Ainsley fit into Society rather well. Amazingly well, actually. He wore civilization like a comfortable overcoat—and Bennett suspected he could remove it just as easily.

"Captain," the duke greeted, cutting him off with apparent ease from the trailing scavengers, "a word with you."

In a moment they were out on the balcony overlooking the Fordham House garden. Kero left his shoulder to scamper along the granite railing, and Bennett took a deep, cleansing breath. "Thank you, Your Grace," he said feelingly.

"One of the mysteries of the female mind," Sommerset drawled with a short grin, "is how they will pursue an adventurer to the ends of the earth, but once they've caught him, they never want him to leave home again."

"Are you speaking from experience?"

"I remain uncaptured, though I suppose I won't be able to put that off forever." Steel gray eyes sent him a sideways look. "You've moved your things to Fennington's residence."

"I wanted to keep a closer eye on him and his publishing partner."

Sommerset nodded. "I think that's wise. And if you dispute the . . . exaggerations of the book at a later time, your association with Fennington will gain you more credibility."

"So you called me out here to approve my living arrangements?"

Running a hand through his raven black hair, the duke snorted. "You're supposed to be proving your worth to your peers. Small talk is essential to that."

"Bugger small talk. What do you want?"

"You should stop by the Adventurers' Club again, Bennett. You can snarl there to your heart's content. Don't do it in public." With a sigh, Sommerset turned his back on the stone railing and leaned his hips against it. "Langley's father is the Earl of Thrushell."

"I know that. I heard about the amount of Langley's likely inheritance for three years."

"Yes, well, Thrushell's petitioning to join the Africa Association. We require a two-thirds approval to add to the membership, and he hasn't quite got it yet. But he will. His son's book has gained us a great deal of favorable attention, despite the fact that he hasn't actually contributed anything to either the Association or England. Except himself, of course."

Cursing, Bennett pounded his fist against the railing. He knew what it meant; once Thrushell sat on the Association board, Langley would have the next available expedition. And the one man who knew for certain that Langley wasn't fit to lead anything would never be allowed within a league of the Association, much less gain their support for another expedition. "I suppose you voted your approval," he growled.

"I did not. I happen to believe your account, and I don't want the father of a fraud helping shape the direction of African exploration. Nor do I want to be associated with that family when you're able to recover your own standing."

Bennett faced him. "Thank you."

"You know, I had a chance to invite Langley to join the Adventurers' Club back when we all thought you were dead. At times I admire my own perception." He straightened, heading for the door back into the ballroom. "Don't disappoint me, Captain."

As the duke left the balcony, Bennett turned to look out over the torch-lit garden. Every instinct he possessed shouted at him to ride to Dover and get back his journals before Langley managed either to destroy them or to put them beyond his reach. He was fairly certain, though, that the journals weren't with Langley. If he went charging about now, David would know precisely what he intended, and he would never see his writings again. He would never have proof that he had led the expedition while Langley had whined and bullied his way through the Congo and nearly gotten them killed on more than one occasion.

No, he needed to stay precisely where he was and make Langley wonder what game he meant to play. And he had to continue allowing his supposed peers to tell their harrowing stories of foxhunting and to chuckle at him behind his back. He would strike when the moment was right, and not until then.

All of which also allowed him to see to something that had taken hold of him and refused to let go, whatever the rest of his troubles. He meant to get his hands on Phillipa Eddison, and he meant to do it soon.

Chapter Seven

For weeks the thick canopy of leaves all but hid the sky. Then one evening we camped atop a ridge. As night fell, the sky opened up. Thousands of stars, thick enough to walk upon. And brightest of all, the Southern Cross. She is a reminder that I am on an adventure unlike any I've ever attempted. I seek her out now whenever I glimpse the sky, for to my eyes she is the prettiest girl in the room.

THE JOURNALS OF CAPTAIN BENNETT WOLFE

Phillipa's pulse jumped as Bennett crossed the room. It seemed, to her at least, as though every other guest present paused in what they were doing to turn and watch him. Large and lean and graceful, even though it seemed too obvious to think so, he reminded her of nothing so much as a panther on the prowl. For her.

He stopped in front of her. "This is our dance," he said, and held out his hand.

"Where's Kero?"

"Back in the palm tree. She seems to like it there. Come along."

Putting on a smile to cover her sudden nerves, Phillipa gripped his warm fingers and allowed him to pull her to her feet. "I'll return in a few minutes, Mama."

"Take your time, my dear. Your father has promised to keep me company."

Curving his fingers around hers, Bennett pulled her toward the dance floor. "Your mother," he said in a low voice, glancing past her. "She's not well?"

"She's recovering from a lung ailment. This is her first outing in over a fortnight."

"You're good to watch her."

Phillipa tilted her head. "You wrote in *Walking with Pharaohs* that your mother died of a chill when you were nine. It made me feel . . . lucky, to still have mine."

Green eyes held hers. "Thank you. You're the first person I've met who's mentioned that book without adding scorpions or poison adders into the same sentence."

"It is an exciting book. Tomb robbers, desert treks, and pyramids and such. Do you truly think it was Bonaparte's soldiers who shot the nose off the sphinx?"

"That was what the locals claimed. I think they may have caused part of the damage." As they reached the dance floor, he faced her. "I don't want to talk about pyramids," he said, sliding a hand around her waist, and twining the fingers of his other hand with hers. The orchestra began playing, and he effortlessly swung her into the waltz. Oh, yes, he could dance.

Phillipa drew a breath, attempting to steady herself. This close, he smelled of leather and, surprisingly, peanuts. Kero's doing, she supposed. "Kero is behaving well," she noted. There. Nothing about pyramids.

"She finds food exceedingly persuasive."

"Is her stomach ever full?"

Bennett chuckled, an arousing, rumbling sound. "Not that I've noticed." He drew her a breath closer. "Tell me, Phillipa, who's been pursuing you?"

The question surprised her—everyone in Mayfair likely knew the answer to that question. Bennett Wolfe, however, had spent the previous three Seasons in the Congo. "No one's pursuing me," she answered.

A line furrowed between his brows. "What's wrong with you, then?"

She snorted, ducking her head to cover the sound. Damnation, she thought she'd managed to stop that habit. Livi teased her about it enough. "I have a very lovely older sister who received all of the gifts of flirtation and charm. I received the gifts of short patience, short legs, and very little tact."

He grinned. "And I repeat, 'What's wrong with you, then?'"

As she didn't feel inclined to ruin this singular moment by delving into the various defects of her character, she shook her head. "I'd rather discuss your explorations."

His arm muscles around her tensed a little, then relaxed again. "One question, then," he returned. "Only one."

Oh, that hardly seemed fair—or adequate. And aside from that, people were watching them. Watching him, rather, but they were attached at the shoulder and the hip. It was all very distracting. And exhilarating, actually. "Very well," she said slowly. "Is there any place in the world that you call home? Not a house, since I know you own Tesling, but home."

He blinked. "Nothing about leopards or crocodiles or hippopotami or cannibals?"

"No."

They danced in silence for a long moment. He continued gazing at her, his intensely green eyes mesmerizing. It was as if he carried part of the jungle with him, as if it had sunk inside his soul and colored him from the inside out in its fierce shading. Beautiful. And she liked when those wild eyes looked at her.

"You are a conundrum," he finally announced.

She smiled. People rarely said anything so flattering to her. "What about me puzzles you?" she asked, genuinely curious. To herself, she felt fairly straightforward.

"That is something I would have to show you," he murmured.

Something in his tone made her blush. After all, she might be practical and logical, but she wasn't ignorant or stupid. "Why did you return to London? You didn't know you'd been declared dead, and John said your expedition crates went to Kent."

"That is a second question, Phillipa."

"You didn't answer my first one."

"Then which one do you want answered?"

She considered that. The first query was about him, while the second had at least a little to do with her. As she was still attempting to decide, though, the waltz ended. Cursing at herself for missing the chance to discover something insightful about this fascinating man, she halfheartedly applauded with everyone else and then headed across the crowded room in the general direction of her parents.

A hand cupped her elbow. "I'm not finished with you yet," Bennett said in a low voice, cutting sideways through the tide of dancers, her in tow, with apparent ease.

"Where—"

"Stop asking so many damned questions."

Phillipa snapped her mouth closed again, settling for frowning as they left the ballroom, hurried down the hallway, and pushed inside an empty upstairs sitting room.

"You agreed that I should ask you a question," she finally snapped, pulling her elbow free.

He faced her. "*A* question, Phillipa. Not a barrage."

"But—"

Bennett gave a half smile. "A complete conundrum," he murmured.

Lifting both his hands, he stroked his fingers along her cheekbones, making her shiver. Softly he ran a thumb along her lower lip, then he leaned down and caught her mouth with his. The sensation—warm, soft, and electric—jolted through her. Phillipa closed her eyes, her breath stopping at the arousing heat that seemed to move from him into her. She tilted her face up and wrapped her arms around his neck.

With a low groan Bennett pulled free of her grip, only so he could close on her again. He'd wanted to kiss her for days, and even with the poor timing and the proximity of possible witnesses, he couldn't wait any longer. He wanted to stroke his hands down her curves, rip the buttons from her pretty yellow gown, and slake himself inside her naked body.

Phillipa curled her fingers into his hair, opening her eyes to look up at him. "This is nice," she murmured unsteadily, lowering her gaze to his mouth again.

She tasted like strawberries and desire. He bent his head to her again, teasing her mouth open, backing her into the wall and splaying his hand on her hips. Arousal crackled at him, sending heat spearing down to his cock. Christ, he wanted her.

Dimly he heard the music to a country dance begin. "I'm supposed to be dancing with someone," he muttered, shifting his grip to pull her against him.

"What?" She leaned her head back, away from him. When he pursued her, she put a hand over his face and pushed. "Stop it."

With a growl Bennett loosened his hold on her. "I'm not finished."

"You have to go dance."

"I don't want to."

Her brow furrowed, her dark brown eyes nearly black in the dim room. "Bennett, if you promised someone a dance, you have to dance with her. I would hate to be standing there, waiting for some man to appear after he'd already promised to do so."

He tilted his head, reluctant amusement beginning to push past his frustrated lust. "I'm in the midst of kissing you, Phillipa, and you're actually ordering me to go dance with some other chit whose name I can't at the moment recall?"

"You promised."

"And with whom will you be dancing?"

"I will be sitting with my mother."

For a moment he considered that. If *she'd* had someone waiting for her, he was fairly certain he would have kept her there. She, on the other hand, didn't seem to have any of the same reluctance where he was concerned. And then there was the question of why no one else found her as fascinating as he did. He didn't have a very high opinion of her fellows, however, and it didn't surprise him that none of them recognized how compelling she was.

Bennett released her and took a step back. "Let's go, then."

Just before he reached the door, she put a hand on his arm. "Will you be kissing her in here after the dance?"

"What?" The thought hadn't even crossed his mind. "No."

She smiled, rocking back on her heels. "Good."

That left him feeling a bit better. After all, that had been quite the kiss, if he said so himself. He sent her ahead, counted to ten, then left the sitting room. And immediately he wanted to return there again.

"Sir Bennett, Sir Bennett, we must take our places for the dance!" a young lady called, waving her dance card at him as soon as he walked into the ballroom.

What the devil was her name? Most of his attention was still on the vanished Phillipa. Miss Penny, or Perry, or something. "Shall we, Miss Perry?" he said aloud, sending up a quick prayer and offering his hand. "Apologies for my tardiness."

Giving her female companions a look of complete triumph, Miss Perry took his hand and pranced onto the floor and into the dance with him. Apparently, then, he'd gotten her name right. She seemed to prance and bounce quite a bit. The up and down movements had the effect of rendering her bosom the most . . . noticeable part of her anatomy, but he began to wonder how she avoided putting out an eye.

"How are you finding London?" she asked brightly as she made the turn around him.

"It's crowded," he returned, sending a glance in Phillipa's direction. Too many people dipped and bobbed between them for him to catch more than the most fleeting of glances. "And loud."

"Oh, I would imagine it is, after the wilds of Africa. And so much more civilized."

He could debate that. "I suppose so."

"Lord and Lady Fordham always manage to host the event of the Season. Of course with no crocodiles or bare-breasted natives, it must seem quite tame."

She was practically bare-breasted herself. They circled away from each other and joined again. "It has its challenges," he observed, looking about again as they neared the end of the line of dancers.

There she was, sitting beside her mother and chatting amiably, the high color in her cheeks the only indication that she might be anything other than cool and collected. For a heartbeat her brown eyes met his before she vanished behind the crowd again. Lust rolled across him like a warm breeze.

"Have you been to the Tower menagerie?" Miss Perry pursued. "They have two lions there. And a giraffe. And some monkeys very like Kero."

"I've seen them in the wild, Miss Perry. I do not need to see them in cages." Truth be told, he felt too much sympathy for the animals. He felt rather like he'd been caged and put on display himself from the moment he'd returned to London. Every time he returned to London.

Her bright smile faltered a little, though she continued bouncing as enthusiastically as ever. "Do you know when Captain Langley will be returning to London? I should very much like to meet him."

"I have no idea."

"Oh."

Finally the dance ended, and he used some of his hunting skills to disappear before she could demand that he introduce himself to her parents. He moved back against the wall and observed the ballroom. They all looked like a colony of ants, moving along the same trails, moving the same way, gathering gossip to use for and against one another as ants gathered leaves.

Under any other circumstances he wouldn't have given a damn what any of them thought of him. Now, however, David Langley had pulled him into some sort of contest of competency and popularity before he'd ever realized a game had begun. Women still looked at him; with the remains of his reputation and most significantly his five thousand a year, he seemed to be quite the attraction. If all he'd wanted was sex, he could have a very large quantity of it.

But there was some indefinable . . . *more* that he seemed to require at the moment, and he knew where to find it. With whom to find it.

A reverberating screech yanked him out of his lustful reverie. He pushed upright. "Damnation."

The palm tree in the corner of the ballroom shook like it was in the middle of a monsoon. "Kero, *siyo!*" he called, striding toward the fracas.

As he neared the tree, Kero leapt ten feet through

the air to land in his arms. She put her head beneath his jacket, handing him a tattered lady's glove at the same time.

"That beast tried to bite me!" a matronly female squawked, clutching at her ample bosom. "I was only attempting to be friendly!"

Bennett held up the glove. "Did you wiggle your fingers at her?"

"Well, yes. How else was I supposed to say hel—"

"She thought your fingers were grubs," he interrupted, and handed the glove back. "They're white, and about the same size."

Several younger members of the crowd snickered. The woman clutching her ruined glove turned beet red and looked as though she might suffer an apoplexy at any moment. Abruptly Phillipa stood beside him.

"Considering that Kero never saw London fashion until four days ago," she said, "I'm surprised she hasn't attempted to eat anyone's hat. You were brave to try to make friends with her, Lady Sefton."

At the sound of more chuckling and some murmurs of agreement, Lady Sefton bit back what was likely another complaint. "You really shouldn't allow a wild animal to roam among civilized persons," she finally said.

Civilized. There was that word again. As though the people around him personified it, while he didn't even know the meaning of the word. He supposed every group of wild beasts thought *they* were the civilized ones. His fingers brushed Phillipa's, but he shifted away again before anyone else could notice. Little tact as she claimed to have, she had more than he did. "I'm fairly wild myself, my lady," he said. "Thank you for your patience with both of us."

"Yes, well, you can't leave an animal sitting about to attack unsuspecting ladies."

"Hopefully everyone will be more wary of her now."

With that he turned his back on her and offered his arm to Phillipa. He felt rather than saw her hesitation, but then her fingers wrapped around his sleeve. Enjoying the sensation, he kept silent as he walked her back to her parents.

"You shouldn't be so blunt with people," she said finally.

"Me? I thought you were the direct one."

"You know what I mean. If you haven't noticed, your reputation is rather uncertain at the moment. Telling viscountesses they have fingers that look like grubs will not make you any friends."

"I have all the friends I need." He drew a breath. "I want to kiss you again."

Her fingers crushed into his arm, then lightened again. "You're being overly blunt again."

"There you are," Lady Leeds said, as he and Phillipa reached the side of the room. "I heard a terrible commotion."

"Oh, that was us," Phillipa returned with a grin. "Kero, actually."

"Heavens. Was anyone hurt?"

"Only Lady Sefton's glove." Phillipa released Bennett's arm. "Do you think Kero will be more tolerant of me?"

He stifled his scowl at her stepping away from him. "Let's find out," he said aloud. Making low-pitched clucking sounds in imitation of any good monkey mother, Bennett scratched Kero behind the ears. "Move slowly," he instructed, gathering the cat-sized monkey into his arms and then holding her out to Phillipa.

"Flip, be careful," Lord Leeds cautioned with a frown of his own. "That monkey has very large teeth."

"Bennett will protect me," she said absently, offering her arms to the vervet. "Hello, Kero."

The way she said those words, so matter-of-factly, as though she had no doubt of the truth of them whatsoever, made his pulse speed. "I will," he agreed quietly, wondering if she had any idea how seriously someone like him—someone who knew very well how fragile life could be and how many dangers lurked about—took a promise like that.

Kero looked at her, tilting her head from side to side, and chittered. Then she reached out, grabbed Phillipa's fingers, and swung across into her arms. "You're so light," she cooed, gently scratching behind the monkey's ears. "And your fur is scratchy."

The vervet patted Phillipa on the cheek, then reached up to begin picking through her hair, destroying the neatly clipped coiffure. "Oh, Flip, it's making a mess," her sister said, abruptly appearing beyond Lord Leeds. "Your hair."

"It's no bother," Phillipa said, actually grinning. "It tickles."

"She's grooming you," Bennett told her, concealing his own surprise. "It's quite an honor, actually."

As he watched Phillipa giggling, scratching Kero as the monkey cooed and picked apart the pretty arrangement of her long chestnut hair, everything else fell away. His missing journals, Langley, the news Sommerset had given him, three years of the hardest living he'd ever done, the still-healing spear wound in his side. "I'm coming after you, Phillipa," he said, making certain she could hear him. He wanted her to know.

Chapter Eight

We've learned never to wash in the river without at least one lookout; crocodiles lurk everywhere in the inlets and slower-moving stretches of water. The natives say there is nothing more placid than a pond with a crocodile just beneath the surface—until it strikes, at which moment nothing is more horrifying.

THE JOURNALS OF CAPTAIN BENNETT WOLFE

Bennett sat in the breakfast room at Howard House and sliced slivers off a peach. Chattering her teeth and chittering happily, Kero accepted the pieces and messily gobbled them down. While pulp and the peach's tart skin landed around her on the polished mahogany table, the butler and his two footmen stood at the opposite end of the room taking turns making disapproving grunting noises.

"You sound like a herd of wildebeest," Bennett commented, glancing at them as he handed over another slice to the monkey. "Or camels. I can't decide."

Evidently he hadn't disguised his anger toward Fennington and his brood very well, because they'd all altered their breakfast schedule to avoid sitting with him. While he wouldn't have minded dining with Geoffrey or his sister, Madeline, he knew himself to be a poor conversationalist—especially with the man who'd conspired with Langley to cut down his reputation. As for Lady Fennington, his aunt had nearly enough personality to fill a teacup.

"The animal is making quite a mess," the butler droned.

"Are you referring to the monkey, or to my nephew?" Fennington drawled, strolling into the room.

"Hm. How long did you lurk outside the room waiting for *that* opportunity?" Bennett asked, handing Kero the remaining quarter of the peach.

"I don't lurk in my own home. Hayling, that'll be all for the moment."

The butler finished pouring the marquis his morning tea. "Very good, my lord." With a gesture he sent the two footmen out of the room and followed them, closing the door after himself.

"You still have a great many admirers," Fennington said after a moment, opening his freshly ironed copy of the *London Times*. "I have to say, I was a bit dismayed by the tone of Captain Langley's book toward your involvement in the expedition."

"You did write that very nice foreword connecting you to me," Bennett said with a nod. "You should have read the book before you agreed to contribute to it."

"For all I knew, his observations were accurate. They may yet be."

Bennett deliberately set the knife aside. "Are you going to attempt to blame me for the fact that this is

the first time I've set eyes on you in seventeen years, Fennington?"

"No. It was merely a comment on the facts."

"How much is Langley paying you for your . . . connection to me?"

"Fifty percent of his profits."

Bennett lifted both eyebrows. "That's generous. Why so much?"

The marquis sighed. "I believe it was so that I wouldn't make an issue over the ownership of the items you gave him on your deathbed. If I had done so, Sommerset might also have made a claim for them."

"And Sommerset would have had the best chance of getting them." Taking a bite of poached egg, Bennett sat back in his chair to study his uncle. He had a vague recollection of the man from a brief visit when he'd been twelve, but that had been only because his aunt and uncle had come by whichever boarding school he'd attended at the time and announced that they were on their way to holiday in Scotland, and that no, he wasn't invited. And then, nothing. Not until three days ago. "I'm somewhat surprised that you're not dissembling."

Fennington shrugged. "I thought you were dead, Bennett. I haven't done anything wrong except perhaps keep my silence about a few papers that may or may not have rightfully belonged to Captain Langley." He dropped a lump of sugar into his tea. "Now, must you encourage that monkey to sit on my furniture?"

"You helped make her famous," Bennett returned. "This is the consequence."

"Just remember, if not for that book, no one would

remember you at all right now. Langley's moment in the sun is purchasing you a moment or two in his shade. Get that thing off my table."

At the angry tone of his voice, Kero faced Fennington, giving a high-pitched, teeth-bared chirp, the hairs lifting on her back. Clearly uncomfortable being at approximate eye level with an agitated vervet monkey, the marquis pushed to his feet. "Control your animal or I'll have it shot and stuffed."

"You could try that, but I wouldn't recommend it." Bennett made a low clucking sound and Kero subsided, dropping the peach pit onto the floor and clambering up his shoulder. Gazing levelly at his uncle, he stood as well. "We'll have to continue this later. Jack Clancy's dragging me somewhere civilized," he continued, unable to keep the sarcasm from his voice. "That should be a treat."

Out in the foyer he handed Kero into the coat rack and pulled on his greatcoat. Once he'd straightened the collar, the monkey returned to his shoulder.

"Ready for a ride?" he asked, flicking her tail with his finger.

"Sir." The Howard House butler reached for the door and, backing as far away from Kero as he could manage, pulled it open.

"Cousin? Bennett?"

Halfway through the front door he stopped, turning around to face the source of the young, hesitant voice. "Geoffrey."

His cousin stood just inside the morning room doorway. He'd barely seen the boy since the day of his arrival, and the rather brusque exchange they'd had then had been their only conversation.

"Did you truly shoot a leopard?"

"I did."

"Did you keep the pelt?"

"It's at Tesling. I do have a necklace made out of the teeth upstairs in my bedchamber." Mbundi had assured him they would keep him safe from harm. He should likely have been wearing them the evening they were ambushed, but the damned things dug into his skin. The one time the leopard had attempted to eat him had been enough without repeating the experience every time he wore the necklace. "I'll show it to you later, if you like."

"Father says I may go foxhunting when I'm twelve."

Bennett had no idea how to reply to that; saying that he considered foxhunting to be the poorest excuse for a sport ever invented would be unkind. "Good for you," he ventured, and left the house.

Jack waited for him on the drive. He rode another of his horses, gray Brody, while he held Jupiter by the reins. "I thought you might need transportation," he said, tossing the leads to Bennett.

"I still haven't decided if I'm accompanying you," Bennett returned, patting the big bay on the flank and then swinging into the saddle. "If the 'civilized' character of wherever we're going is its highest recommendation, I'm not interested."

The marquis's son flashed him a grin. "Trust me."

With an exaggerated sigh Bennett settled Kero against his chest and trotted off behind Jack Clancy. In truth he didn't have much in the way of plans, and that aggravated him. He was accustomed to having something to accomplish, whether it was making it to the foothills before nightfall or discovering whether a certain species of lizard was red all the time or only when it was seeking a mate. At the moment, however, he needed to wait. Wait for Langley to reappear.

Of course, he also needed to convince the Mayfair herd that his previous books weren't fictional or exaggerated, while Langley's Africa book was both of those things. And he needed to talk to the Africa Association before they voted to sponsor another expedition that did not include him.

The entire damned thing involved him being charming and patient and social, when he was more comfortable with, and more eager for, throwing punches and brawling. London felt so bloody small. Small space, small minds, and nothing new under the sun.

Ahead of him, Jack slowed a few hundred feet into St. James's Park. Bennett looked where he indicated, and lifted an eyebrow. Perhaps there was something new under the London sun. "Lawn bowling?"

"Very civilized, don't you think?" He dismounted. "And a rather attractive selection of young, unmarried ladies playing it."

Bennett didn't answer. He'd already seen her. Phillipa. This morning she wore a pretty green and white sprigged muslin, and absolutely looked like springtime. She said something to her sister and then took a step forward, squatting a little to roll the green bowl forward. It was a grand shot, glancing off someone else's bowl to land right against the kitty.

"If anyone asks, I've been showing you the sights, and we stumbled across the game," Jack said, pulling the reins over Brody's head and loosening the bit, leaving the gray to stand and graze.

Finally Bennett glanced over at him. "Why are

we here actually?" he asked, dismounting as Kero clambered up to his shoulder. "Not that I'm complaining."

"Because if I came by myself and stood about watching Livi Eddison, it would be frightening. With two of us, it's an innocent excursion. And I'm more charming, so I'll make the better impression." He frowned. "Stay away from Olivia Eddison, by the by."

"I have no interest whatsoever in Olivia Eddison."

"Good. You'd never suit anyway. In fact, the only person I can conjure who'd be less likely to want to go traipsing off on one of your expeditions than Livi is her sister."

Bennett slowed his approach. "Why is that?"

"Flip is one of the most intelligent people I know, male or female. But she's very . . . attached to her library. In fact, a group of us went fishing a few weeks ago, and asked her to join us. She declined. Flip said she would rather read a book about fishing than engage in the practice."

The information jolted him. Since he'd first heard her voice he'd set himself on a trail that led to him having her. For that reason it shouldn't matter that she didn't like travel or adventure. But part of him, evidently, had been looking beyond the end of the bedposts. And that part didn't like what he was hearing.

"Look who's found us!" Olivia sang, prancing over to take one of Jack's hands and one of his and tow them toward the green.

"I was showing Bennett the sights," Jack said with a smile. "You surprised us."

"I told you yesterday that we were going to be

bowling in St. James's," Phillipa said, her brown eyes turning to Bennett. "Good morning, Captain. Kero."

"So you came to find us?" the other sister was saying. "That's even better. Sir Bennett, you must be on my team. Flip is handing us a pounding."

"I already promised your sister I would join *her*," he heard himself say. "Take Jack, or you'll hurt his feelings. He was always the last one chosen for cricket at university."

"Captain, do you remember Wilhelmina Russell?" Phillipa was saying to him. "She met you at John's book reading club."

Ah, the hatchet-faced chit, still up to her chin in muslin, blue this time. He nodded. "Miss Russell."

Twin red blotches appeared on her cheeks. "Sir Bennett. What a great honor."

"I thought you said I was a savage," he pointed out, unable to resist.

"That's why I like you," Phillipa put in, reaching up to his shoulder to scratch Kero's stomach.

"Do you now?" he breathed, the scent of citrus touching him. Lust stirred deep in his gut, sharp and intoxicating.

"I was talking about Kero," she whispered back, her eyes dancing. "Now. Do you know how to bowl?"

"Put the green bowl as close as you can to the white ball. The kitty, yes?"

"Very good. And you roll underhand. No throwing at anything."

Good God, she was flirting. Teasing. Arousing as he found it, this morning was going to be a test of every bit of control he owned. "No throwing," he repeated, lifting Kero into the nearest tree and handing her an apple from his pocket.

They began the game over, each of them taking turns rolling their three irregularly shaped bowls at the kitty target. Phillipa might prefer books to fishing, but she was the devil of a bowler. Perhaps it was her grasp of logic and mathematics. Personally he didn't care, as long as he got to watch her.

He stood back beside her as Miss Russell took her turn. "I want to kiss you again," he murmured, waiting for the soft blush to touch her cheeks. It was absolute torture to not be able to put his hands on her.

Phillipa looked up at him. "You've been away for a very long time," she returned in the same low tone, twisting her fingers into one another. "I told you where you could go to . . . slake your lust. You should find a lady who knows what she's about."

" 'Slake my lust'?" he repeated, chuckling.

"Yes. Don't laugh. There are myriad other young ladies here, Bennett. I don't understand why you kissed me."

"I kissed you because I wanted to kiss you."

"Have you wanted to kiss anyone else since you returned?"

With any other chit he might have asked whether she was jealous, but he had the feeling that Phillipa genuinely wanted to know what he was about. Curiosity. Another trait he found very compelling, despite the blow to his self-esteem. "No."

"You see? That's what I mean. You haven't met anyone but me."

He folded his arms over his chest. "So if I knew better I wouldn't be drawn to you?"

Rich brown eyes widened a little. "You're drawn to me?"

"Yes."

"How so?"

Sweet Lucifer. "I want you." She claimed to prefer straightforward conversation. "Naked. In my bed. In any bed. On the floor. That part doesn't really matter. Just the naked bit. Naked with me."

Phillipa opened her mouth, then closed it again. A moment later she cleared her throat. "That's . . . that's very scandalous."

"Is it? I don't actually care."

"It's because you've been away for so—"

He reached out and grabbed her wrist. "No. It's not. I've danced with two dozen chits since I've returned. I've chatted—if that's what it's called—with fifty more. You're the one I kissed."

"But you can't simply ruin me," she returned, her voice squeaking a little.

She pulled her arm free and walked forward to roll her bowl. This time her aim was terrible. Then it was his turn. With barely a look he tossed the green bowl out onto the grass and moved up even with her again. "That's all that troubles you? That I not ruin you?"

"That's not what I mean." She scowled. "You . . . the . . . there are steps. And rules. You haven't even said anything nice to me, except that you liked my laugh. And now you want to . . . well, you know."

"Steps."

"You said you were after me. Just for . . . intercourse? That's not very flattering."

"I beg to differ, but I don't like to waste time. Courtship is overrated."

"To whom?" she demanded. "I've never been courted, so I couldn't say, myself. And if you're not interested in seeing me unless I'm naked, then I seem to have wasted a great deal of conversation with someone I admired."

"You admire m—"

"I've spent time, you know, imagining what it would be like to talk to the great Bennett Wolfe. He would be suave and charming and witty. He wouldn't after four days say, 'I want to see you naked,'" she went on, doing a poor imitation of his voice, "and then say that spending time getting to know me is overrated."

He glared at her. She might as well have thrown cold water on him. This wasn't about being back in London for a few days, or even about being practically alone in the jungle for three years. This was about her. And he'd clearly stepped into a very large pile of elephant shit in telling her that. "I'm going now," he announced, turning to face the rest of the bowlers. "I have an engagement."

"You do?" Jack asked, looking perturbed.

"Yes. You may as well stay here, because you're not invited." He glanced back at Phillipa's confused, hurt expression. "Good day."

"We'll see you tonight, for our dinner," Olivia called after him.

"Seven o'clock," he returned, collecting Kero and returning to Jupiter.

"And please bring the monkey!"

Yes, everyone liked the monkey. He kicked Jupiter in the ribs, and they galloped out of the park. He didn't have a particular destination in mind, but he did feel in the mood to be surly—which, given the restrictions he had to place on his own behavior, left him with only one place he could go. Other than back to Africa, which he couldn't do at the moment, either.

Ten minutes later he stepped down and tossed Jupiter's reins to a liveried groom at Ainsley House. Kero loosened her grip on his cravat and clambered down the length of him to pull a peanut from his pocket. Bennett walked along the front of the house to the second, vine-obscured entrance.

He pulled the small key from his pocket and unlocked the door, then stepped inside. "Hervey," he said, greeting the dark-clothed servant walking toward him.

"Captain. Make yourself comfortable. Is there anything you require?"

"A glass of whiskey, if you please." Barely noontime or not, he wanted a damned drink.

"Very good." Hervey turned away.

"Hervey, is Sommerset about?"

The servant paused. "I haven't seen His Grace today, Captain. Should I inquire?"

Bennett shook his head. "No. That's not necessary." While he wanted to know whether Lord Thrushell had yet been able to bully his way onto the Africa Association board, there remained nothing he could do about it. For the moment, anyway.

"Well, if it ain't the man with the monkey!" Thomas Easton waved from halfway across the room.

Ignoring both the comment and the sarcasm in the man's voice, Bennett took a seat close to the shelves of books. Three other men had taken refuge in the Adventurers' Club this afternoon, though Easton was the only one he recognized. That suited him; he wasn't in the mood for conversation, witty or otherwise. Not even from men who had an understanding of what the devil they'd all mired themselves in, coming back to London.

The chair opposite him pulled out, and Easton took a seat. "Finished Langley's book," he said, draining a mug of beer and gesturing Hervey to bring him another. "What I can't figure is why you got the Sommerset royal invitation to join this little club, while Captain Langley didn't."

"Bugger off."

"I've heard that before." Easton chuckled. "At least people know where you went. I mean, whether you bungled it or not, you did survive the Congo. No one knows what I was up to."

"I don't care." Bennett took the glass Hervey handed him.

"Ah." Easton sat forward. "But if you ever attended a ball, you would. All them pretty gowns, that silk from the East. That's because of me."

If he'd provided the yellow silk that Phillipa had worn last night, perhaps Bennett did owe him a vote of thanks. He nodded. "Well done, then."

"Did you know that Muslims don't drink?" Easton pursued. "Not a damned drop of liquor. How the devil do you deal with men who don't enjoy a good brandy in the evening?"

"I presume you're going to tell me," Bennett said dryly, taking a swallow of whiskey.

"Oh, I am. You don't drink for a bloody year, and then you return to London and find a place where you can drink as much as you want, gratis." He picked up his new mug of beer and drained half of it.

Bennett looked at him for a moment. "Was it worth it?"

"The not drinking?"

"The pretending to be a Muslim for a year."

Easton shrugged. "I think I saved the entire social Season."

"Then you should go and enjoy it." Kero climbed down his arm to dip one finger into his drink. She tasted it, then snorted, flinging the remaining droplets onto the tabletop. Evidently she wasn't a whiskey drinker.

"I enjoy it more when the chits take those damned silks off." With a short laugh, Easton took another swallow of beer. "So now I get to see pretty gowns and I get to drink." He slapped the flat of his hand on the table. "And in exchange, I only had to give up my God, my religion, and a half-dozen friends who thought donning Muslim attire and custom would be sacrilegious."

"Stop whining, will you, Easton?" a tawny-haired man said from his seat at the center of the room. "You chose to stay alive. You might have chosen otherwise, and then we wouldn't have to listen to you."

Easton pushed to his feet. "Out there," he snapped, pointing at the outside-leading door, "you may be an earl, Hennessy, but in here you're another damned misfit."

"A misfit who doesn't whine about the misfortune of surviving."

"Gentlemen."

They all looked up as the Duke of Sommerset strolled into the room from the direction of the main house. He carried a riding crop and wore his beaver hat, evidently just in from or just about to go riding.

Bennett eyed him. At two-and-thirty Nicholas Ainsley might be younger than half the men in the room, but he doubted very many of any age would dare take him on. Well, *he* might, but he couldn't imagine Easton, for example, brawling with His Grace.

"Easton's whining again," the Earl of Hennessy stated, going back to his cigar and newspaper.

"His prerogative, I believe." The duke shifted his gaze to Bennett. "I'm going riding. Care to join me?"

"Certainly." A bit of action suited his mood better than listening to other men arguing, anyway. He stood, handing Kero back up to his shoulder.

"Care for more company?" Easton asked.

"No. Go pester someone else," the duke returned without heat.

They left the club through the outside door. Jupiter and the duke's huge black gelding waited for them. "You're lucky I agreed," Bennett commented, swinging into the saddle.

"I knew you'd agree. You wanted to talk with me." Sommerset mounted the black, and led them out to the street. As Bennett drew even with him, the duke pulled a peanut from his pocket and handed it over to Kero, who clicked her teeth at him. "I assume that means I'm one of the family," he observed.

"I thought I was the only one who carried fruits and nuts about in my pockets."

"I have a very loud macaw upstairs who blathers all sorts of nonsensical things except when he's eating." Sommerset watched the monkey for a moment as she held on with one foot and one hand and shelled the peanut with the other two limbs. "That's handy."

"She's hell at plucking insects off my jacket, as well."

The duke gave a short grin, then sobered again. "Langley's in Cornwall. He's expected back in London by Tuesday."

Less than a week. "Good."

"He's bound to know by now that you're not dead. He may just burn the journals."

"If he does, I'll begin asking if he has any proof that he was in Africa at all," Bennett returned, trying to keep his voice even when he wanted to bellow. "I, at least, have a monkey. And all my artifacts and specimens at Tesling."

"The proof of *his* presence being in your journals."

"Mm hm."

"That sounds a bit sticky for Langley."

"Good. Little liking as I have for him, I wouldn't have abandoned him in a mud hut on some damned riverbank to die."

"Are you going to be diplomatic about this?"

"I'm not a diplomat."

"Bennett, you can't—"

"That's not why I'm here, anyway."

Sommerset rolled his shoulders. "Enlighten me, then."

"I need some advice."

The duke lifted an eyebrow. "Am I your confidant now?"

"I can't chat with my uncle, and Jack Clancy's half convinced I eat raw meat. Which I've done, but I didn't like it."

"Very well. What is it, then?"

Now came the difficult part. "I find myself . . . interested in Lady Phillipa Eddison." Obsessed with was a more accurate description, but he didn't wish to come across like an escapee from Bedlam, or Sommerset would be advising Phillipa how best to flee from him.

His Grace shrugged. "You're an earl's nephew; there's nothing unacceptable with a union."

"You're getting a bit ahead of things, don't you think?" Bennett began to wish he'd finished off that glass of whiskey back in the club. "I tried approaching her, but clearly I'm less of a gentleman than she's accustomed to."

"What did you do that she found so unpleasant?"

"I kissed her. She seemed to enjoy that, though."

"No sweet nothings whispered into her ear?"

"I don't know any damned nothings. Generally chits approach me, breathe my name, and lift their skirts."

"Ah. Did you happen to mention to Lady Phillipa that you liked her?"

"Yes. I told her that I wanted her."

Sommerset fished out another peanut for Kero. "That's hardly the same thing."

"Yes, it is." Bennett blew out his breath. "You can't expect me to . . . sit in the morning room and chat about the weather with her mother, and hold her yarn while she knits, and . . . wait five weeks before I attempt to hold her hand."

"It may not be life or death, my friend, but that doesn't make a courtship unimportant. If it's a courtship. If you're attempting a seduction, well, pick another female. I sponsored your expedition, and you're attempting to recover your reputation. Don't ruin a girl from a noble family."

"But—"

"Decide what you want. That's my advice. And try flowers, possibly accompanied by an apology for chewing on her after five days of acquaintance."

It had been four days before he kissed her, but he wasn't going to admit that. "Flowers."

"I believe in polite circles it's referred to as a bouquet. And not one pre-dined upon by the monkey."

"I'll consider it."

"Do that." The duke looked at him for a moment. "Have you ever considered, Bennett, that in trying to accomplish so much in your life, you may be missing what lies along the way? In my experience, some moments are to be savored. And not only the ones you expect. Up, Khan!" Sommerset flashed him another grin and then kneed the black into a gallop as they reached Rotten Row in Hyde Park.

Flowers. Kissing. Seduction. Courtship. Savoring— savoring what, not having her? A bloody pile of words between himself and Phillipa Eddison. If she hadn't made it clear earlier that she found his approach insulting, he likely would have continued the path of his pursuit without a second thought. Apparently finesse was called for. And expressions of admiration. It all seemed like a waste of time when he knew so clearly what he wanted. Not easy for an uncivilized man such as himself, but he was nothing if not determined.

Chapter Nine

In my estimation, the deadliest animal in Africa is not the lion or the leopard or the serpent. Rather, it is the hippopotamus. Not only is it unpredictable and territorial and short-tempered and larger than a bull, but from a distance and to unaccustomed eyes it has the appearance of a round, benevolent jester. This jester, however, has eight-inch incisors and can rip a canoe in half. I don't believe even a Society chit's angry mama can do that.

THE JOURNALS OF CAPTAIN BENNETT WOLFE

For the last time, Livi, I don't know what Captain Wolfe prefers to drink! I would imagine anything that hasn't had wild animals swimming in it would be sufficient." Phillipa closed her eyes, but fleeing from Livi's nervous prattling would only allow more room for her own thoughts to intrude.

She considered declining to attend tonight's dinner at all. While she'd chosen remaining home over sitting about at some soiree or other before, though, this time the event was at Eddison House. If she hid, Livi would never forgive her. More than that, Bennett Wolfe would know that a few naughty, direct words was all it had taken to send her fleeing. Hardly practical or logical of her.

That kiss. Oh, that kiss had been magnificent. Perhaps that was the difficulty—when Bennett kissed her, it hadn't had anything to do with either logic or practicality. It had been . . . Well, it had positively curled her toes, heated her in places that ladies weren't supposed to mention, and she wanted to experience it again. Several more times, in fact.

But then the big beast had marched in and announced that he wanted her naked on his bed. Or on the floor—it hadn't mattered where. The suave, charming man she'd imagined from reading his books had the finesse of a rhinoceros.

What, then, was she supposed to do? Turn her back on him? Attempt to convince him that if he wanted to court her—and good heavens, she couldn't quite imagine that—there were rules to be followed? Why had he set his gaze on her, anyway? There were certainly more flirty, bubbly females in abundance all about him. If it was because he saw her as pitiful and awkward, well, then he deserved a punch in the nose.

Livi stuck her head into the morning room. "You didn't need to yell at me," she said, her expression halfway between excitement and nervousness.

"Apologies." Phillipa set aside her embroidery. "What might I do to help you, then?"

"Oh, thank goodness." Her sister sent her a relieved smile. "Come with me into the drawing room. I don't like the way the chairs are arranged, but . . . well, you'll see."

"You've invited twenty-seven people, all with whom you're already acquainted," Phillipa said, trying to sound soothing as she followed her sister upstairs to the drawing room. "I don't think anyone will care about the arrangement of the furniture."

"Yes, they will. The ones farthest from Sir Bennett will think they're being slighted, and the nearest ones will wonder whether his current reputation weighs more heavily than his previous one, and how their own standing will be affected."

"You've spent far too much time thinking about this."

"I'm beginning to think I shouldn't have arranged for this dinner at all, but he is so very compelling." Her sister twisted her hands together. "And he has a good income, of course—unless Prinny feels embarrassed by all this and takes away Sir Bennett's stipend."

"Bennett hasn't given anyone any reason to feel embarrassed," Phillipa returned. Except perhaps for her, but at least no one had overheard their last conversation.

"Oh, and then there's Mama," Livi continued, twirling. "She plans to sit with us. Do you think she's well enough to attend a dinner and a gathering afterward?"

Immediately Phillipa knew what that meant. And despite the fact that she'd half decided it would be wiser to spend the evening upstairs alone, she didn't like that she'd just been assigned a task. One that would more than likely keep her well away from Bennett Wolfe. She sighed. "I'll sit with Mama and make certain she doesn't become overly tired."

Olivia swooped in and kissed her on the cheek. "Oh, thank you. That's one thing I don't have to worry about, anyway."

From the drawing room doorway she heard the front door open downstairs, and a rush of heat and ice ran through her before she could remind herself that it was twenty minutes yet until anyone was expected for dinner. What was she supposed to do? She'd never even been kissed before, much less had a beau. Perhaps if she had a bit of experience she would know whether every man kissed with that . . . passion, though she had a fair idea that gentlemen did not go about telling females that they wanted to see them naked.

It was too much to think about. After all this she would be lucky not to faint or vomit from nerves when he walked into the room.

"I was attempting to be fashionably late," the low drawl of Lord John Clancy sounded from the doorway. "Apparently everyone else is more fashionable than I am."

Phillipa took a deep breath and opened her eyes again. Pasting a smile on her face, she turned around. "Hello, John. I would say that you're fashionably on time. Are you alone?"

He grinned. "My famous friend has fled Clancy House for his uncle's." His light green gaze moved past her to Livi. "Good evening, Lady Olivia."

She waved her fingers at him. "John. Nice of you to come tonight," she said, and went back to counting chairs.

"You did invite me." Pursing his lips, he strolled over to her. "Anything I might do to help?"

"I keep thinking that rows of chairs are too

formal, but if I simply scatter them about, it looks very shabby."

"Ah. Perhaps a half circle, all facing toward your focal point."

Livi smiled. "Oh, you're a dear, John. Do help me. Flip is snapping at crickets. She's no assistance at all."

"I am not cranky," Phillipa returned. "You change your mind every two minutes, and it's making me dizzy."

With a muffled smile John began picking up the chairs and shifting them, forming a half moon facing the room's eastern wall.

A moment later Olivia breezed up to her. "Since John is here and is much more help than you are, why don't you go and change for this evening?" she whispered.

"I already did."

"Flip, please. This isn't one of your reading club meetings."

Phillipa scowled, looking down at her blue muslin. "What's wrong with what I'm wearing?"

Her sister sighed. "Nothing. If you don't see anything wrong, then nothing's wrong." She hugged Phillipa. "Would you go make certain dinner is on schedule?"

"Yes. Certainly."

She hurried down to speak with Cook, then headed back up to the drawing room. Inside she could hear conversation; Sonja Depris and her sister had arrived, together with what sounded like Henry Camden and the Elroy sisters. For a moment she paused, looking down at her gown. *Damnation*. What she wore was perfectly acceptable for a small, informal dinner party. None of the guests other than John was likely even to notice her presence.

Oh, for heaven's sake. Taking a breath, she opened the door and strolled back into the room. In small groups the remainder of Livi's guests arrived, while she watched from one side of the room. She knew them all by name, and they were all perfectly nice, but other than the weather she couldn't think of a thing about which she could converse with them. Well, the weather and Bennett Wolfe, but she didn't want to talk about him. Not at the moment. She was too occupied with thinking about him.

"You danced twice with Sir Bennett," Sonja said, stopping in front of her.

Phillipa blinked. So much for silent contemplation. "Did I?"

"No one else danced two dances with him last night. How did you manage it?"

"I'm sure I have no idea," Phillipa returned, putting what was hopefully a baffled smile on her face.

"And he let you hold his monkey. *And* he joined your team for lawn bowling. You must have some insight into his likes and dislikes."

"Sonja, I—"

Miss Depris took her arm. "You can't mean to save your information for Livi. That's hardly fair for the rest of us. We all deserve an equal chance to charm him, don't you think?"

"I . . . yes. Certainly. But I don't know anything."

"Oh, bosh. At least you must tell us which one of us he's spoken about the most."

"What little conversation I've had with Captain Wolfe hasn't been about his preference in ladies." Not directly, anyway. She freed her arm and made a show of being interested in the chair arrangements.

All Livi's friends completely discounted her as a romantic rival. It never occurred to anyone that Bennett Wolfe might be interested in kissing her. For a moment she was tempted to inform Sonja that, according to Bennett, *she* happened to be one of his likes. Or she had been, until she'd spoken her mind to him today. But he'd deserved it, dash it all, for saying such things to her.

"Oh, he's here! He's here!"

Phillipa jumped at Livi's pronouncement. Clearly she was even more unsettled than she'd realized. She set herself to inching chairs this way and that, making certain they formed a perfect half circle. Of course she'd been offended by his conversation. He'd said he wanted her, and after less than a week of acquaintance. Gentlemen did not say such things.

"Good evening, Sir Bennett!"

"How pleasant to see you!"

"What is the monkey's name again?"

After the first few greetings, however, an odd silence swept across the room. Phillipa frowned, hoping he wasn't staring at her or something. She concentrated on breathing, and on rehearsing her cordial, indifferent greeting when she happened to turn around and see him. Then a hand touched her shoulder, and she froze.

"Good evening, Lady Phillipa."

She found herself facing a large bouquet of red roses. A very large bouquet. Of very red roses. For an odd moment she stared at them. No one in the entire world had ever given her flowers before. And certainly not red roses.

She finally lifted her gaze from the posies to look

at the lean, dark-haired man holding them out to her. From his expression she couldn't tell whether he was nearer amusement or annoyance, but his jungle-colored eyes were very, very intense.

"What are these for?" she asked, her voice quaking a little as she realized that absolutely everyone in the room, including her parents, was staring at her.

"To apologize for any affront I may have given you," he said quietly, and tilted his head. "And to woo you," he continued in a more carrying tone. "It was suggested that steps should be taken, and flowers presented."

"Woo . . . me?" Phillipa squeaked.

Bennett nodded, the slightest hint of a grin touching his mouth. "Woo you."

Everything went fuzzy and very loud and figures swarmed in her direction. The last thing she saw was the flowers hitting the floor as Bennett stepped in to catch her. That was a shame; they were very pretty flowers.

Good God, he'd killed her. Bennett swept Phillipa into his arms, then caught sight of her sister rushing forward. "Somewhere quiet," he barked.

"This way. Oh, dear. This way." Olivia hurried for the drawing room door, Bennett on her heels. Behind him he could hear muttering and jabbering and, closer by, the angrier voices of her father and mother.

Kero leaned out a hand and patted Phillipa on the cheek, much as she did when she was concerned over him. It was so damned odd, the way the monkey had taken to the chestnut-haired chit.

When they reached the small sitting room he strode over to the sofa and carefully lowered Phillipa onto the cushions.

As he reluctantly let her go and backed away a step, Phillipa's mother slapped him. "How dare you?"

"Move away from my daughter, you blackguard," the marquis snarled, pushing forward.

Bennett straightened to his full height, using that advantage to look down at Phillipa's father. "I just expressed my intention to court your daughter." He glanced at her supine form again. "With the idea of marriage, if that wasn't clear enough. How, precisely, does that make me a blackguard?"

"Hush," the marchioness snapped. "Get out of this room, Captain. Family only."

Narrowing his eyes, Bennett hesitated long enough to let them understand that they never would have been able to force him out if he hadn't acquiesced to it. Then he nodded and retreated into the hallway.

Someone shoved him against the wall. Kero fled, yapping like a dog, onto the nearest wall sconce. "You stupid man," Jack's low voice came. "What the devil are you about? You should be locked in a damned cage."

Bennett shoved back, sending Jack staggering a few feet. "Stop pushing," he growled. "And enough with the damned insults."

"I know everything's become life or death and galloping into gunfire with you, but you can't go about circumventing rules and propriety like that. And you can't toy with people. Especially not Flip."

"I'm not— What do you mean, 'especially not Flip'?" Bennett narrowed his eyes. From everything

Jack had said, his interest was completely focused on the other sister. If not, they were going to have a disagreement. A large one.

"I mean, she's . . . odd. You've conversed with her; you know. She's brilliant, but she has no prospects. Everyone's waiting for Livi to make her choice, and then it's just expected that one of the men left behind will offer for Flip. Make a fool out of her, and she'll end up a spinster."

No one seemed to be able to comprehend that he'd been serious. He'd brought flowers because she required them, and he required her. The end. "I brought bloody flowers and I stated my intentions. The rest is between Phillipa and me."

"It's one thing to be unconventional, Bennett. And I know you were practically raised by wolves. But you're no virgin. You know the proper way to do this." Jack glanced down the hallway toward the noisy drawing room. "Don't you?"

"What do you want me to say?" Bennett hissed back. "I've had women on more continents than you can name. I know how to get a woman into my bed. I've never had any other use for one." *Until now.* Whatever he wanted from Phillipa, it didn't end or begin in the bedchamber.

"If your intention is to get Flip into your bed, you're going to have to go through me, my friend. I won't see her hurt, or ruined. Is that clear?"

His first instinct was to smash Jack in the face and tell him that no one stood between him and what he wanted. Bennett clenched his fist, then eased his fingers open again. He'd seen them conversing. Jack and Phillipa were friends. More than likely Jack was one of the few friends she had. He might not

The Care and Taming of a Rogue ❀ 141

know exactly what he wanted, but he did know that he had no intention of hurting her. "You're a brave man, Jack. But give me some bloody credit."

So attempting to do the correct thing to get Phillipa still got him slapped and shoved and threatened. At the moment he couldn't decide whether he'd been away from London for too long, or for not long enough. Walking out the door and returning to Howard House seemed the wisest response to all this nonsense, but he seemed to be the raison d'être for the dinner, and angering the sister further wouldn't help him gain Phillipa.

He cursed, pacing back and forth along the hallway. How was he supposed to know that the heretofore practical, logical Phillipa Eddison would faint when he handed her a fistful of posies? It concerned him—not only because she'd fainted in his arms, but because of what others had said. That she was timid, that she lived through her books and wasn't interested in or capable of actual adventure. If that was true, they would never suit.

Her reaction to the flowers supported that, and yet . . . It had been only a handful of damned days. How had he become so smitten with her so quickly? She'd dashed through every preconceived notion he'd ever had without even slowing down.

"She wants to see you," Lady Olivia stated from the doorway of the sitting room.

Christ. They made it sound as though he'd sent her to her deathbed or something. He was the one who'd had a spear rammed through his gut. She'd received flowers. Through his deep annoyance, though, he was relieved. Relieved that she was well, and relieved that she still wanted to see him. With a last, hostile glare at Jack, he returned to the sitting room.

To his relief she was sitting up, a glass of water in one hand. Her parents stood nearby, their expressions closed. They might as well have been rooted to the floor, because clearly they weren't going anywhere.

"I'm alive," she said helpfully, offering what was likely supposed to be a smile. Her face still looked pale, which alarmed him.

"Someone told me that flowers would be an acceptable way to approach a chit I like," he stated, stopping a few feet short of her. "Which is something that I already knew, but hadn't thought of until he mentioned it."

"My parents think you're lonely and misguided," she noted.

He glanced over his shoulder at them. "Perhaps your parents could give us a private moment to spare anyone any further upset."

"You should be embarrassed, Captain, flinging a courtship at my daughter like that." The marchioness crossed her arms over her chest.

"Mama, please give us a moment. Nothing will happen; everyone knows he's in here."

After another moment of glaring, Lady Leeds nodded. "Five minutes." She stomped out of the room, the marquis on her heels.

Bennett waited until they quietly shut the door behind them. "I'm supposed to be embarrassed for being interested in you?" he asked.

She looked at him, taking a sip of water as she did so. "You told me this morning what part of me interested you. I found that insulting."

"So you said," he returned, clenching his jaw. "Hence the flowers."

"You weren't raised in the jungle, Bennett. Don't you know what red roses mean?"

"As a matter of fact, I've spent more time out of England than in it, and my mother died before she could give me any posy lessons. Red roses. Red for passion, and roses because they're fragrant."

"They signify love. And ten thousand of them together signify—"

"Two dozen. Not ten thousand."

"It looked like more than that when you flung them in my face."

He stalked toward her, feeling his own expression darken. "I didn't fling anything. I said I intended to woo you, and I attempted to hand them to you."

She stood, the glass still gripped in her fingers—likely for self-defense. "I am confused," she announced.

"Well, so am I."

"I mean, what you said this morning was a private thing, between two people. Two dozen red roses given in front of two dozen dinner guests is not private. It says that your intentions are . . . honorable."

"Then they must be honorable." Beneath all the frustration, this conversation began to seem somewhat amusing. He'd been correct in calling her a conundrum, anyway.

"But you don't even know me! How do you know you want to woo me? I don't like the idea that I'm so simple and easily decipherable that after five days—your first five days back in London after three years—you could point at me and say, 'Yes, I'll take that one.'"

"That is not—"

"You might have said something first, regardless. I told you before, there are steps. You take me driving, you dance more than two dances with me, y—"

"I attempted to."

"At more than one soiree," she countered. "You tell me that my appearance is at least satisfactory, you call on me to sit and chat, you—"

"That's all nonsense."

Phillipa blinked, looking hurt. "Oh. I think, then, that you might consider giving those flowers to someone else."

Bennett took another step forward, close enough to take the glass from her hand and set it aside. "Phillipa, I spent three years obsessed with one thing. And then I spent two months after that fighting every day to stay alive. And now I'm doing everything I can to arrange to captain another expedition. I don't dawdle about with anything. In the places I've been, indecisiveness is deadly. And time is too precious to waste on sitting and chatting about nonsense or in telling pretty lies."

"Then why—"

"Why should I bother with saying I find you— what did you say—satisfactory, when I find you mesmerizing? Why should I drive you in a circle around some park when I want to taste you and hold you naked in my arms?"

"Good heavens." Paling once more, Phillipa reached out to steady herself against the back of the nearest chair. "You cannot flout the rules like that."

For a long moment he gazed at her. "Your complaint, then, is not that you don't want to be wooed or courted or seduced by me," he said slowly, "but that I'm not doing it correctly."

"Well, other than a general disbelief that an adventurer would find me mesmerizing, yes, I suppose it is."

"Then I have two things to say. First," and he reached down to take her hands and draw them up to his chest, "I do find you mesmerizing."

He slid his own hands down her shoulders, then leaned in and covered her mouth with his. He felt her hesitation, then the softening of her mouth as she leaned into him. She sent his sensibilities swirling with just the uncertain grip of her fingers into his jacket; it was as though she worried that he *had* made a mistake in wanting her, that she feared he would change his mind and leave her standing there alone.

Bennett shifted to place kisses against the sensitive corner of her mouth. Then he swooped in again for another heated, openmouthed kiss. Finally he lifted his head an inch. "Are you going to faint again?"

"I should," she returned unsteadily. "At least it would stop you from behaving in such a manner."

He smiled. "You would think so, anyway."

Phillipa chuckled a bit breathlessly against his mouth. "You are a rogue, sir."

"Which brings me to my second statement. If you want me to follow your rules and behave like a proper gentleman, you'd best convince me just how I would be benefited."

"Bennett."

"Because at this moment I can't help but think that kissing you is better than chatting about the weather." And if he pulled her any closer, she would feel just how interested he was in continuing this particular debate.

The door rattled and opened again. "Your five minutes are— Flip, get your hands off that man!"

At least she seemed recovered enough that she could blush now. Belatedly she fisted her hands and shoved at his chest. Bennett lifted an eyebrow, but took a step back from her—because she wished it, not because of her parents.

The marquis and his wife looked as though they'd been arguing over which of them would renew their attack against him first. "What do you think you're about, Captain?" Lord Leeds finally demanded.

Bennett returned his gaze to Phillipa. "I—"

"It was a misunderstanding," Phillipa interrupted. "Apparently in Egypt red roses are a sign of esteem. Nothing more. "

"This is not Egypt," the man retorted. "I suspect that Sir Bennett knows precisely the meaning of red roses. And the repercussions of presenting them to a young lady in public."

"Not precisely," Bennett countered, "but I assure you there was no misunderstanding. Not on my part. As I said, I mean to court Phillipa."

Her father actually blustered. "You . . . you can't simply say such things and expect them to be accepted," he stammered, his face growing red. "You haven't asked permission of her parents."

Bennett shrugged. "I'm only concerned with Phillipa's feelings in this matter."

"You are uncivilized, sir," the marchioness stated.

"So I've been told."

"I will not have anything scandalous connected

with our Flip. She is not prepared to face the censure of Society. And I believe you have your own reasons for not wanting to appear foolish to your peers." The marquis took a breath. "We will therefore tell everyone this was indeed a misunderstanding."

For a moment Bennett weighed whether the marquis knew something about Langley's fraud, or whether he was speaking generally of the dents put in his reputation by the book. The latter made more sense, but it didn't leave him any more inclined to agree. "It is not a misunderstanding, damn it all."

"Tonight we will call the roses a . . . a jest," Phillipa said, stepping up beside him and putting a hand on his arm, "because I had bragged to Bennett this morning over lawn bowls that nothing ever overset me. Livi's friends will believe that."

"And tomorrow?" Lord Leeds asked skeptically, his gaze on his daughter's hand where it rested on Bennett's arm.

"By tomorrow we will all have had time to consider developments," she returned. "And if Bennett is serious about courting me, then he will call and take me driving."

Bennett looked down at her. As surprised as she'd been, Phillipa kept her wits about her. And unless he wished to end his pursuit of her, for the moment he was going to have to play along. "Very well."

"Back to the party, then," her mother said, her expression easing just a little. "Tell your tales, and make an attempt not to embarrass Olivia in front of her friends."

The family walked for the door. Reaching out, Bennett grasped Phillipa's hand, stopping her. He leaned over her shoulder to whisper in her ear. "After the way you kissed me back tonight, you'd best not call this a misunderstanding tomorrow. Especially if you're forcing me to take you driving."

Through his hand he felt her shiver. "If my parents will let me see you again, I believe I have some lessons in propriety and the rules of courtship to deliver."

His hand grazed her hip as she slipped through the door. "I have a few things in mind to teach you as well, Phillipa."

Chapter Ten

When a girl of the T'ngula tribe comes of age, she stands inside a circle of tribesmen who all spit date palm seeds at her, with the idea of ensuring her fertility. While I see the symbolism, in practice the spitting is done so enthusiastically that the poor girl ends up stained and bruised from head to toe and in no mood to marry anyone. Perhaps a gift of a sack of seeds might be more practical, but who am I to counter tradition?

THE JOURNALS OF CAPTAIN BENNETT WOLFE

H ayling, I'm not asking much," Bennett said, attempting to keep his voice pleasant and even. "Just hold the apple slice in your fingers, and she'll take it with her fingers."

"She will bite me," the Howard House butler returned faintly, his hands still firmly clasped behind his back.

"Kero won't bite you if she doesn't think you'll bite her."

"I won't bite her."

Bennett took a breath. Damnation, it wasn't as

though he was attempting to be rid of the monkey. All he needed was someone to look after her for an hour or so. Wooing Phillipa would be difficult enough as it was; with Kero hooting and jumping about, he'd never get close enough to kiss the chit again.

"I know you won't bite her, but she has to believe it, as well. You look fairly fierce." The butler actually looked as though he was about to wet himself, but he was the only possibility. Fennington had already threatened to shoot and stuff the vervet, and the rest of the Howard House servants were even more unsettled by Kero than Hayling was. "You only have to manage her for an hour; perhaps two."

"Put her in a cage, then, where she can't injure anyone."

"No." Bennett cleared his throat, offering Kero the apple slice Hayling had declined. "She does not go in a cage. Ever."

"Then my apologies, Sir Bennett, but all the tea in China couldn't make me let that beastie on my shoulder."

"I'll watch her for you."

Bennett turned around as the diminutive figure of his cousin Geoffrey appeared from down the hallway. His chin lifted high and his gait stiff, the ten-year-old was clearly uneasy, but he nevertheless continued forward.

"If you're certain she won't bite, that is," the lad added.

Well, this was unexpected. "Do you think you could keep an eye on her for an hour or more?"

"No, he will not." Fennington stepped up behind his son. "For all I know, the animal is rabid."

"But Father, it's Kero. You read Captain Langley's book. She saved the expedition once."

And the fact that Langley had included that incident continued to surprise Bennett, considering the animosity between man and monkey. Hiding a frown, he reached out and tousled the boy's dark hair. "Thank you for the offer, Geoffrey, but on second thought Kero might enjoy a bit of fresh air after all. Perhaps when I return you might join us for a walk."

"Oh, yes."

Bennett took his hat from Hayling and lifted the satchel he'd had sent to him from Tesling. So he would bring Kero along with him. Phillipa seemed to like her, and Kero had clearly found no fault with Lady Phillipa. "Good morning, then."

Even though he'd requested assistance with the morning's outing, he was still somewhat surprised to find a high-perch phaeton emblazoned with the red and white crest of the Duke of Sommerset waiting for him just beyond the front steps. He only hoped he remembered how to drive. He'd ridden camels more recently than he'd tooled about in a phaeton.

As soon as he climbed onto the high perch and settled the satchel beneath the seat, Kero left his shoulder to scamper about the small vehicle until she settled for perching on the folded-up canopy directly behind him. Nodding at the groom holding the head of the pretty bay gelding at the front, he gathered the reins and flicked the ends forward. With a jolt and a roll, they were off.

Last night he'd gritted his teeth and gone along with Phillipa's story that the roses had been a jest. The most bloody frustrating part of that had been that everyone believed it. Apparently Phillipa Eddison was not expected to make a match, much less have anyone pursuing her. That information, however, made him even more determined to do so.

If calmer heads prevailed at Eddison House and he wasn't met at the front door with a pistol for daring to declare his liking for the chit, he would do as Phillipa wished and take her driving. If calmer heads didn't prevail, he would see her anyway, but her parents would be less happy about it.

At this moment the only thing that troubled him was the notion that Phillipa herself didn't seem to take his declaration seriously. It wasn't as though he told a woman every day that he wanted her, and he supposed that he felt a bit insulted by her response. He could manage that, though, if she could manage to understand that he'd meant what he said.

Both the marquis and Phillipa stood on the front portico as he reached Eddison House. She wore yellow again, and looked like sunshine and warm summer. He smiled at her as he pulled up the phaeton; he couldn't help himself.

"Oh, look, he's brought the monkey," Lord Leeds grumbled.

"I would have left her behind," Bennett returned, "but she's still not well-enough acquainted with anyone to trust them to carry the requisite number of peanuts."

"She's hardly a chaperone, either," Leeds stated. "And I do notice you've driven a vehicle that won't allow a third party aboard."

"Papa," Phillipa broke in, putting a hand on her father's arm, "considering that I ordered Bennett to take me driving today, I think he's done quite well."

"Even *without* considering coercion," Bennett muttered. For Lucifer's sake, he was driving a carriage owned by a duke.

"He can't even let loose the reins or the horse will bolt. I believe my virtue and reputation are both safe."

"They would be safer if you stayed inside."

She lifted up on her toes and kissed her father on the cheek. "Yes, but then my sanity would come into question."

Bennett leaned down, offering her a hand as she clambered onto the seat. Only when he had her fingers in his did he relax a little. This was insane; she made him insane, and had nearly from the first moment he'd heard her voice. And the only time he truly felt free of the mess that had both accompanied and followed him from Africa was when he was in her company.

"Where are we off to?" she asked, primly folding her hands in her lap.

He urged the bay into the street. "This was your idea. You tell me."

"Well, I've never really been taken driving before. Livi seems to like Hyde Park, but it's so crowded there." She sent him a sideways glance. "What about Hampstead Heath?"

Bennett turned them up the next north-heading road. "The heath it is." The heath was known for highwaymen, but he doubted anyone would care to go up against him and Kero in broad daylight. Phillipa had requested a more private location, and he would give it to her.

Reaching into her little green reticule, Phillipa produced a peanut. "May I?"

His mouth curved. "If she's seen it, then you'd best give it to her. Otherwise I won't take responsibility for the consequences."

With a swift smile she handed the peanut over her shoulder, and Kero snatched it out of her fingers. "She doesn't hang from her tail."

"No, that's only monkeys from the Americas." For a moment he concentrated on navigating through the heavy midmorning traffic. "How much driving about is expected in a courtship before we do more than chat about parks and the weather?"

"I haven't even mentioned the weather." She glanced up. "It is nice, though."

"Mm hm."

She looked about them for several minutes, the nervous twitch of her fingers telling him that she had something else on her mind. He stayed quiet, waiting. Finally she shifted a little in the seat, turning to face him. "Why are you doing this?"

"Doing what? Riding about in a carriage? Because you made me."

"Don't insult me, Bennett. You know very well what I'm talking about."

Ill-equipped as he felt to confront feelings he didn't quite understand himself, he did admire her directness. "I told you last night. I'm set on wooing you."

"Stop saying that. It sounds silly."

Bennett scowled. "Wooing is not silly. Not unless I'm doing it very, very poorly." He looked sideways at her. "Am I?"

"How the devil would I know?" Phillipa clenched her fists, then relaxed her fingers again. "I don't want to sound foolish or like I'm fishing about for compliments, but honestly, Bennett, why me? My sister is the one every man notices, and you've been surrounded by ladies who would welcome your courtship. All I've done is tell you that I read your books."

"This is why I didn't want to go on a damned drive with you," he growled, yanking on the reins to halt the bay. Drivers behind him began yelling, but he favored them with a two-fingered salute and otherwise ignored them. "I knew you would sit there and ask a thousand questions, and if I didn't have the answer you wanted, you would . . . run. What, then, is so deficient about you that I shouldn't be interested?"

"Drive on," she said.

"No."

Phillipa looked over her shoulder at the growing line of vehicles behind them. "Bennett, drive on."

"Answer my question."

Her cheeks paled. "I already told you. Go. Please."

Irritated, Bennett snapped the reins, and the bay took off at a brisk canter. "You told me that your sister is pretty, that you're not tall, and that you speak more directly than tactfully. I don't find any of those things to be a black mark against you, Phillipa."

"But—"

"Hold a moment." Another thought abruptly occurred to him, and he frowned. "Are you protesting because you think there's something wrong with you, or because something is wrong with me?"

"You? Nothing is wrong with you. You're . . . perfect, Bennett."

He snorted. "Aside from quite possibly being a buffoon lucky to have survived walking out my own front door." Bennett slanted another glance at her. "Is that it, then? You believe Langley's tripe?"

Her expression eased a little; no doubt she was happier to be discussing a book rather than her own life. That seemed significant, but he would consider it later. "Captain Langley's book is exceedingly well-written, for the most part."

That snagged his attention. " 'For the most part'?" he repeated.

She grimaced. "I've read your books, you know. Several times. And there were several occasions as I read Captain Langley's book that I could swear you had written it—except for the passages when everything changed. The setting became very dramatic, and Captain Langley became exceedingly heroic, and you became . . . less so."

"What does that mean to you?"

Instead of answering, Phillipa reached into her reticule for another peanut and handed it to Kero. Then she sat forward again, folding her hands in her lap.

"What does it say to *you*?" she finally asked. "Because I don't think Bennett Wolfe would return to London for no reason. You don't like it here. You haven't mentioned anything about writing a book concerning your own experiences in the Congo, you've gone out of your way to not discuss Captain Langley, and you're driving a phaeton owned by the Duke of Sommerset, who happens to be the head of the Africa Association—which would seem to have every reason to want nothing to do with you, considering that you were the one meant to return with information to bring *them* fame and glory."

For one of the few times in his life, Bennett found himself speechless. He'd thought it had been his alleged reputation that was giving her pause; it had certainly affected her parents' opinion of him. But she'd figured it out, without his prompting or protestations of innocence, without hints or kisses to persuade her.

"Langley stole my journals," he said quietly. "I was wounded, unable to get out of my cot, and he walked in and said he would see that my writings and sketches went where they would do the most good, and he sailed off down the river without me. I came to London to get them back. I had no idea he'd claimed them for himself and turned them into that damned book."

"My goodness," she whispered. "What will you do now?"

"He'll be back in London next week. I'll settle it then."

"You make that sound very deadly."

"Do I? I'm not very civilized." He turned them onto the road winding through Hampstead Heath. "And I would truly appreciate an explanation of what I'm doing wrong here. With you."

"Where do I begin?" she muttered under her breath.

"I heard that."

She faced him again. "Very well. To begin with the most obvious, whatever your reputation at the moment, you are one of the two most famous men in England. If you haven't heard it, the general consensus is that for the most part your wealth and previous fame outweigh your . . . less than sterling performance in the Congo. You should be wooing a princess, or a duke's daughter, or at the least, the most celebrated beauty of the Season. Not me."

"Ballocks."

"It is not. And stop cursing in my presence. It's not gentlemanly."

"That, I can manage." He wanted to touch her, and wrapped his hands hard into the reins to stop himself. "But I would appreciate if you wouldn't tell me in whom I should be interested. If your complaint is that I don't know you well enough to like you, or if you don't know me well enough to let me kiss you again, well, here we are."

"So today you'll answer my questions?"

He drew a heavy breath. At least she remained curious enough about him to *ask* questions, even though she had to realize that the prospect of ridicule still hung about his neck. "Yes."

With every molecule of his body attuned to her, he knew precisely when she scooted an inch closer to him. That was so much better than when she flung up every excuse she could think of to keep her distance. And well worth answering a few of her questions.

"What was your childhood like? Were you always adventurous?"

"Going back that far, are we?"

"Bennett, you gave your word."

He hadn't, not precisely, but it was close enough, he supposed. "My mother died when I was nine years old. My father was an army major who went to India without bothering to take his family with him. He died . . . well, I'm not certain when he died. I hadn't seen him since I was six. So if you're asking whether I went hunting for toads and beetles, no, I don't recall that I did."

"I'm so sorry," she breathed, laying a hand on his arm. "Do you have any siblings?"

Bennett shook his head, doing his best not to drive the phaeton into a ditch at her soft, concerned touch. "Just me."

"What about your uncle? Lord Fennington wrote very warmly about you in that book's foreword. Did you live with him?"

With a snort, Bennett detoured them around a barouche full of bonnets and parasols. "No. His sister married a career soldier. I believe he told her that she received precisely what she deserved."

"Who raised you, then? Badgers?"

"You've guessed it."

"Very amusing. You're educated. I've read your books, remember?"

"I'd rather talk about you, Phillipa."

She lifted her palm to lightly slap his arm. "This is my turn. And I'm going to be ruthless."

"I'll remember that when it's my turn."

Color touched her cheeks. "Come now. Who raised you?"

"I did." He shrugged. "I had a small stipend thanks to my grandfather, the former Lord Fennington, and went from boarding school to boarding school to university, which is where I met Jack Clancy. Then I joined the army, and used my . . . agility with language to see most of Europe and then India, Istanbul, Egypt, and eastern Africa. I wrote the books to further fund my expeditions, found myself knighted and given a gift of a country estate by Prinny, applied to the Africa Association to sponsor an expedition to the Congo, and here I am."

"I think you left out some things."

He grinned briefly. "You've read my books. That's where the rest of it is."

"What about ladies?" she asked, looking down at her feet. "You've never married?"

"No."

"Have you been in love?"

"That's a work in progress."

The blush of her cheeks deepened. "You shouldn't say such things."

The number of vehicles around them had shrunk considerably, and as Bennett spied a small stream to one side of the road he turned the phaeton onto the grass. Pulling up behind a large, low-limbed oak tree out of easy sight of the road, he held the reins out to Phillipa. "Hold these a moment, will you?"

She started to reach out, then pulled her hands back again. "I don't know how to drive a carriage."

"You don't have to. Just pull on the ribbons until I tie the horse off to a tree."

"But I don't have a chaperone."

A muscle beneath his left eye began to twitch. "I would like to chat with you, as you instructed, and I don't want to drive into the shrubbery while doing it."

Sighing, she took the reins from his hands and kept them taut. For a heartbeat Bennett watched, waiting to see what the bay would do with a different driver holding him. When the phaeton didn't lurch into motion again, he jumped to the ground and secured the animal. Kero leapt onto a low-hanging branch and practically flew up into the top of the oak tree, where she promptly set a quartet of sparrows into flight.

"You can let go now," Bennett said, moving up to her side of the phaeton.

Phillipa looked at him as he raised his hands to help her down from the high seat. *Oh, goodness.* How had all this happened? One of the men she most admired in the world, he wasn't at all what she'd expected. He was forward, direct, disdained most of the niceties of polite society, and seemed to be infatuated with her. She scowled for a brief moment. No, not infatuated, because he was quite aware of all her faults. She'd told him about them. Absorbed was perhaps a better word. But the why of that continued to elude her.

With exaggerated care she draped the reins over the seat and stood. Perhaps if she kept talking she wouldn't be able to consider how very nervous she was at being in his company, especially after his announcement of yesterday. Especially when he still seemed perfectly serious today about wooing her.

She held her breath when he settled his hands around her waist and lowered her to the ground. Bennett gazed into her eyes, then leaned down. "No," she said, pushing out of his grip. "Rules, remember?"

"And steps," he added, looking equal parts annoyed and amused.

"Yes. Precisely. So whatever we may wish to do, we have to proceed properly."

" 'We'?" he repeated, taking her hand in his. "We wish a kiss then, do we?"

"Yes. But while you might not care about propriety or convention, I wish to know more about your goals and motivations before I allow you to lead me down the garden path, Captain Wolfe."

"We're not all the way back to that, are we?" He reached beneath the phaeton's seat and lifted a small satchel. "Because I brought you a gift."

"A leather bag?"

Bennett lifted an eyebrow. "I suppose you may have the bag, but I thought you'd be more interested in what's inside it. Shall we?" He gestured to the pleasant-looking grassy bank beneath the scattered shade of the surrounding oak trees. Together with the gentle burble of the stream beside it, the setting was desperately romantic.

Phillipa clasped her hands behind her back. "Are you attempting to seduce me?"

"I told you that I was." He sat on a fallen trunk, and gestured for her to join him there. It seemed far too close to him, given the way her heart was pounding, but for heaven's sake. He wasn't a lion. He wasn't going to eat her.

"Well, it's very pretty here. I'll grant you that."

"You know, the last time I sat this close to a riverbank, a crocodile tried to eat Langley. A shame I stopped it, now that I consider it."

"You shouldn't talk that way, Bennett. And you know that in the book it's he who saves you." She seated herself.

"Yes, I recall." Bennett shifted a breath closer to her before he set the satchel on his lap and opened the flap. "One of the friendlier tribes traded this to me for a mirror," he said, pulling out a small wooden carving and holding it out to her. "What do you make of it?"

She held out her hand, and he put it into her fingers. The squat figure was approximately the size of an ostrich egg, though the thick-looking fur, flat nose, and menacing teeth little resembled any kind of bird she'd ever seen. "It looks a bit like a chimpanzee," she offered, "but not quite."

"I thought the same thing. My housekeeper wrote me a rather nasty note about me terrorizing her after I had her open the crate and send it here to me."

"Well, I'm not surprised. It's rather frightening." She turned it this way and that. "You never came across any animal that looked like this?"

Bennett shook his head, one dusky lock of hair falling across his eyes. "Nothing even close. Baboons were the largest monkey in the area."

"Perhaps it's a mythological creature."

Frowning thoughtfully, he ran his finger along its spine, as though petting it. "About twenty-three hundred years ago," he said, examining the creature's flat, wide face, "the Carthaginian explorer Hanno wrote that he came across some very large, very hairy individuals on the West African coast. He called them 'gorillae.' This could be a rendering of one of them, I suppose." He flashed her a grin. "Or it could be the result of an artist drinking too much fermented berry juice, and is actually a carving of his wife."

"Mm hm."

"At any rate, I thought it was interesting, and I thought you might find it the same. So there you are."

She looked up at him. "You're truly giving it to me?"

"I can't think of any other female who would wish to touch it, much less be interested in its origins."

Phillipa smiled, closing her hands around it. There might be nothing else like it in the world, and he'd given it to *her*. "Thank you, Bennett. It's remarkable."

"Remarkable and frightening." With another short smile that sent her heart into dizzy loops, he reached into the satchel again. "And something a bit prettier, I think."

He held a necklace in his hand. It couldn't be anything else, with brightly painted wooden beads and shells interspersed with what looked like a trio of large claws. "I got this after a challenge where I had to knock the tribe's chief warrior out of a dirt circle using nothing but a large stick. Which may not seem like much, but those damned things sting against bare skin."

"Your skin was bare?" she asked, deciding at the same moment that Livi never would have asked that question.

"From head to toe. Part of the challenge." He looked down at it. "The claws belong to a leopard, apparently killed by this warrior using the same kind of stick. I actually think a spear might have been involved, but he wouldn't admit to it. Hence the fight in the dirt circle."

"You argued with a warrior over how he killed a leopard."

Bennett shrugged. "I killed a leopard, too, you know. Only I used a Baker rifle." He held the necklace out to her. "It's supposed to be protection against evil spirits. And it's one of the prettiest pieces I've ever seen."

She began to reach for it. She wanted it, not just because it was primitive and beautiful, but because he wanted her to have it. Phillipa set the carving aside and folded her hands in her lap. "You can't give me jewelry."

"It seems that I can."

"There are two reasons why you can't."

He sighed. "I can hardly wait. Enlighten me."

"First, you're simply not thinking clearly. And when you do realize where a more advantageous match lies for someone in your position, you'll want these things back. I don't want to be embarrassed, and I don't want my heart broken."

"I'm not here to break your heart, Phillipa." He set the necklace down across his knee, freeing his hand. He ran a finger along her cheek, making her shiver. "Though I am somewhat relieved that your heart is involved. Continue."

Phillipa shook herself. After his touch, she'd nearly forgotten what she'd been saying. "Second, jewelry is too . . . personal a gift. There are r—"

"There are rules," he interrupted, scowling. Before she could move, he had both her hands in his, their faces inches apart. "Don't put me off, Phillipa. I've given you my one warning; I am after you. If you wish me to proceed your way, I will. To a point. But if you continue throwing up that damned—blasted— 'you can't do that' protest and still look at me with that same . . . passion in your eyes, I will put you back in that phaeton and not stop driving until we reach Gretna Green. Is that clear?"

She swallowed, her breath coming fast and shallow. Every muscle longed to tilt her face up just a little so their lips would touch. He was too direct, too confident, to fit in with his Mayfair peers. And that made him very appealing to her, whatever she might tell both him and herself.

"Do it, Phillipa," he whispered. "Kiss me."

Though she had the distinct feeling that she would regret it for the remainder of her life, she held where she was. "I won't tell you what you can't do," she murmured back at him, her voice shaking, "but I will tell you what you should be doing. If you mean to . . . do this correctly. If you're serious about . . . wooing me."

"Don't say that," he returned in the same intimate tone. "It sounds silly."

Phillipa cleared her throat at the soft, compelling sibilance. "Bennett."

"I've been alone for a very long time, Phillipa, and I mean to marry you. That is how serious I am."

She pulled away from him while she still had an ounce of sense left to her. "A woman likes to be pursued," she began, realizing at that moment how very little she knew about the topic in which she'd decided to instruct him, "but not literally."

"No chasing you down the street," he agreed, a slow smile pulling at his sensuous mouth.

"Correct. Poetry, picnics, dances, drives—things that can be shared, but aren't gifts. Then flowers, and then more intimate gifts like jewelry."

"You fainted when I brought you flowers."

"Not two dozen red roses, for heaven's sake. Up until that moment, you'd called me a conundrum and made some comment about chasing me. Then just like that, red roses."

"What is the least threatening flower, then?"

Phillipa scowled. "You're teasing me."

He lifted an eyebrow. "I said I would go along with the rules to a point. And nice as it was to carry you in my arms, I'd prefer that my future actions not cause you to faint."

Apparently he meant to rush through the non gift-giving portion of the courtship. If he was truly serious, she actually didn't mind all that much. "Daisies, then," she decided. "White or yellow."

"Daisies," he repeated, reaching over to tuck a strand of her hair behind her ear.

As she shivered, he leaned in, replacing his fingers with his lips, brushing lightly along her temple. She kept still. If she protested, he would stop. If she continued to push him away, he might stop looking for other ways to pursue her, and then she truly would have accomplished the stupidest action in the history of stupid actions. If they didn't suit, it should be because they'd found they weren't compatible, and not because she was foolish.

"I'm something of a hunter, you know," he murmured, his breath skimming warmly along her cheek. "You trying to run only makes me want you more."

"I'm not trying to be coy," she managed, her eyes closing at his touch. "I'm trying not to be ruined."

"I know that." With a sigh of his own he backed away, placing the necklace back into the satchel. "You'll get this later, then. Will the carving suffice as an object of intellectual curiosity?"

She smiled. "Yes. I shall keep the carving."

"Good."

Because now she wanted to kiss him again, Phillipa stood and wandered over to the edge of the water. "Did you bring luncheon?" she asked over her shoulder.

He walked over beside her. "I have peanuts, an apple, and a peach," he said, patting various pockets. "I didn't actually think of luncheon."

"Well, if Kero will share, I'm satisfied with the repast."

His fingers touched hers, twining with them. "*I'm* not satisfied yet," he returned quietly, "but this is a very good start."

Chapter Eleven

Today Langley asked me about the danger of lions. This isn't the first time his lack of experience has troubled me. I finally answered that one always looks out for the large predators, though lions aren't well-known jungle dwellers. Of more danger are the small ones that no one sees: the spiders and snakes and crawling things that are invisible until the moment their fangs pierce the skin. And then, of course, it's too late.

THE JOURNALS OF CAPTAIN BENNETT WOLFE

Bennett walked back into Howard House, favoring Hayling with a short nod as the butler opened and shut the door for him, then offered him a tray full of invitations. "All for me?" he asked.

"All addressed to you," the butler returned, extending his arm as far as he could while keeping his body well back from Kero's apparently terrifying and intimidating person.

"I thought I was being viewed cautiously," Bennett muttered to himself, taking the stack of cards and parchment and heading upstairs to his borrowed bedchamber.

Apparently it was as Phillipa claimed, and his yearly stipend from the Crown made him more acceptable than Langley's book damned him. Still, he needed to choose the events he attended with care; an appearance at the wrong soiree could send him sliding back to infamy. He'd have to pay a call on Jack for a bit of guidance. And in more than one field, since he seemed to be even more uncivilized than he'd believed.

As he topped the stairs, he dug his fingers into his right side just above his hip. The spear wound was fairly well healed by now, but driving a carriage and pulling on the leads of a spirited animal used muscles that he'd been fairly careful with previously.

With a concerned chitter, Kero patted his cheek. Bennett reached up and scratched her between the ears. "Don't worry," he muttered at her. "Nothing broke loose, so the exercise is likely good for me."

"Cousin."

For a moment Bennett though he'd imagined the nearly inaudible whisper, until the sound repeated. He turned his head to spy the figure lurking behind a hall table. "Good afternoon, Geoffrey."

"Shh." Backing away, the ten-year-old gestured for Bennett to follow him along the hallway back toward the house's west wing, where the family's bedchambers lay.

With a glance about to make certain the disapproving Fennington wasn't somewhere waiting to club him over the head, Bennett followed his cousin into what was clearly the lad's bedchamber. Lead soldiers, wooden swords and muskets and pistols, even what looked like a genuine American Indian bow and sheaf of arrows, littered the walls and floor and shelves.

Books, jars of rocks and glass marbles and seashells—he'd had much the same collection himself at nearly the same age. Shortly after that, however, his worldly belongings had been pared down to what he could tote from school to school in one battered trunk.

The boy closed the door once they were both inside. "I wanted to speak with you," he said in a low, conspiratorial voice.

Bennett pushed back against his general dislike of the entire Howard family. "What is it?"

"My father says you should be more understanding of his position."

Hm. Considering that he had no intention of pummeling a ten-year-old, this seemed to be one of those occasions that Phillipa had mentioned, when patience and diplomacy were both called for. "And?" he prompted.

"And I think you should be nicer to him. He's had a very bad time of it, you know. Lord Mason purchased his favorite team, a sterling pair of grays, and Mama stopped speaking to him for a fortnight because he wouldn't allow her and Madeline to holiday in Paris last spring to purchase the latest fashions."

Money troubles? In all the imaginings of his relations he'd entertained over the years, Fennington and his brood had always been wealthy and privileged and condescending. Apparently he'd been in error on one of those counts, anyway. Whether that explained the marquis's eagerness to received fifty percent of Langley's book profits, he didn't know.

Even if it did explain his actions, it didn't excuse them.

The boy continued to look up at him, all gangly elbows and knees and dark eyes set above high cheekbones. "I'll make an attempt to be nicer," he hedged.

Geoffrey smiled. "Splendid. Because I read Captain Langley's book, and I would very much like to become acquainted with Kero, even if Papa doesn't wish me to."

Langley's apparent affection for Kero was one of the largest surprises in his book, considering that the two of them couldn't abide each other in the Congo. Bennett supposed it was a matter of David being unable to conjure any writing talent on his own. He sucked in a breath. "Shouldn't your father and I make amends first?"

"I thought about that, but it may take some time. And your disagreement shouldn't keep Kero and me from becoming friends."

Bennett considered in silence for a moment. While he didn't particularly care whether he angered Fennington, putting Geoffrey into the middle of their feud hardly seemed fair. On the other hand, he didn't want Kero sitting on his shoulder while he attempted to woo or court or seduce Phillipa—whatever they were calling it at the moment.

Perhaps Geoffrey had a point; a bit more civility toward Fennington might well benefit both of them. "Let's sit on the floor, shall we?" he suggested, sinking down cross-legged.

Across from him, young Geoffrey followed suit, his eyes shining as he focused his attention on the small vervet monkey. "I have some peanuts," he said, and leaned under the bed to pull out a small box stuffed with them. "I gathered them in case you agreed."

"Good thinking." As soon as Kero recognized the contents of the box she began to bark, bouncing up and down on Bennett's shoulder. "You could put a few of them on the floor in front of you," he commented. "She's just as likely to grab the box and run, though, so you might as well dump them all out right beside you."

The boy did as instructed, and Bennett lowered his shoulder, the usual signal for Kero to disembark. She bounded onto the floor and began gathering peanuts into her arms, her teeth chattering in absolute delight.

"Hold one out to her in the flat of your palm."

"Will she bite me? Father says she will."

"I can't swear to anything, but she's good-tempered and very bright. Move slowly and keep your voice gentle until she becomes accustomed to you."

Geoffrey nodded, looking nervous. Even so, he held out his open palm, and Kero grabbed his thumb for balance while she removed the peanut with her other hand. "It feels like an infant's hand," the boy announced in a carefully hushed tone.

"Except much stronger, especially when it comes to opening things that contain food. Offer her another."

Within five minutes his instruction had been reduced to "Don't worry, she won't pull your ear off," and "She prefers being scratched between the ears."

"Oh, she's brilliant," Geoffrey laughed, hunching

his shoulders as Kero sat on his head and rained peanut shells down on him.

"You are two of a kind, I think."

Finally, Bennett stood. At least two of the invitations Hayling had handed over to him seemed to be for that evening, and he needed to find Jack before he accepted the wrong one.

"Can she stay?" Geoffrey asked, handing up another peanut.

Damnation. He couldn't leave the house until he was certain the vervet wouldn't panic, and he didn't want to split them up if they were becoming friendly. Very well, he'd had to have Jack come to him. "We'll give it a try. Kero, *utangoja*," he instructed. "Stay" was the one command she tended to listen to, since the first incident with the leopard. Only, though, if he said it in Swahili.

He left Geoffrey's door open in case she became anxious and wanted to find him, then made his way back downstairs. "Writing paper?" he asked Hayling as the butler appeared in the foyer to meet him.

"The desk in the morning room, sir."

"Thank you. And I'll need someone to deliver a note to Clancy House."

"I'll see to it."

To his surprise, Jack knocked at the Howard House front door before the messenger had even returned. "That was prompt," Bennett observed, escorting him to the billiards room.

"What's amiss?" his friend prompted.

"Nothing's amiss."

"Your note said," Jack returned, pulling it from

his pocket and unfolding it, "and I quote, 'I require your assistance.'"

"And I do. I have invitations, and I don't know which ones to accept."

Jack blew out his breath, sinking heavily into a chair. "Christ, Bennett. You fight crocodiles bare-handed. When *you* need assistance, *I* get frightened half out of my wits."

Bennett laughed. "Apologies. I'll attempt not to abuse my reputation for animal wrestling in the future." He tossed the stack of cards and invitations at Jack. "Help."

With a put-upon frown, Jack glanced through them. "What are you looking for?" he asked. "Are you trying to avoid Langley's family? If so, I would send my regrets to L—"

"I want to know which parties Phillipa is most likely to attend."

Jack looked up at him. "Phillipa Eddison? Flip?"

"Yes. Secondary to that, I don't want to be seen anywhere that will raise more questions about my judgment or competence. When I come face-to-face with Langley, I want the high ground."

"Flip?" his friend repeated, lifting both eyebrows. "I mean, I know you shoved roses at her, but you're serious, aren't you?"

Bennett walked to the nearest window and sat back against the sill. "I'm getting somewhat tired of you—of everyone—dismissing the idea that I find her attractive. That she is attractive. You keep claiming to be her friend. I hadn't realized you were such a shortsighted one."

"I *am* her friend. That's why your interest in her

worries me, Bennett. You're a damned adventurer. What do you want from her? A warm bed? A traveling companion? A family?"

Walls abruptly began to close in, and Bennett turned to shove open the window and stick his head outside to draw in a deep breath. "I don't know," he finally said, ducking back inside the room.

"You'd best figure it out."

"Why? Why do I have to think that far ahead? I like her, and I want to be close to her. And at this moment, that is all I require. She and Sommerset said that implies marriage. So I'll marry her to have that."

"Do you know how many steps and rules you've just crushed beneath your soddy old boots?"

"I'm becoming aware of that. So are you going to assist me, or not?"

"Oh, the stories I'll be able to tell my grandchildren," Jack muttered, sifting through the stack again. "I once helped the great Bennett Wolfe choose a soiree to attend."

"It'll be an even better story if I don't punch you in the nose for excessive cheekiness. Where will she be tonight?"

Finally the Marquis of Emery's youngest son picked out a heavy, folded card and flipped it to him. "The Beckwith recital. Millicent Beckwith is her cousin. And Livi's attending, so Flip's likely the one who bullied her into it."

"Then you'll be attending, as well." Of course Jack would be, if Lady Olivia planned to appear. Bennett considered pointing out that he found his friend's interest in the one sister as baffling as Jack likely found his interest in the other, but the timing seemed poor. After all, he still needed advice on another dozen invitations.

"Yes, I'm attending. I'll come by for you at seven o'clock, shall I?"

"Thank you." Bennett gestured at the stack. "Continue. Phillipa first, then respectability."

"I'd rather help you fight crocodiles," Jack grumbled, but went back to his task.

"Flip! Are you ready?"

Phillipa blinked at the reflection in her dressing mirror. She couldn't recall how long she'd been standing there, staring at herself, but she did know it was more than likely longer than all the minutes she'd previously spent there all Season. "Yes," she called, then took another look at herself. "No. Livi, could you come in here for a moment?"

Olivia opened her bedchamber door and entered, Mary, the maid they shared, following. "You're the one who said we must be on time tonight. And don't you dare beg off."

"I'm not begging off," Phillipa protested. "I wanted your opinion about something."

"About what?"

Phillipa glanced at her pale blue-clothed reflection again. "My gown. I'm not certain it's terribly . . . flattering."

Silence. Then Olivia practically leapt into the air, pirouetting as she landed. "It's a miracle," she exclaimed, laughing excitedly.

"No, it isn't," Phillipa returned with a scowl. "I only want to know what you think of me in this dress."

"You're fine. The dress is hideous. The color is all wrong for you, and the neck is far too high, and—"

"What do you mean, it's hideous? I wore it last month and you never said anything!"

"Yes, I did. You just couldn't be bothered to listen. Mary, go fetch Flip's peach and green gown, the one with the lace sleeves. And my faux emeralds."

The maid curtsied. "Right away, my lady."

"Oh, and my green hair ribbons."

"Yes, my lady."

Oh, dear. "Do I look that awful?" Phillipa asked, attempting to look at herself critically and seeing the same not-quite-easy figure who always looked back at her.

"No, you don't look awful." Livi made a circle around her, one eye narrowed thoughtfully. "But you could look better. I don't know how much difference it will make at Milly's recital, but I've always found that when I know I look nice, I feel . . . confident."

Mary reappeared with the gown and the jewelry, and Phillipa found herself in the unusual position of being fawned over. The simple knot she and Mary had fashioned for her hair became an elaborate tangle of delicate, dripping curls. The pale blue dress vanished, apparently never to be seen again, and instead she found herself in her new, daringly low-cut peach and green silk gown with matching green stones ringing her throat and hanging from her ears.

"Oh, Flip," Livi exclaimed, putting both hands to her cheeks as she finally stepped back. "You're my Mona Lisa."

"Mona Lisa has no eyebrows." She faced her reflection once more. To her relief the image was still clearly she, not obscured by face paint and beauty patches. For one of the first times in her life, though, she felt . . . well put-together. Her rough edges hidden a bit better. The fact that she didn't quite fit in, disguised.

"You know what I mean. Now let's be off. No one will believe their eyes."

Frowning again, Phillipa hurried down the stairs after her sister. "Do not go about announcing that you've improved me or some such thing."

"I won't." Olivia spun about to take her hands and pull her out the front door. "But you do look very nice. It's almost a shame there's no dancing."

A smile pulled at Phillipa's mouth. "I will be more than happy just to sit and be admired."

"Speaking of being admired, is Sir Bennett planning to attend, by chance?"

Her heart began pounding. "A recital? I very much doubt it."

"Good. That will give the other gentlemen present a chance to look at you."

That hadn't even occurred to her. For heaven's sake, she hadn't wanted to look nice to impress anyone. Not directly, anyway. In fact, she realized as she took her seat in the coach opposite Livi, what she seemed to have achieved tonight was looking on the outside the way she felt on the inside when Bennett looked at her.

And yes, she did wish he could see her tonight, dull recital or not. He heated her blood and spun her mind, neither of which she was accustomed to. It was intoxicating for someone who'd been born with both feet firmly planted on the ground. He was intoxicating. And if she could have believed for a second that she could possibly be more than a passing fancy for such a famed and worldly adventurer, she would more than likely be absolutely terrified.

She knew that she should take his interest for what it was, enjoy it while it lasted, and use the opportunity to learn what she'd agreed to teach him—those silly rules of decorum, propriety, and courtship. Whereas she'd thus far been able to be as direct and blunt as she pleased because no one paid her any mind, *his* mistakes would be noticed. He did need her help, then, if only to recover his journals and his reputation so he could stride off to enjoy his next adventure.

"If you keep frowning, your face will crease."

"I'm not frowning," she retorted. "I'm thinking."

The coach lurched to a stop. "Well, think later, because now you must be pretty and charming."

The music room of her aunt and uncle's house was lined with chairs, and thankfully there seemed to be enough people in the room to occupy most of them. Given that Millicent hated playing the pianoforte in public, the only thing worse than a large crowd would be a very small one.

She hurried forward to kiss her older cousin on the cheek. "Look how many people have come!" she exclaimed.

The petite brunette smiled, the expression pinched. "I think it's the desserts Mama always serves," she whispered. "And the Robbins twins are going to play a duet."

"Well, I'm here to see *you*."

"I'm a bit nervous," Milly confessed, nodding as Livi joined them. "You'll never guess who sent an acceptance this afternoon. Of course there's no chance for a match between him and me, but can you imagine?"

Phillipa began to frown, then remembered Olivia's warning and attempted to smooth the expression away. "Who's coming?"

"Oh." Their cousin's gaze went past them, her already fair complexion paling to an alarming degree. "Him."

She and Olivia both turned around. Phillipa's heart stopped, then resumed beating again in a rather fluttery manner. John Clancy was there, but he wasn't the man at whom everyone was looking. At whom she was looking. Bennett was absolutely . . . edible in a well-fitted black jacket, gray and black flecked waistcoat, and tan breeches. An arrested look on his face, Bennett gazed directly back at her.

He walked toward her, his stride long, his gait smooth and confident. No wonder he drew every female's attention merely by virtue of his presence. And those eyes, deeper green than the faux emeralds around her neck. She felt as though she'd run her stockinged feet along the carpet on a windy day, full of sparks and electricity.

"Hello, Livi," John's voice came from beside him. "Flip, you look lovely this evening."

"Thank you, John," she returned, though she couldn't pull her gaze from Bennett's. She didn't want to.

What was wrong with her? She couldn't recall that she'd ever been at a loss for words before. Fighting the urge to simply wrap her hands into his lapels and kiss him, she cleared her throat. "Good evening, Bennett," she managed.

"Good evening." Kero on his shoulder clicked her

teeth. "She would like for you to scratch her," he translated after a moment.

Someone tugged at her skirt, and Phillipa shook herself. Milly stood beside her, brown eyes wide. "Bennett, this is my cousin, Miss Beckwith. Milly, Captain Bennett Wolfe. And Kero, of course."

"Pl-pleased to meet you," Milly stammered, curtsying.

Finally Bennett looked away from her. "Miss Beckwith," he said in his low drawl.

"How lovely of you to come and hear me play," she continued, offering another of her tight, uncertain smiles.

"Lady Phillipa always chooses interesting outings," he returned, "so I attempt to follow her lead."

Milly sent her a surprised glance. "She has interesting friends, as well."

John stirred. "Come along, Bennett," he said, nodding at the ladies. "I'll introduce you around."

For a moment Phillipa wasn't certain he would leave her side, but with a breath he turned and followed his friend across the room. Immediately Millicent grabbed her arm. "I heard that he gave you roses, Flip, but everyone said it was a jest. It's not though, is it?"

She watched him for a moment, nodding at the various guests, mostly female, to whom John introduced him. He simply dominated the room, and he didn't even seem to be aware of it. "He says he's courting me," she whispered, still not quite ready to say the words out loud.

"Good heavens." Milly continued staring at him as well. "I have to say, I can't think of a better way for him to shore up his reputation than by associating himself with the most brilliant and sensible young woman in London."

Phillipa blinked. "What?"

"Oh, Mama's waving at me." Millicent hugged her. "I need to go take my place."

"Good luck," Livi said, taking Phillipa's arm as Milly released her. "Don't listen to her," her sister continued in a quieter voice. "You know how jealous she gets. And you do look very fine tonight."

With a forced smile, Phillipa nodded. "We should find seats."

"You're thinking about it, Flip," Livi chastised, leading her toward the rows and rows of chairs. "She probably spent three days thinking up what she would say to you. Now she won't have anything else to contribute for a week or more."

Despite her abrupt concern, Phillipa snorted. "Goodness, your fangs are sharp tonight," she told her sister.

"You ask yourself enough questions about everything," Olivia returned, taking a chair and pulling Phillipa down beside her. "You don't need anyone else inventing mischief."

If Milly's theory was an invention, it was one that made a certain amount of sense. Bennett's star burned far brighter than hers, but she knew what some of her peers said about her. She knew they called her a bluestocking, more interested in books than in anything actually going on around her.

A large, muscled form sank onto the chair beside her. "I don't think I've ever attended a recital before," Bennett said in a low voice. "Does one throw money?"

If a lady skilled in charm and conversation had the

questions that Phillipa did, no doubt she would find a way to ask around them, to peel away the layers and discover the truth without saying a cross word or offending a soul. Phillipa turned in her seat to face Bennett. "Are you courting me in order to quell the talk about your performance in the Congo?" she asked.

Milly sat at the pianoforte, and Phillipa turned forward again to join in the applause. Even without looking directly at him, she could still feel him gazing at her. No, not gazing—glaring. A heartbeat later, his glass of vodka spilled down the side of her dress.

Startled at the sensation of cold running down her leg, Phillipa shot to her feet. Bennett stood at the same moment. "My apologies," he said, just loud enough so those directly around them could hear. "Let me help you get something for that." He lifted Kero from his shoulder and handed her and an apple to John. Then he wrapped a hand around Phillipa's wrist and pulled her away from the chairs and through a door into a hallway.

"You ruined my dr—"

She couldn't finish her complaint, because his mouth found hers. He tilted her face up with his hands, kissing and retreating, kissing again, until she couldn't think of anything but how exciting it felt. When her hands slid around his shoulders, he uttered a low moan that made her shiver.

This long, hard, dark-haired lion of a man made her yearn for things she couldn't quite put a name to, made her lift up on her toes to follow him when he retreated for breath. "This is rather rash, don't you think?" she managed, her voice as unsteady as her legs.

"You need to stop thinking so much," he returned,

kissing her hot and openmouthed. "What's in here?" he asked, gesturing at the door beside her.

For a moment she couldn't even remember. "It's where the chairs are stored," she finally answered.

"Good." Still holding on to her with one hand, he opened the door and pushed it open, then pulled her with him into the room.

"Bennett, you're going to ruin me."

He lifted her around the waist, setting her down on a sheet-covered table. Now his hands splayed over her thighs, slowly drawing her dress up past her knees. When he parted her legs to step between them, she gasped at the intimacy of the position.

"Stop." Grasping for logic again, she pushed against his shoulder.

Bennett lifted his head. "Why?"

Yes, why? "Because I asked you a question, and you haven't answered me."

His long fingers caressed her face again. "You've read my books, Phillipa," he said quietly, his eyes searching hers. "You know me. Would I use you to fortify my own standing in front of these people?"

The kernel of doubt Milly's comments had sent into her chest crumbled away. "No," she returned.

"Then what is your objection?"

Phillipa forced a smile, attempting to pretend that having him so close and so set on . . . having her, didn't make her more than a little nervous. "You haven't even brought me daisies."

"For God's sake." Blowing out his breath, Bennett rested his forehead against hers. "Being civilized has very few merits." Slowly he backed away a little, tugging her skirt back down to its proper place. "I'll purchase you a new dress."

She glanced down at the damp streak on the gown's right side. "You buying me a gown would definitely raise eyebrows. It will survive."

"I hope so. You look radiant in it."

It was entirely possible that that was the nicest compliment she'd ever received. Every time she saw him, he said something even better. "Thank you."

Silently he helped her back down to the floor. As he held open the door for her, though, he put a hand on her shoulder and turned her to face him. "I hope you appreciate that I am being very, very patient," he whispered, delivering a soft, slow kiss. "And that I am not a patient man. Not where you and propriety are concerned."

Chapter Twelve

I have discovered the most annoying thing in the world. It is the West African mosquito. Unlike its English cousin, this beast is large enough to carry away an elephant, and thirsty enough to drink dry the Thames. My only consolation is that the things seem to prefer Langley. Perhaps I should be more compassionate, but then Langley shouldn't have attempted to drown my monkey.

THE JOURNALS OF CAPTAIN BENNETT WOLFE

Someone knocked at the front door as Phillipa sat down with her book. Reading *Walking with Pharaohs* again seemed silly, considering she'd already read it five times in the past five years, but now that she'd met Bennett, she could hear him speaking the words on the page. It made the adventure feel more immediate, and it let her feel close to him even though she hadn't heard a word in three days.

She glanced up as Sonja Depris and Lucy Elroy swished into the morning room. They weren't there to see her, and she had more significant considerations today—according to the newspaper, Captain

David Langley would be back in London tomorrow. His family was even holding a soiree in his honor—one to which she'd been invited.

"Good morning, Flip," Sonja said brightly, making her jump.

"Good morning," she answered. "Livi will be down in a moment."

"Yes, we're here to take her shopping. Would you care to join us?"

The invitation was more than likely merely a kind gesture, but it surprised Phillipa, and it made her more than a bit suspicious. In the past two years Sonja had never once invited her to join them anywhere. Livi, yes, but not any of her friends. "Thank you, but no," she replied.

"Oh, no, you must join us," Lucy put in, plunking herself down on the sofa next to Phillipa. "Livi told us that Sir Bennett ruined your pretty peach gown. We'll find you the material to make another."

"It was only a bit of a spill."

Sonja sat on her other side. "Yes, but we also want to hear all about Sir Bennett. Captain Langley's family is saying that he's parading about London with his monkey trying to earn sympathy, and that everyone should reread the captain's book to remember the truth about him."

"The truth about Bennett Wolfe is that he's no one's fool," Phillipa retorted. "And the truth about Captain Langley's book is that he needs to answer a few questions about it—to Bennett."

"You see, Lucy?" Sonja giggled, leaning around in front of Phillipa. "I told you that she was infatuated with Sir Bennett. He *is* wooing you, isn't he?

Does the monkey sit on his shoulder while you hold hands?"

Phillipa scowled, actually rather relieved they'd begun the accusations by making her angry. "We don't hold hands. The flowers were a jest, if you'll recall." She refrained from announcing that he was not wooing her, though, because it had very much begun to seem that he was.

"I thought it must be, really," Lucy Elroy put in. "Because, well, you and Bennett Wolfe are as different in temperament and character as any two people can be, don't you think? I mean, he's an adventurer."

"I—"

"I heard that the Duke of Parnessy's youngest daughter, Lady Melanie, wants to meet him. Can you imagine? With her income he could travel anywhere."

"As long as he doesn't mind that one of her eyes travels independent of the other." Sonja chuckled, covering her mouth. "He could send her red roses, and they'd be married before sunset the next day."

Gritting her jaw, Phillipa pushed her book into the cushions and instead grabbed up her embroidery to jab her needle into the cloth, continuing her loops. "That's not very nice to say about either of them." Nearly as annoying was the way they so easily dismissed the idea that Bennett was actually pursuing her. She'd been attempting to dismiss it herself, of course, but her skepticism was being seriously undermined by those delicious kisses.

Olivia glided into the room. "You aren't teasing my Flip, are you?" she asked her friends, putting a mock stern look on her face.

"We're only attempting to find out where Sir Bennett's interest truly lies," Sonja said, standing again.

"I think his interest lies in returning to his adventures," Livi commented. "Flip, do come shopping with us. I heard that Perrington's has received a new shipment of Egyptian silks. A deep burgundy would look so very lovely on you."

A new dress. Generally she allowed Livi to drag her shopping for gowns at the beginning of the Season on one or two occasions, after which she avoided the awkwardness of attempting to appear highly fashionable when so much of it simply looked— and felt—silly. But Bennett had certainly admired her gown at Milly's recital. In fact, he'd kissed her senseless.

On the other hand, she did not want to spend the entire morning being teased and belittled by Livi's friends. "I—"

The morning room door opened, and Barnes the butler stepped inside. "A delivery for you, Lady Flip."

Her heart sped. "I'll come get it," she said quickly, setting her embroidery aside and rising.

As soon as she entered the foyer she saw it, bright as sunshine on the entryway table. Dozens of white and yellow daisies, wrapped together in paper. He'd sent her daisies. Nearly a hundred of them, by her count. *Oh, my.*

"Oh, Flip, they're beautiful!" Livi, followed by her friends, crowded into the foyer behind her. "Are they from Captain Wolfe?"

"A note!"

Before Phillipa could reach it, Sonja plucked the card from beneath the daisies. Her heart jolted. If they made fun of it, of Bennett, or of her—it could spoil what she'd begun to imagine. "That's mine, if you please," she stated firmly, holding out her hand.

Sonja giggled, dancing backward and unfolding the note at the same time. "*For Phillipa,*" she read, evading Phillipa's increasingly aggravated grabs. "*I hope—*"

Olivia snapped the note out of her friend's fingers, folded it again, and placed it in Phillipa's palm. "You know," she said, rubbing her temple, "I've a bit of an aching head. I'm so sorry, but I don't think I'm up to a shopping excursion today."

"Oh, Livi, don't be angry."

"I'm not angry, Sonja." She lowered her hand a little. "I did hear, in fact, that Captain Wolfe might be at Tattersall's this morning. He also mentioned the Duke of Sommerset. If—"

Sonja grabbed Lucy's arm. "Bennett Wolfe and Nicholas Ainsley," she whispered, her cheeks darkening. "Can you imagine?"

"Excuse us, then," Lucy put in, heading for the door. "Feel better, Livi. If we hear anything at Tattersall's, we'll let you know."

"Thank you," Livi called after them. As soon as the door closed, she faced Phillipa. "I like my friends," she said, her smile dimming, "but on occasion I almost want to pull their hair."

"You dealt with them better than I would have," Phillipa returned. "But you didn't have to send them away on my account."

"I sent them away on *my* account. I'll see them tonight, anyway." She gestured at Phillipa's hand. "Now read your note, and don't even tell me what it says."

Phillipa blew out her breath. Running a finger

along the soft flower petals, she unfolded the note. *For Phillipa*, she read to herself, *I hope adding yellow daisies isn't too forward. I asked Lady Fennington for their meaning, and she said white means "purity," while yellow means "slighted." I'm taking them to mean "frustrated." Because I am frustrated that you are still pure. Bennett.*

She snorted, clasping the note to her chest. Thank heavens Sonja hadn't read the rest of it. As Livi busied herself with collecting vases, Phillipa looked at her reflection in the hallway mirror. Unspectacular brown eyes. Brows more curved than her sister's. Hair somewhere between red and brown and black, and more blond in the sunlight, but none of those. She did like her mouth, though her chin was a bit sharp. Not ugly, but not spectacular. Except, apparently, to Bennett Wolfe.

"Livi, does your head truly hurt?" she asked.

"No. Unless you're going to make me read something, then yes, it does."

Phillipa grinned, excitement flitting through her chest. "Let's go shopping for a new dress, then."

Olivia clapped her hands together. "Burgundy?"

"I shall be your mannequin. Whatever you think."

"Oh, this is a marvelous day."

"You don't have to purchase a mount," Jack Clancy said, taking a step back as a groom led a striking bay gelding between them. "Borrow Jupiter for as long as you like."

Bennett watched the animal as it and its handler entered the main pen at Tattersall's. "I may be about for a while if I can't settle this business with Langley. And if it gets nasty, I'd rather not be seen as so feckless I don't even own my own horse."

"And if you do settle it? Without killing Langley and getting hanged for murder, of course."

"Then I'll gift you with the animal," Bennett answered absently, moving up to the chest-high wooden railing as bidding began.

"If you're going to give him to me, then bid on that one. Sullivan Waring's stable is the best in Britain."

"Thank you for your selfless concern, Jack." With a grin, Bennett lifted his hand.

"Seventy-five pounds to Captain Sir Bennett Wolfe," the auctioneer acknowledged.

Faces turned in his direction, though thanks to Kero he hadn't precisely gone unnoticed. He listened to the chattering and muttering even as he kept his attention on the auction. A bunch of parrots yapping and mimicking one another with nothing to say in the first place. And he still needed to make a good impression with them. He offered a slight smile and nodded, hearing the acknowledging increase of sound. At least it was simple—thus far.

A minute later his purse was eighty-seven pounds lighter, and he owned a big bay gelding with the promising name of Ares. He turned to follow Jack and collect his horse—and found his way blocked by two young ladies. Olivia Eddison's cronies, he recalled quite clearly from that useless evening of questions and answers. One of them, Sonja, he thought, had seemed obsessed with discovering his favorite color. And judging from the bright yellow muslin gown she wore, he'd finally given in and told her.

"Sir Bennett," she said, curtsying. The second chit mimicked the motion. "How splendid to find you here!"

"Miss Depris," he returned, madly trying to remember the name of the other girl. "And Miss Elroy, isn't it?"

"Oh, yes." Miss Elroy giggled in a manner he found rather alarming. "You've bought a horse."

"Yes. I needed my own mount."

"We heard that the Duke of Sommerset might be in attendance today," Sonja put in, barely sparing Jack a glance.

"No, just us villagers," Jack contributed with a short grin. "Is Livi with you?"

"She said she didn't feel well, so instead of going shopping, we've come here." Miss Elroy sent him a sly smile. "*I* think her feelings were hurt because a certain someone sent flowers to her sister, and not to her."

"I'm a bit jealous, too," Sonja added, smiling sweetly and batting her eyelashes at him. "I'm a far better dancer than Flip Eddison, you know."

Jack cleared his throat, stepping between them. "Come along, Bennett. I'm curious to try out your Ares."

Bennett, though, abruptly began to find this little chat interesting. "You're jealous of Phillipa?" he asked, ignoring the nonsense about the dancing.

"I . . . Which young lady wouldn't want to receive a hundred daisies from an admirer?" she returned, blushing a little.

"Tell her that." Bennett inclined his head. "I think she'll find it amusing. Good day, ladies."

He led the way around the back of the stables to

where Ares stood with a groom. While Jack admired the animal, Bennett paid for him, signed for him, and took the beast's papers. Ares was a fine animal, and it made him consider that this was the first horse he'd ever actually owned. In the army he'd ridden several, but they'd belonged to the Crown, and in school he'd either rented animals or borrowed them. Of course he'd never owned a house, either, until Prinny had granted him Tesling. Before that he hadn't even lived in a family home since he'd been nine, and he'd never felt the need to do so.

It was . . . comforting, though, to know that his specimens and artifacts were safe, in a place that no one else could take from him. And that was mainly what he'd used Tesling for—as storage. The longest he'd ever stayed there had been two months, after he'd received it and before he'd finalized the details of the Congo expedition. And now he had an estate and a horse. And a monkey who thought he was her mother. Very domestic of him.

"You shouldn't have said that, you know," Jack commented from the far side of Ares.

"Said what?"

"That bit about Flip finding Sonja's jealousy amusing. Sonja's fairly obvious, but she excels at being the most admired chit in the room. She may very well attempt to embarrass Flip, now."

Bennett looked across the gelding's back at his friend. "You should have said something."

"I just did."

"Before."

"I tried to get you to leave, if you'll recall."

Slowly Bennett gathered the line at Ares's halter. "I'll go have a word with her, then."

"For God's sake, Bennett, you can't go roaring at her. You'll make her cry or something, and then both you and Flip will end looking ill. Just leave it be." Jack sighed. "I'll have a word with Livi. If anyone can smooth out your mess, she can."

Together they walked back to where they'd left their horses. "I won't tolerate anyone speaking against Phillipa," Bennett said matter-of-factly. "Particularly not on account of my stupidity."

Jack stopped, taking a quick look at the thinly scattered crowd around them. "You know, I never thought of you as the marriage-minded sort, Bennett. What's changed?"

"Do I have to know the answer to that? I like Phillipa. I don't want to see her ruined." From the displeased look on his friend's face, Bennett could tell precisely where this conversation was going to lead. And if he was in for an argument, he preferred to be the one on the attacking side. "How long have you been in pursuit of her sister?"

"Don't change the subject."

As they reached the horses, Bennett tied Ares off to Jupiter's saddle and swung aboard. He'd have to borrow a saddle until he could purchase one for himself, but that didn't concern him overly much. "I'm not changing anything. You've been after Olivia for . . . what, three years? And have—"

"Four years."

"Four years, then. And have you offered for her?"

"If I did that now, she'd refuse me. She's already refused seven other gentlemen. And I did propose, a week after we met. At least we could laugh that nonsense off."

"I've known Phillipa for nearly a fortnight, now.

I don't want to blunder and then have to chase my tail for the next four years while she possibly finds someone else."

Jack snorted. "As if you'd stay in England for the next four years chasing anything."

"I did just purchase a horse."

"And decided in the same second how you mean to dispose of it when you go."

Whether Jack's intention was to point out that he had no business pursuing where he had no idea what to do when he finally caught his prize, or to demonstrate that he had no business engaging in that kind of a hunt in the first place, Bennett didn't like it. They both led to the same conclusion; that he should leave Phillipa Eddison be. And he couldn't do that. She meant something. Something important. And he could no more let her go without a word then he could have left Africa without knowing the source of the Congo River.

"Well?" Jack prompted.

"Mind your own affairs. Until you can do that, stay out of mine."

For a long moment they rode in silence. Of course Jack's argument made sense; Bennett didn't stay anywhere for long. He never had. And if Phillipa was as book-bound as his friend seemed to think, one of them would be pulled in a direction they didn't want to go. But he couldn't decide any of that in twelve days. All he could know for certain at this moment was that he wanted her, and he apparently seemed willing to do whatever it took to achieve that goal.

"So you sent her flowers?" Jack finally ventured.

Bennett nodded. "Daisies. She requested them."

"What's your next step, then?"

"Almack's, I suppose."

With a choking sound, Jack pulled ahead. "Sweet Lucifer, you *are* serious about this."

"You have no idea." He wanted to see her. Immediately. And he had some choice words for Society's damned rules in the meantime—the rules that said there were hours for social calls and numbers of dances two people could share in an evening. But if Phillipa wanted him to follow the rules, he would. For as long as she did. And he meant to encourage her to pay as much attention to them as he always had.

"I simply don't think we should attend," Phillipa said, nudging the newspaper in her mother's direction.

"When the *London Times* describes a party that hasn't even taken place yet as the likely event of the Season," Olivia said from the opposite side of the dining table, "you *have* to attend. Everyone else will."

"And that doesn't take into account the fact that we've already accepted the invitation." Their mother gestured for a refill of her cup of afternoon tea as she glanced through the article.

"But you didn't ask me about it first, and it's being held by Lord and Lady Thrushell." Phillipa stirred her tea as she had been for the past twenty minutes. She had yet to drink any; with her nerves as they were, putting even tea into her stomach would likely make her ill. "On behalf of Captain Langley."

Olivia laughed. "If we asked you which event we should attend before we accepted, we would be spending the Season in musty old museums and book reading clubs."

"David Langley is the Thrushells' son, my dear. Of course they're holding a soiree in his honor."

"But Mama, we don't attend every party ever thrown by someone's parents for their offspring."

"David Langley isn't just an offspring," Livi countered. "You know he returned from Africa a hero, *and* he's been celebrated all over England for his book."

The book he hadn't even written. Phillipa sent her sister a glare. "And that's why we shouldn't attend. That book makes Bennett look foolish. I don't want to be seen endorsing either it or Captain Langley."

The marchioness put her hand over Phillipa's. "The difficulty with refusing, my dear, is that it may well be seen as a slight, *because* you've been seen with Captain Wolfe."

"It will definitely be seen that way," Olivia agreed.

"Livi, fetch my blue shawl, will you?"

Olivia stood. "You might simply tell me to go away, you know," she said with a smile.

"Well, go away, then, but return with my shawl," their mother amended lightly.

Once the door closed again, Phillipa stood to pace. "I will feel like a traitor."

"Because Captain Wolfe says he's courting you?"

When Phillipa drew a breath, she could still smell the fresh scent of daisies in the air. "Because I think he truly is courting me," she returned.

"And if you're wrong, we will look doubly foolish. Not only would we be seen as siding with Captain Wolfe, but we would look as though our loyalty had been purchased for the price of a few daisies and some vague promises."

A hundred daisies was a great deal more than a

few. "I can hardly believe that someone I admire could also admire me, Mama, but I'd hoped that perhaps *you* would believe it."

"Flip, that is not what I mean. Regardless of whether Bennett Wolfe does or doesn't attend, are you certain you want to risk being looked at askance? You're twenty-one years old. Both you and Livi should have married already. With Livi, I'm not worried. But I don't want you to have to end up alone."

"Oh. Oh."

She understood that. As it was, she was already regarded as something of an oddity. If she made a show of siding with a man of uncertain reputation simply because he was the only man who'd ever looked twice at her, and if he either turned out to be unworthy or decided against marrying her after so public a pursuit, she would fall from eccentric to laughingstock.

"Don't look so serious, Flip," her mother was saying. "All we need do is attend the soiree."

Phillipa turned for the door. "I'm going for a walk. I need a bit of fresh air."

"Yes. Of course. Make certain you take Mary with you."

She fetched a bonnet and the maid, and went outside. Early afternoon meant everyone was out visiting, paying calls, returning calls made earlier, or simply making certain they were seen out being social, but she didn't much care about any of that. It had always seemed insulting that the main goal in visiting wasn't actually seeing someone, but being seen seeing someone. Well, she wasn't paying a call on anyone, but she supposed she still received credit for doing so, simply for being out-of-doors.

"Where are we off to, my lady?" Mary asked.

"Nowhere in particular. I just want to stretch my legs."

"Very good, my lady. It is a lovely afternoon. And I think your peach gown will survive its dousing the other night. It wasn't nearly as bad as I thought at first look."

"Good. I'm fond of that gown."

Phillipa kept walking. Yes, the soiree at Langley House would be extremely popular, if for no other reason than people liked to associate with the famous and celebrated. None of them would likely have the slightest inkling that Captain Langley was a thief, much less an outright fraud and a liar.

As for the damage done to Bennett's reputation, she'd heard the questioning remarks made behind his back, the comments about whether he'd adopted the monkey, or the monkey had adopted him. It was all nonsense, and anyone who'd read his books would know that. Clearly it was more amusing for her peers to think the worst, whatever the evidence to the contrary.

She knew the truth. Even if Bennett hadn't told her, all it would have taken was a few of their conversations for her to gain all the proof she required that he wasn't incompetent and that Captain Langley's version of events wasn't the accurate one. The only difficulty with knowing that Bennett was a brave and honorable and intelligent man was then accepting that he was completely serious about chasing after her.

If she'd been pursued before, if she were the kind of woman that men longed for, she supposed she would have accepted him at his word. But men didn't long for her; she frightened some of them, as far as she could tell. She did have male friends, like John Clancy and Lord Murdock, but that had more to do with common literary likes and opinions than with the fact that she was a female.

When she finally slowed and looked up, they were more than three miles from Eddison House. In fact, she and Mary were on Lees Mew, directly outside Howard House. Bennett's temporary residence. Phillipa took a deep breath, her heart hammering. How in the world had she ended up here? She wasn't a great believer in providence, but coincidence had its limits, as well.

She wanted to talk with him, though. With Bennett. After the daisies and not seeing him for nearly three days, the urge to set eyes on him again had burrowed itself into her chest, nagging and aching. "What a lovely garden," she heard herself saying aloud. "Let's explore for a moment, shall we?"

"But—"

"Come along, Mary. It's only a garden. Not a lion pit." As she spoke, she walked through the open gate. And immediately she looked up toward the house, to see a startled pair of emerald eyes looking back at her through one of the windows.

Chapter Thirteen

While Langley huddled beneath a tarpaulin in an attempt to avoid the rain, I joined the bearers beneath the trees. From there I heard a symphony played by frogs and crickets and other creatures which have never yet been named. Unexpected and magnificent, it for some reason brought to mind the hard, jolting awareness of life, as when one first sees from across the room that woman. *The* woman.

THE JOURNALS OF CAPTAIN BENNETT WOLFE

B ennett turned away from the window so quickly that Kero jumped. "Geoffrey, look after her for a bit, will you?" he asked, tossing his young cousin a peach and striding for the lad's bedchamber door.

He told Kero to stay, and then charged down the stairs and out the servants' entrance adjoining the Howard House kitchens. Whatever reason Phillipa might have for seeking him out, her presence sent his heart pounding. If she was as ready to throw over the damned rules as he felt at that moment, he wasn't about to leave her standing there in the garden. And he knew precisely where he wanted her to be.

As he came around the back of the house into Lady Fennington's large garden, he didn't see her. For a moment he thought he might have imagined her, and he stopped, listening. Even with all the loud London sounds around him, he knew he would recognize her voice—and then he heard it. Angling toward the center oak tree, he made his way around the tangle of vines and roses until she came into view again.

"Phillipa."

She turned away from her maid to face him. "What a pleasant surprise, Captain!" she exclaimed, tension and excitement radiating from her so powerfully he could almost touch it. He *could* feel it.

"Come in and see Kero," he heard himself say, as he reached out and took her hand. He needed to touch her. He wanted to touch her.

"Oh, of course." She glanced back at her maid. "Wait here for a moment, Mary. Kero's timid around strangers."

"But my lady, you—"

"Wait here," Bennett stated.

With a faint squeak the maid sat on the bench that encircled the oak tree's trunk.

Before Phillipa could come to her senses and begin protesting as well, Bennett wrapped his fingers around hers and towed her around the back of the house and in through the servants' entrance. "What are you doing?" she finally demanded, her voice hushed. "And you're not supposed to order my maid about."

"Shh." With a quick look around them he pushed

open a door at the far end of the back hallway. He took a lit candle off a hallway sconce, pulled her in after him, and shut the door with them inside. After another assessing glance at her, he shoved a broom across the doorjamb, effectively locking them in.

Sacks of flour, dried herbs, pots and pans, and jars of assorted other spices and jams lay tucked into shelves or stacked on the floor. "Why are we in the kitchen larder?" Phillipa asked, pulling her hand free from his.

Bennett set the candle on a shelf. Closing his eyes, he took a long, deep breath, excitement, arousal, the hard feeling of just being alive all pounding at him. Then he opened his eyes again and turned around. "I was going to say something clever," he murmured, studying her face and the glint coming into her brown eyes, "but nothing comes to mind."

With one long stride he reached her. Before a protest could come to her mind, he slid his arms around her waist and lifted her onto an upturned barrel. Then he kissed her.

She opened to him, lips and teeth and tongue, with a passion that both reassured and thrilled him. The blood pounding through his veins felt molten, all flowing down to his already alert cock. "Phillipa," he murmured against her mouth, lifting his hands to undo the half-dozen buttons running down her back. He wanted her bare skin against his.

"Bennett, I think this is a very bad idea," she moaned, digging her fingers into his shoulders.

"Stop thinking, then."

"That's not very helpful." Her voice hitched as he tilted up her chin and began kissing her throat.

"Did I mention how patient I've been attempting to be?" he returned, pulling the front of her gown forward to bare her shoulders. Good God. Her skin smelled of citrus. "Do you always bathe in lemons?" he breathed, baring his teeth to nip a little at her soft skin.

"Oh." She jerked, shifting her hands to twine her fingers into his hair. "Lemon slices. I like the way they smell."

"So do I."

"I thought we were working on you behaving in a civilized manner." To his delight, she began pulling at the knot of his cravat.

"I'm not civilized, Phillipa. Not at all. And certainly not today." After another deep kiss, though, he backed away a fraction, resting his forehead against hers. Whatever he wanted, and however badly he wanted it, he wasn't about to force her into anything. "I want you, Phillipa," he whispered. "And I mean to have you. So tell me yes, or tell me no. Now."

He actually felt her breathing deepen. "This is very naughty," she murmured, nearly breaking his neck as she yanked his cravat free. "Yes."

Thank Lucifer. Finally he let his breath out again. "Good."

One by one he pulled her arms free of her gown, then tugged the plain green muslin down to her waist. Glorious. His hands shook a little as he ran his fingertips in slow circles around her warm breasts, drawing closer and closer until he could slide the pad of his thumbs across her nipples.

At her soft gasp of pleasure his own blood began pounding. It took every ounce of control he owned to resist the primal urge to lay her down on the floor, lift her skirts, and bury himself in her. But this was her first encounter with intimacy, and he did not want to send her fleeing.

And so he kissed her again, molding his palms over her breasts, listening to the changing pattern of her breathing. "I want to see you naked," he whispered, moving his mouth against her ear and down the line of her jaw.

"I *am* naked," she returned in the same tone.

"Not nearly naked enough."

He lifted her again, setting her feet down on the floor. Then he squatted down, pulling on the hem of her dress until it fell past her hips in a rumpled green pool of material. He wanted to stay there, to taste her, but that would wait, as well. Slowly he straightened, setting her back on the barrel. Leaning in between her legs, he licked her left nipple.

Phillipa gasped, arching her back and pressing herself closer against him. He did the same with her right nipple, then took it into his mouth, sucking gently. Placing his hands on her bare thighs, he ran them slowly down to her knees and up again.

"I'm beginning to think that being ruined is underrated," she murmured in a shivery voice that made him ache. "But I am quite nervous."

Bennett pulled off his coat and waistcoat, dumping them with her clothes. It made an odd pile, he decided, all the cloth that had been keeping him from her, lying there together on the floor.

"I encountered a tribe along the Congo," he said quietly, kneeling down to pull off his boots, "where women decorate their bare breasts with blue and yellow river clay to signify their availability." He ran the tip of his tongue back and forth across one sensitive nipple again, and she shivered, groaning and tangling her hands into his hair.

"Did you now?"

"I did. At the time I found it rather . . . exotic, but now I'm thinking the stuff must have tasted awful." He licked her nipple again.

"I . . . I promise not to paint myself blue, then," she managed shakily, throwing her head back, then gasping again when he sent his hands trailing up the insides of her thighs.

"You're no longer available." With a growl, pushed nearly to breaking by the aroused sounds she kept making, he ripped his shirt off over his head, then pulled her down to the floor in front of him.

Phillipa stared at the bare, muscled chest before her, mesmerized. Slowly she lifted one hand to touch his warm skin. Muscles jumped beneath her touch. "Oh, my," she breathed, fascinated by the dusting of dark hair on his chest that narrowed as it descended his abdomen and disappeared beneath the band of his trousers. Then she noticed the puckered white scar just below his rib cage on the right side. "This is where you were wounded."

"Yes. Hurt like the devil. I don't want to talk about it." He moved over her, taking her hands and lowering her onto her back, then kissed her again. "Touch me."

The deep huskiness in his voice sent waves of excitement through her. "I don't want to do anything wrong, Bennett."

"You can't do anything wrong. There aren't any rules."

As he lowered himself over her to take her mouth

again, Phillipa slid her arms around his shoulders, kneading her fingers into his muscles. He felt so alive, and so arousing, that she could barely remember to breathe.

Then one of his own wandering hands slipped between her thighs and brushed against her most intimate place. Phillipa couldn't help jumping, but she was rather proud that she didn't yelp. Until he slid one finger inside her, and she *did* yelp.

"Shh," he cautioned, desire and deep amusement in his voice. "You want me, don't you?"

Phillipa nodded, every nerve in her body centered on his finger rubbing against her. Inside her. "Oh, yes."

"Then unbutton my trousers, Phillipa."

If he wanted her to stop thinking so much, he'd certainly found the way to accomplish it. With his fingers down there and his mouth on her breasts, she couldn't think at all. And all she wanted was to know what came next. With shaking fingers she reached between them. Her fingers grazed the engorged part of him that strained at the seams of his trousers, and he hissed in a breath.

"I'm sorry," she whispered. "Did that hurt?"

He wiggled his finger. "Does that hurt?"

Her eyes almost rolled back in her head from the sensation. "N-no."

"From your expression, I would say they felt about the same. Unbutton me, Phillipa."

Trying to find enough control to open each button left her moaning and panting as though she'd run a race. Finally she managed the last fastening. He straightened, his knees between hers, and she helped him shove his trousers down past his thighs. "Oh, my," she breathed, fascinated all over again at the sight of his large, aroused manhood.

"That's better," he said, lifting one leg at a time to yank the last bit of clothing off either of them.

"Are you certain it doesn't hurt?" she asked, lifting up on her elbows to get a better view. "It looks swollen enough."

He snorted. "You say the most romantic things."

Still barely able to breathe, Phillipa frowned up at him. "Don't tease me."

"I'm not." Bennett went down on all fours again and leaned in to kiss her. "And no, it doesn't hurt. It will hurt you, though. The price of your virginity."

"I'll pay it, but I still think you're teasing."

Bennett smiled, the expression making her heart do excited flip-flops all over again. "The more I want you, the more swollen it is. Judge for yourself whether I'm teasing." He twisted sideways, giving her a very nice view of his muscular arse, and dug into the inside pocket of his discarded jacket.

"What's that?"

He held up the brown, tubular thing with a red ribbon at the open, top end. "A French condom. To keep you from getting with child. That, I would not tease about."

"Let me, Bennett."

She reached up. After a brief hesitation, he shook his head. "Next time."

"You think I'll do it wrong?" she asked, indignant.

"I think you'll drive me over the edge and therefore make its use unnecessary." Swiftly he pulled it over the end of his large manhood and tugged it up like a stocking, using the ribbon to pull it closed and tying it.

"It's very festive." She lifted her gaze to his face again, to find him studying her. "I would drive you over the edge?"

"Mm hm." He sank down again, lightly brushing hair from her face and then kissing her on the mouth. His finger slid inside her again, its rhythm matching that of his tongue. "Like this," he murmured, moving in deeper, pressing his palm against her curls as he did so.

She drew tighter and tighter inside, arching her hips up against his hand. "Oh, *oh*," she breathed, shaking. Then everything shattered in pulsing, shivering ecstasy.

Bennett angled his hips forward as she clung to him. Slowly, very slowly, he slid inside her. As she still shuddered from the . . . whatever he'd done to her, he met her gaze, his jungle-colored eyes glinting in the candlelight. "Hold on, Phillipa," he murmured, making her name into a kiss.

He pushed forward, entering her fully. Sharp pain cut through exquisite pleasure. She yelped again, but Bennett caught the sound against his mouth. In a moment she nodded.

The sensation of him inside her simply had no words. His weight, the scent of him, the slide of his bare skin against hers—she'd never known anything like it. And immediately she had no idea how she'd ever gone through life without it.

"How do you feel, *nyonda*?" Bennett asked, beginning a slow, rhythmic thrust and retreat.

She tangled her fingers into his hair again, pulling

him closer against her. "Ruined," she panted, tilting her head back as his pace increased.

"Put your legs around me."

His words were cut off, short, the rising tension in him flowing through to her. As she locked her ankles around his thighs he seemed to move even deeper inside her, and she moaned again, shifting to grip him around the shoulders.

She could feel every inch of him, tight and hot and exquisite. When he kissed her again, warm and openmouthed, the deep pull began in her once more. He sped his thrusts until they seemed to meet the hard, fast beat of her heart. Their gazes locked, and Phillipa dug her fingers into his back. Then it happened again, that exquisite release, and she moaned breathlessly.

Muscles flexed, their bodies seeming to merge into one writhing, heated, hungry beast. Faster, harder, deeper—and then with a fierce low growl he pressed into her, his eyes closing and pure ecstasy etched on his lean face.

Breathing hard, he lowered his face against her neck. Phillipa stroked her fingers along his back, memorizing his contours and the flex of his muscles. "So this is what you meant," she managed, "when you said you would woo me."

He shook his head, lifting up to meet her gaze. "No. This is desire. Wooing has a different aim."

She closed her own eyes, wondering if she'd ever be able to move again. *Delicious.* "Which aim?"

Bennett kissed her softly. "Marriage, *nyonda.*"

"Marriage?" Phillipa squeaked, her pretty brown eyes widening. "You didn't just say that to keep my father from clubbing you with the fireplace poker?"

Bennett shook his head. Still inside her, resting most of his weight on his elbows, he reflected that most people would think he'd gone mad. Better than three years in the Congo with very limited female companionship, lovers here and there around the world as he'd traveled, and now he'd decided on marriage to essentially the first woman he'd set eyes on since his return to London.

But he hadn't decided it today. Sex with her had simply confirmed that he'd made the correct decision. By God, she'd been worth ten years of traveling across three continents.

"I didn't walk over here for a proposal," she said. "And you asked me whether I wanted to participate. Don't feel obligated." She pushed at his shoulder. "Truly. Don't."

"Have I ever said anything to make you believe that bedding you would be the end of my interest?"

"No."

"You don't have to sound so begrudging."

"I'm a bit . . . overwhelmed."

At least she didn't sound suspicious or hostile any longer. He reluctantly pulled away from her and sat up, grabbing for a rag to clean himself off. "What stage of courtship have we entered, considering two bouquets of flowers, a drive in the country, two dances, and a recital? And sex, of course."

Phillipa scooted on her pretty bare bottom back against a shelf so she could sit up. "You can't count the first bouquet, because you didn't follow the rules." She smiled briefly. "This shouldn't count, either, but I find that I'm unwilling to discount it."

"Well, that's something." Bennett shifted onto his

hands and knees and pursued her, stopping only when he was close enough to touch her soft lips with his. "It all counts, Phillipa. I've told you from the beginning what I want of you. But I haven't proposed to you. Yet. If you want me to follow the rules, I'll send you more flowers and take you driving every morning."

She kissed him back. "The rules are for *your* benefit, you know. You can't walk about London swinging an axe through propriety. Not when you're trying to recapture your reputation."

"And now we have your reputation to consider, as well."

When she lifted one hand to stroke his cheek, he leaned into the caress. Bennett couldn't fault her for being concerned about his reputation, but she had to realize that he was equally concerned with hers. He would proceed as slowly and carefully as he could, but in the end someone would find out that she was no longer a virgin—especially when he didn't intend that this should be anything less than the beginning of their intimate relationship. She was the one. He knew that as well as he knew anything.

While he waited for her to conjure a logical reply to his concern, she sat forward and brushed her lips against his. She retreated, then closed again, her tongue flicking against his teeth—a delicate, exquisite promise of future ecstasy. *Good God.* It was a promise he intended to have her keep, and at the next, earliest opportunity.

"Speaking of reputations, what will you do when you run across Captain Langley? You know it will happen."

"I'm looking forward to it. Sex isn't the only thing

with which I have a considerable amount of experience." He lifted one hand. "I can kill a man with my
little finger, you know."

She chuckled, taking his finger and pulling it into
her mouth. Oh, that was enough of that. He was
taking her again, immediately.

"We should—"

The loud squawk directly outside the door startled both of them. Tiny hands yanked at the door
handle, hammering and clawing, as Kero shrieked
at the top of her lungs.

"Damnation," he hissed, leaping for the door.
Geoffrey could be following the monkey. At worst,
half the kitchen staff had already heard and were
running to the larder to investigate. "Get dressed,"
he snapped over his shoulder, yanking aside the
broom and pulling the door open a crack.

Kero leapt through the opening onto his bare
shoulder, and he swiftly closed them inside again.
The vervet bounced up and down, barking in distress, while he dove into the pile of clothes to find
his jacket and the peanuts he carried in one pocket.

"Here, Kero," Phillipa said softly, holding up an
apple from one of the myriad barrels.

The monkey stopped making noise in mid bark,
then jumped from Bennett's shoulder to Phillipa's.
The vervet took the apple and climbed onto one of
the shelves to begin obliterating it.

"Very nicely done," he said, grinning at Phillipa
even as he bent down and tossed her the dress. "And
you looked very lovely for a naked chit with an apple
and a monkey on her shoulder. Paradise's Eve."

She smiled back at him. "Likewise, except for the
bit about being a female."

216 🁢 Suzanne Enoch

Bending down again, he reached for his discarded trousers. "We'd best hurry. I doubt that anyone could miss hearing that."

"She's not jealous of me," Phillipa noted, stepping into her gown and wriggling her hips as she drew it up over her waist.

The sight of her wriggling made it difficult for him to shrug into his pants. Of course he'd bedded women before, but this was . . . different. His fingers didn't tingle or his breath catch from simple lust. He should be sated, he supposed, and he did feel satisfied. But underneath that, he wanted her again. And again. And again.

"Why is that, do you think?" Phillipa prompted.

He shook himself. She was clearly thinking again, and he needed to catch up. "I'm not her mate," he replied belatedly. "I'm her mother. She's still young, but I don't think her perception of me is going to alter. I hope not."

"So do I. I have no desire to get my hair pulled by an angry monkey every time we're together."

Bennett caught her arm, turning her around so he could fasten the buttons up her back. Leaning in, he breathed the citrus scent of her hair. "Does that mean we'll be seeing each other naked again?" he asked, kissing the nape of her neck.

"Mm. Perhaps you might bring me some lilies," she said, smiling slyly as she looked over her shoulder at him.

Lilies. Not precisely a declaration of undying love, but then he hadn't precisely proposed. Yet. As he pulled on his boots, the door handle dipped. Someone pushed, but the broom held. Thinking quickly,

Bennett yanked on his shirt. "Hold a second. Kero's made a shambles in here."

He motioned Phillipa to turn over the bottles along the closest shelf, and she silently complied while he buttoned his waistcoat and yanked on his jacket. After he'd scattered a few apples across the floor, he noisily pulled aside the broom and allowed the door to open.

Geoffrey and Hayling both stood looking from him to Phillipa to the larder. "Lady Phillipa and I were in the garden chatting when we heard Kero screeching," Bennett explained. "We followed her in here, but she's apparently even more fond of apples than I realized." He scooped up the monkey and hoisted her into his arms.

Phillipa bent down and picked up the apples he'd just scattered. "I'm just thankful she didn't rip open the flour sacks during her rampage."

"I'll see to that, my lady," the butler put in, motioning them both to leave the larder.

"We were playing hide-and-seek," Geoffrey said, looking woefully at Kero, "and then I hid under a blanket. When I jumped out, I think I frightened her. Will she still like me?"

"Give her an hour or so to forget, and I imagine you'll be fast friends again." After a hesitation, Bennett ruffled the boy's dark hair. Geoffrey hadn't been deprived of his parents, but Bennett very clearly recalled how welcome a kind word from an adult would have been at that same age. "Lady Phillipa, we should go find your maid," he continued, offering her an arm.

He held his breath until her warm fingers closed

around his sleeve. "Yes. We no doubt frightened poor Mary half to death when we began running to the house."

Once they were outside, she slowed and pulled her fingers free. "My family received an invitation to Lord and Lady Thrushell's party welcoming Captain Langley back from his book tour. They accepted it without asking me."

Bennett narrowed his eyes. "I wasn't invited. Funny, that."

"I would imagine that Langley will do everything possible to stay away from you."

"If he's wise, he will. But I don't intend to wait for him to stumble across me." He shook himself. Thoughts of justice and revenge could wait until he wasn't in the company of a very compelling young woman. "Thank you for telling me about the party."

"I told my mother I wouldn't be attending," she said, "but then I thought you might be able to use me as a spy."

"You don't need to spy for me, Phillipa."

She smiled. "Bring me some lilies, and I will consider it an even trade."

Chapter Fourteen

The water roiled in front of me. As I lurched back, the great beast surged forward—twenty feet of hungry crocodile. I had no time to aim my rifle, so I dove sideways, thwacking the animal hard across the eyes with the butt of the weapon. The predator clearly didn't expect to be attacked in return and it retreated, giving me time to get ashore and realize that my shirt sleeve was missing. Thus is the difference between life and death in the Congo; the thickness of a cotton shirt.

THE JOURNALS OF CAPTAIN BENNETT WOLFE

I don't appreciate you befriending Geoffrey behind my back."

Bennett looked up from brushing down Ares. Fennington, dressed in a quality blue jacket and gray waistcoat and trousers, stood in the stall entrance. With a frown, Bennett glanced toward the stable's wide doorway. It was dark outside. He'd lost track of time again, after a ten-mile ride across London and cooling down the big gelding. That was another thing he didn't understand about the peerage—their nearly completely sedentary lives.

"He's my cousin," he said aloud, dropping the brush into a bucket and straightening. "Do I need your permission to converse with him?"

"I won't have you speaking against me."

"If I have anything to say against you, I'll do so to your face. I have no need to wield children as weapons." Bennett scooped the dozing Kero off a bale of hay, then stopped. "Are you on your way to Langley's gala?"

The marquis frowned. "Yes. It's nothing against you, Bennett. The captain and I are partners."

"The captain and I *were* partners. Don't turn your back on him."

"Bennett—"

"I'd like to join you," he interrupted. "Will you give me a few minutes to change my clothes?"

"You weren't invited," his uncle countered, following him out of the stable and back into the house.

"Yes, and why is that, considering that I'm a former companion presumed dead? I haven't said a word against him since my return." *Not in public, anyway.*

He heard the marquis's heavy breath. "Guilt, I would imagine. What about your friend? Won't Lord John Clancy allow you to use his invitation?"

"Jack offered. He even said he would decline the invitation if I asked him to. I thought it would be more . . . seemly, I suppose, to attend with my relations. I am staying under your roof, after all."

"Or you could remain here tonight."

He'd thought about that as well. Langley, however, had to know by now that he was back in London. This hadn't been an oversight. David likely meant to use the opportunity to encourage the view that he had led the expedition to success, and that Bennett was superfluous. Bennett didn't intend to allow that to happen.

And of course Phillipa would be there, as well. And knowing her, if he didn't appear to defend himself, she would more than likely charge in to do so. Though he appreciated the support, he didn't want her to be put in that position. Not for him.

"I could simply arrive unannounced," he mused. "They might attempt to keep me out, but if I make enough of a stir, I suppose I'll make my point. Or *a* point."

Fennington regarded him for a moment. "We'll wait for you." In fact, his uncle followed him up the stairs and down the hallway to the bedchamber he'd been given over.

Kero had fashioned a mound of pillows— apparently taken from throughout the house—into a nest of sorts beside the bed, and he plopped her into the center of it. His wardrobe had increased slightly over the past days, but he knew his uncle still considered it woefully inadequate for a gentleman during the Season. During his first days back in London he hadn't given a damn what he looked like or how anyone else perceived him, but recently he'd altered his opinion. Phillipa felt awkward in public, and he had no intention of adding to her discomfort.

She'd asked for him to behave like a gentleman, and with several rather large stumbles, he'd been attempting to do so. On the other hand, she'd never said a word about his appearance. It more than likely hadn't occurred to her any more than it had to him. But it mattered to the people around them, and after the fiasco with the roses he'd realized that he had to win over her parents with nearly as much care as he'd been using to win her.

"What's made you decide you don't hate me?" his uncle pursued, shaking his head at the contents of the wardrobe but otherwise keeping silent.

"I don't have time for it."

"So schedule permitting, you would continue to detest me?"

Bennett glanced over his shoulder, then went back to dressing. "I detested you when you couldn't be bothered to take me in twenty years ago. And yes, it made me angry that when you've wanted so little to do with me in life, you were quick to step in for a share of the profits after I was presumed dead."

"I did n—"

"I reckon I've made my own way in the world, and I will continue to do so. Don't stand in my way where Langley is concerned, and I'll attempt not to ruin your reputation as you've allowed him to injure mine."

"I see." Fennington shifted, then settled against the door frame. "And this is why I should allow you to share a coach with your aunt and me tonight."

"And your invitation to the party. Don't forget that."

"Yes, it's all about self-preservation for me. You might have told me instead that you're attempting a reconciliation, so that I would be more likely to support any action you take."

"Should I have? Phillipa keeps telling me I need to learn better manners."

"You should listen to her."

"She keeps telling me that, as well."

He pulled on a dark gray jacket and walked back to Kero's nest. Lowering his arm, he clicked his tongue at her, and she swarmed up to sit on his shoulder. The knife already rested in his boot, though his uncle might have forgotten that fact. Bennett hadn't; whatever Langley was or wasn't likely to do in a room full of people, *he* wasn't going anywhere near Langley House empty-handed.

Five minutes later he was in the coach, letting Kero stand on his knee and chitter at the sights they passed in the dim light of streetlamps. He sat back, declining to join the chat between his aunt and uncle. Even though Lady Fennington had been helpful with the daisies, he had nothing in common with her at all.

"I was chatting with Lady Timgill this morning, Bennett," she said unexpectedly. "And I thought you should know that people are talking about you and Lady Phillipa. She said that Lady Jersey said the sister would be a much more suitable match. What's her name?"

"Olivia," Bennett supplied.

"Yes. She's lovely. And very sought-after. Phillipa seems . . . pleasant enough, but, well, she's bookish, isn't she?"

"Yes, she is."

"Be cautious. It would be dreadful if you were to be matched with her in everyone's eyes simply because she's read your books."

A week or so ago Bennett would have told Lady Fennington exactly what he thought of her opinion and her tongue-wagging friends. This evening he gave a noncommittal nod. He'd brought roses to Phillipa, and she'd fainted. He would follow the steps she wanted, and those steps did not include informing his gossiping aunt of his intentions.

"You know," his aunt continued, "this would be the perfect time for you to marry. Although your . . . behavior in the Congo lacked a bit of bravado, everyone loves a wedding."

His jaw clenched. "I'll keep that in mind."

"If you have no one in particular under consideration, I would be happy to make some inquiries. I know, for example, that Lady Elizabeth Chendle is about to come into her inheritance. Three thousand a year. With that in addition to your own income, you could likely fund your own expeditions. Ideally you should have begun courting her before Captain Langley's return; no doubt he'll be looking for a bride as well—and he is very celebrated at the moment."

"I'll manage my own matrimonial affairs." In the back of his mind he could almost see Phillipa scowling at him. "Thank you for the offer," he added belatedly.

"Yes, of course. But make certain you consider Julia Jameson. Oh, and Millicent Beckwith plays the pianoforte exceptionally well, though her face is a bit . . . pinched."

"I've heard her play." And he'd seen the results of what a little chat with Millicent had done for Phillipa.

As Bennett wondered whether Lady Fennington actually considered skill at the pianoforte to be something that would encourage him toward marriage, his aunt continued on and on about the various eligible females wandering about London. Graceful gazelles all, unaware of the lions prowling in their midst and ready to pounce—except that he was quite cognizant of the fact that the gazelles knew precisely what they were doing, and the prowlers-about more closely resembled hyenas than lions.

He'd danced or attempted to chat with a number of the mentioned females, and they hadn't impressed. And yet his aunt kept talking, promoting what seemed like every chit in Mayfair except for the one he wanted. Clearly Phillipa was a mystery to her peers, if no one had bothered to notice her in the three years since her debut. He had noticed, however, and she fascinated him in a manner that no one and nothing else in the world had managed. And she would be in attendance tonight.

In a way, he was glad for the conversation. By the time the coach stopped outside Langley House his nerves had been worn to a sharp point, and every muscle ached with suppressed tension and anger both at the slights to his own character, and at the less subtle ones to Phillipa.

The butler accepted Fennington's invitation, then sent Bennett a curious look. "Lord and Lady Fennington and . . ."

"And guest," Bennett supplied. "With monkey."

Given the talk about London, Kero's presence was probably enough to identify him to the butler. The only question was whether said servant had been told to look out for him or to notify Langley if he made an appearance. The man looked more affronted than nervous, so Bennett guessed he didn't know anything.

"There's Miss Jameson," Lady Fennington said as they entered the ballroom, indicating a pretty, black-haired chit. "Shall I introduce you?"

"No. I'll manage."

From his swift survey of the room, David Langley hadn't yet appeared to greet the admiring throngs. He did see Phillipa, though, seated beside her mother against the near wall. The sight of her actually calmed him, though the new imaginings she awakened pushed at him with equally strong, albeit more pleasurable, force.

"Excuse me," he said, leaving his relations without a backward glance.

"Oh, hello, Sir Bennett!" Sonja Depris blocked his path and sank into a deep curtsy that showed off a considerable portion of her bosom. Olivia Eddison stood a step or two behind her.

"Miss Depris." With a nod he started around her.

"I was just telling Livi about the magnificent horse you purchased."

Olivia nodded at him. "What was his name, Sir Bennett?"

"Ares. Pardon me."

Henry Camden stepped in between him and Olivia, as though protecting her from him. The idiot was guarding the wrong sister. "Will you purchase a pony for the monkey to ride?"

"No."

"I wonder," Camden continued, tapping his chin with one finger, "why you didn't leave the monkey behind tonight. Won't Kero abandon you when she sees Captain Langley?"

"Oh, that's true," Sonja piped up. "I read the book. Kero and the captain are good friends."

Lucy giggled. "Perhaps you should have purchased her a pony, after all."

Fingers brushed his hand and then retreated again. At the same moment, the hair on his arms lifted. Heat and desire began their slow trail along his veins. With a breath he turned to see Phillipa standing beside him. "That's always troubled me," she said, offering a thoughtful frown. "If Captain Langley is so fond of Kero, why did he leave her behind? You'd been declared dead, so she was essentially orphaned."

Bennett wanted to hug her. He was tempted to announce just how highly Langley and the vervet regarded each other, but restrained himself. This would seem to be one of those instances where a picture would suffice better than any words he could conjure. "I imagine Langley can explain their bond better than I," he offered, and faced Phillipa. "Might I have a word with you?"

"Certainly." She took his arm.

Her fingers shook a little. He felt the electricity between them himself, and had to work harder than he expected to keep from leaning sideways to smell her hair. "I want to kiss you," he murmured.

"Well, you can't," she returned, with a quick smile that looked more worried than amused. "We won't find anywhere private here tonight."

"What's wrong?" he asked, settling for stopping to gaze at her. What he wanted to do was to take her into his arms and not let her go for at least several hours.

"You shouldn't be here. That's what's wrong. I told you that I would look about and try to determine what Captain Langley has in mind."

"And I told you that I didn't want you spying for

me." He placed his hand over hers where it rested on his arm. "And how better to judge his game than to see how he reacts to me?"

She sighed. "Clearly it's too late to talk you out of attending."

"Clearly." He gave a short grin.

"Your friend the Duke of Sommerset is here. And there's to be dancing. In fact, His Grace asked me for a waltz."

Ah, the evening was getting better and better. He handed Kero a peanut, hoping to keep her silent for the next few minutes. "You do prefer the civilized savages, then. How many dances does *he* get?"

Her pretty brown eyes widened just a little, something very like excitement touching them. "Are you jealous?" she asked.

Jealous. Closer to volcanic, but in all fairness that wasn't entirely Sommerset's fault tonight. "Yes, I'm jealous. What do you exp—"

"No one's ever been jealous over me before." Her mouth swooped into a smile.

That stopped the retort he'd been about to make. What was wrong with the damned London noblemen, that they'd let her roam among them unnoticed for three years? "Are there any other waltzes being offered tonight?"

Phillipa nodded. "Two more. Apparently Lady Thrushell isn't entirely pleased with the large number, but Captain Langley is particularly fond of the waltz."

"Give me both of them."

"No. It wouldn't be seemly."

"Even if I mean to marry you?"

"Shh," she cautioned, her cheeks darkening. "You

can't bandy that about. You said it when we were . . ." She looked around, lowering her voice still further. "Naked."

An unexpected smile touched him. God, she was an original. "I would argue with that, but I want a dance, and you've already ignored my request for a kiss." Behind the cover of a half-open door and a potted plant, he reached up to brush his fingers along her cheek.

"You didn't request a kiss. You said you wanted one."

He moved still closer, putting his free hand on her hip. "I'll play with words if you want," he whispered, "but there are other things I'd rather be doing with you, Phillipa."

"Bennett, stop," she murmured back, taking his hand away but holding on to his fingers.

"Then give me your damned dance card."

She glanced down to pull the card from her reticule. It wasn't only Sommerset; four other dances had been claimed, as well. And he didn't like that one bloody bit. "Who is Francis Henning?"

"A friend of a friend of John's, I believe. He's rather amusing, though I'm not certain he realizes that."

"No. I mean, point him out to me." He wrote his name down beside the evening's last waltz.

Phillipa shook her head. "Considering that you look very like an angry panther whose antelope dinner has been stolen, I'm not pointing out anyone to you."

"Are you certain?" he asked, only half jesting. "Pummeling this Henning would warm me up nicely for Langley."

"Stop that." She took back her card.

"Then distract me with something else."

"Very well." She stayed silent for a moment, considering. "These last few weeks have been full of new experiences for me," she continued in a thoughtful voice.

Bennett held himself still. "Any particularly memorable experiences?" he asked. If she mentioned meeting a monkey or receiving daisies, he was going to put his fist through a wall.

"Mm hm." With a quick glance at their shadowed retreat, she moved closer in his arms. "I keep thinking that everyone who sees me must know. Is the experience always so . . . exquisite? I can't seem to think about anything else."

Now he felt better. "I can only think of one way we can be certain that a second experience would be as enjoyable, *nyonda*." He ran a finger down her bare forearm. "In fact, I think you should open your morning room window when you return home tonight and then wait there for a time. Beginning at two o'clock, say."

Her shoulders rose and fell as her breathing deepened. "It would be wise to find out for certain if we . . . merge as well a second time," she breathed.

"I already know the answer to that, but I'm more than happy to demonstrate on every possible occasion. You fascinate me, Phillipa, and I want you. No one but you."

She smiled, the expression lighting her eyes and doing some interesting things to his nether regions. "You make me feel like a butterfly, Bennett," she whispered, reaching up to touch his cheek.

They'd been in hiding for several minutes now, and the odds grew every moment that they would be seen. Frankly, Bennett didn't care about that. She was his, whether she felt ready yet to say it aloud or not. As long as he could recover his reputation, regain the trust and backing of the Africa Association or the East India Company, he would be able to go exploring again. And that was the only thing that troubled him. Not that his butterfly would spread her wings and fly away, but that she wouldn't.

The orchestra played the opening of a country dance, and Phillipa abruptly broke away from him. "This is my dance with Mr. Henning," she said, backing out of their tiny hiding place before he could stop her.

"I'll keep you company until he appears," he said, following her and offering his arm.

"Bennett, you don't—"

"Don't the monkey ruin the line of your coat?" a short, round fellow queried, then stuck out his hand. "Francis Henning."

Abruptly Bennett felt a bit easier about this particular dance. He shook Henning's hand. "Until this month, it's been three years since I've worn a formal coat," he said. "I don't actually give a damn about its line."

"I say, that's brave of you," Henning returned, taking a half step back. "I suppose next to angry leopards the *ton* don't much impress."

"No, it doesn't."

Henning blinked. "I, ah, I'm here to collect Lady Flip for the country d—"

"Of course, Mr. Henning," she said, brushing past Bennett and gesturing for the short fellow to lead the way to the dance floor.

Bennett stayed where he was, watching. He knew

how to be more subtle, but tonight he couldn't seem to manage it. At any minute David Langley would walk down the main staircase into the arms of his adoring guests, and at this moment all Bennett wanted to do was see Phillipa dance. All around him the well-dressed natives of this land chattered, so much noise that it made his head ache. Each one fought to be the prettiest bird in the flock, too self-concerned to notice anything but the outward plumage of the fellows around them.

"Sir Bennett, you must join me at White's tomorrow," one of the crowd, Lord Hay-something, he thought, rumbled. "I've no doubt we'll have you in as a provisionary member by noontime."

I would rather eat elephant shit, Bennett thought. "My schedule is full at the moment," he said aloud.

"You should come by without delay," the fellow pursued. "You've already been in Town too long without accepting a membership somewhere. Strike while the iron is hot, don't you know. I'll be happy to sponsor you."

"What about the current rumors that I'm a fool?" Bennett asked.

Hay-something looked affronted. "One never admits to that, Captain. And if you're to be in London indefinitely, you should make an attempt to fit in, don't you know."

"Thank you for the invitation," Bennett returned, facing the dance floor again, "but I don't expect I would be spending much time at a club where everyone fits in." And thank God for the Adventurers' Club. In fact, a drink there after this bloody party and before his rendezvous with Phillipa might be just the thing he required.

"Have you ever *been* to a club?" the viscount retorted. "There are scores of gentlemen clamoring to
get through the front doors of places like White's."

"Ah. There's your problem," Bennett retorted. "I'm
no gentleman."

"You—"

"Ladies and gentlemen," the butler bellowed
from the ballroom's main doorway, "Lord and Lady
Thrushell, and Captain David Langley."

Chapter Fifteen

Today I met the man to whom I will be entrusting my life for the foreseeable future. Captain David Langley is like myself a veteran of the Peninsular War, though his service was to Wellington rather than on the battlefield. Given that, now I can only hope that his aim will prove as sharp as his tongue is glib. I have my doubts about him; he seems too vain to want to risk his skin being worn by someone else.

THE JOURNALS OF CAPTAIN BENNETT WOLFE

Kero, up," Bennett muttered, handing the vervet into a chandelier.

Then he turned to look. He wanted a little visit with Langley without Kero's opinion coming between them. Though with the number of people crowded around the doorway, that wouldn't be quite as simple as he'd imagined. As he'd spent the past five months imagining.

That was when the cautious dislike he'd long felt toward this man—whose life he'd saved several times and who had more than once saved his—had deepened into hatred. He'd never called himself a gentleman, but that was precisely what Langley, who'd attempted to grind his name into the dirt and then stand on it, prided himself on being.

Well, Bennett would see how long that lasted. Sidestepping a footman and Lord Hay-something, he strode across the room. Despite the amused and speculative chatter of the nearest guests, they at least had enough sense to move out of his way.

And then someone didn't move.

"No, Bennett," Phillipa said, looking as though she was ready to knock him down. Or attempt to.

"Move aside," he grunted, his attention immediately divided.

"I thought you had a plan to rescue your reputation," she muttered back at him. "Something about not reacting the way everyone would expect a slighted man to behave."

"That was before I saw him. Now I'm going to beat him senseless."

When he started around her, she actually put a hand against his chest and pushed back. "That will not get you justice. Or your journals."

"No, but it will make me feel better." He drew in a sharp breath. "He doesn't need his teeth to hand me my journals."

Her pretty face paled, and she lowered her hand again. "Fine. If beating him is what you want most in the world, then do it. See what happens to your reputation and your future."

Apparently he'd acquired a walking, talking conscience. Bennett narrowed his eyes. "I thought I made it clear yesterday what my intentions toward Langley were. You might have attempted to dissuade me then."

"Yes, well, I thought that was merely manly bluster. And you weren't planning on being here. Now you have murder in your eyes."

"I won't kill him until I have my journals again. Excuse me, Phillipa."

He stalked straight at Langley, just visible now in the crowd. Light blue eyes lifted, caught sight of him, and widened. Apparently the butler hadn't informed David that his formerly deceased partner was in attendance tonight, after all. Good.

"Langley," he half growled as the darling golden-haired viscount's son faced him, "you are a son of a bitch."

Langley's jaw flexed. "Wolfe!" he exclaimed, smiling with all his teeth. "You aren't dead, after all!"

"No damned thanks to you. I appreciate you leaving me my boots, by the way. I expected to find them stolen along with my journals and my Baker rifle."

"Your recovery hasn't improved your disposition, I see. Or your memory. The only journals I left with are my own."

Bennett opened his mouth to demand that Langley produce them. A match of their handwriting would prove to whom they belonged. If he said that, though, Langley would have another reason to destroy them. "I read my—I mean, your—book. A very entertaining fiction. At least you had the tribal names spelled correctly—though with those journals, how could you not?"

"What is it they say about the worth of one man's opinion?" Langley commented smoothly, still smiling with everything but his eyes. "I don't recall exactly. Something about it being rubbish. In the—"

With a loud threat bark, Kero scrambled across the

floor and jumped—onto Langley's head. Shrieking, she yanked out a handful of golden hair and sank her teeth into one perfectly shaped ear. Screaming, Langley threw her off. She hit the floor running, then scampered up Bennett's leg and onto his shoulder.

"You damned devil!" Langley snarled, pulling his fingers away from his ear and eyeing the blood on them. "You should have drowned that vermin, Wolfe!"

"Yes, I should have, but before I could manage it he left me for dead and sailed away with most of my possessions." Bennett scratched Kero behind the ears as she cowered into the side of his neck. Clearly he'd underestimated the generally good-natured monkey's hatred of Langley. He was buying her a damned peach tree. An entire orchard. "What a shame that Kero doesn't seem as fond of you as you wrote. But then you did leave her behind, as well."

Snatching a handkerchief from his simpering mother's fingers, Langley pressed it to his pierced ear. "I want blood for blood," he snapped.

"I was hoping you would say that." Bennett shot out a fist and punched Langley flush on the nose.

Langley fell backward, hitting the ground with a satisfying-sounding thud. Spewing curses, blood now trickling from two orifices on his pretty face, he scrambled back to his feet again. "You damned bastard," he spat, his face reddening to nearly the color of his blood.

"Now you can leave the little monkey alone and come after me," Bennett said coolly, every muscle singing with the urge to do battle.

At least three chits had fainted, though he didn't know whether that had happened because of the blood, the violence, or the excitement. Bennett noted them on the periphery of his mind, just as he did the rest of the guests who pressed forward like circling vultures. Of more interest and concern was Phillipa.

She would be angry, of course, not because he'd taken action but rather because she saw a more logical course of action. If there was one thing Bennett had learned during three years in the Congo, however, it was that the strongest, most aggressive males were the ones who survived. Langley would not outflank him, betray him, or play on his trust again.

"You bloody twat," Langley snarled, still putting on a display of courage without actually advancing on him. "You simply can't stand anyone thinking you less than a hero, can you?"

"I think you've used more than your and my share of words combined," Bennett goaded. "Come at me. Or do you want to continue dancing with me, instead?"

"I'd rather be wiping your guts off my sword, Wolfe."

"Excellent." He made a low ruffing sound, and Kero jumped off his shoulder and fled. Predictably the vervet headed straight for Phillipa and jumped into her arms.

Langley followed the monkey's retreat with an angry gaze. "Well, isn't that interesting?" he drawled, the sound nasal through his pinched nose.

Bennett bent down, then straightened, in the same motion pulling the long, slender, horn-handled blade from his boot. Another woman whose name he couldn't recall fainted. The so-called gentlemen around her allowed her to fall to the ground before they even noticed her distress. "Let's get to it, shall we?"

"Put that away," a lower, more commanding voice ordered. Bennett didn't move, except to glance sideways as the crowd parted like the Red Sea and the tall, black-haired Duke of Sommerset strode through the opening.

"No."

"You two were sponsored by the Africa Association. If there's some sort of dispute, we'll hear it. But attacking a man at his homecoming is unacceptable, Captain Wolfe, however badly you think you've been wronged."

"Not wronged. Stolen from."

Langley sketched a bow, elegant and proper despite a blackening eye and a ragged kerchief pressed to his ear. "I have nothing to hide, Your Grace."

"Then I'll see you both at Ainsley House, at ten o'clock. Sharp. In the meantime, conduct yourselves in a civil manner." His gaze rested on Bennett. "If you are unable to do so, stay away from public events. Especially those held in honor of the man you're threatening."

Bennett realized he still grasped the knife handle. He took the moment of distraction as Sommerset turned his back and walked away to shove the blade back into his boot.

"Leave this house," Langley hissed, a half-dozen footmen approaching at his signal, "or I'll have you thrown out on your arse."

Abruptly Jack Clancy stood between them. "I'll see to it," he said, and wrapped a hand around Bennett's upper arm.

Bennett allowed his friend to pull him aside, toward the door, before he yanked himself free. "I don't need a rescue." Anger still pushed at him—and he couldn't leave Phillipa standing there with his monkey.

"Well, don't stab me, but I wasn't rescuing you. I mean, I was, but only from being hanged on Tyburn Hill for murdering an earl's only son and heir in front of two hundred witnesses."

He took a deep breath. "Thank you then, Jack."

"Very sensible of you. Let's depart, shall we? I'll buy you a glass at Jezebel's."

It made sense. Jack made sense. Bennett rolled his shoulders. In the jungle it all would have been much simpler. As Jack—and Phillipa—had pointed out, however, they weren't in the jungle. "I need to get my monkey."

"Flip and Livi are going outside to meet us."

"Why didn't you say so?" Bennett muttered, striding for the exit again.

Both Eddison sisters stood in the drive among the carriages when he left Thrushell House. He kept walking until he was directly in front of Phillipa, close enough to touch. He wanted to touch.

"I—"

Olivia slapped him. "How dare you let everyone know you're courting Flip and then begin a brawl in the middle of a ballroom," she snapped.

Kero barked, and she immediately backed away a little. "No, Kero," he said in a low voice, holding out his arm. All he needed was for the monkey to begin attacking everyone who touched him—they'd be asked to leave the country, rather than a damned party he hadn't wanted to attend in the first place.

"Livi, I can speak for myself," Phillipa said, lifting her shoulder toward him. Kero hopped from her to him, and he offered her a peanut. "If I'd known you meant to go about punching and stabbing people willy-nilly," she continued, "I would have made certain my family didn't attend."

Bennett frowned. "I didn't stab him."

"You would have if Sommerset hadn't intervened."

"Perhaps."

Clenching her jaw, she continued glaring at him. Clearly he'd broken several rules, but he couldn't be sorry for it. In fact, the only thing that concerned him about the evening was the idea that he'd done something to push her away from him.

"Phillipa, he stole my future from me," he finally said, wishing he knew how to look vulnerable and irresistible.

"So you've told me. I don't think you gained any converts to your way of thinking tonight."

"No. But I think I made my feelings fairly obvious." He blew out his breath. "I'm rough around the edges. He's not. I'm not likely to earn any allies in that house regardless of my restraint."

"Except that now he's more than likely inside that house reminding two hundred people that your monkey bit him and that you punched him in the nose when all he did was welcome you home. He's going to call you a blackguard and a rogue who argues with your fists."

Bennett narrowed his eyes. "So I should have listened to you."

"Yes, you should have." Slowly she reached up and tugged on Kero's tail. "You don't have to win friends, Bennett, but you do have to appear credible." When Kero hummed at her, she smiled. "And you, you silly thing. You weren't any help, either. I thought you and Captain Langley were friends."

"Never were," Bennett countered, handing over another peanut for her to give the monkey. "We had an overloaded boat on the way downriver. When we hit rapids, we started to swamp, and had to throw several boxes overboard to stay afloat. Langley grabbed Kero and threw her into the river, as well. Kero doesn't like water."

She gasped. "What happened?"

"I fished her out with an oar and told Langley I'd stake him out over an anthill if he touched her again. Langley is one thing about which Kero and I are in complete agreement." Of course he and Kero also agreed about something else—they were both becoming irretrievably fond of Lady Phillipa Eddison.

"I would have bit his ear as well, then."

He took her hand and drew it to his lips. "I suppose I'll be going."

"Yes, I think you should." She lowered her head, then darted a look up at him through her thick lashes and pulled him a few feet away from Jack and Livi. "Until two o'clock, then?" she whispered.

Heat rushed through him. So she still wanted him to come calling. "Leave your morning room window open, and I promise to be very prompt."

Phillipa smiled slowly. "Good."

And whatever his other difficulties, however much he wanted to finish his beating of David Langley and retrieve his journals and his reputation, that smile seemed the most significant thing of the entire evening. Life had taken a damned odd twist since he'd left the Congo.

* * *

Bennett slipped out of the Clancy House garden, retrieved Ares from where he'd left the bay hidden behind the stable, and rode for Eddison House. Jack's mother wouldn't be happy to find two dozen of her white and purple lilies missing, but he'd leave that for her son to explain. Jack would think of something. Lady Fennington didn't grow lilies, or he would have been able to save himself the detour.

He liked riding through London at night. Most of his fellows avoided it—especially on their own—but he was quite familiar with the sense of danger coming from the shadows, the heightened awareness of smell and sound, and the heavy feel of darkness around him.

Carriages still rolled through the streets as the occupants finished their evening's festivities, but the curtains were closed and the doors securely latched. And the few pedestrians outside hurried along, far more interested in their own concerns than in his. He wasn't interested in them, either.

Two streets away from Eddison House he found a suitable clearing behind someone's stable yard, and he tied Ares off in the shadows to wait for him. Then he walked the remaining distance, feeling a bit unbalanced without Kero on his shoulders. He'd left the monkey sleeping in Geoffrey's room, though, with a selection of fruit and nuts available for the boy or the vervet to sort through if either should awake.

Silently he turned up the white house's carriage drive to wait in the black shadows of the stable. By the distant sound of the church bells it was two o'clock. He'd said that he meant to be prompt, but one light still shone in an upstairs room.

Abruptly, though, it went out. As muffled excitement and arousal stirred through him, he wondered if it was Phillipa's bedchamber, and if she was on her way down to wait for him in the morning room. There was one way to find out.

Crossing the carriage drive, he swiftly made his way through the shadows and shrubbery to the morning room. Four windows meant four chances for him to worry that she'd come to her senses and changed her mind, but he'd never been much for hesitation.

He touched the first windowpane, and it shifted beneath his fingers. Relief ran through him, heady and welcome. It might well have been a mistake, a latch the servants had missed, but he preferred to believe otherwise. Slipping his fingers around the frame, he pulled the window open. The light green curtains lifted, flowing into the room, as he hopped onto the sill, swung his legs over, and stepped down onto the Eddisons' morning room floor.

The window couldn't be seen from the street, but he reached back and closed it anyway. No sense risking being caught. Then he turned back again. The interior of the room was darker than the moon-lit night outside, and for a moment he stood blinded, looking, listening, and inhaling for any trace of her. Above the sweet scent of the lilies in his hand, citrus touched his nostrils, stirring his blood. "Phillipa," he murmured, facing the dark fireplace.

A match flared, blinding him all over again. "I knew it," a female voice hissed.

Bennett took a half step back. *Damnation.* "Lady Olivia."

Phillipa's sister lowered the glass flute of the lamp, then stood up. "Are you here to ruin my sister, or have you already done so?" Only the barest quaver at the end of her question gave him a sense of how nervous she must be.

"Where is she?" he asked. Setting a trap didn't seem in Phillipa's nature; it was more likely that if she'd changed her mind, she would have sent him a note telling him precisely that. Of course he hadn't returned to Howard House to look for a missive, but that clearly didn't signify if she'd found a third option. One that he hadn't considered.

"Don't worry about Flip. Answer my question."

Annoyance and frustration beginning to replace his surprise, he shook his head. "No. You answer *my* question. Now."

This time *she* took a step back, but she kept her chin lifted in a gesture that reminded him of her younger sister. "I knew she was up to something when I found her in here. I told her to go up to her room or I would tell Mama and Papa. And then I sat down here to wait for you."

She had meant to meet him there. "And what do you intend to do now?"

"Tell you to leave. I won't see Flip ruined simply because your unconventional ways appeal to her."

"Mm hm. Her unconventional ways appeal to me, as well."

"That doesn't signify." Olivia jabbed a finger toward the window. The appendage shook only a little. "You need to leave."

Getting by her would be a simple matter, but that wouldn't stop her from shrieking an alarm to rouse the household. And he had no intention of hurting her, so grabbing and gagging her was out of the question.

Actually, this little midnight confrontation had lifted her a few notches in his estimation. "So, Lady Olivia," he ventured. "You think I'm no good for your sister?"

"You made a spectacle of yourself this evening. I'm certain you flatter her and say all sorts of lovely things, but she doesn't fit in well as it is. Being ruined by a man whose only goal is to leave England with all possible speed couldn't possibly do her any good."

The damned chit made a good point. "Very well," he growled. "For the sake of Phillipa's reputation." He took one sharp step forward, to let her know that he could have gotten past her—or *to* her—if he'd chosen to do so. "But just between you and me," he continued, "since no one else seems to believe me, my aim here is not to ruin Phillipa. It never was. I'm not playing about." He turned for the window.

"So you would ruin her and then marry her?"

"I meant the red roses." Bennett set the now rather tightly squeezed lilies onto the nearest end table. "Please tell Phillipa these are for her."

Without a backward glance he retreated out the window and into the well-groomed shrubbery. Damnation. He'd spent the evening conjuring Phillipa's touch, her scent, and her warm body spread beneath his. Now he'd had a cold bucket of sisterly advice dumped over his head.

Bennett looked up at the row of second-floor windows. She was up there, but he had no more than a vague idea of where, precisely. "Bloody hell."

"Giving up already?"

He whipped around, just barely keeping from yelping like a startled chit. Phillipa stood behind him, garbed in nothing but an excited grin and a flimsy-looking night rail. The seasoned explorer, nearly given an apoplexy by a slip of a female.

She hadn't gone to her bedchamber to wait for her sister to dispose of him. She'd come looking for him. Her eyes dancing in the moonlight and her gown nearly as transparent as mist, she opened her mouth. "You look surprised," she whispered, chuckling.

He put his hands on her shoulders, pushing her back against the wall and taking her mouth in a hungry kiss. He couldn't get his fill of her. Five minutes ago he'd been contemplating taking himself into hand, so to speak. Damned poor substitute though it would have been, it might have allowed him to sleep.

Phillipa flung her arms up around his shoulders, pressing herself along his body. Hard arousal crashed into him. "Where can we go?" he murmured, leaving her mouth just long enough to utter the question.

"Mm." She pushed him away, twisting her hands into his lapels so he couldn't go very far, not that he had any intention of doing so. "This way," she returned, pulling him toward the back of the house.

He'd half thought she'd climbed out of her window, but of course practical, logical Phillipa had found a better way. She opened the kitchen door, peered inside the dark room, then grabbed his hand and tugged him inside the house. Even if her sister had remained lurking about downstairs to see whether he would break down the front door, she wouldn't have been able to hear them silently climbing the servants' stairs at the back of the house.

On the second floor he followed her down a short hallway to a door on the east side of the house. "Here," she breathed, opening the door and slipping inside.

His body had been on a bumpy ride tonight— the fury at seeing Langley, anger and frustration at being denied a fight, hope and anticipation, more frustration, and now the heated arousal as he followed her into her bedchamber and latched the door behind them. They'd best hope the house didn't burn down tonight, because he was not going to be turned away now.

She faced him again. "I'm sorry about Liv—"

"Later."

Bennett kissed her again, more slowly this time as he relished the soft warmth of her mouth. Thank God he'd stumbled into Jack's reading club that first night, or he might never have gotten close enough to Phillipa to know her. And that would have been a damned shame for every reason he could conjure.

Shrugging out of his jacket, he sat her on the edge of her bed. Her hair was down, shimmering dark chestnut and gold in the light of the small fire in her hearth. Bennett strummed his fingers through it, breathing in the soft citrus scent of her.

He wanted to set her on her back, push up her skirt, and take her. A rogue would do that, or an animal. He tried to steady his breath. At her behest, with her assistance, he was attempting to be neither of those things. That was why he sat beside her now, enduring her amateurish attack on his waistcoat and cravat.

The thing he most marveled about, other than Phillipa, was the way she made his past fade away. Three years in Africa, when he'd thought to return to England with no family to cheer his success, when he thought he'd be off again before the end of the year. And all the years before that, when he'd gone from place to place, country to country, lover to lover, with never enough time or inclination to create a lasting bond with any but a select few acquaintances. He'd felt so damned hollow, sometimes. And now, with her, he didn't.

Drawing the strap of her night rail down to her elbow, he kissed her shoulder up to her throat and around her jaw to her mouth again. She moaned, curving closer to him. When he pulled the other strap down, she slid her arms free to continue undressing him. The gown fell to her waist, and he leaned in to flick his tongue first against one pink nipple, then the other.

Finally, unable to stand it any longer, he pushed her hands away and finished unbuttoning his waistcoat himself. With her eager assistance he yanked it off along with his shirt. His boots and trousers followed. Then he pressed her backward, skimmed his hands from her shoulders past her breasts to her waist, and pulled her night rail off past her waist and down over her feet when she arched her hips for him.

"I want you," he murmured, parting her knees and dipping down to taste her. She was wet, and from her strangled yelp she wanted this as much as he did.

"Now," she breathed, grabbing him by the hair and yanking his face back up to hers. "Put that"—and she brushed her fingers against his cock—"inside me. Now."

"This?" he whispered back, settling over her to rub the tip of his cock against her folds.

She threw back her head. "Yes. Oh, yes."

He was not about to wait for a second invitation. With another deep kiss he pushed forward, entering her fully. The tight, hot slide was so exquisite that he nearly lost control. *Steady,* he ordered himself. He wouldn't allow himself to let go until she did.

The animal in him kept fighting to spill himself inside her, but he clenched his jaw and began a slow rhythm, in and out, in and out. With Phillipa panting beneath him, her eyes shining, he couldn't imagine anything closer to perfection. Then she wrapped her ankles around his thighs, digging her fingers into his shoulders. God, she felt good.

As her muscles tightened around him, he deepened his stroke, gazing into her eyes, waiting for her to climax. Abruptly she shook, shivering inside and out. "Bennett," she breathed, clutching him. "Bennett."

Breathing harder, he increased his pace, pushing himself to the edge. He kissed her as he came, holding himself against her, deep inside, two joined as one. Finally, perfection.

Chapter Sixteen

Exhausted as we were, we pushed on. We were so close to Mbundi's village that spending another night away was unthinkable. We pushed too hard. The Ngole had no crates to carry, no tents or trinkets to bear, and they caught us at the edge of the river. I didn't feel it at first. How odd, to look down and see a spear protruding from my side and realize that I was dead. That is what I most remember about it. Surprise.

THE JOURNALS OF CAPTAIN BENNETT WOLFE

And here," Bennett murmured, trailing a finger along her ribs, "we have the Congo River."

"Oh, really?" Phillipa held her breath, trying not to giggle at the sensation.

"Mm hm. Ah, but wait." The trail moved up the outside of her right breast, halting at its peak. "A plateau. And beyond, a deep valley." He continued his tour across the dip of her breastbone and up the slope of her left breast. "Well, that's unexpected," he murmured. "I don't remember this being here." Slowly he bent down and closed his lips over her nipple.

"Oh, goodness. Is the expedition over, then?" she managed, as his fingers stroked in a lazy circle around her right breast. "Or are you looking for a route to the ocean?"

He chuckled, the sensation reverberating into her. "I'd planned on heading south."

She would have enjoyed that, but despite her best efforts to halt time, the night continued to creep toward dawn. Phillipa pushed Bennett off his elbow and onto his back. Large and hard-muscled as he was, he gave in to her fairly easily. She had the distinct feeling that he didn't give in often, or to just anyone. "What will happen in the morning? When you and Captain Langley meet with the Africa Association?"

Bennett slid an arm around her shoulders, drawing her against him. "We'll shout at one another, I'll point out the very close resemblance of the wording of my other books to his, and logically they'll demand that he produce the journals in which he wrote his original observations. Which he won't be able to do."

"So you'll win."

"That's the idea."

She twisted her head to look up at him. Despite the . . . satisfaction she felt in his company, his own countenance was far from relaxed. Behind his vibrant green eyes, behind the whispers and secrets of the jungle and all the other exotic places he'd been, he wasn't as confident as he claimed. "And if they don't believe you?"

"They will."

"But if they don't?" she repeated.

"Then I suppose I'll have to find employment in Northumbria. Sheep herding, perhaps."

Phillipa sat up. "You shouldn't jest."

He tugged her back down beside him. "I'm not jesting. Without the support of the Africa Association, no one—not a private party, not the East India Company—will sponsor me to lead another expedition even as far as Cambridge." Slowly he twined his fingers through her hair, the gentle tug and pull sending delighted goose bumps down her arms. "Tell me something, Phillipa. Would you be willing to be a shepherdess?"

For him, she thought she could be a fishmonger. "I like sheep," she admitted with a slight smile, though at the moment she didn't feel much like smiling.

Bennett being successful tomorrow would mean, without a doubt, Bennett gone. How was she supposed to wish him well? Being a shepherd, or an ordinary landowner, would undoubtedly make him miserable—but that was exactly the life she'd imagined for herself.

"I suppose," he said quietly, "that I should wait to propose to you until I know for certain whether I'm a lion or a lamb. Or rather, which one I'll be chasing after. What do you think about all this?"

Her heart skittered in an unsettling mix of joy and apprehension. "I think I admire you very much, and that if anyone deserved to have his dreams realized, it's you."

He chuckled. "So now you're my dream, are you? You're very sure of yourself."

She hadn't been referring to herself. "I meant—"

Before she could finish, he pulled her into his arms,

kissing her until she decided it would be best to kiss him back. He'd said before that he meant to marry her, and the idea had at first seemed mad. Then she'd begun to believe that he meant it, and considering her own reaction to his presence, the realization had been heady and glorious. And now . . .

And now, she found her own courage being tested. Could she be selfish and marry him and ask him to remain in England? Could she somehow find the wherewithal to join him in his adventures? Or worst of all, could she watch him go while she remained behind?

With a groan she flung her arms around his shoulders, kissing him everywhere she could reach. Whether she could manage any courage or not when the time came, she had no intention of missing this moment. Not for anything.

Bennett chuckled against her mouth, rolling them both so that he lay on top of her, his growing arousal pressed deliciously against her inner thigh. "You *are* my dream, Phillipa," he whispered, kissing her again, "and at moments like this I never want to wake."

"Neither do I," she said feelingly. Here in her bed, with him, everything was perfect.

Their waking circumstances, though, were rather different. As he slid deep inside her, daylight troubles faded away. Moving, shifting in and out, hard and warm and insistent, he made her forget what she'd been worrying over. She forgot everything but how very good it felt to be in Bennett Wolfe's arms. And that was very good, indeed.

* * *

Bennett returned to Howard House as the eastern sky began to lift from black to gray. Inside the stable he brushed down and fed Ares himself. Lucifer knew the bay wasn't the only one who needed a few moments to cool down. He'd never regretted leaving any house since he'd been nine years old—but leaving Phillipa asleep in her bed, her chestnut hair framing her pretty face, had been one of the most difficult things he'd ever had to do.

Once back inside his borrowed room at Howard House he stripped and lay down, hoping for an hour or two of sleep before the rest of the household awoke. Before he could do more than close his eyes, though, his door began rattling and a distinctive chittering sounded in the hallway beyond.

"Oh, good God." Rolling to his feet again, he went to the door. "Come on, then," he muttered, as Kero scampered in, bypassing him in favor of her pile of pillows.

Almost immediately she began emitting her dainty little snore. Bennett blew out his breath and returned to bed. At least one of them would begin the day well rested—though it would likely be best if she didn't accompany him to Ainsley House. Langley could stand to lose the rest of his ear, but Kero wouldn't win the argument for him. Logic would see to that.

He sat up again, giving up on sleep. Kero lifted her head to eye him, then sank back into the soft pile once more. Thankfully she'd become much more at ease in Howard House, though she'd first explored every inch of it for predatory birds and snakes. Once she'd deemed it predator-free, and after finding . . .

another sibling, he supposed, in Geoffrey, she'd stopped insisting that he be within view at every second.

At breakfast he made certain Kero ate well, which would leave her less likely to insist on accompanying him to Ainsley House. Before he could track down his cousin and ask whether he'd be amenable to looking after her, Geoffrey strode into the breakfast room. "There she is." He walked up to scratch her on the chin, while she hummed at him. "I thought she'd gone looking for you this morning, but I didn't want to go barging about the house." He leaned on his elbows, stretching across the table toward Bennett. "Father doesn't like when I go barging about."

"That's understandable," Bennett returned with a short grin. Even if he hadn't been in an exceptional mood thanks to several hours spent in Phillipa's bed, he rather liked Geoffrey Howard, young Lord Clarkson. And that was surprising, considering that what little thought he'd spared the lad over the years had been less than charitable. "Would you do me a favor and look after her for a bit this morning?"

"I don't want my son bitten by that rabid beast," Fennington stated, as he walked into the room. From his expression he didn't feel any more affection for his nephew than he did the monkey. After all, he'd provided Bennett with the means to attend the soiree last night. And by now, everyone in London probably knew it.

"She's not rabid." Bennett returned his attention to his cousin. "She just ate half a bowl of strawberries, however. You may want to encourage her to take a stroll in the garden in half an hour or so."

"I'll be happy to. And I caught some crickets for her."

"She'll adore you forever, then."

Fennington, still looking displeased, selected his own breakfast and sat at the table. "So now you've got my son catching insects for a monkey," he noted.

"I only told him what she ate. The rest was his idea. He's learning the Latin names of all the insects in the area, if that makes a difference."

"Not particularly. There isn't much use for that in the House of Lords."

"I'm not going to sit in the House of Lords," Geoffrey contributed. "I'm going to be an explorer, like Bennett. I'm particularly interested in Africa."

"Well, isn't that splendid." The marquis curled his fingers around his fork as though he wanted to stab Bennett in the eye with the utensil. "You *are* going to sit in the House of Lords, because you *are* going to be the next Marquis of Fennington. You are *not* going to Africa, nor are you going to return from there to begin fights with people whose reputation exceeds your own. Now sit down and eat your eggs."

That was a bit blatant. "After this morning, Fennington," Bennett said, keeping his tone low and calm, "Langley's reputation won't be an issue, because he won't have one. My purpose last night was not to embarrass you."

"I wrote—" The marquis stopped. "Geoffrey, I've changed my mind. Go walk the monkey now."

"But I thought you—"

"Now, son."

Geoffrey sighed heavily, then grinned. "Come along, Kero," he said, offering his shoulder.

The vervet patted Bennett on the cheek, then scampered up the boy's arm. "Be good," Bennett instructed, and the two of them were off.

"As I was saying," Fennington continued, "I wrote the foreword to Langley's book. His reputation and mine are intertwined. And I don't like this."

Bennett shook his head. "You thought I was dead, did you not?"

"Of course I did. But . . . I did know that he had possession of your journals. I knew that he would use them in writing his own book. I used *his* popularity and *your* reputation because I knew it would be profitable."

That surprised Bennett. Not that his uncle had gone along willingly with a fraud, but that he would now admit to it. "I suppose if I was dead, I wouldn't care," he said after a moment. "And thank you for telling me."

"Yes, well, you're welcome." The marquis drew in a breath. "If it comes to it, I give you permission to inform the Africa Association that I saw your journals, and that Langley said they were yours, given to him on your deathbed."

For a moment Bennett looked down, making a show of cutting the ham on his plate. "You're friends with Thrushell."

"Yes, I am. So don't say anything if you don't absolutely have to."

This was damned odd. A decade ago—hell, a month ago—he would have gone out of his way to cause trouble for Fennington and his brood. Now, though, that urge seemed to have left him. "May I ask you a question?"

"What is it? Why am I trusting to your discretion after the display you put on last night?"

"I'm more interested in why you didn't want to take me into your household after my mother died." Bennett clenched his jaw; he didn't like feeling vulnerable. And however little regard he'd ever claimed to have for this man, Fennington seemed long ago to have acquired the ability to wound him.

"We don't need to dredge up that nonsense now."

"Yes, we do."

With a scowl, Fennington lifted his head and made a sharp gesture at the footman who stood ready to refill their tea. Immediately the servant left the room, closing the door behind himself. "My father—your grandfather—had willed your mother five hundred pounds a year. That amount went to you after she died."

"I know. As I reckon it, that money is the only reason I didn't end up in a workhouse."

The marquis glanced up at him, then returned to contemplating his breakfast. "Five hundred a year, regardless. It didn't matter if one year the fields flooded at Fennington Park, or if some sort of rot ruined all the wool we took from the sheep another year. Before anyone else earned anything, could put anything into repairs or schooling or taxes, you received five hundred pounds. And so honestly, Bennett, I didn't want to have anything to do with you."

"Hm. You would rather have had the blunt, and I would rather have had a family." Bennett pushed away from the table. "I'll attempt to be discreet during the meeting."

"I would hope so."

So that was it, Bennett reflected as he made his way out to the stable and collected Ares once more. Fennington resented a nine-year-old orphan the income to put himself through school and keep food in his belly. That explained why the marquis had been so eager to profit from the publication of his—or rather, Langley's—book. How odd, that he'd grown up detesting his relations, while they'd had the very same opinion of him.

Phillipa would call it irony, and point out that if he'd grown up differently, he might have learned to favor cattle over travel. And since travel had ultimately brought him back to London, and to her, he couldn't dispute that his life had its merits.

From the number of carriages and horses crowded around the large stable yard at Ainsley House, most of the Africa Association had arranged to attend the meeting. Good. The more men who could thereafter attest to Langley's theft and slander, the better.

"Good morning, Captain Wolfe," the duke's butler said, stepping aside to let Bennett into the house. "I'll show you to the conference room."

They went upstairs and down a corridor that apparently passed over the top of The Adventurers' Club below. He wondered briefly how many other members of the Association knew about the sanctuary Sommerset had created. Or what shape this meeting might have taken if it had been Langley rather than himself who'd impressed the duke enough to merit a membership in his private club.

"Wait here, if you please." The butler left him in the hallway and slipped inside the nearest room.

Sommerset had said ten o'clock, and it was still two minutes before the hour, according to his battered pocket watch. Apparently they'd needed to discuss events before the participants arrived. That was well and good, as long as they meant to wait on making a decision until after they'd heard him speak.

The abrupt furor of voices inside the room didn't sound all that welcoming. If he needed to apologize for his actions at the soiree, then, he would do so—to the Africa Association. Not to Langley. Fleetingly he wondered whether the room had two entrances, one for him to stand behind, and the other for Langley. Sommerset didn't seem to approve of fisticuffs, though he'd found it rather satisfying, himself.

While he waited for permission to enter the meeting, he took a moment to study his surroundings. Additional trinkets from foreign travel stood out among the more mundane vases and clocks and paintings. It was an eclectic mix, and he found it appealing. If he spent any time at Tesling, he imagined his house would look rather similar. And of course he would have books, because Phillipa loved them.

Would she remain there if he secured sponsorship for another expedition? Would she wish to join him? Did he want her exposed to the dangers that he'd encountered on an almost daily basis? Bennett frowned. He wanted her in his life. His general approach to problems was that with the appropriate application of weaponry, they would work themselves out. Phillipa was much more complex and important than anything else he'd encountered, however. And he didn't have any answers. None that left him feeling any easier, anyway.

The door opened again. "This way, Captain," the butler said, gesturing him into the room.

From the servant's face alone, Bennett knew that something was afoot. Anyone employed by Sommerset would have learned to school his expressions. The man hadn't batted an eye when he'd first arrived with Kero on his shoulder. Bennett stepped forward.

Thirteen men were in the room. He'd met them before, when he'd first applied for their sponsorship of his Congo expedition. But the Association had eleven members. The other two, Lord Thrushell and his son, were new. And they'd clearly been in the room for a time.

"Have a seat, Captain," the Duke of Sommerset said, gesturing him to the one empty chair at the large table.

"Was I in error about the time for the meeting?" Bennett asked. "You seem to have begun without me."

"We wanted to discuss the matter of your outburst last evening," Lord Talbott stated.

"Do you also want to discuss the reason for my outburst last evening?"

"Bennett. Sit down." Sommerset sent him a hard look.

"If I'm going to be ambushed, I prefer to stand."

"This is not an ambush," Thrushell put in. "We of course want to discuss the entire matter of the expedition."

" 'We'?" Bennett repeated, his confidence melting into frustrated anger. "Are you on the Association board now?"

"I am."

Damnation. "Ah. Congratulations, my lord."

Langley evidently hadn't had any reservations about seating himself. He lounged in the chair between his father and Lord Hawthorne, looking like a well-fed baboon unable to decide between napping and scratching his arse.

"I'll begin, shall I?" David said, dropping a tattered book onto the table. "My journal."

"Captain Wolfe, do you recognize it?" Hawthorne asked.

Bennett nodded. "I recognize it. I believe you'll find some pages missing—Langley had a bout with incontinence."

The Duke of Sommerset cleared his throat. "What is your complaint, Captain Wolfe?"

As far as Bennett knew, Sommerset was his only ally in the room. Not at all what he'd expected this morning. He hadn't thought he'd be the conquering hero—not when no one but Sommerset had bothered to see him since his return—but what he sensed at the moment was . . . hostility.

"My complaint is that Captain Langley left the Congo four days after I received an injury, and that he took nine completed journals, authored by me, with him. Without my permission."

"Captain Langley, do you have any of Sir Bennett's possessions?"

"What are we, in the nursery?" Bennett muttered.

"I do not," Langley said smuggly. "My book, *Across the Continent: Adventures in the Congo*, was written based—"

"Do you get royalties when you say the entire title?" Bennett asked.

"—based on my journal and my recollections. I never even saw Wolfe writing in anything resembling a journal."

"Ballocks."

"Captain Wolfe," Lord Talbott chastised, "we are civilized gentlemen here. Please control yourself."

"I am controlling myself. If I wasn't, Langley would be dead."

The duke sat forward. "That's enough of that," he said, the touch of a growl in his deep voice. "I would like to hear if you have any proof of this wrongdoing, Captain Wolfe."

Bennett shook himself. Words now. Fists later. "We spent three years in the Congo. I filled nine journals with information on everything from rainfall to elevation to descriptions of plants and animals. My—"

"God, that sounds dull," Langley interrupted with a chuckle. "This is your imagination, Bennett. Surely you can conjure something more exciting than that."

"*You* couldn't," Bennett shot back at him. "Those things—well, the ones that didn't take much intelligence to figure out—all appeared in that book of yours."

"I was in the Congo, as well. Of course they appeared."

Taking one step forward, Bennett reached the table and grabbed Langley's journal. He flipped it open. "Let's see how well David strips away Africa's mysteries, shall we? 'Everything is hot and wet and covered with thorns and vines,'" he read, dodging Langley's reach. " 'The damned natives smell, and the women are ugly.'" He looked up. "And that is . . .

three months of observations, judging from the date of the next entry."

"I said that the book is also based on my recollections."

"It's just a coincidence that *I* have thirty crates of artifacts and specimens waiting for me at Tesling, then, while you have . . . this." Bennett tossed the journal back at him. "In addition to the coincidence that the monkey you so touchingly befriended tried to take off your ear last night. And that you didn't see fit to bring her with you to England after I died. Hm. Ah, that bit didn't happen either, did it?"

"I suppose you can say anything you like," Langley retorted. "You have no proof."

"I have an idea," Bennett pushed, anger building in him like water behind a dam. "I enjoyed that sketch you did of Mbundi. Draw it again, why don't you? In fact, we should each take a pencil and paper and see whose work more resembles the one in your book. Let's do that now, shall we?"

"I—"

"And we can't forget the two books I wrote before we ever met. I don't suppose *you* kept any of the papers you wrote at Cambridge. Or that you'd want these men to compare them to the language of your book. Or your book to my books, which is where the closest resemblance lies."

"That's sufficient, I think," Lord Hawthorne said.

"I agree," Sommerset commented, his own eyes glinting. For a brief moment Bennett wondered which of them was closer to jumping Langley.

"The difficulty with deciding whether Captain Wolfe had any journals and whether Captain Langley knows of their whereabouts," Lord Thrushell said in a cool voice, "is that the book has gained us all an unprecedented level of popularity. It is my understanding that both the scientific community and Prinny are clamoring for another expedition to begin, and for my son to lead it."

"Your son couldn't lead a horse around a track," Bennett retorted.

"Make your point, Thrushell," the duke asked, over the growing muttering. "Because we were supposed to receive research materials and artifacts from the expedition. Captain Bennett has reiterated that he will be sending us specimens once he returns to Tesling. From Captain Langley we've received . . . applause, I suppose."

"Has the Africa Association ever been the focus of so much fame and acclaim?" Thrushell countered. "Not since Mungo Park's return, I'll wager. Are any of you willing to let such an opportunity go by in exchange for—for what? For pointing a finger and saying this man wrote one word and that man wrote two other words?"

"An uproar over the authorship of Langley's book would consume any discussion and deflect the attention from any accomplishments made," Hawthorne put in. "And we would all be subjected to ridicule. Perhaps even by Prinny. Our reputations and that of the Association could suffer. Would suffer."

"Does the book contain any lies, Captain Wolfe?" Lord Thrushell demanded.

"About who the bumbling fool of the expedition was, yes."

"Any factual untruths, Captain."

Bennett clenched his jaw so hard the muscles

creaked. He could lie, but that would put him in the same bucket of slop that Langley already occupied. "No. Dramatic flairs and hyperbole, but no lies."

"I won't sit for this," Talbott snapped.

"I wouldn't either," Hawthorne put in, "if Captain Wolfe hadn't exhibited such poor behavior last night. That, taken together with his damaged reputation and the overall furor calling the book's authorship into question would cause, is far outweighed by the positive publicity and interest and donations we've received because of Captain Langley's new fame."

"Donations?" Bennett snarled. "You mean that Lord Thrushell has bought your silence."

"He hasn't bought mine," Sommerset cut in, though he looked more resigned and disgusted than self-righteous.

"Why don't we take a vote?" Thrushell suggested. "Do we admit that Captain Langley's book is a perjury? Well, no it's not, but he didn't write it, except that he did and only borrowed a few details from a man believed to be dead. Do we admit that the Association was wrong to support the popular, well-respected son and heir of a well-respected and very generous earl? That Bennett Wolfe, a supposedly-deceased, hostile rogue who can't conduct himself with any sort of propriety and decorum, is our man?"

"And wouldn't you be hostile, if upon returning to England after an extended time away, you discovered that your reputation and your work had been stolen from you?" Sommerset rose, walking to one of the room's tall windows to gaze outside.

"I thought he was dead," Langley protested.

"Yes, of course I would be angry." Sighing, Lord

Hawthorne sent a glance around the room—at everyone but Bennett. This was bad. Very bad. "But for the good of the Association and its future, I believe we need to be . . . discreet."

The others were nodding. Bennett's chest felt hollowed out, as though these men had ripped everything out of him, heart and soul. "You're condemning me to remain here in England, then, with no reputation."

"I think we can work in a word here and there to indicate that perhaps Captain Langley was having a bit of fun with his description of you." Thrushell's smug expression made Bennett want to hit him. "Should we put this to a vote? Or does anyone disagree? Sommerset?"

"I abstain," the duke snapped. "There is no reason for a vote here."

"You bloody hypocrites." Bennett turned on his heel and left the room. *Bloody, bloody hell.* He should have realized. The laws of London were nothing like those of the jungle. In the Congo, at least there had been a certain logic. Survival was always a good thing.

"Captain."

Bennett stopped halfway out Ainsley House's front door. "I don't think you want to talk with me right now, Sommerset."

"No doubt." The duke joined him in the doorway and then led the way onto the front drive. "I am outvoted."

"You didn't vote."

"There was no point, except that I look better by abstaining than by losing outright."

Clearly Sommerset had spent more time in the jungles of London than he had. "At least you're honest."

"Bennett, you know I believe you."

Bennett snorted, gesturing for a groom to bring Ares up. "I'm touched."

"I'm also going to give you some advice. Take it, or don't. But listen to it." The duke scowled. "I suggest that you keep your opinions about Langley and his book to yourself. Otherwise you'll have the Association after you, and you'll never find your way out of England. They are all men with a great deal of influence. Second, f—"

"Excuse me, Your Grace, but go shit yourself."

"Second," Sommerset hammered in a harder voice, "find your damned journals and show them to the *London Times*, or go home to Tesling and learn how to be a landowner. Or fund your own damned expeditions with your charm. That should see you to Brussels."

The duke returned to the house. Bennett wanted to curse him again, but one thing stopped him. Sommerset was correct. The journals were still his way out of England. And fleetingly he wondered which way Phillipa would want him to proceed.

Chapter Seventeen

Langley and I are the first white men here. David expected we would be greeted as gods. I'm less surprised to find that the natives think us sickly, and require visual proof that we are indeed men. Some rules hold true everywhere—one good poke with a stick is curiosity; more than that is ill manners. And rather uncomfortable.

THE JOURNALS OF CAPTAIN BENNETT WOLFE

I hope you're not angry with me," Livi whispered, taking Phillipa's arm as the two of them left Eddison House the next morning. "You know he would have ruined you, Flip. Yes, you think he's fascinating, but what if Mama or Papa had seen you sneaking into the morning room? It would have been you to face the consequences. Not Sir B—"

"For goodness' sake, Livi, stop talking and take a breath before you faint."

"But I want to know if you forgive me."

Phillipa sighed. "I forgive you." She had a strong suspicion that she wouldn't have felt as charitable if she hadn't managed to get Bennett into her bed, but she had, and the fact that Livi had voluntarily faced off against the formidable adventurer spoke well for her sister. "And you gave me the lilies, which was nice."

"I shouldn't have given them to you. Bennett Wolfe is a beast. And even if you marry him, he'll still be a beast."

"He isn't a beast."

"Flip, he climbed through the window."

Settling for a noncommittal nod, Phillipa increased her pace a fraction. Going for a walk had been Olivia's idea, more than likely her way of finding a moment for the two of them to speak in private. The problem was, it was just after ten o'clock. Bennett was speaking with the Africa Association. And her heart was beating as fast as if she'd run all the way to Marathon.

"You do realize that if you want him to continue courting you, you cannot give in to his seductions. A man may say things, but it's a test. He'll never offer for you if he knows you'll . . . succumb without first having a ring on your finger."

Phillipa snorted.

"I'm serious, Flip."

Attempting to gather her thoughts back in, she took her sister's arm. "I know you are. And silly as most courtship rules are, I do understand that you're looking out for me." She sighed. "The lilies were very pretty."

"Yes, but they're only flowers. You must trust me. I have more experience with these things than you do."

Her sister most decidedly did not have more experience with men than she did. Not any longer. In fact, Phillipa reflected, she could more than likely tell Livi a few things that would make her blush. "I have listened to your advice," she said aloud, wishing she had a pocket watch to check the time, "and I'm most definitely not ready to give Bennett up." Even the thought of not seeing him again left her queasy.

"Have you spoken with Mama or Papa yet this morning?" Olivia continued, waving at a passing acquaintance. "They weren't happy with what happened at Langley House last night."

She wasn't, either. "Kero was trying to protect Bennett, I think. And then Bennett had to protect Kero."

"But Captain Langley nearly lost an ear. And then Captain Wolfe flattened him."

Rather effectively, too. "I don't want to talk about it."

"You may have to, when we return."

Phillipa sighed. "Then let's make this a long walk, shall we?"

Livi agreed. At least walking and chatting about Paris fashions—a mysterious and elusive topic, as far as she was concerned—kept her from dwelling on what Bennett was doing. By her guess, Langley should be apologizing for literary theft, and the Africa Association would be placing Bennett at the top of their list for leading the next expedition, whenever that might be.

"Are you listening to me?" Livi asked, breaking into her reverie.

She shook herself. "Mostly," she conceded.

"What has you so distracted?"

Well, how was she supposed to answer that? By

admitting that Bennett had spent most of the night with her, and that she was very concerned that, however satisfying she found the situation, he couldn't seem to wait to leave on another adventure? "You may be accustomed to having beaux," she said aloud, "but it's a bit unusual for me."

"Especially ones who climb in through the morning room window," Livi added.

"What?" a low voice squawked.

Phillipa jumped as Lord John Clancy swung down from his horse behind them. Oh, good heavens.

"Who's climbing through windows?" he asked.

"Your friend. Captain Wolfe." Olivia folded her arms across her chest, the image of affronted sisterhood all over again.

"He climbed into your morning room? Did he forget how to use a damned door?"

"Well, how are we supposed to know that?" Olivia retorted. "And good morning to you, John."

With a swift grin, he took Livi's hand and bowed over it. "Good morning. I do not climb through windows, if that ever comes into question."

Olivia grinned back at him. "I'll keep that in mind."

"Oh, please." Phillipa resumed her walk, heading back now toward the house. If they continued any further in the opposite direction, they would end up in the Thames.

"Flip," John said, speeding up to catch her, "if Bennett is harassing you, please tell me. I'll have a word with him, no matter what sort of wild animals he's capable of wrestling."

"He's not harassing me," she blurted, annoyed. "He's courting me, just as he said. No one believes it, I know, but he actually likes me."

"I believe that he likes you," her friend returned, his expression abruptly more thoughtful. "He seldom speaks of anyone or anything else in my company."

"Truly?"

"John, don't tell her things like that, or next time she'll have him climbing up the chimney."

"As you wish, Livi. May I at least see the two of you home, then?"

"That would be acceptable."

He offered Olivia an arm, the two of them walking ahead and leaving her to converse with John's horse, Brody. "And how are you this morning?" she asked.

The gray gelding snorted at her. That made this conversation nearly equal to half the ones she'd had at various parties through the Seasons. John glanced over his shoulder at her, but she motioned him to return to his chat with Livi. If she had her way, she would steal Brody from John and ride to Ainsley House to discover what had happened.

Good news for Bennett would be bad news for her, and vice versa. Claiming he meant to propose while he was stranded here in London was one thing, but what would he say when he had the chance to leave again? Would he want her to go along? Did *she* want to go along?

As Eddison House came back into view, she slowed. Bennett's big bay Ares stood in the drive. The meeting was finished. "Oh, dear," she whispered, as the man himself came into view on the front step.

"That is not a happy-looking man," John muttered.

At that moment he turned and saw them. Saw her, because once his gaze found her, it didn't waver. He strode back down the steps and across the drive. "Phillipa."

"Bennett, what happ—"

He grabbed her arm. "I need to speak with you."

"I say, Bennett. Unhand Flip."

Bennett glanced at John. At his black expression, though, Phillipa held up one hand. "It's all right, John. What about the garden, Bennett?"

"Yes."

Now that she was moving in his direction, he loosened his hold, sliding his fingers down to grip her hand. More than his fierceness, it troubled her that she couldn't decipher what he might be thinking, other than it hadn't gone well. "What happened?"

"Firstly, your father wouldn't let me into the house. I was about to break down the door when you appeared."

She frowned. "What? Why would he do that?"

"According to your butler, I'm an uncivilized rogue who begins fights unprovoked, and I'm not to go anywhere near you."

"But—that—I—" Phillipa snapped her mouth closed. For heaven's sake. Her parents had been wringing their hands for three years over her inability to attract a beau. It made no sense that now, because of one perfectly understandable altercation, they would attempt to drive away the one man who'd ever been in pursuit. "I'll talk to him," she said aloud, stopping with him as they reached the oak tree at the center of the garden.

"I would have spoken to him, if he'd come to the bloo— to the door."

She squeezed his fingers. "Bennett, you can't attack my father. Now you're clearly upset with more than being banned from my house. What happened with the Africa Association? Didn't they send Langley skulking away in shame?"

He gazed at her, his jungle-colored eyes glinting with poorly disguised anger. Thank goodness it wasn't aimed at her. His passion was overwhelming enough; she couldn't even imagine facing the full force of his fury.

"Bennett, tell me," she urged when he kept silent. "It's why you're here, isn't it?"

Bennett shook his head. "I'm here because you . . . remind me that this town does have its merits." With a deep breath he released her hand and dropped onto the stone bench.

Phillipa pushed aside the thought that he'd just given her one of the nicest compliments she'd ever received. She sat down beside him. "What happened? Didn't they believe you?"

"They did believe me."

"They . . . that's wonderful," she exclaimed, then frowned. "Isn't it?"

"Not particularly." Absently he twined his fingers with hers again. "Langley's a popular fellow, and he's brought a great deal of positive attention to the Africa Association. I, on the other hand, am apparently untrustworthy and uncivilized, *and* I own a monkey who attacks people."

"But—"

"In short, the Association feels they are better represented by David Langley than by Bennett Wolfe, regardless of his qualifications." He blew out his breath, his shoulders lowering a little. "It doesn't hurt that Langley's family has money, and that Lord

Thrushell got himself a seat on the Association's board."

"Oh, that is blatantly unfair!" Phillipa shot to her feet and strode in a circle around the tree. "They let themselves be bribed! And I respected them!"

For heaven's sake, the Association for Promoting the Discovery of the Interior Parts of Africa had seemed the epitome of what civilization should be—intelligent men searching for knowledge in the unknown lands. And yet there they were, as self-serving and greedy as anyone else.

"I called them hypocrites."

"Good. That's what they are."

Bennett eyed her. "The Duke of Sommerset suggested in private that I still attempt to find my journals. If I make them public, the Africa Association won't have any choice but to admit that Langley fooled them."

"Well, that's something, anyway. I've always liked His Grace."

"Have you now?" Bennett stood. "It slipped my mind that you waltzed with him last night." Moving in front of her, he took one of her hands and slid the other around her waist. "Tell me all about it, Phillipa."

Her cheeks heated. "We waltzed."

Bennett turned her, sending them both into a silent dance in her garden. "Like this?"

"Except for the lack of music, yes, this precisely. Now what about—"

"Did he hold you this close?" Her chest very nearly touched his. "Or this close?" He drew her nearer, her skirts tangling about his legs.

Now she had the dismaying wish to smile, which was of course wrong given what had just happened to him. "The first one."

"Ah." He lowered his head, brushing his cheek against hers. "I asked you if you would herd sheep with me, and you said you would. I neglected to ask if you would tread across mist-shrouded rivers and jungle-filled valleys with me. But I suppose I don't need to ask that now, do I?"

Phillipa pulled away, back to the proper waltzing distance. "No, you don't need to ask."

Slowly he stopped, dropping her fingers. "But would you?"

Her heart hammered. "I . . . I don't know," she finally said, her voice cracking. "I want to, but I don't know."

He sighed, his gaze lowering. "Thank you for being honest."

For a moment she imagined him walking away, leaving her to wallow in her cowardice while he did everything he could to abandon England once and for all. Phillipa stepped forward, grabbing his lapels. "I said, *I don't know*," she repeated, shaking. "The same way you don't know what it would be like to stay in one place. Don't give up on recovering what's yours, Bennett." She tugged on his jacket as a tear ran down one of her cheeks. "And don't give up on *me*. Please."

And he'd been about to ask her not to give up on him. Bennett wrapped her trembling body in a hug, holding her close against him. After all, he'd failed this morning. He'd attempted to prevail through reason and logic, and he'd been defeated by the baser needs of greed and pride. Funny, actually, considering that he was supposed to be the animal in the group.

"I find that being close to you is more important than anything else I can imagine, *nyonda*," he murmured into her hair. "So if you promise not to give up on me, I will make the same promise to you."

"Oh, I promise," she whispered against his shoulder. "I very much promise."

"Then we're in agreement. We will figure something out."

"Bennett, for God's sake," Jack's affronted voice came from the front of the garden. "Let her go before you ruin her."

"Too late for that," he breathed, so only she could hear him. Jack was correct, though, and he reluctantly pulled away from her.

"Why don't we go inside and have some tea?" the sister suggested, though she glared at him through narrowed eyes and clearly preferred to see him gone.

"Bennett can't come into the house until after I talk to Papa," Phillipa said, wiping at her eyes.

"Did Lord Leeds find out about the climbing through the window incident?" Jack asked.

Bennett swore to himself. Apparently this had become a four-person conspiracy. "How did *you* find out about it?"

"I mentioned it," Olivia said loftily, "and John overheard."

"That isn't it, anyway." Phillipa wrapped her hand around his arm. "It's because of the fight."

Olivia put her hands on her hips. "You see? I told you that would happen."

Bennett rolled his shoulders. Very well. If Phillipa wanted her sister and Jack included, then so be it. And as badly as he wanted to punch someone, Phillipa's father made a poor target, given that he intended to be related to the man. "I can't stay, anyway. I'm taking you driving tomorrow, so I need to purchase a carriage."

"Borrow mine, nickninny," Jack suggested.

"No. And I'm not borrowing Sommerset's again, either. From now on I'm paying court using my own possessions and on my own merits. Such as they are."

"You don't need to do that," Phillipa whispered.

"Yes, I do. If I'm to stay in England, I need a curricle. They're more civilized than phaetons, are they not?"

"There's room for a chaperone, if that's what you mean."

"It is." There were several other things he needed to see to, as well. He raised his voice. "And Jack's coming with me."

"Hm. Tea with two lovely young ladies, or buying a rig."

Bennett lifted an eyebrow. "And?"

Jack sighed. "I'll be on the drive, waiting for you. Huzzah, we're purchasing a curricle."

However improper it was, Bennett couldn't resist kissing Phillipa. Her mouth was so soft and so sweet, parting from her was physically painful. "I'll talk to your father in the morning," he said, ignoring Olivia's gasp. "I can explain myself. You shouldn't have to do that."

"I enjoy setting things right," she returned with a smile.

"Mm hm. I'll see you at eleven o'clock. And I'm bringing luncheon."

He made himself turn around and leave the garden. Whether they'd resolved anything or not, he felt calmer and steadier after seeing her. Most females wouldn't appreciate being thought of as ballast, but Phillipa would more than likely think it both hilarious and touching.

"Why the devil do you need me to go with you?" Jack complained as they headed down the street. "You wrestle lions; I wrestle calling cards."

"Because you know people, and I don't."

"I'd rather have tea with Livi."

Bennett glanced sideways at him. "You said you've been after Olivia Eddison for four years."

"Yes. Nearly since her debut. What's your point?"

"And you've made it as far as tea? That's pitiful." He couldn't imagine sitting back and watching other men pursue Phillipa while he simply bided his time.

"Don't criticize my strategy just because you barge into a room swinging crocodiles by the tail and bellowing. Livi has dozens of suitors. Subtlety is required."

"And Phillipa doesn't require subtlety?"

"Oh, no, you don't." Jack pulled up Brody. "Fight with someone else. I like Flip. As a friend. She's unique. And no, she hasn't had suitors. But I'll tell you one thing. She's as sharp as a tack, and everyone knows it. If she supports your side of an argument, it's because your side has more merit."

Bennett circled his friend. "You don't need to convince me to like Phillipa. And I'm not using her to gain some sort of damned credibility." He drew Ares to a halt. "And yes, I want a fight. But not with you."

"Thank God for that."

"What I want from you, my friend, is information. I want to know everything you know about Langley's life in England."

For a long moment Jack looked at him. "The Africa Association is backing Langley, isn't it?"

"Yes. And without my journals I can't do a damned thing about it. Which is why I'm going to get them back." Bennett dug his fingers into the leather reins. "I honestly don't think Phillipa cares what everyone else thinks of me, but I want to be in a better position for her sake."

"And so you can leave England again."

"Perhaps. It's a bit of a complicated kettle of fish, Jack. Are you going to help me?"

Jack kneed Brody into a trot. "Yes. I only hope I don't regret it."

"So do I."

By the evening he had a curricle, a horse to pull it, and the beginnings of a plan. If their positions had been reversed, he would have burned the journals to keep Langley from getting his hands on them. But over the last three years he'd come to know David Langley as well as anyone could. And Langley was something of a coward, and he liked power—which was why Bennett was fairly certain that the journals' wouldn't be going anywhere. At the moment, they were leverage. Against him.

Without the lure of the journals, Bennett would have no reason to maintain the pretense of civility. And David would be worried about preserving his pretty face—and his reputation. If Langley headed another expedition to Africa, he wouldn't want Bennett running free in England spreading . . . well, truths. The journals were the only assurance the dear fellow had of keeping Bennett at bay, and his mouth closed.

The House of Lords had had a late session, and with no parties planned for the evening, Mayfair was quiet. He could go to the Adventurers' Club, he supposed, but at the moment he wasn't particularly in the mood to run across its benefactor. And climbing through another window to see Phillipa, though highly appealing, didn't seem wise. Olivia would more than likely be sitting up all night with a pistol across her knees. While she wasn't much of a problem, he should likely be proceeding in a more honorable manner.

And so he found himself in the unusual position of having idle time. He and Kero retreated to his borrowed bedchamber, and he sat at the small table there to read. With one hand he turned pages, and with the other he tickled the hooting, teeth-chattering vervet monkey. At least *she* was content.

He tried to imagine more nights like this. Quiet, ordinary, each one like the next, where the only part of the world he could see would be the one passing by his front window. And he knew one thing for certain. He couldn't do it. Not alone. With Phillipa there, however, he didn't see how everything—anything—could be . . . dull. She brought her own light with her into a room. And after all the time he'd spent walking through deserts and jungles and so many solitary places, he craved it. He craved her.

A knock sounded at his door. "Come in."

He expected Geoffrey, wanting to play with Kero again, but the figure at the door was taller and sterner. Fennington. "I wanted to ask if you would be joining us for dinner."

"Do you want me to?" Bennett asked, surprised. He generally either avoided being about when the family sat down together, or he went down to the kitchen to scavenge something.

Fennington cleared his throat. "Yes. I think it would be . . . pleasant."

"Then yes." Standing, he held down one hand and then swung Kero up onto his shoulder. "Thank you."

"I had luncheon with several fellow members of Parliament," his uncle commented, stepping out of the way as Bennett left the room. "Including Thrushell."

"Ah."

"Yes. I had to listen to a great deal of drivel about you contesting the authorship of David's book. It seems that since you had no proof, your claims were considered ridiculous and dismissed out of hand."

So that was the story. "Something like that."

"It occurred to me that you did have proof, and you declined to mention it. Why?"

Bennett glanced over his shoulder at his uncle. "The overall opinion was that Langley makes a better representative of the Association than I do. I don't think it would have mattered if I *could* have produced my journals for them. I didn't see the point of dragging you into a lost argument."

"That was good of you, Bennett. I wasn't . . . anticipating a rift between Thrushell and myself."

He settled for nodding as they walked into the

dining room to find his aunt, Geoffrey, and fourteen-year-old Madeline already seated. Even Madeline mustered a smile as he took the seat beside Geoffrey and Kero jumped over to his cousin's shoulder.

It was all so damned odd. He and Fennington having a civil conversation, after his uncle actually offered to speak against Langley. And he hadn't used the opportunity, even when it would have made trouble for a man he'd hated for most of his life.

"I saw your new rig, Bennett," Geoffrey said with a grin, handing Kero up a slice of potato. "It's sterling. What's the mare's name?"

"Sally. Which I don't like. I was thinking of Usiku. That's Swahili for 'night.'"

"Oh, I like that. And she's a pretty black, so it fits. I'd been meaning to ask you, what does Kero mean?"

"Nuisance."

Geoffrey laughed. "That's a perfect name." He leaned forward. "Maddie, you should feed her. She's very friendly."

"No, thank you. She's a dirty beast."

"You're such a girl." The lad chuckled again. "I think you're settling into London, Bennett. A carriage, two horses, and a monkey. Next you'll have chickens."

"Not in this house," Lady Fennington put in.

"I think I'll wait on purchasing chickens." Bennett stifled an unexpected smile. "What else should I get, then, to fit into Society?"

"A cane," Madeline suggested. "And a hat."

"Gambling debts," came from Geoffrey. "All the rakes have gambling debts."

Bennett took a breath. "Actually," he said, looking down at his plate, "I'm planning on getting married."

"What?" Fennington sat forward. "You don't know anyone. To whom could you possibly be getting married?"

There was one woman he did know. And thank God he'd met her. "I think I've mentioned her to you already. Lady Phillipa Eddison."

Chapter Eighteen

Langley went down to the river to shave, despite the disappearance of a porter two nights before. Mbundi and I had scouted ahead at daybreak, and upon our return I sighted the paw print. A leopard, and a large one. Keeping downwind, I stalked the animal. Finally I sighted a spotted shoulder, firing my rifle just as the animal leapt. It died as it fell, one clawed foot covering Langley's boot. I'd never heard as hair-raising a shriek as Langley emitted, and hope never to hear it again.

THE JOURNALS OF CAPTAIN BENNETT WOLFE

A re we back to roses?" Phillipa asked, as Barnes opened her front door to reveal Bennett standing there wearing a smile and holding a large bouquet.

"They're pink," he returned, handing them to her. "I researched it. Pink is sweetness and admiration."

She grinned back at him. "They're beautiful. Thank you."

"You are most welcome."

When he didn't enter the house, but instead craned

his head to look down the hallway, she turned to follow his gaze. "What?"

"I thought your father might be waiting with a pistol."

That had very nearly been the case. "I told you that I would set things right. I explained that you and Kero were defending her honor."

"Oh. Wonderful. Now I'm uncivilized and completely mad."

"I'm certain it didn't sound that way." At least she hoped not. "He would like to speak to you, but he had a meeting. I told him you would make yourself available after our picnic."

"I'll do that." He spent another heartbeat or two gazing at her, then offered his arm. "Shall we?"

Phillipa handed the roses to Barnes. "See that these are put in water, will you? And send Mary down."

"Of course, my lady."

Bennett escorted her down the front steps, and then left her breathless as he put his hands around her waist and lifted her onto the curricle's seat. And a few short weeks ago she'd thought amorous pursuit was overrated. Ha. Now she wanted to tremble just looking at him. Part of her still couldn't believe that he was looking back at her—though he'd several times proven that his interest was sincere and ongoing.

"Hyde Park?" he asked, handing Mary onto the narrow seat at the back of the carriage and climbing up himself.

"Might I suggest somewhere else?"

He lowered one eyebrow, but nodded. "Wherever you like."

She smiled, encouraged and a bit nervous at the

same time. After all, at the moment he was trapped here. It seemed a fine line between showing him there were things to enjoy in London and attempting to bribe him to stay put. "The British Museum."

"Can we get in without an appointment?"

"Oh, yes. They know me. I go all the time."

"Ah." He snapped the reins, and the smart black mare trotted down the drive. "So we're going for *my* sake."

"Firstly, don't be angry with me before you even set eyes on the inside of it. Secondly, I said that I go all the time, which I would think implies that I enjoy myself there."

His mouth twitched. "Very well. Consider me humbled."

"I'll consider you chastised. I don't think you've ever been humbled."

Bennett laughed. Oh, she liked the sound of his amusement. It lifted her inside, made her feel cherished. She reached over and touched his sleeve; she couldn't help herself.

"Don't distract me," he said, chuckling. "I don't know where I'm going as it is."

"Turn here." She pointed. "Up Oxford Street." Phillipa smiled again. "You find me distracting?"

"You have no idea." He shifted closer to her. "Do you want to take the reins?"

"I told you that I don't know how to drive."

"I'll be right here," he returned. "And Usiku has a very good temperament. That's why I chose her."

Phillipa looked at him. "You chose this mare because you think I can manage her?"

His mouth curved. "Since we're all to be part of the same household, I thought it made sense."

Part of her felt very warm and tingly at hearing that. The other part, though, was abruptly troubled. "You haven't given up on locating your journals, I hope."

"I haven't. I'm developing a strategy even as we speak. But forgive me if I've found something that seems of even more immediate import."

He meant her. She almost felt guilty that she could be so happy and excited even knowing how abysmal he must consider his own prospects. When she could prefer that he remain in England no matter how badly he might wish to be elsewhere. "When you retrieve the journals," she said, mentally shaking herself, "will you write another book? One to counter Langley's? I'm certain there are things—discoveries—he must have left out. Your expedition couldn't have been day after day of heroic posturing."

"It was for him," Bennett commented. "And no. Other than details of who did what and the more scientific observations that no one wants to read about, my book would essentially be identical to his."

"But what good will it do if you only use the journals to blackmail the Association and not to make the rest of London respect you again?"

He shrugged. "I'm an explorer. It's not up to me whether anyone believes what I tell them or not. Let the scholars debate. The journals are only important because, well, they're mine, and because they are what will convince those who control the purse strings and make the decisions about who is asked to head which expedition."

For a minute she made herself pretend that all this didn't mean he wanted to leave again. "I still think it's a shame," she said quietly. "I so much enjoyed reading your books. I could actually feel the sun burning my skin when I read about you seeing the pyramids for the first time."

"I could take you to see them with your own eyes, you know."

She shivered again, this time with nervousness. Could she travel to Egypt and brave sandstorms and bandits and thirst in exchange for such an amazing sight? Phillipa drew a sharp breath, shutting her eyes for a moment. When she opened them, brilliant green eyes were gazing at her.

"Oh, turn here," she said abruptly, although there was still plenty of time to maneuver. "Up Tottenham Court Road, and then right onto Great Russell."

He didn't bring up traveling again as they went inside the museum, but as far as she was concerned, it colored every bit of their conversation. Why had the greatest adventurer in England decided to pursue her? And why couldn't she stop worrying about whether she would disappoint him? Oh, books were so much easier.

"I've never been to Greece," he commented, pulling her out of her reverie.

They stood in the gallery filled with the Elgin Marbles. "I love looking at these sculptures," she said. "But you would have left them at the Parthenon, wouldn't you?"

"I don't know." He eyed the closest of the figures speculatively. "I might have made off with one or two of them. They are exquisite."

She took his arm as they wandered through the museum. This was the way she liked to explore. From his expression at least he wasn't bored, but she could imagine how displays with description cards must pale compared to seeing lions running on the savannah or being handed a carving of an unknown figure by the man who'd fashioned it.

"What's that?" he asked, stopping before a black block of stone with letters and hieroglyphs carved into it. Several men stood around it, eyeing it and sketching it as though they expected it to get up and walk away.

"That's the stone from Rosetta. Bonaparte's men found it. Everyone's been trying to translate it, but it's written in at least three different languages, only one or so of which anyone's ever been able to decipher."

"Hm. It looks like one of those damned decrees they used to post in Spain—the same orders, repeated in Spanish, English, and French. Only wordier."

One of the men closest to them made a sound, then began muttering furiously with his colleagues. Phillipa tried to listen in, curious, until Bennett headed them off toward the African collection. In quick succession he named off the tribes to which a rack of spears belonged—Masai, Zulu, Turkana, and Samburu.

"Which kind stabbed you?" she asked.

"The tribe was Ngole, but I didn't keep that particular spear." He looked for a moment. "It's closest to that one, I think." He pointed at the sharp-looking, narrow, eight-inch head of the Turkana spear.

"Dear heavens, I can't imagine how much that must have hurt." Tears gathered in her eyes. Seeing the spear made it seem more real. She'd already seen the scar, and it was devastating to realize how very close she'd come to never meeting him at all.

"I'm only thankful I was stepping into a canoe at the time." He looked down at her, then stroked a finger softly along her cheek. "Don't cry, *nyonda*," he murmured.

Phillipa took a deep breath. "What does that mean, anyway? *Nyonda*?"

His green gaze held hers. "It's Swahili. It means 'beloved.'" A small smile touched his mouth, and he brushed her cheek again. "You do know I love you, Phillipa. To an alarming degree."

Her heart did a somersault. "I very much want to kiss you, Bennett," she whispered back.

"I'm not stopping you."

Oh, propriety was such a silly thing, anyway. She leaned up on her tiptoes.

"Lady Phillipa," Mary exclaimed.

She jumped. For goodness' sake, she'd forgotten the maid was even there. Bennett lifted an eyebrow, but settled for reaching out to straighten her sleeve. "Damned shame, that."

He was cursing again, but she rather agreed with the sentiment. "Perhaps we should find a park and have our picnic," she suggested.

"If you'll attempt driving the curricle."

"Very well." After all, driving a curricle was a less alarming prospect than traveling to a different continent. Or than losing Bennett Wolfe to his adventures because she was too much of a coward to share in them.

He needed to stop pushing so damned hard. Bennett handed over a leftover apple to Usiku, looking beyond the black mare's head to Phillipa seated on the driver's bench and holding the reins as if she thought the mare would fly away if she let go.

"Relax your fingers," he instructed. "I'm holding her head, so she's not going anywhere."

"I made it to the park without killing anyone. Are you certain you wish to press your luck?" she asked, though her mouth quirked up at the corners.

The Bennett fresh out of Africa would have said that he lived by pressing his luck, but he'd more than likely pressed her limited thirst for adventure enough for one day. "Only if you want to. I'm actually somewhat surprised that Usiku hasn't chewed her way out of the harness and escaped."

"Very amusing."

An odd chill ran down his spine. As he looked up again, Phillipa was gazing past him, her rosy cheeks paling. Abruptly she glanced down at him. "Langley," she mouthed.

Bennett turned around. Langley, mounted on a swift-looking chestnut hunter, trotted directly for him. That in itself would have been a surprise, except that Lord Thrushell's darling son wasn't alone.

"Ah, Bennett," he drawled, stopping out of reach despite the superior numbers he'd brought with him. He had always had a fairly strong sense of self-preservation. "Introduce me to your pretty friend, why don't you?"

Or perhaps he didn't wish to stay alive, after all. "I will if you will." Releasing Usiku, he strolled over to stand in front of the wheel, putting himself between Langley and Phillipa.

"That's right; you haven't spent much time in London." Langley gestured at the broad-shouldered man mounted beside him. "Bradley, Lord Frizzel; Lord Louis Hedges; and Lord Warren Hastings."

"Lady Phillipa Eddison," Bennett said reluctantly, not moving.

So Langley had brought a pack of lords with him. David would be the highest ranking of them; he wouldn't be wearing that air of cool superiority otherwise. Bennett understood pack dynamics and the rules of hierarchy. They held true everywhere, and for every species he'd ever encountered. As someone frequently ruled by his baser emotions, he also understood the look in Langley's eyes. Whatever victory he'd won with the Africa Association yesterday hadn't been enough for him.

"You were with him the night Wolfe and his beast attacked me."

A proper, typical female would more than likely agree that they'd attended the same event, but not that she was "with" him or any other gentleman. Phillipa, however, wasn't typical. Bennett held his breath, ready to react to whatever she might say.

"He promised to introduce me to you," she said in a breathy, excited voice. "That wasn't at all what I had in mind. Oh, and you have a black eye. Does it hurt?"

Langley puffed up like a damned peacock. "Not much. Will you be attending the assembly at Almack's tonight, Lady Phillipa?"

Lord Frizzel whispered something at him, but Langley made a dismissive gesture. At the same time, Bennett was trying to keep his jaw from dropping.

Phillipa giggled, a rather engaging if unsettling sound. "I'll be there if you will, Captain."

"Then save me the first waltz." With a nod and a half smile for Bennett that didn't touch his eyes, Langley led his pack off in the direction they'd come.

As soon as they were out of sight, Bennett whipped around to glare up at her. "What the devil was that?" he demanded, climbing up onto the seat and taking the reins from her.

She fanned her face with both hands. "Do you think he believed me?" she asked, her voice still unsteady and sharp with excitement.

"Believed what? That you're mad? A complete lunatic?" He clucked at Usiku, and they set off back toward Eddison House.

"But I was attempting to sound like Livi."

When he glanced at her, her expression was affronted. "You didn't sound like you. I'll grant you that."

"I wasn't actually flirting with him, you know. It occurred to me that being friendly with him might gain us more information than you going about punching him in the head."

Bennett pulled the reins so sharply that Usiku nearly skidded onto her haunches. "You are not going to seduce him to find out where my journals are."

"I'm certainly going to attempt it," she retorted. "I may have to ask Livi for some advice. I'm not very good at flirting."

A stab of jealousy nearly gutted him. "I don't want you going anywhere near him, Phillipa. And I like the way you flirt."

"Thank you. But I think this is a good idea. Admittedly I had no time to plan it, because it only just came to me when he and his overbearing friends rode up."

"No. No, no, no."

She brushed his thigh with her fingertips. "I may not be certain where I . . . see myself with you, but you need those journals. And I have a better chance at figuring out their location than you do."

Bennett opened his mouth to repeat his protest, then closed it again. As Phillipa had said on several occasions, she loved to set things right. And skittish as she'd been today about discussing adventures past and future, it was entirely possible that this little escapade was more for her sake than for his.

"It would be more satisfying for Langley," he said slowly, pushing aside the strong feeling that he was going to regret this, "if we made it clear that he was stealing you from me." He took her chin in his fingers, making certain she looked him in the eye. "Which he is not."

Pretty brown eyes gazed deep into his. "Which he is not," she repeated.

"And he's dangerous."

"He's dangerous in the wild, perhaps, but what would he possibly do here? He's already dented your reputation and gotten away with it. Winning me should be exactly what he wants and expects to do next."

"You've done some studying of behavior in the natural world, yourself," he acknowledged grudgingly.

"I've read your books."

They drove in silence for a moment. Bennett didn't like it. He didn't like it with every fiber of his being that both wanted her and wanted to protect her. And if it was gentlemanly to step back and let the woman he adored do something that could be harmful to her reputation if not to her safety, then he would rather be a rogue and a beast.

"What are you going to do if he wants to kiss you?" he finally asked, the question coming out in a growl.

"A proper female wouldn't allow a gentleman to kiss her until after they became betrothed."

"Oh, really?"

"Absolutely. Isn't that so, Mary?"

The maid behind them nodded so vigorously that Bennett could see her out of the corner of his eye. "Yes, Lady Flip. Nor any touching. Barely any holding hands except for assistance climbing in and out of carriages."

Belatedly Phillipa returned her fingers from the edge of his coat to her lap. *Damned chaperones.* "What if I simply tell you that I appreciate what you're willing to do, and then you don't do it?" he suggested.

She shook her head. "No. I need to attempt this. If he . . . if we don't match well tonight, then of course we'll have to think of something else, but I—"

"Promise me one thing," he said. "If you feel uncomfortable, or if he says something that makes you suspect he's realized you're up to something, you will give me a signal."

"A signal? Should I shoot a pistol into the air?"

"Don't jest. Brush your hair behind your left ear. Like this." He gently tucked a strand of her chestnut hair behind her ear, ignoring the disapproving cluck of the maid. "Will you?"

"How will you see that?"

As if he would be more than ten feet away from her all evening. "I'll see it. Will you?"

"Yes. If I feel that something is wrong, I will tuck my hair behind my left ear."

One thing was for certain. After he left Phillipa and sat for her father to remind him what a damned beast he was, he was going to the Adventurers' Club. Because he was not going to survive the night at Almack's without a drink and an hour or two to cool down and find some patience. Or rather, David Langley wouldn't survive the night if he didn't do those things.

Chapter Nineteen

Leopards are solitary creatures, prowling the night at the fringes of herds or lurking in trees waiting for their unsuspecting prey to pass beneath. It is known that men are killed by lions every year, but I suspect that many, many more are dragged off by leopards. It's much easier to see a pride coming than one lethal animal.

THE JOURNALS OF CAPTAIN BENNETT WOLFE

I'm telling you, she has no suitors."

David Langley sank back against the far wall of Almack's assembly room to examine his fingernails. "She has one suitor, Bradley." He gave a slow smile. "Well, actually, at this moment she has two."

Another group of chits approached to chat with him, the third since he'd arrived. They all held on to one another in their excitement at meeting such a famous fellow. He'd lately been encouraging Bradley and his other friends to refer to him as the Conqueror of the Congo, but it didn't seem to be catching on yet.

He wrote his name on the dance cards of the prettiest ones, telling the others that his own card was filled. As he was assessing whether the stunning redhead in the lead admired him enough to take off her clothes, Lord Frizzel nudged him.

Lord and Lady Leeds and their daughters entered the main room. His eye went immediately to the honey-haired older sister. She had just come out into Society when he left for Africa, and he had danced with her a handful of times. How the lovely chit had thus far avoided marriage, he had no idea, but he did know which of the Eddison sisters he would be after if he had a choice.

"I'd best go say hello," he muttered, pushing away from the wall. He paused, and a second later Frizzel joined him. Generally he enjoyed hangers-on, but in this instance cronies were vital. Wolfe could make an appearance anywhere, and he refused to be attacked again by the heathen.

As he approached Lady Phillipa, he wondered why Wolfe seemed to have focused his attention on her. Yes, she was pretty enough, he supposed, but she might as well have been a tree stump with her sister present. She wasn't as willowy as he liked, though her curves were certainly generous. No suitors, Frizzel had said. Did she lack refinement? Grace? Conversation?

It was a curiosity, though it didn't much signify. Bennett Wolfe kept company with her, and that was all that mattered. Because he'd spent three years in Wolfe's company, and if he'd learned one thing it was that the man didn't give up. Whether he could steal the chit away or not wasn't as important as whether he could coax, charm, or trick her into revealing everything she knew of Wolfe's plans and intentions.

More than anything he wanted to burn the damned journals and sketches, but he wasn't ready yet to give up the only leverage he had. Little liking as he had for the man, he'd be foolish to ignore the fact that Bennett Wolfe was a formidable opponent. And he was not a fool.

"Good evening, Lady Phillipa," he said with a smile as he reached the family.

"Captain Langley. Oh, you've come after all. I thought you might have been teasing." She patted him playfully on the arm. "You've met my family, haven't you? Lord and Lady Leeds, and this is my sister, Olivia. Everyone, Captain David Langley." She gave an excited giggle. "The Conqueror of the Congo."

Ah, so the moniker *had* begun to spread. Excellent. He took her hand and bowed over it. "I'm only hoping that Captain Wolfe hasn't stolen your heart completely, and that there's a bit of room still for me there."

"Keep saying such nice things, and I shall forget him completely."

Not completely, he hoped, deepening his smile.

Out of the corner of her eye, Phillipa could see her family looking at her like she'd grown a second head. For the moment she pretended not to notice; it was difficult enough to be . . . giddy without having to worry about them.

Bennett hadn't yet arrived—which was unsurprising considering that she'd asked him not to make an appearance until half nine. He would distract Langley when she needed to charm the captain, and he would distract her. Having him walk in just before the first waltz would serve them best—however much she might prefer to be conversing with him and gazing at him rather than at Langley.

"May I escort you to the refreshment table?" the captain asked, everything about him impeccable, from his manners to his dark blue trousers, light blue waistcoat, and gray jacket. Everything except for a fading bruise beneath one eye and the bandage still covering the tip of one ear.

For a moment she wondered whether Bennett would bring Kero with him. She almost hoped so, however counterproductive it would be to her—their—plan. "That would be delightful," she exclaimed.

For a second she worried that Livi would insist on joining them, but then Sonja and Lucy appeared to drag her away. She took Langley's arm, very aware that she was on her own in this, except that she wasn't. In fact, she wouldn't be at all surprised if Bennett was spying on her through one of the tall windows that lined the near wall. She risked a glance in that direction, but the room was too well lit for her to be able to see anything on the far side of the glass.

Generally when she wanted to know something, she asked a question. That was one of the things that many of her peers didn't much appreciate, and while Bennett did, she couldn't risk being so obvious with Langley. "I read your book," she said instead, fluttering her eyelashes at him. She nearly stumbled, and had to catch herself.

"Did you now? You did say this morning that you were looking forward to meeting me."

"Oh, yes. When I met Sir Bennett I asked whether

304 🌸 Suzanne Enoch

he would be able to make an introduction. He assured me that he could, but then he made several cutting remarks about you." She leaned closer. "I think your assessment of him in *Across the Continent* is rather accurate. He does seem a bit . . . unsophisticated."

"Unsophisticated?"

Oh, dear. Had she already made a misstep? She needed to find words with fewer syllables. "I think that's the right word. At least, he walked straight up to me without an introduction, and I never know when he's going to appear, or whether he'll have that monkey on his shoulder or not." Inwardly she hesitated. "Shouldn't Kero be yours, anyway?" she ventured, unable to resist a little jab. "Your book tells how fond she was of you. What happened?"

"Ah, yes. Kero. Wolfe's the one who rescued her, but he hadn't a clue how to keep her fed and healthy. That fell to me. She had disappeared at the time I left, and I can only suppose that he taught her to fear everyone but himself."

"How terrible." An even worse lie, but this was all about charming him. The truth could come later, after she'd discovered the location of the journals. "I thought it must be something like that."

"You're not interested in being pursued by Wolfe, then?"

This was where she had to be careful. Bennett had said Langley would enjoy the idea of stealing her away, so she couldn't make it too easy. "Well, he is quite handsome," she said slowly, as though genuinely considering. "And I like adventurers. And he does have five thousand a year."

"So you're waiting to receive a better offer."

She giggled. Heavens, what an awful, shallow person this Flip was. "I have to look out for myself, don't I?"

"Indeed you do." He handed her a chocolate-dipped strawberry. "And I hope you've saved that waltz for me."

"You're the first gentleman I saw when I came in." Pulling the card from her reticule with her free hand, she gave it and a pencil to him. As he wrote in his name, she took a bite of the sweet strawberry, attempting to form her lips into a kiss the way Livi did. And she dearly hoped she wasn't drooling.

He looked up from the card. "I wish I could have a dozen dances with you," he said, his gaze on her mouth.

Hm. The lip trick actually worked. "That would be terribly improper, I'm afraid."

"Flip?"

She'd been concentrating so hard that her sister's voice startled her. "What is it?"

Livi stood behind her, Lord John accompanying her. Clearly they both thought she'd gone mad. "Mama wants a word with you."

Langley gave a slight bow. "I'll see you for our waltz."

Phillipa led the way to her parents, setting a course that would take them by a less crowded side of the room. No one could be allowed to overhear whatever it was Livi wanted to say to her.

"What in the world has gotten into you?" Livi demanded, just as she'd expected.

Squaring her shoulders, Phillipa turned around. "I don't know what you're talking about."

"Captain Langley? Bennett—" Livi lowered her voice and stepped closer. "Bennett Wolfe has practically proposed to you. They are enemies."

"So you support Bennett's suit now? That's good to know."

"He is not a man to play about with, Flip," John put in, his expression more serious than she was accustomed to seeing him wear.

She sighed. Clearly they were alarmed and intended to save her from herself. She would have to tell them something. In a moment. First she wanted to enjoy her unexpected fame for the tiniest second. "Are you certain you're not jealous because I'm being pursued by two of the most famous adventurers in England?" she asked aloud.

"All I know is that someone is going to get killed, and that it's more than likely to be me." John put a hand on her shoulder. "Do you have any . . . *any* idea how much Bennett cares for you?"

Abruptly this wasn't amusing any longer. "Before I answer that or say another word, you have to promise me something. Both of you."

"What are we promising?" Livi demanded, glancing around them.

"Promise that you'll help me, and not hinder me."

"In breaking Bennett's heart? In collaborating with the man who ruined his future? I think not."

"Hush, John. This is *for* Bennett."

Silence. "Now I'm even more confused," John whispered.

"I'm looking for clues about where Captain Langley is hiding Bennett's journals. To get any clues, I have to speak with him. I therefore have to be nice.

And charming." She frowned. "And I have to let him think that he's stealing me away from Bennett."

"You cannot do this," Livi hissed.

"I *am* doing this. So kindly don't ruin it."

"Flip, you could get hurt."

She swallowed. "I know."

Yes, she could get hurt, but not in the way Livi was imagining. Because if she succeeded, she would have to choose. She would have to decide whether she had any real courage. Compared to that, fooling David Langley for a few days seemed . . . easy.

"I think you need to explain this a bit further," John said, offering an arm to each of them.

"Promise me first."

"As long as Bennett isn't going to kill me, then I promise."

Livi looked as though she'd swallowed a bug. "I will promise unless it looks as though you will be hurt. Then I do not promise."

"You'd best take me over to Mama, then, or Langley will become suspicious. But walk slowly. And stop scowling, Livi. For heaven's sake."

Phillipa didn't like him cursing in her presence, so Bennett made good use of every word of profanity he knew in every language he knew as he paced outside Almack's. He could curse himself, as well, for allowing her to entangle herself in this mess between him and Langley, but it hadn't precisely been up to him.

He'd fought off a crocodile with the butt of his rifle and his hunting knife. He'd walked a thousand miles through jungles and deserts and savannahs.

And that slip of a woman had him befuddled and dazzled and twisted in so many directions he didn't know which way to go.

This had been her idea. The problem was, it was also her risk. And he didn't like that. Not a damned bit. He flipped open his battered old pocket watch again. Twenty-two minutes after nine. Bloody close enough.

Passing by the footmen at the entrance, he strode into the main assembly room. Trying to look like an about-to-be-thrown-over beau made him feel stiff and awkward, but entering the room like a charging rhinoceros wouldn't get him anything but an invitation to leave.

The level of his obsession was such that he searched for and found where Phillipa stood before he even thought of Langley. That idiot held court in the center of an admiring circle, mostly chits, all of them cooing and preening like doves.

Phillipa, on the other hand, stood a short distance away from her parents, Olivia and Jack her only companions. And while her color was high and her hands fidgeting with nerves or excitement or both, the other two looked decidedly dismayed.

Slowing his pace to a more respectable stroll, he approached her. She'd worn an ivory and blue silk that shimmered with beads in the chandelier light. Stunning. Nearly as lovely as she was. "Good evening," he said, taking her hand and drawing it to his lips. Kissing her knuckles wasn't nearly enough. His body craved her as much as his heart did.

"Flip says this nonsense is all her idea," Jack said in a low voice. "I find it difficult to believe that you didn't have something to do with it. You being the one who most benefits, after all."

"Ah. She told you, then. We thought we might have to let you two in on it so you wouldn't step into the middle of everything and ruin it."

"Speaking of ruined," Phillipa's older sister began, her voice stiff and low, "you do realize you're sending her to feign an affection for the man you intend to ruin. There are her marital prospects to consider here, Captain Wolfe. You may plan to trot off to Africa or . . . or . . . Siberia, but what about Flip?"

"I told you this was *my* idea," Phillipa stated, before he could conjure a defense that didn't exist. "I didn't actually give Bennett a choice."

"You." Jack raised an eyebrow. "You ordered Bennett Wolfe to assist you. And he agreed."

Bennett sighed. At the same moment he glimpsed Langley leaving his admirers to head toward them. Two of his cronies from earlier in the day flanked him. At least Langley had learned one lesson about approaching him alone. "Unless you wish to stand here and play 'state the obvious,' your prince approaches, Phillipa."

"Oh. *Oh.* Walk away, you two. Bennett and I have to argue now."

"I think I'll stay to protect you," Jack commented.

"No, no." Phillipa nudged him a little closer to where Bennett stood. "If you're staying, then protect Langley from Bennett."

"I don't want to."

"The more convinced Langley is that Phillipa will side with him, the sooner we can be done with this bloo—blasted charade." Bennett risked a quick glare at Jack. "So hold me back."

"Ah, Phillipa," Langley said smoothly. "It's time for our waltz, unless you've changed your mind."

"She has changed her mind," Bennett retorted, wishing both that they'd had a bit of time to rehearse this, and that he actually could take a swing at Langley. "She's going to dance with me."

"Bennett, Captain Langley asked me first."

He pinned her with his glare. "You'll do as I say."

Her eyes flashed, and for a moment he worried that he'd said the wrong thing and turned the argument real. Then she stomped her foot in a very un-Phillipa-like manner. "You do not get to dictate to me, sir. I'll dance with whomever I please. And I please to dance with Captain Langley, and—"

"David," Langley interrupted smoothly.

"—with David. In fact, if you cannot conduct yourself like a proper gentleman, I don't wish to see you at all."

"I don't believe that. And this fool certainly doesn't deserve you."

"Steady now, Bennett," Jack put in, a touch too dramatically.

"Lady Phillipa, we'll miss our dance." Langley offered his hand.

At least Langley didn't seem to notice the theatrics. Her chin in the air, Phillipa strutted by him. And disguised by the folds of her pretty skirt, she brushed her fingers against his. And then she was gone onto the dance floor. With Langley.

One thing was for damned certain. She wasn't going out there alone. "You two," Bennett growled, jabbing a finger at Jack and Olivia, "go dance. Now."

Olivia blinked. "But I—"

"He's correct," Jack broke in, offering his arm. "We should attempt to stay close by Flip."

"Yes, you're right. Of course." The sister took Jack's proffered arm, and they stepped onto the dance floor. Just before they twirled away, Jack managed to send him a grateful look.

It was well and good, Bennett supposed, if his—and Phillipa's—tribulations aided Jack in his pursuit of Olivia, but his friend had best remember that that was not the aim of this dance. Bennett turned around. Luckily he was supposed to be jealous and annoyed, because he doubted he was capable of acting any differently.

He spied a chit standing fairly close behind him, no partner in view. "Waltz with me," he said the moment he reached her.

She blushed furiously. "But we haven't been introduced."

"Bennett Wolfe. And you?"

"I . . . uh . . . Catherine. Miss Patterson."

Bennett took her hand and placed it over his arm. He wanted to be on the floor already, but he couldn't drag her there. The rules at Almack's were fairly strict about that. "Now we've been introduced, Miss Patterson. Shall we?"

After some more stammering she apparently gave up and allowed him to lead her onto a corner of the well-polished dance floor. Without any further ceremony he put a hand on her waist, took her other hand, and began dancing.

"I've read your books, Captain Wolfe," she blurted, as he tried to angle them toward the center of the floor. That was where Langley danced with Phillipa, holding her hand, touching her waist, gazing at her.

"Did you?" he returned absently.

"Oh, yes. And I don't believe you made all those missteps of which Captain Langley accused you in his book."

He blinked. None of these machinations concerned Miss Patterson. And he had no reason to be rude to her, simply because he wanted to be dancing with someone else. "Thank you."

"You can ask anyone, and they'll tell you what a great admirer I am of yours." She nodded eagerly, as if affirming her own conversation.

"Thank you again." Four couples danced between him and Phillipa. Another sharp turn, and he cut past one pair.

"I can even recite the passage you wrote when you first saw a pride of lions." She took a breath. " 'The tall grass, golden in the unforgiving sunlight, rippled in waves—an ocean of gold and yellow broken only by the acacia trees and the occasional massive anthill. I—' "

"That's very impressive," he interrupted, not in the mood to hear words he'd written nearly eight years ago quoted back to him.

"But I can recall the rest of the passage, as well. In fact, I've read your books so many times I can repeat almost all of them from memory. And when I heard the news that you'd been killed, I embroidered all my handkerchiefs with your initials and the dates of your expeditions. And I only stopped wearing black after I read in the newspaper that you were alive."

Somewhere this had gone from being a good idea

and become something of a nightmare. Phillipa had told him that she'd read his books, but he doubted she could quote much more than a word or two back to him verbatim. He doubted *he* could recall any of it word-for-word. When Phillipa had discussed them, she'd talked about how she'd felt, the mental images the written words evoked. She hadn't turned them into some kind of . . . bible.

But then he turned them again, and found himself catching Phillipa's gaze. Time stopped for a heartbeat, and then she made a face and said something to Langley that Bennett couldn't make out. A second later, the captain was facing David.

"This is pitiful, Wolfe," the captain said. "Unless you mean to begin another brawl, keep your distance."

"You're a damned poacher, Langley."

"It isn't poaching if the lovely creature in question goes willingly."

"Don't make a scene, Bennett," Phillipa said, sending an appraising glance at Miss Patterson. "Dance with your partner. I think you'll find that you and Catherine have a great deal in common."

Yes, one of them worshiped him, while the other *was* him. And considering that Phillipa seemed to know Miss Patterson, he meant to ask a few pointed questions of the clever, maddening chit.

"I won't warn you again, Wolfe," Langley said flatly. "Stay away."

"Yes, Captain Wolfe," Phillipa echoed. "Stay away."

With every fiber of his being he wanted to sweep Phillipa into his arms and not let her go. This, however, was *her* game, and putting an end to it now might well also put an end to them. And so he scowled. "This isn't over with," he stated in a low voice, and swept Miss Patterson back in the direction from which they'd come.

"That wasn't very nice," Miss Patterson noted. "I thought Flip was another admirer of yours."

"She used to be," he said carefully, already planning how and when he would be calling on Phillipa Eddison after this damned party was over with. No one had best come between them then.

Chapter Twenty

It's been said that humans are the only creatures who set traps. But isn't a spiderweb a trap? Or when a crocodile lies in wait just beneath the surface, is he not setting a trap? Of course spiders and crocodiles only want a meal. The motives of humans aren't always so pure. Not in my experience.

THE JOURNALS OF CAPTAIN BENNETT WOLFE

Phillipa read mainly histories and true accounts. On occasion, however, she indulged in a different sort of book—either the new comedic romances (of which *Emma* was her favorite), or those terribly overwrought gothic tales.

As she and Olivia returned home from Almack's, she distinctly recalled one in particular. The heroine of *Cliffside Manor* had been pursued by two mysterious men—the scarred, brooding Stephen, and the handsome, brooding Hector. Judith's dilemma had seemed terribly romantic, though of course it was Hector who'd won her affection, and Stephen who'd eventually ended up killed by the monstrous horse he rode.

Her own circumstances were a bit different; Bennett already had her affection, while she could barely tolerate David Langley. But she had no idea how Judith had survived to the end of the book when she actually had feelings for both men. Goodness, it was nerve-wracking enough just pretending to like Langley and watching Bennett dance with an admirer.

"I'm not happy with this," Olivia said, as they said good night to their parents and ascended the stairs.

"It's not up to you. All I ask is that you not say anything."

"Just tell me how anyone could convince you to act so . . . unlike yourself and to risk your own reputation."

"Firstly, I don't have much of a reputation for anything but being a bluestocking and a poor conversationalist—and your sister."

"That is not so, Flip."

"Of course it is. And secondly, Bennett didn't even want me to do this. It's my idea, and I'll see it through."

Olivia stopped outside Phillipa's door, blocking it. "Has he seduced you?"

"Livi, don't—"

"Answer me, Phillipa Louise."

Oh, dear. Her full name. For a moment she considered the question. Had Bennett seduced her? Nearly from their first meeting he'd made it clear that his intentions were honorable, though she was fairly certain that marriage had very little to do with why she'd wanted to be intimate with him, or why she . . . ached to be near him.

"I would call it partially seduction and partially mutual interest," she decided.

"You—but—" Livi scowled. "Are you ruined?" she whispered.

"Yes." Quite thoroughly and quite deliciously, actually.

Her sister stared at her. "I don't even know what to say to you."

"It's more than likely too late to say much of anything."

"Oh, and now you jest about it. I'm going to bed. But consider that if you're successful in this foolish plot of yours, you're giving Captain Wolfe the means to leave England again. You've barely been farther than Surrey. You've barely lifted your head out of your books. Are you planning on going with him to Africa? Or are you hoping he'll miraculously become domestic for the first time in his life?"

Olivia vanished down the hallway to her own bedchamber. From the slam of the door, she wasn't finished with expressing her irritation. And she'd asked a good set of questions. Sooner, rather than later, Phillipa was going to have to answer them.

She opened her door and slipped inside her bedchamber. Mary had lit a small fire in the fireplace and laid out her night rail on the down-turned bed. The rest would be up to Phillipa; Olivia was the one who'd always required the maid for brushing out her hair and changing into her nightclothes. Olivia always looked fashionable and well-groomed. Until the past few weeks, Phillipa had barely spared a thought for any of that.

As her eyes adjusted to the dimmer light of her

bedchamber, she noticed the figure seated in her reading chair beneath the window. She gasped, grabbing for the fireplace poker, until she recognized both him and the deep green eyes gazing at her. Her heart continued to pound, but for another reason entirely.

"Bennett, you nearly frightened me out of my skin," she whispered, returning the poker and dropping her reticule onto the writing table.

"I only want you out of your clothes," he returned in a low, intimate voice. "Not out of your skin." He sank back in her deep, comfortable chair. "Come here, Phillipa."

Little as she liked being ordered about, he seemed to be just what she needed after the evening she'd spent. Phillipa walked over, placed her hands on either arm of the chair, and leaned in for a warm, lingering kiss. All the bad things of her day melted away in the rush of arousal and excitement of being with him.

Bennett wrapped his hands around her waist and drew her down onto his lap, holding her close against him as he kissed her again and again. Finally she lifted her head a little, stroking her fingers along his stubbled cheek. "Did you come in through the servants' stairs again?"

"Through the window. I hate repeating myself."

"Then the next time you'll have to descend the chimney."

"That could be a bit warm, but I'm willing to risk it." He kissed both of her cheeks, then touched her lips again. "I heard Olivia out there. She has a very good point."

"I don't care about that. Those journals are yours. And I think I've figured out a fast way to find them. Fast enough to avoid having the Association name Langley to head their next expedition."

"What about after that, Phillipa?"

"Later is later."

He closed his eyes for a moment. "Recite a passage of one of my books to me, will you?" he finally asked, opening his pretty eyes again.

Phillipa scowled. "What?"

"Recite a passage of *Walking with Pharaohs* or *Golden Sun of the Serengeti*. You told me you've read them."

"I don't have any passages memorized, Bennett. I have a few words here and there that I remember fairly closely, like the way you said the setting sun turned the desert sands into an endless, burning sea. It creates an image."

He grinned, kissing her again. "Thank you."

"What is this about? It's not like you to be in my bedchamber and want to talk about books. Yours in particular."

"Catherine Patterson is a great admirer of mine."

With a snort, Phillipa buried her face in his neck. "Oh, that. I thought I might spare you. I had no idea you'd drag her onto the dance floor."

"If I'd had any idea, I wouldn't have." He gazed at her. "I asked Jack to sponsor me at White's," he finally said. "We'll see if my income rates higher than my present reputation."

He was trying. He was making an effort to fit in, to join London Society. And what was she doing? "If you could do anything you wanted to, Bennett, go anywhere, what would you do?"

"I can't answer that any more than you can answer my question. We seem to be stuck." He took a slow breath. "So tell me your plan."

"Langley—David—invited me to come and see his stuffed animal collection. The ones he shot in Africa."

"Yes, he had a great many hides."

"So I will go and see them. And I'll bring my book for him to autograph. All I'll need to do is get away from him for a few minutes, and I can search Langley House."

"No."

Blast it all. He might at least have taken the time to consider it. "And how did you think I was going to find the journals?"

"I didn't want you to go looking for the journals. They're *my* problem."

"And you can't go in and tear Langley House apart and burn it to the ground. Not if you want your reputation back."

"And yet somehow the more I see you chatting and dancing with him, the better that particular suggestion of yours sounds."

She frowned. "That was not a suggestion, and you know it." When he didn't reply to that, she elbowed him in the ribs. "I already accepted his invitation to visit. The only thing I need from you is the return of my book."

His muscles had tensed considerably since she'd first joined him in the chair. Clearly he wasn't happy, and he was growing even less so. "Phillipa," he finally said, "you may have read his book, but you haven't read my journals. And where Langley is concerned, the two tell a very different story."

"I'm not falling for him, you know. I'm trying—"

"He wears a polite and pretty face better than I do," he interrupted. "But don't think he's anything but a self-concerned, vicious bastard." Bennett tightened his grip on her. "And I swear to you, if you'll leave this be, I'll stay. You don't have to ask yourself whether you could travel with me, because we won't go any farther away than Kent."

So there it was. Bennett would give up his dreams for her, and in exchange all he asked was that she not make any sacrifice, herself. Her adventurer would become a gentleman farmer, not even because she asked him to, but because he knew she couldn't manage if he attempted anything more.

Bennett brushed his fingers along her cheeks, and she realized she'd begun crying. Of course he would think they were tears of gratitude and joy. She, on the other hand, had never been as disappointed with herself as she was at that moment.

That, however, didn't diminish his sacrifice. Until she'd heard him say it, she wouldn't have been able to imagine any man willing to alter his life for her. And for this extraordinary man to do so . . . Her heart ached, both for him and for his voluntary loss. "I love you, Bennett," she whispered, her voice shaking.

"And that is all I needed to hear," he returned, sliding his palm up her leg, drawing her skirt with it. "Because you know I love you."

"Yes. I think you've demonstrated that." Better than she had.

"I'd like to demonstrate it again," he said, clearly misunderstanding what she'd been referring to. "Several times, if we have that long tonight."

She twisted a little so she could reach his knotted cravat with both hands. "Will you still want me in Kent?"

He smiled against her mouth. "I'll even want you in Yorkshire."

Slowly she slid his cravat free, dropping it to the floor so she could pull his shirt from his trousers and run her hands up the warm skin of his abdomen and chest. "In that case, I think we should move to the bed."

She felt his thighs bunch beneath her, and then he stood, holding her in his arms. "An excellent suggestion, *nyonda*. My swollen parts are beginning to feel a bit confined."

Phillipa chuckled. "We must see to that immed—"

Her door handle rattled. "Flip?" Olivia called in a low voice. "Are you asleep? Let me in!"

"Damnation," she cursed, grabbing Bennett's shoulders and pushing until he released his grip on her and her feet touched the floor again.

He reached for her as she headed for the door. "Send her away."

"What is it, Livi?" she asked through the door. Thank goodness she'd latched it; she'd only begun doing so in the last few nights.

"Let me in, or I'll scream."

"All right. Give me a moment, will you? I'm half dressed." That bit was nearly true, anyway. She faced Bennett. "Go! Out the window."

He frowned. When she gestured at him to flee, though, her heart hammering, he backed a few steps toward the window. From the tent at the crotch of his trousers, he was going to have to be very careful climbing down, or he would damage something.

"Send your regrets to Langley," he murmured, sliding over the windowsill and swinging his legs outside. "You and I are going for a drive at two o'clock. Promptly."

She nodded, throwing the cravat out the window after him. As Livi knocked once more, louder, she yanked the clips out of her hair, straightened her skirt, and unlatched the door. "What in the world is wrong?" she asked, opening the door.

"After our conversation, I did some thinking," her sister said, striding past her to glare suspiciously around the room. "If Sir Bennett ruined you, it was accomplished either by him sneaking in here, or you sneaking out." She walked over to the far side of the bed and ducked down to look beneath it. Then she straightened, sat on it, and slid under the covers. "I am therefore sleeping in here until you either marry him, or he leaves the country."

Considering that she'd been minutes away from being naked with Bennett in that same bed, Phillipa decided her exasperation was understandable. But with him more than likely still climbing down the trellis outside her window, it was also somewhat amusing. She snorted.

"It's not funny," Livi retorted, throwing her night rail at her as she wriggled out of her dress. "I may not be able to keep you from stepping between Bennett and Captain Langley in public, but I can certainly keep your reputation safe in our own house. No more adventures for you, Flip."

Phillipa started to reply that she no longer had a reason to step anywhere near Langley, but she stopped herself. Instead she pulled the thin night rail over her head and climbed into bed beside her sister. "Thank you," she said, imagining she could hear Bennett swearing down on the ground outside.

"You're welcome."

"Do you truly think I've been adventuring?" she asked after a moment, surprised to hear Livi refer to all this mess as an adventure.

"That's certainly what I would call it. Carrying about monkeys, deciphering conspiracies about book authorship, engaging in an illicit affair with one man while flirting with another—you'd never catch me doing any such thing. Now go to sleep."

Phillipa curled onto her side, but sleep was the last thing on her mind. So Bennett had conceded, declared her victorious, and removed any reason for her to risk anything on his behalf. Tomorrow she could sit in the morning room and read until after he had his sponsored luncheon at White's. Then he would take her for a drive promptly at two o'clock, and quite probably propose.

Or she could find another copy of Langley's book, go visit the captain at ten o'clock on the pretext of seeing his silly dead animals and obtaining an autograph, and take that one opportunity to look for Bennett's journals. With or without discovering their location, she could still be home in time for their drive. And then she could say she'd done her best—and mean it. Even more importantly for her, she could say she'd had an adventure, risked . . . something, and it would be true.

It wasn't difficult at all to slip out of Eddison House with Mary at shortly after half nine. Despite her recent popularity, her parents were still far more accustomed to her attending book reading luncheons or going on visits to museums than anything else. And Livi, of course, was already out on Bond Street shopping with Sonja.

Since Olivia had taken the barouche and her father the coach, Phillipa opted to hire a hack. Her first stop was to the bookstore to purchase another copy of *Across the Continent*, however little she liked the idea of further supporting the book or its supposed author. Then she had to turn all the pages, break the spine, and do whatever else she could think of to make the book appear well-read.

"If you dislike that book so, Lady Flip," Mary said, watching from the opposite seat of the hack, "why did you purchase it?"

"I do not dislike this book," Phillipa returned, sitting on it and wiggling to loosen the bindings a little. "I adore this book. You've barely seen it out of my hands since I purchased it—which was weeks ago. Make certain you remember that, Mary. Will you?"

"Yes, my lady."

"Good. Now when we reach Langley House, I want you to hang back a little. Captain Langley needs to be able to speak to me freely. And if I should . . . vanish from the room at some point and Langley notices, you are to say that I went seeking a privy. Is that understood?"

"I think so, my lady."

Mary looked as though she would rather have been off toting boxes for Livi, but it couldn't be helped. Without a maid she couldn't go calling at Langley

House. If the captain's parents didn't also reside there, she wouldn't have been able to go at all.

When the hack jolted to a halt and the driver rapped on the roof, she rubbed a hand against her suddenly constricted throat. This was for Bennett, and it was for her, she reminded herself. All she needed to do was watch Langley and take a quick look about for the most likely hiding place of the journals. Once she had that information, Bennett could do with it as he pleased. The important part was that she go looking, that it not be her cowardice toward this and toward life that made him stay in England.

Captain Langley pulled open the door of the hack just too late to catch her sitting on his book. "David!" she exclaimed, with what she hoped was a bright smile. He must be eager to see her, which was good—however uncomfortable it made her feel.

"You are very prompt, Phillipa." He took her hand and helped her down to the drive. "I've heard that your friends call you Flip. May I also have that honor?"

Anything that set him more at ease. "I would like that."

"Flip it is, then." He placed her hand over his arm as they walked past the butler and into Langley House. "Your sister couldn't join us?"

"Oh, no. Livi had a prior engagement."

"Well, that leaves more time for just you and me, doesn't it? Splendid."

As they ascended the stairs Phillipa couldn't shake the feeling that she'd walked unarmed into the enemy's stronghold. *Relax,* she ordered herself. She couldn't panic and be charming at the same time, and she needed to be charming.

"I brought your book," she said, trying to sound breathless and excited rather than wary and nervous. "I do hope you'll inscribe it to me."

"I would be delighted to do so. Did Captain Wolfe sign his books for you?"

She flipped her hand dismissively. "You know, I looked for our household copies after he reappeared, but I couldn't find them anywhere."

"Perhaps the servants used them to level the furniture." He laughed, so she joined in.

"So you didn't welcome his attentions at all, Flip?" They left the stairs and traveled along the balcony to the west wing of the house.

"Truthfully, he is quite handsome," she replied, "and people do notice him. For the first few days it was interesting." Phillipa stopped herself before she could begin to wax poetical. "But he's so . . . unrefined. In fact, I'd begun to worry that I would find you to be the same. Thank goodness it's not so."

"I imagine you can take the savage out of Africa, but you can't take Africa out of the savage. Or however that saying goes." They stopped before a set of double doors. Stepping forward, he threw them open and moved aside. "Thankfully, I am not a savage."

Phillipa took a step inside the room. And stopped.

To her right a large crocodile reared on its hind legs, its jaws agape and menacing. On the left, a leopard stood with its tail arched over its back, a household cat grown to giant and deadly size. The room was the house's library, she realized after a moment, the center of it gutted to make room for at least two dozen stuffed animals of various sizes. *Not a savage, indeed.*

"Oh, bless me!" Mary exclaimed behind them. "I

ain't going in there. I'll never close my eyes again as
it is, seeing those beasties!"

"Why don't you wait down in the foyer for me?"
Phillipa suggested, torn between interest and horror
herself.

"Go down to the kitchen and have some tea,"
Langley amended, otherwise ignoring the maid.
"My display has that effect on some people."

"It's very . . . primal," Phillipa forced out, as she
took another few steps forward and came face-to-
face with a pair of vervet monkeys perched on a
trunk and both staring at her, glass-eyed. Oh, thank
God it was Bennett who'd found Kero. But David
still claimed that he and the monkey had begun as
friends. Anything she could learn to prove him a
liar could be helpful. "These aren't Kero's parents,
are they?"

"What? Oh, no. I shot these before we met up with
Kero." He took her arm and pulled her forward. "I'll
wager you've never set your eyes on one of these
before."

Briefly praying that it wouldn't be an African
tribesman, she went with him. What she saw was a
small creature with short legs and a very long tail,
a catlike head, and faint spots running from its ears
and darkening as they progressed down its back. It
had been posed as though it was about to pounce on
something. "What is it?"

"No idea. I thought it might be a new kind of
weasel, but Wolfe seemed to think it lives in the
trees. I shot it while it was devouring a bat."

She swallowed. "It sounds as though you and Bennett argued about it."

"We argued about a great deal." He pointed a finger over his shoulder, indicating the vervet monkeys atop their trunk. "Those especially. He didn't see the point. I told him that just because an animal is known, doesn't mean it shouldn't be collected."

Phillipa forced a warm smile as she faced him. "You're very proud of these, aren't you?"

"They're better than the beads and bones and carvings Bennett boxed up. I know that." He held his arms out in an encompassing gesture. "This is Africa. Come in here at night and see if your heart doesn't race a little."

"My heart's racing right now." *Though not for the reasons he thought.* "Would you mind if I browse for a bit?" She handed him the book. "Perhaps while you think of something . . . personal to write for me?"

He grinned. "I do like a chit who appreciates the primal. I'll be back in no time. Remember, they don't bite. During the day, at least." With that he gave a jaunty salute and trotted out of the room.

Unfortunately he'd left the door open, but she couldn't take the time or risk being noticed by shutting it. This room was his pride and joy. This was where the journals were most likely to be.

She leaned behind a large antelope, but the books on the shelf behind it were all almanacs. The poor beast stank, as well. They all smelled. She would be taking a bath before her drive with Bennett. That was for certain.

The fact that this was an altered library with a great many of its books remaining didn't make her search any easier. Neither did the fact that the smaller animals all stood upon faux boulders or authentic-looking crates and trunks, no doubt David's way of reminding everyone that he'd been the one to kill the beasts and bring them back. They blocked her view, made her feel watched, and left myriad additional hiding places.

She swept her gaze along the shelves, practically running. Nothing, nothing, and nothing. Then she stopped. Whatever his book claimed, Langley *hated* Kero. Probably as much as he detested Bennett. No doubt if he'd had his way, she would be looking at a trio of vervets rather than a pair. A pair perched on a large trunk.

Glancing at the door, Phillipa approached the monkeys. It was all very Shakespearean, hiding one enemy's treasure beneath the bones—or skin, rather—of an equally hated enemy. She reached out, reluctant to touch the small animals that looked so much like slightly larger versions of Kero.

"Oh, dear," she breathed, then resolutely took one around the waist and set it on the floor, followed by the other. Surprisingly they were heavier than Kero, but it likely wouldn't do to have stuffed monkeys tipping over every time someone walked by them.

She knelt down, then opened the lid. Nearly a dozen leather-bound journals lay inside, together with innumerable sketches and maps. Bennett's treasures. She'd found them. Thank goodness. Now all she needed to do was go tell him that he could find his journals beneath the monkeys, and then if he wanted them, he could retrieve them. She wouldn't be the one keeping him in England. He would be doing it, because he chose to do so.

"Well, isn't this interesting?"

With a gasp, she twisted around. David Langley leaned against the door frame, her book in his hands and his light blue eyes gazing at her.

"I'm going to have to change some plans," he continued, and walked forward.

Chapter Twenty-one

Animals, I've observed, have two reactions to danger. They will either flee from peril, or they will charge straight at it. I once saw a quintet of baboons drive off a leopard in such a fashion. Bravado does occasionally have its rewards.

THE JOURNALS OF CAPTAIN BENNETT WOLFE

B ennett looked about the crowded main dining room at White's again. Loud, filled with cigar smoke and the nauseating odor of supposedly masculine colognes, the damned place could serve as a study on monkey dominance behaviors. The top-ranking males—the dukes of Sommerset and Melbourne—sat in the center of the room, while those of lower rank sat as close to them as possible, hoping to be acknowledged.

He and Jack—and Kero—sat close by the window, where he could at least see the out-of-doors. "And there's a waiting list to become a member here?" he asked, slicing his way through an overcooked pheasant.

"Yes, and keep your voice down. You're not terribly popular at the moment, and I don't want to be run out of the club at the point of a pistol." Jack downed half his glass of wine.

"I think I'm behaving quite admirably," Bennett returned. "And I am grateful to you for sponsoring me."

"I'd be more grateful to you if you'd bother to tell me why you suddenly want to join all my gentlemen's clubs."

"It's complicated."

"Is this part of the same plan wherein Flip charms David Langley?"

"No." Bennett reached for his own glass and drained it. When Kero clicked her teeth at him, he handed her a slice of the peach he'd requested for her benefit. The footman had seemed happy to comply; evidently the monkey was more popular than he was, despite the fact that he'd only bloodied a nose while Kero had attempted to remove an ear.

"How goes that plan, anyway? Is she out chatting with him as we speak?"

Bennett narrowed his eyes, anger grinding into his gut. "That plan is over with. She was worried that I would regret staying in England and wanted me to have my journals. I told her that I'm staying in England regardless."

"I'm somewhat relieved she's done with it then, because frankly I didn't like the way Langley looked at Livi."

"At Livi? That's your own damned fault, Jack."

"*My* fault? I didn't punch anyone in the nose and make an enemy."

"No, but you've been mooning after Olivia for too bloody long. It's time to fish or cut bait, don't you think?"

"I keep telling you, it's a delicate process. I have to prove myself steady and considerate, undemanding yet available."

"You sound like an Irish setter."

Jack sat forward. "Just because you roar into Town and claim the first chit you set eyes on doesn't mean you've the right to criticize those of us who are following the rules of civility."

"I don't see the point of hanging back and watching someone else sweep in and take what I want." Bennett scowled, knowing what Jack was going to say about that. "And Phillipa has no interest in Langley, so don't throw that in my face. She was only trying to do a good deed for me." And that one night of torture had been more than enough for him.

"What do you do now, then? Aside from joining clubs."

Bennett shifted. He didn't like revealing his hand before he'd played it, but Jack was a good friend. A trusted friend. He reached into his inside breast pocket and pulled out the ring. It was a delicate little thing, crowned with a single blue-tinted diamond, and it had once belonged to his mother. One of the few things of hers he'd been able to keep with him over the years. "I sent to Tesling for this better than a week ago," he said, evading Kero's grasp and her excited chittering at seeing something sparkling.

"Well." Jack looked at it for a moment. "So you marry Flip and spend your afternoons here eating pheasant? I wouldn't waste a penny on that tale, Bennett."

Why the devil did everyone have such a difficult time believing he could stay in England? Just because he'd never chosen to do so before didn't mean he was incapable of the action. "With her or without her," he said aloud, "I'm not going to be heading any expeditions for some time. And considering that I adore her, I find marriage to be the wisest and sanest and most acceptable action on my part."

Jack eyed him over his glass of wine. "I truly hope you've thought this through, my friend. Because I'm quite fond of Flip myself, and practical as she may be, she has a very tender, untried heart."

"I'm aware of that."

"And you know she's never come close to having a beau before this. Much less marriage. If you disappoint her, or hurt her, I'll have to come after you. And I'd really rather not do that."

"You're safe, Jack. I will do anything to make certain she doesn't regret meeting me."

He closed his eyes for a moment. Yes, he wished Phillipa wasn't quite so happy to read about adventures rather than experience them, but she'd certainly never attempted to mislead him on that count. He could drag her along with him, he supposed, but that would leave both of them miserable and resentful.

Bennett shook himself, pulling out his pocket watch. Twenty minutes of two. "I need to go. Do I receive an engraved card, or does someone teach me a secret handshake if I'm admitted to the club?"

"You'll receive a letter." Jack stood when Bennett did. "I think I'll follow along and visit Livi while you're proposing."

"That sounds romantic." They left the club together. "You're risking becoming her pet rather than her lover, you know," Bennett offered as he stepped up to the curricle's seat. Kero climbed down his shoulder to sit beside him.

Jack swung up on Brody. "Why don't we simply agree that different women require different approaches?"

"Fine." Although he would never have had the patience to watch for months, much less years, while other men attempted to win Phillipa's affections. Never.

At one minute past two he left Usiku and the curricle standing with one of the Eddison House grooms and walked up to the front door. He supposed he should be nervous, but what he actually felt was anticipation. Beneath that, well buried where he meant to keep it, was also the smallest bit of pain and panic. Not that she would refuse him, but that he might not be able to live up to his part in all this.

For the first time he wondered if that was what had become of his father. Had Randall Wolfe tried to settle down with a wife and a young son, and had he failed? Had he fled England simply because he'd tried and been unable to remain in one place?

Jack clamped a hand on his shoulder. "You look a bit pale. Haven't changed your mind, have you?"

Bennett shook himself. "No. I just realized I'm asking for Phillipa's hand without getting Lord Leeds's permission first."

"The fact that that even occurred to you at all stuns me. You *are* becoming civilized."

The front door opened as they reached it. "Lord

John, Sir Bennett," the butler said as he inclined his head, "good afternoon."

"Barnes. I'm looking for Lady Olivia, and he's after Flip."

"If you'll wait in the sitting room, I shall inquire."

As soon as they entered the front room, Kero jumped onto the back of the sofa. From there she inched her way forward to peer at the pair of fish swimming in the bowl by the window. He'd debated whether to leave Kero with Geoffrey, whom she'd apparently adopted, but Kero was his charge, and she would be a part of the future he and Phillipa would have.

"Damn," he muttered, as he caught sight of the bouquet on the end table. "Roses. I should have brought red roses."

"That didn't work out so well the last time."

"Yes, well, I've worked back up to them this time."

The sister pranced into the room. "Good afternoon, gentlemen," she said, smiling at Jack and sending Bennett a suspicious look. Considering the discomfort the chit had caused him last night, he wasn't feeling terribly friendly himself.

"Hello, Livi. I was wondering if you'd care to join me for a stroll."

"Oh. I'm actually sorting out my hair ribbons. You're welcome to join me, John."

Bennett lifted an eyebrow as Jack glanced at him. If his friend had required evidence that he was not being looked at romantically, Olivia had just provided it.

"Livi, you have a maid for that," Jack said, squaring his shoulders. "I want to go walking with you."

338 ❀ Suzanne Enoch

"Oh." She blinked. "Well, I suppose I could stand to get some air. But you know I've been sorting all by myself, because Mary's gone off somewhere with Flip."

Across the room, Bennett went very still. "Gone off where?" he asked carefully. Phillipa knew he would be calling at two o'clock. And although he hadn't given a specific reason for the visit, she would have figured that out. Had she changed her mind about him? Or was he overreacting because he was a damned idiot? After all, this wasn't the Congo. A missed rendezvous didn't mean disaster or death here in London.

"I don't know where she went. I invited her to go shopping, but she never wants to do that. I wish she hadn't taken Mary, though, because I detest untangling ribbons."

"When did you last see her?"

With a frown, Olivia looked at the mantel clock as though realizing for the first time what the hour was. "I left early, to see the new hats at Madame Costanza's. A little after nine o'clock, I think."

Five hours ago. In two long strides Bennett reached the doorway. "You," he snapped at the butler, "when did Phillipa leave this morning, and did she say where she was going?"

"I hired a hack for Lady Flip at approximately half nine," Barnes returned. "She did not say where she was going, though I presumed it to be one of her reading clubs."

"There's no need to be hostile, Sir Bennett," Olivia put in from behind him. "I don't think it's possible for Flip to remember the clock when she's reading. Or discussing what she's reading."

"No. She wouldn't forget today."

He'd survived for most of his life by virtue of his instincts. And the tension in his muscles, the clench of his heart, the chill running down his spine—all told him the same thing. Something was amiss. And with Phillipa absent, his thoughts went to one man, one reason for her not to be where she said she would be. *Langley*.

"Why do you think it was a reading club she went to?" he asked the butler, doing his damnedest to keep from hurling people about the room.

"Perhaps we should inform Lady Leeds of your concerns." Looking a bit unsettled himself, the butler started for the stairs.

His one source of information was not going anywhere. Bennett grabbed the servant by the collar and shoved him against the nearest wall. "Answer my bloody question," he snarled, ignoring Olivia's alarmed yelp.

"I—I heard Lady Flip tell Mary they needed to stop and purchase a book. Please let me go, sir."

Bennett released him. "Kero!" he barked, and the monkey scampered into the foyer and onto his shoulder.

"Bennett, where are you going?"

"I'm going to Howard House for my horse and my rifle, and then I'm going to find Phillipa."

"With your rifle?" Olivia squeaked.

"If I'm correct, she's with Langley. And if she's not there willingly, I'm going to kill him."

Phillipa sat squarely in the middle of the coach's seat and glared at David Langley lounging opposite her. The blasted blackguard had even taken the forward-

facing seat, which left her facing backward and feeling distinctly queasy.

Of course she likely would have been feeling ill
even in the coach's good seat. With her feet tied together and strung to her bound hands, and a gag
across her mouth, if she wasn't so . . . furious, she
would be terrified. More terrified—since to herself
she could admit that she was terribly frightened.
Letting Langley know that, though, would give him
yet another advantage, so she continued to glare.

"If you'll promise to be civil, I'll remove the gag,"
Langley said, gazing at her.

She nodded.

Langley leaned forward and yanked the cloth
down past her chin. "There. Now, what shall we
chat about?"

"Where were we when you threw my maid out of
the carriage?"

"Somewhere near Charing Cross. With no money,
if she's resourceful, she should make it back to Eddison House by nightfall."

Thank goodness for that. Now, though, came the
question she likely shouldn't ask. Even under the circumstances, however, she couldn't convince herself
that ignorance was more comforting than certainty.
"Are you planning on murdering me?"

The captain laughed. "Good God, no. Unless you
force me to, of course, which I suggest you don't."

"Then where are we going?"

"Well, as far as anyone else knows at this moment,
I'm going to my family's estate. Thrushell Manor is
just west of Carlisle. Have you ever been to the Lake
District?"

"No."

"It's rather breathtaking, even to me. And I've seen quite a few amazing sights."

"If you're going to the Lake District, where am I going?"

"Well, that's the clever part. Because just a few hours almost directly north of Carlisle is the Scottish border. And *just* beyond that, is Gretna Green."

Phillipa stared at him. "You're kidnaping me into *marriage*?"

"Frizzel said you were intelligent. Actually he said you were a sharp-tongued bluestocking, but I'm attempting to withhold judgment." He grimaced briefly. "I would have wished that it was your sister who'd attracted Wolfe and then found the journals, but I don't suppose it signifies."

"What?" Some of what he was saying made sense, but the more talking she could get him to do, the better. Information was always good, whether she actually wanted to hear any of it or not.

"I'll be returning to Africa within the next few months. And though I don't wish to kill you, I do need you to keep your mouth shut about the journals, whose work went into *Across the Continent*—all of that nonsense. Thus, marriage."

"So I can't testify against you? You're kidnaping me! Of course I'll say something."

"I'm showing you my familial estate, and we're continuing on to Gretna Green, spurred by our genuine, if unexpected, love."

"Oh, please."

Langley lifted an eyebrow. "Don't make me gag you again."

Phillipa stopped the very unflattering retort she wanted to make. He seemed to be proceeding along a logical path—logical to him, anyway. Perhaps logic could sway him, then, to let her go.

"What if I simply gave my word not to say anything about the journals? Then you could wait and actually marry someone because you wanted to do so."

"Ah. If only I could believe you, Flip."

"You can believe me. I don't lie." And she'd only been speaking hypothetically, because she had no intention of standing by silently while any of this went on.

"You do realize that by the time we arrive at Gretna Green you will have been in my company, unchaperoned, for a bit over two days. In fact, it's already been six hours. You're ruined, I'm afraid."

She blinked. "I—"

"So I'm actually doing the gentlemanly thing." He snapped his fingers. "And I almost forgot. If you say anything against me, you'll be stomping all over your own future, as well. Because we'll be married. And because I can accuse you of something nefarious, like a clandestine affair with Wolfe. If I say it happened while I was away on my triumphant return expedition to Africa, you'd be so detested, you wouldn't be able to show your face in London."

All of the information he was giving her so freely was supposed to be helping her, giving her the means to escape or to talk her way out of this trouble. Instead, cold despair began creeping down her spine. For a plan he'd apparently thrown together in a few minutes, it all seemed very tightly woven together.

"You're forgetting something," she said, feeling choked.

He sat forward, elbows on his knees. "What did I forget?"

"Bennett. He'll come after me. And he'll start at Langley House. He'll tear your home apart looking for me. He'll find the journals, just as I did."

"Oh, I imagine he *will* tear my parents' home apart. I hope he does. The more people who see him as a beast and a menace, the better. And he won't find the journals, because I brought them along." He patted the fat satchel on the seat beside him. "So I suppose I did think of everything."

"But I don't want to marry you."

"I know that. You want to marry Bennett."

"Do you hate him that much?"

He took a deep breath. "I didn't. I hated the damned monkey, but Bennett was more of an . . . annoyance. But then he got hit with that spear, and he blamed me—*me*—for upsetting the idiot tribesmen."

Phillipa made a noncommittal sound, and he scowled at her. At least he didn't put the gag back on her.

"And then I had to sit there," he continued, "waiting to see whether the glorious leader of our expedition would survive. I was bored, so I picked up one of the journals he was constantly scribbling in." Langley paused, a brief look of what might have been pain crossing his handsome face. "It's very interesting to read someone's unedited opinion of you. And then to realize that he was going to write another of his books, and that I would be the jester of the piece."

"So you beat him to it."

"Yes, I did. I bested him. And now I have you, so I've bested him twice. Three times if we take into account the new expedition I'll be leading. And don't worry; I'm not taking you with me to Africa. I wouldn't dream of dragging a complaining female somewhere I couldn't get away from her. You can stay here and continue to defend my reputation against Wolfe's accusations, if he dares to make any more of them."

"I can still refuse to marry you."

"My dear, you've already passed the point of no return. You'll marry me, because that is the only thing that will make you acceptable to Society again. Just as I'm marrying you to make certain I *stay* acceptable. It's a mutually beneficial situation."

"If one overlooks the theft and the fraud and the kidnaping."

Langley clucked his tongue. "Now you're being unpleasant again." He leaned forward, grabbing her chin with one hand when she tried to pull away, and lifted the gag once more. Then he sat back to pull out his pocket watch and flip it open. "We'll change horses in a bit, and then again before midnight. We should be at Thrushell Manor by afternoon tomorrow."

They weren't stopping. Sharp dread cut through her again. She hadn't continued with her list of what Bennett would do, mostly because she didn't want to remind Langley now if he *had* forgotten something. But she knew what would happen after he tore through Langley House. He would figure out where Langley would be taking her, and he would come after them. After her.

But now she had another worry. He would be at least a few hours behind them. What if he couldn't catch up in time?

Phillipa clenched her jaw. It seemed she was going to have to rescue herself. It never occurred to her to give in and allow herself to be married to Langley. She'd spent years thinking she would end up alone with her books and perhaps a cat or two. And then Bennett had found her. And she wanted him. No one else, under any circumstances. Only Bennett Wolfe. Now.

And to think, Olivia had called her previous few weeks an adventure. What would her sister call this?

Chapter Twenty-two

One law that holds true in both England and the
Congo is one of the most basic, though the reasoning
behind it is different. The law: Never leave a wounded
animal alive. The English reason for this is that it looks
dishonorable to leave the job half finished. In Africa,
the reasons are a bit more practical; there is nothing
more dangerous to a man than a wounded predator,
because we as a species are easier to kill than nearly
anything else found in the wild.

THE JOURNALS OF CAPTAIN BENNETT WOLFE

B ennett jabbed his rhinoceros-horn knife through
the middle of the large, stuffed antelope. Piles of
rags spilled out the opening and onto the carpeted
library floor.

"I'm not telling you again, Wolfe!" Lord Thrushell
squawked from close to the doorway, all bluster and
no balls. "Cease destroying David's specimens or I
will have you shot!"

Swinging around to pin a glare at the earl, Bennett flipped the knife into the air and caught it again
by its handle. "Tell me where David's gone, or I will

bring this house down around you." He couldn't stop the deep growl that touched his voice, but he didn't particularly want to. Phillipa had been here; the bloody-nosed butler had admitted to that, and he could practically smell the citrus scent of her in the air.

"You expect me to reveal my son's location to a knife-wielding madman? I think not. And I've sent for Sommerset, since he seems to be the only man who can control you, you animal."

He had no idea. "Your son," Bennett bit back, "has Lady Phillipa Eddison with him. According to your groom, she was bound, and he had luggage."

Thrushell's ruddy face paled a little. "I only returned here an hour ago. I have no idea where—"

"Cumbria, Bennett."

Bennett whipped around as Jack strode into the room, Olivia and a bedraggled-looking maid with him. He stalked up to the servant, slowing his approach only when her already distressed gaze lowered to his knife. "You're certain?" he asked, attempting to soften his tone.

She nodded. "Oh, yes, sir. I heard the driver telling the tiger with him when they dragged me out of the coach. They were grumbling about driving all the way north to Carlisle in the middle of the Season."

"What's in Cumbria?" he demanded, rounding on Thrushell again.

The earl backed away a step. "You have no proof of any of this. That girl's a servant, for God's sake. She'll say anything for a shilling. How do I know that you have any reason to be here at all?"

"Is that the stance you mean to take?" Bennett shot back, fury heating his blood.

"Thrushell Manor is in Cumbria," the lower voice of the Duke of Sommerset came as he, too, stepped into the room. The duke was armed with a pistol; apparently he had a better sense of danger than did Thrushell. "You've killed the damned animals twice, Wolfe." He glanced at the extensive carnage in the room. "Seems a bit harsh."

"I didn't shoot them the first time. And I'm going to Cumbria." Bennett shoved the knife back into his boot and headed for the door.

"I'm going with you," Jack said, grabbing his shoulder. "If he's taken Flip, he needs to be stopped."

"I don't need your help, Jack." Nor did he want anyone attempting to reason with him or slow him down.

Sommerset moved sideways to block the doorway. "Wait a moment," he murmured, then looked up at the earl. "Do you know anything about this, Thrushell?"

"No, Your Grace. As I told Wolfe before he began destroying my home, I only returned here an hour ago. No one was here."

"We arrived at ten o'clock," the maid piped up, her voice stronger now. "We were gone again before eleven. I tried to stay inside the coach with Lady Flip, but Captain Langley wouldn't allow it. He said I wouldn't be required."

Olivia covered her mouth with both hands, stifling a sob. "Go!" she ordered him. "For heaven's sake, go find my sister!"

"I am." He faced Sommerset again. "Get out of my way."

The duke moved aside. "I'll join you."

As they left the room, Jack fell behind, putting an

arm across Olivia's shoulders and guiding her out with him. "Tell your parents what's happened, and make certain they stay at Eddison House. We'll be back with Flip before you know it."

"Not before the rest of London knows it." She sobbed again. "She's ruined, John. How could Captain Langley do that? Drag her off without a chaperone?"

"Jack!" Bennett barked, descending the stairs at a near run. Now that he had a destination, he was not about to dally.

The battered butler remained slumped in a foyer chair. Bennett noted that the servant was no longer a threat, and otherwise ignored him. Nothing else mattered but finding Phillipa. And if she was headed for Cumbria, then so was he. He swung up on the waiting Ares.

"Bennett, wait until Livi's safely away from here."

He snarled at the delay, but nodded. Putting one sister in danger because he couldn't wait two minutes before he galloped off to save the other—Phillipa would never forgive him.

Jack ushered Olivia and the maid into their barouche and spoke to the driver. Once the vehicle left the drive, the other two men mounted, Jack on Brody, and Sommerset on his monstrous black thoroughbred, Khan. Bennett could spend time arguing that he didn't need them along, but in truth both of them more than likely knew the roads better than he did. "Keep up," he snapped, and set off north at a gallop.

Nicholas Ainsley, the Duke of Sommerset, had known a handful of men like Bennett Wolfe in his lifetime. A half dozen of them were members of his Adventurers' Club. The rest were either scattered about the world, or they had run across one obstacle they couldn't overcome, and it had killed them. The one currently riding point while he and Lord John Clancy stayed close behind, he preferred to keep alive.

"Why Cumbria?" John asked, sounding as though he was winded and too stubborn to admit it. It had been full dark for an hour, and neither they nor their horses were nearly as fresh as when they'd begun.

"Don't care," Wolfe grunted from in front of them. He hadn't even looked back since they'd left Town.

"I've been considering that," Nicholas commented. "No chaperone, driving north in a coach, and toting luggage. If I didn't know that Thrushell Manor lay in this direction, my guess would be—"

"Gretna Green," Clancy supplied.

Up ahead, Wolfe's head lowered briefly. A string of multilingual muttered curses drifted back on the wind. "A marriage is better than murder," the duke agreed. "And it will preserve her reputation."

The big bay skidded to a halt. His face a mask of anger and worry, Bennett rounded on both of them. "She is not marrying David Langley," he snapped. "I won't allow it, and she won't do it. We will therefore bloody well catch them before they reach Scotland." He kneed Ares, and they sprinted off again.

"You shouldn't say things like that where he can hear them, Your Grace," Clancy noted, urging his mount back into a gallop. "Bennett already has a ring. He meant to propose to her this afternoon."

It wasn't only pride at stake, then, but Nicholas

hadn't thought so. That did make this rescue considerably more dangerous. Nothing in his life had been overly dangerous for far too long, however. A deep excitement, the thrill of the hunt, edged into him, and he sternly pushed it back down. This was a rescue; nothing more. And Wolfe was far past the line of civility at the moment. They couldn't afford for two of them to be so. "The inn where they would most likely change horses is about a mile ahead," he said aloud. "We should rent fresh mounts, as well."

"Yes," Bennett grunted over his shoulder. "If they aren't stopping, neither are we."

Phillipa started awake as the coach stopped. Dread speared through her, still sharp even after nearly a full twenty-four hours. It seemed too soon to be at Thrushell Manor, much less in Scotland, but then she couldn't be certain how long she'd been asleep.

"We're changing horses again," Langley said, sitting up straight and stretching out his arms in a way that made her distinctly jealous. He flashed her a grin. "You're glaring again, my dear. Is there something you wish to say?"

Oh, there were several things she wished to say, but she had more immediate concerns than venting her spleen. Phillipa nodded. Leaning forward, Langley pulled down her gag. "I would like some water and something to eat," she stated. "And my legs and my arms are very cramped."

He stood, looming over her. "I imagine so." Then he pushed open the door and hopped to the ground. Beyond him she caught a glimpse of a small, muddy courtyard and some chickens. "I'll send Arnold to purchase a jug and some bread. Don't think of trying to attract anyone's attention, because I'll be directly outside here, stretching my legs."

"Bastard," she muttered.

"What was that?"

"Yes, David," she amended.

"Mm hm." He shut the door.

It was the first time she'd been left alone in a day. Sometime late last night he'd untied her and allowed her outside to relieve herself in the shrubbery, but she'd been surrounded by all three men and, as far as she could tell in the dark, in the middle of nowhere.

This was not the time, however, to lament her fate. Scooting to the edge of the seat, if she stretched out her hands and her feet she could just reach the satchel holding Bennett's journals. It wasn't the same as having him present, but it was the closest she could get. And there they were, the items that had brought him back to England from the Congo— carelessly dumped into a pile of David Langley's luggage. The blackguard had even brought copies of his own book with him.

She knew Bennett was looking for her. If poor Mary had managed to return home to Eddison House, the maid would be able to provide her family with some information. Hopefully it would be enough. After weeks spent attempting to help Bennett civilize himself, she almost wished that now he would forget all the rules and simply get there.

When she heard Langley speaking with Arnold the tiger directly outside, she sat back again. Kero had had the right idea where David Langley was concerned. And while Phillipa didn't want to bite off anyone's ear, she wasn't about to surrender.

With nearly every one of their odd little conversations, Langley had managed to mention her fate if they should fail to marry. She would be ruined; she would be ostracized; she would never be invited to soirees, and if she ever was, no one would ever ask her to dance.

What he clearly didn't realize, and what she had no intention of enlightening him to, was that she didn't care. For heaven's sake, she'd never been popular, she'd rarely danced until Bennett's arrival, and her indignation and anger over the theft of the journals far outweighed her worry over how Society might view her. She didn't view Society terribly favorably.

The coach door swung open again. Langley climbed in, toting a jug and a sackcloth. "Water and bread," he announced, as Arnold closed the door from the outside and he seated himself again. "And some cheese."

"Thank you." With her hands strung to her feet she couldn't reach her mouth without curling into a very undignified ball, so she had to be polite and wait to be fed—which Langley seemed to find amusing, and she didn't.

Pulling a knife from his boot, he sliced into the wedge of cheese and held the piece out to her. As she took it in her teeth, the coach rocked into motion again. Her tired muscles protested, but she tried to keep her weariness from showing on her face.

"Are we in the Lake District yet?" she asked.

"We are. It's rugged country; perhaps we can take more time to view the sights on our return from

Scotland." He handed her more cheese, and then granted her a drink of water.

She deliberately dribbled. "Blast it," she grumbled. "Might I have one hand free so I can feed myself? If the country's as rugged as you say, I'm not going anywhere."

"There's nowhere to go. And if you tried running without knowing the countryside, you would be likely to fall off a cliff before you could get twenty feet from the coach."

Phillipa swallowed nervously. "I've read about Cumbria's geography. It sounds very treacherous."

"Oh, it is." Giving her an assessing look, he reached across and untied her left hand.

Immediately she stretched out her arm, flexing her fingers. "Thank you again."

"We *are* going to be married. Mutually beneficial or not, it is an alliance. And it would be better for both of us if we could deal cordially."

A marriage to him was ostensibly beneficial to her only because he'd kidnaped her, but she refrained from mentioning that. "May I have more cheese?"

He sliced off another bit and handed it to her. She put it into her mouth, waited for the coach to go over an especially rough patch of road, and began choking. Her heart pounding so loud she thought he might be able to hear it, Phillipa grabbed her throat, then made to reach into her mouth.

"You don't expect me to believe this, I hope," Langley commented, leaning back in his seat.

She coughed, spitting out a portion of her bite, and then held her breath so her face would turn red. Making some wheezing sounds, she clawed at her throat again and rolled her eyes back in her head. Good God, she'd never seen an actress put this much effort into a part; if he didn't believe her now, she would never get another chance.

Langley cursed. "Lean forward," he ordered. "I'll try patting you on the back."

She leaned forward. As he lifted up over her, she rammed her head into his chin. He fell back with a grunt. Immediately she yanked the knife out of his hand and sliced off her ropes. Then as he growled and came at her, she stabbed him as hard as she could in the thigh.

"You bitch!" he yowled.

Phillipa grabbed the heavy satchel at the top of the stack, flung open the coach door, and jumped. She hit the road hard, rolling and ending up with her skirt around her waist. Shaking herself, she climbed to her feet, slung the strap of the satchel around her neck and across one shoulder, and began running.

The country was rough indeed, and before the coach had even stopped behind her she'd managed to make it over a hill and out of sight of the vehicle. Rocks and boulders, cliffs, and old, tall trees—a great deal of cover, but she wanted some distance between her and Langley before she attempted to hide. Bennett had best arrive soon, or she'd just made things much worse for no good reason at all.

Bennett began stripping the tack off his mount as soon as they stopped in the inn's courtyard. The duke headed for the stable to rent them additional mounts, while Jack limped into the inn for food. As soon as he'd finished, Bennett went on to Sommerset's animal. The less time they had to waste changing their gear, the better.

His two companions had stopped attempting to talk to him sometime in the middle of the night— apparently they'd realized he was no longer capable of human conversation. They were on the trail, because three innkeepers now had described Langley's coat of arms and a northbound coach in a hurry. No one had seen a woman, though one groom had noted that at least one of the three men had remained close by the coach during the entire time the horses were changed.

"Bennett!" Jack called, returning from the inn with half a loaf of bread and more energy than he'd shown a moment earlier. "Twenty minutes ago."

His heart ground to a halt, then began beating again. By changing horses approximately every ten miles they'd been able to keep up a grueling pace, and finally they were seeing results. For that reason he was glad Sommerset had joined the hunt; his name alone had gained them more cooperation than he would have received on his own.

The duke returned as well, leading one gray gelding and with two stable boys and two additional horses in tow. "The coach horses back there are still wet," he said.

Jack nodded. "The innkeeper said he rented them horses and sold them some food and water not twenty minutes ago." He scowled. "He also said there's not another station for fifteen miles. These horses are going to have to last us a bit longer this time."

"Not if we're twenty minutes behind," Bennett grunted, saddling one of the new mounts while the servants worked on the other two animals.

"Wolfe, if he's bothered to take her all this way,

he's not going to hurt her," Sommerset commented. "Not until she refuses to cooperate in Scotland, anyway."

"She doesn't travel," he snapped, buckling on the bridle. "She's never been farther from home than Devon." He couldn't explain it. Not at the moment, when all he could think of was having her safely in his arms again. But for the devil's sake, she'd been nervous over the idea of traveling anywhere with *him*. In Langley's company . . . With a growl he swung back into the saddle. He needed her back.

With an ill-stifled groan, Jack mounted beside him. "So are we going to simply run them down, or do we have a plan?"

Bennett kicked the gray in the ribs. "Run them down."

He heard the other two fall in behind him, but otherwise paid no attention. Twenty minutes. Three miles? Four? And they would still be traveling. An hour, then, until he was able to catch up. Langley therefore had an hour to live.

"Wolfe, as far as London knows, this is a mutually agreed upon elopement," Sommerset said, interrupting his thoughts as he scanned the road for recent wheel and horse tracks.

"I don't care what London thinks or knows," he sent back over his shoulder.

"You'll care if you murder Langley. He's an earl's son. An earl's heir."

"He stole Phillipa."

Langley hadn't grown any better at disguising his trail in the time since he'd been tracked by that leopard in the jungle. And from the widely spaced hoof prints, the coach was going at top speed. Did he

know he was being chased? Part of Bennett hoped so, even if would make the catch more difficult. It would make the ending more satisfying if Langley was afraid.

Deep down, he was afraid, as well. Afraid that David would hurt Phillipa. And afraid that his practical, logical Phillipa would decide that marriage to Langley made sense if it kept him from harm, if it left him free to travel, if it kept her family from scandal. She'd been alone with Langley for more than twenty-four hours now. If the bastard had so much as touched her . . .

They rounded a wide curve in the road, and he allowed the end of that thought to drift away, unfinished. Half a mile in front of them a coach stood. And he recognized the yellow coat of arms on the door. Langley's coach.

"Bennett, slow down," the duke ordered, charging forward to grab for his bridle.

"Get the bloody hell away from me." He kicked out, but Sommerset avoided the blow.

"It could be an ambush."

Jack drew even on his other side. "A damned good place for one. There's cover everywhere."

"Angry and self-righteous or not, you can't stop a bullet or a lead ball from killing you."

With a scowl, Bennett pulled up. "Fine," he said, jumping down from the horse and pulling his Baker rifle from its scabbard. Not his favorite Baker rifle; Langley had never returned that one. He had two pistols in his coat pockets in addition to the rifle and the knife in his boot, but at the moment he could likely kill Langley with his bare hands.

Jack had a musket, as did Sommerset. They would

be able to reload more quickly than he could, but he intended to end the fight before they had the chance to do so. Using one hand to tie the gelding off to an oak tree, he cut left, heading up the hill to the far side. A second later he heard Sommerset and Jack going right to help him flank the coach.

The ground was rough and stony, and as they'd left the inn, he'd spotted a lake to the northwest and tucked low into the surrounding mountains and cliffs. He kept low, using the brush and the rough terrain for cover as he swiftly moved forward. Ahead he could hear the horses blowing, and all around the sound of birds and the wind brushing through the trees. No voices, and that worried him.

He came in along the left rear wheel, crouched, and yanked open the coach's door as he spun to aim inside. Empty. "It's empty," he said aloud, cursing. Stepping up inside the vehicle, he looked for signs of Phillipa.

It took only a second to find them. A torn bit of lace, a few strands of hair—and rope. "He had her tied up," he growled as Sommerset appeared in the doorway, Jack behind him. He flung the bindings back down onto the seat. And then he saw the blood. "Christ." His fingers abruptly shaking, he brushed them along the stain that edged one seat. Still wet.

"You don't know that it's hers," Jack said in a low voice.

"It had better not be." He jumped to the ground again, gazing at the surrounding terrain. "They had to have stepped off here. The wheel ruts and hoof prints are deep, so they halted the horses, rather than letting them stop on their own."

Sommerset put a hand across Jack's chest, backing

them both down the road a step or two and away from the chaos of prints. "This is your hunt, Bennett. What do you see?"

Bennett left the road, shifting his gaze to the soft ground immediately around it. Boot prints. One set, then two more. Moving quickly. And more drops of blood, irregular and widely spaced. "It's not her blood," he muttered. He noted every track as he followed beside the pathway, but they weren't what he was looking for.

Then he spotted it. A smaller, softer-edged print. A lady's walking shoe. "This way," he growled, and began running.

Chapter Twenty-three

Mbundi and the porters gave both David and me names in their native Swahili. They called me Msafiri, which means "traveler." Langley they named Ushari, which I told him meant "strong." In reality, it is Swahili for "an aggravation." By the end, though, they had shortened it to Shari, which means, simply, "evil."

THE JOURNALS OF CAPTAIN BENNETT WOLFE

Phillipa knew the inn lay to the south, and she started back in the direction the coach had already traveled. But out of sight of the road and with the overcast sky, she wasn't certain whether she was still heading south, or whether she'd veered more to the west.

Though she would have preferred a place with doors that could be locked and barricaded, it actually didn't matter where she was, as long as she could keep hidden from Langley and his men. As long as she could stay free and out of Scotland until Bennett arrived.

No, it wasn't much of a plan, but hopefully that

meant Langley wouldn't have much of a response. Hiding behind a trio of boulders in the middle of rugged Cumbria was certainly the least logical thing she'd ever done. At the edges of her mind, though, she was rather surprised that she wasn't panicking. She was planning, thinking—where to go next, which way to turn if one of them detected her. She couldn't say she was enjoying herself, but it was certainly . . . invigorating.

Having read Bennett's previous books she knew about leaving tracks, and so as soon as she could she'd begun moving from rock to rock and along the fallen trunks of trees. It wasn't perfect, but it should make her trail more difficult to detect.

At the moment the most troubling realization was that she was already cold. If she managed to stay free until past nightfall, the chill in the air would become even more worrisome. In the dark, however, she might well be able to move closer to the road and find the inn—if she could figure out in which direction, precisely, the road lay.

"Flip," Langley's carrying voice came, not for the first time, "this is ridiculous. I said I wouldn't harm you."

From the sound he was several hundred feet away, and he wasn't happy. But then, she hadn't answered him in the better than two hours she'd been running. At least she thought it had been that long. He seemed to love the sound of his own voice, so she let him indulge himself.

Abruptly a hand reached between two of the boulders and grabbed her arm. "I've got her, Captain!"

With a shriek Phillipa tore away, leaving part of her sleeve behind. She grabbed up the satchel and began running again. Heavy boots pounded behind her, and she veered sideways to leap through a narrow gap in the trees.

"Phillipa!"

Her heart crashed into her ribs at the familiar voice. "Bennett!" she screamed, but kept running. He would be behind her somewhere, but she couldn't allow herself to get caught. Not now.

A rock shifted from beneath her foot and she stumbled, rolling forward to keep from losing momentum. As she came upright, though, she suddenly realized that momentum was the last thing she wanted. Phillipa dug her heels into the earth, twisting and grabbing onto a tree root as she continued to skid forward.

Inches in front of her, the landscape opened up. Two hundred feet below her toes, a large lake rested at the foot of the cliff. Beyond that, she thought she could see all of Cumbria.

Still clinging to the tree, she faced back the way she'd come. Arnold, the liveried tiger, leapt over a boulder and came straight at her. Before she could yell at him to stop or he'd kill both of them, another figure launched through the air from one side.

Bennett slammed into Arnold's rib cage, taking him into the ground with a sickening thud. Twisting quickly onto one knee, he lifted his knife.

"Don't kill him!"

He looked up at her, his jungle-colored eyes direct and distant. "Why not?" he snarled.

"Because you don't need to. And because he was following orders."

With a curse Bennett straightened, shoving the knife back into his boot. He grabbed up the rifle that had landed beside him and began scrambling toward her. "Come here," he said, glancing at the edge of the cliff just beyond her. He held out his free hand.

A sob ripped from her chest. She'd known he would come, but he'd arrived at the exact right moment. "I'm very glad to see you," she said shakily.

"Not so fast."

Above Bennett on the cluster of boulders, Langley appeared. He also held a rifle, and it was pointed at the back of Bennett's head. Phillipa froze. She'd been frightened before, but now . . . now she was terrified. For him. For Bennett.

"We seem to have a problem, Wolfe," Langley said coolly.

"Give it a minute," Bennett returned in that low, deadly voice he'd used a moment ago. "You won't have any problem ever again."

"That's very brave, but considering that my driver has your friends pinned down and I have a weapon aimed at you, perhaps you should rephrase that."

"I'm going to kill you. Is that any better?"

"Bennett, stop it," Phillipa ordered shakily. "This is over with, David. Lower the rifle, and we'll all go our separate ways. We'll never speak of this again. You have my word."

"And you, Bennett?"

"I'd rather kill you."

Phillipa wanted to grab Bennett and shake him, though she could more easily move a mountain. "Give him your damned word, Bennett."

A muscle in his cheek jumped. "You have my damned word," he echoed.

"Well, that's a start," Langley put in, his expression easing a little, "but I have one more condition."

"No m—"

"What is it?" Phillipa interrupted.

"Throw that satchel over the cliff, Flip. Then neither of you will have any proof of the other thing, and I'll sleep much better."

Bennett looked from Phillipa's exhausted, dirt- and sweat-streaked face to the satchel over her shoulder. His journals. She'd not only escaped Langley, but she'd taken his journals with her. God, she was remarkable. And in comparison to a life with her and a life without her, nothing in that satchel mattered worth a damn. "Drop them," he said.

Phillipa furrowed her brow. "You'd let them go?"

Langley shifted behind him, and he tensed, ready to move. "You heard Wolfe, my dear. Drop them. Now. Or I'll put a bullet through *your* head, and you'll drop them, then."

"Langley, if you do anything—*anything*—to hurt her—"

"Shut up. I'm negotiating with the chit, now. I assume she'll be more reasonable than you are."

Phillipa's gaze, though, remained on Bennett's face, as though she hadn't even heard Langley speak. "Your reputation. You'll never lead another expedition."

The animal anger that had pushed him through the last hours broke apart, and he straightened. "Phillipa, *you* are my adventure."

"Don't make me ill," Langley said.

Bennett shook his head, willing her to understand. "I've been searching my entire life for something to make me want to stay in one place. For someone to be my . . . My home is where your heart is, Phillipa. Let the satchel go."

Slowly she pulled the strap off over her head. "You're certain?"

"I'm certain."

Taking a deep breath, Phillipa held the satchel up over empty space.

"Wait, wait, wait," Langley said unexpectedly. "Hold for a second. I want to see Bennett's face when you let it go." He moved off the rocks, limping badly as he came around the front of them. At least the damned gun was pointed at Bennett again, he reflected, where it should have been all along. "Much better. Swing it out wide, and then let it drop. Now, Flip."

Bennett didn't watch them go. He kept his gaze on Langley. But he heard it. He heard Phillipa's small gasp as she released her hold, heard Langley's deeper sigh of satisfaction. And he saw Langley's attention shift away from him for a fraction of a second as the satchel dropped.

He leapt forward, slamming his shoulder into the side of the rifle and sending it skidding. With his momentum he took Langley to the ground, curled his hand into a fist, and struck.

Langley kicked up at him, but he simply took the blow. It didn't matter. He hit the captain again, squarely in the face. Then he did it a third time.

"Bennett, stop!"

"My word doesn't count," he snarled, letting Langley up only so he could smash him down again. "He pointed a weapon at you."

She grabbed his arm, pulling against him. "Stop it! No killing anyone for me!"

He ignored her, until Sommerset and Jack scrambled into view and threw themselves on top of him, pulling him off Langley. "Enough, Bennett. Stop!" the duke ordered. "It's done."

Langley crawled to a boulder and used it to pull himself into a seated position. Blood running freely down his face, he smiled anyway. "It *is* done. And I'll have you arrested for assault. You have no proof that I've ever done anything ill to you."

"You kidnaped Flip," Jack broke in.

"You think she'll admit to that? It'll ruin her reputation."

Bennett turned his back on Langley to find Phillipa. He gazed at her for a hard beat of his heart, then pulled her into his arms. "You're not hurt?" he asked roughly, burying his face in her tangled hair.

She nodded against his shoulder. "I knew you would come for me," she said in a muffled voice. "I had to stay out of Scotland until you came." Phillipa pushed back from him just enough to free one hand. Tangling her fingers into his hair, she pulled his face down to kiss him. "I love you," she whispered.

"I love you." He gazed into her eyes. "You are my heart. Do you understand that? There is no me without you." There was only that rogue, that animal who couldn't think of anything but survival and revenge.

"Yes."

"The next time you have to drop something of mine to save yourself, do it, for God's sake."

"But I didn't." She kissed him again.

Bennett scowled. Still refusing to release her, he lifted his head a little. "You didn't what?"

"Drop them."

"They went over the bloody cliff," Langley chortled. Jack kicked him in his wounded leg, and the captain yelped again.

Phillipa turned her head to look down at Langley. "Your books went over the cliff. I hid Bennett's journals up there in the rocks."

"You . . ." Bennett snorted, then lifted her into the air, bringing her back down for another kiss. "You are a remarkable chit," he murmured, brushing his fingers through her hair. "But my decision doesn't change. I'm finished with traveling."

She laughed against his mouth. Of course she was happy to hear that. And he was happy, as well. Happier than he could ever recall being in his life. Because of her.

"May I make a request?" she said in a low tone, a smile in her voice.

"Anything."

"Might we continue on to Scotland? If you mean to propose to me, of course."

Truly startled, he glanced over at Jack, who shrugged. "She *is* ruined."

Sommerset was actually smiling. "Go to it. We'll deal with this, and your journals. I have a man or two with the *London Times* who will be willing to make threats—and follow through with them if necessary."

"We'll meet you back in London next week," Bennett said, lifting Phillipa into his arms.

"You still have to ask me," she commented, tears in her eyes.

At the top of the hill, he set her down, then sank onto one knee. All of the beautiful, rugged Lake District lay below them. "I meant to bring you red roses," he began, his own voice catching.

Phillipa ran a finger along his cheek. "You already did that. Skip to the good part."

He chuckled, digging into his pocket to pull out the ring. "Phillipa, my heart, my blood, my everything, will you for God's and my sake marry me?"

She held out her hand, her fingers shaking. "Yes," she breathed.

When he slipped the ring onto her finger, she collapsed against his chest, nearly sending them down the hill again. And he didn't care. Everything was an adventure with his Phillipa. Everything.

Three weeks later

Phillipa sat on a comfortable sofa in the morning room of the small house Bennett had rented for them in London. They were supposed to have gone for a brunch with her family, but then Sommerset had sent over a note, and Bennett had gone off to see him. She'd informed Livi and her parents that they would be along shortly, but in the meantime she had some reading to do.

With a slow breath she pulled the journal onto her lap and opened it to where she'd left off. A few short weeks ago she would have devoured the nine books in two days, foregoing sleep and food until she'd read every last detail. How things had changed. She was only on the second journal, and she would be surprised if she finished it before the end of the week.

The front door opened, and she looked up as Bennett, Kero on his shoulder, strolled into the morning room. "Hello," she said, smiling.

He set Kero onto a chair with an apple to occupy her and sank onto the couch beside Phillipa. "Hello," he returned, and kissed her. "I attempted to bring you roses again, but Kero ate them."

She laughed. "It *is* the most novel excuse ever. But you know I'm just as happy with the monkey."

"Thank you for that."

Phillipa took his hand, twisting her fingers around his. "Well, what did they say? Did they grovel?"

"There was no groveling, but at least three apologies. One of them was, I believe, sincere."

"And all it took was the threat to publish your journals verbatim in the newspaper. You know, I once thought very highly of the Africa Association. And now I don't even know why I d—"

"They offered to sponsor me on another Congo expedition," he interrupted, lifting his hand to look at their entwined fingers.

Her heart skipped a beat. Several beats. If he wanted to go, though, she couldn't and wouldn't be able to stop him. He would be lost to her, in spirit if not in body. "When do you leave?"

Green eyes met hers. "I don't. I have found recently that life is rather precious. I would like to be about for as long as possible."

Deep satisfaction wound through her. "You're certain."

"You don't need to keep asking me that, *nyonda*. I'm certain."

She put on a faux frown and sighed. "Oh, well. It can't be helped then, I suppose."

His scowl looked very genuine. "What can't be helped?"

"It's only that I thought it might be interesting to see the Parthenon—or what's left of it—in person. And you said you've never been to Greece. But if you aren't interested in any more adven—"

Bennett put a broad hand over her mouth. "You're certain?" he murmured, holding her gaze, the jungle deep in his eyes.

She nodded, and brought his hand down into hers. "I've discovered something of a taste for adventure, it seems. And for a certain adventurer."